ACCLAIM FOR RACHEL MCMILLAN

THE LONDON RESTORATION

"*The London Restoration* is a wonder of a novel. With the resplendent combination of Mozart, cathedral architecture, a mysterious ancient relic, a love story, and wartime recovery, *The London Restoration* takes us on a journey to both London and to our own hearts. While reading this novel, one feels as if they are traveling through the streets of London as purely and simply as if one had been dropped into 1945 and the bombed-out spaces of the beloved city. This novel is as immersive as it is thrilling. Brent and Diana Somerville will lodge themselves into your heart and not let go. At the helm of this journey, McMillan's deft prose navigates the story from battlefield to crumbling cathedral to London's finest establishments. McMillan taps into all that matters most to us: love, loyalty, survival, and spirit. Mystifying, immersive, and dazzling."

—PATTI CALLAHAN HENRY, *NEW YORK TIMES*
BESTSELLING NOVELIST OF *BECOMING MRS. LEWIS*

"Elegant writing, beautiful imagery, and wonderfully complex character relationships make this latest novel by Rachel McMillian an insightful look at what remains to us after war, not only in the outside world, but inside the very core of who we are. A perfect blend of love story, mystery, and self-discovery."

—SUSAN MEISSNER, BESTSELLING AUTHOR
OF *THE LAST YEAR OF THE WAR*

"A beautifully compelling tale, illuminating love's fragile renewal among the ruins of war's destruction."

—KATE BRESLIN, BESTSELLING AUTHOR OF *FAR SIDE OF THE SEA*

"*The London Restoration* is about coding and decoding—not only the literal codes that Diana works with at Bletchley Park but also the symbolic codes embedded in the architecture of her beloved churches and her war-scarred husband. This meticulously researched novel is also a poignant love story that surprises its protagonists with the beauty arising from their fractured world. *The London Restoration* will appeal to fans of Anna Lee Huber's Lady Darby mysteries and Kate Quinn's *The Alice Network*."

—CLARISSA HARWOOD, AUTHOR OF *BEAR NO MALICE*

"*The London Restoration* is McMillan's love letter to the city of London and its churches, and what a love letter it is! An insightful exploration of the broken places within and around us, and the resiliency of the human spirit, even in the face of tragedy and war. Affecting, beautifully written, and soulful."

—ANNA LEE HUBER, BESTSELLING AUTHOR OF THE LADY DARBY MYSTERIES AND VERITY KENT MYSTERIES

"What a love story! *The London Restoration* is a beauty and compelling tribute to a city, a people unconquered by the horrors of WWII, and a couple still fighting the good fight for King and Country, and for each other . . . Rich in detail and history—and with a love story that gives all the feels— this story enchants."

—KATHERINE REAY, BESTSELLING AUTHOR OF *THE PRINTED LETTER BOOKSHOP* AND *OF LITERATURE AND LATTES*

"To read *The London Restoration* is to be swept entirely away by Rachel McMillan's captivating way with place, character, intrigue, and heart. These impeccably woven elements make for a tale that will plant its readers in the postwar pews of St. Paul's, with strains of Mozart bolstering wonder and inviting listeners to lean in and hear what lies beneath the notes. McMillan shines a light on the breathtaking history of the "patchwork churches," rebuilt with painstaking care in the wake of war. Her treatment of these cathedrals and the people beneath their domed roofs cause us to take heart at this timeless and oh, so timely hope: buildings aren't the only things gathered up and rebuilt, with their scars telling a deep and true story. The hearts that beat within us do the very same."

—AMANDA DYKES, AUTHOR OF *WHOSE WAVES THESE ARE* AND *SET THE STARS ALIGHT*

"*The London Restoration* is a clever and deeply moving novel about a pair of married academics who never aspired to life outside of a college campus. Diana Somerville is dedicated to the history and architecture of churches, but in the aftermath of World War II she is charged with helping plan the restoration of the ruined cathedrals in the city she loves so well. The crisis of the war has damaged more than just the cathedrals of London; it has introduced the scars of doubt and wounds into a marriage that may not survive the war. Rich with historical details and a cast of intriguing secondary characters, *The London Restoration* is a wonderful testament to the human spirit and the challenges of rebuilding a world that can never be quite the same."

—ELIZABETH CAMDEN, RITA-AWARD-
WINNING NOVELIST OF *THE SPICE KING*

"*The London Restoration* is an elegant and beautifully researched novel, as rich in history as it is in romance. Set in post-World War II London, Rachel McMillan's passion for historic cities and churches shines through every page. She brings the architecture to life, ravaged by war, but strong at its foundation—just like the marriage of Brent and Diana Somerville. Brilliantly done to the last word."

—MIMI MATTHEWS, AUTHOR OF THE *USA TODAY*
BESTSELLING PARISH ORPHANS OF DEVON SERIES

"A captivating story of a singular love forged in the peeling of church bells, *The London Restoration* drifts through the postwar streets of London to wrap around readers' hearts. McMillan's evocative yet delicate prose is a testament not only to the power of love, but to the unfaltering resilience of the city itself, which she captures so beautifully."

—J'NELL CIESIELSKI, AUTHOR OF *THE SOCIALITE*

"*The London Restoration* is a vividly rendered exploration of the intricacies of love and the resiliency of a city. From the first page, I was transported to postwar London, in all its rubbled streets and indefatigable spirit, and into the world of a couple struggling to reconcile the newfound texture of their love with the life-shaping changes wrought by war. Atmospheric and rich, with characters both nuanced and captivating, the story seamlessly weaves the wonder of falling in love with a journey of rediscovery. Steeped in meticulous research and written in a voice as soaring as the churches depicted and as intimate as the romance between Diana and Brent, this is immersive historical fiction at its finest."

—AMANDA BARRATT, AUTHOR OF *THE WHITE ROSE RESISTS: A NOVEL OF THE GERMAN STUDENTS WHO DEFIED HITLER*

"This is a book for our times. McMillan holds a mirror up to an era when fear ran rampant, a society was on the brink of collapse, and people desperately wanted to believe in something again."

—SIRI MITCHELL, AUTHOR OF *STATE OF LIES*

MURDER IN THE CITY OF LIBERTY

"Rachel McMillan paints her portrait of 1940 Boston with brushes of poetry, humor, and care for historical detail. In this sequel she brings us home, not only to a city she clearly loves, but also to her winning cast of characters. Protagonists Hamish DeLuca and Reggie Van Buren are each a dear blend of passion and vulnerability as they continue their journey toward purpose, liberty, and love (and a few favorite supporting characters are back too!). Flavored with quipping nods to *The Thin Man* and imbued with insecurities and prejudices of the time and place, *Murder in the City of Liberty* is an irresistible read."

—AMANDA G. STEVENS, AUTHOR OF *NO LESS DAYS*

"What a fantastic ride through historic Boston! With evocative descriptions, dialog that snaps, and layered characters so real you just want to hang out with them, Rachel McMillan has penned a beautifully complex mystery that not only entertains but confronts the very real racial injustice and corruption of the time period with a deft hand. Another delightful addition to a solid series!"

—ABIGAIL WILSON, AUTHOR OF *IN THE SHADOW OF CROFT TOWERS*

MURDER AT THE FLAMINGO

"*Murder at the Flamingo* is a dynamite beginning to McMillan's newest series. Both a coming-of-age tale and a twisty case of whodunit, readers will fall in love with her delightfully complicated characters. Nineteen thirty-seven Boston leaps to life in vivid detail, while the author's portrayal of anxiety and panic disorder is both heartbreaking and inspiring. I cannot wait to read Hamish and Reggie's next adventure."

—ANNA LEE HUBER, BESTSELLING AUTHOR
OF THE LADY DARBY MYSTERIES

"Rachel McMillan's *Murder at the Flamingo* is an extravaganza of fabulous characters and prose that transported me to 1930s Boston. McMillan has quite a talent for immersing the reader in a profound historical experience. Highly recommended!"

—COLLEEN COBLE, *USA TODAY* BESTSELLING AUTHOR

"In *Murder at the Flamingo*, McMillan, author of the Herringford and Watts Mysteries, offers us a new generation of sleuths. And in her skilled hands, 1937 Boston comes to life with rich sensory detail and clever winks to books and films. You'll love the happening and opulent nightclubs, the fast-paced dancing and daring, and especially the two sleuths who will steal your heart."

—KATHERINE REAY, AUTHOR OF *DEAR MR. KNIGHTLEY*
AND *A PORTRAIT OF EMILY PRICE*

"On its surface, *Murder at the Flamingo* is a fun and engrossing prewar murder mystery that will keep readers turning pages. It's beautifully atmospheric, taking us to late 1930s Boston in such vivid detail you can almost taste the decadent cannoli cream so beloved by McMillan's amateur sleuth protagonists. The pacing is taut without sacrificing development of the endearing cast of characters. But more significant than this, McMillan gives us a story that highlights the struggles of people living with anxiety and panic disorders long before the conditions were properly understood. Her portrayal of Hamish's challenges is sympathetic and uplifting, and only serves to make his character richer. This delightful series is one I will be following for what I hope is a very long time."

—AIMIE K. RUNYAN, INTERNATIONALLY BESTSELLING AUTHOR
OF *DAUGHTERS OF THE NIGHT SKY* AND *PROMISED TO THE CROWN*

"A perfectly flawed hero and a liberty-seeking lady are the backbone of this delightful and lively mystery novel. Grounded in a city that is no stranger to independence, Hamish and Reggie seek what it means to be free beneath the lights of Boston's glitziest nightclub . . . and a murder that taints its opening night. Fast-paced and at times humorous, the satisfying ending leaves the reader content and anxious for more all at the same time."

—HEIDI CHIAVAROLI, AWARD-WINNING AUTHOR
OF *FREEDOM'S RING* AND *THE HIDDEN SIDE*

"Adventure—the very thing both of Rachel McMillan's lovable characters seek is exactly what she delivers, sucking the reader back to the '30s with distinctive style. Fans will be clamoring for the next installment!"

—ROSEANNA M. WHITE, BESTSELLING AUTHOR
OF THE *SHADOWS OVER ENGLAND* SERIES

"Boston comes roaring to life with fullness and flair, a character in its own right. Endearing protagonists carry the tale with wit, charm, and struggles that make them human. Bursting with rhythm, *Murder at the Flamingo* is a toe-tapping, heart-pumping immersion into the world of Reggie and Hamish. A delightful experience."

—JOCELYN GREEN, AWARD-WINNING AUTHOR OF *A REFUGE ASSURED*

"You will want to add Reggie Van Buren and Hamish DeLuca to your circle of friends when you've read this book. This highly original story is a delight. Excellent historical detail and setting."

—MAUREEN JENNINGS, AUTHOR OF THE *DETECTIVE MURDOCH* SERIES, WHICH INSPIRED THE *MURDOCH MYSTERIES* TV SERIES

"With a crowded mystery and suspense market, it's hard to stand out from the pack. Rachel McMillan manages to do just this. She revives the classic 1930s-era amateur detective–whodunit set in a gloriously atmospheric Boston nightclub—The Flamingo . . . [*Murder at the Flamingo*] manages to cross the bridge between 'issue fiction' and 'commercial fiction' seamlessly. It's an immensely enjoyable and important read that I can't recommend highly enough. I simply loved this book!"

—*TALL POPPY WRITERS*

"A delicious mystery chock-full of 1930s charm and romance. I can't wait to find out what Reggie and Hamish get up to next!"

—CHERYL HONIGFORD, AWARD-WINNING AUTHOR
OF THE VIV AND CHARLIE MYSTERY SERIES

"*Murder at the Flamingo* sweeps the reader into a world of liquid-silk gowns, snazzy gangsters, smoke-filled dance floors, and star-crossed romance. Not to mention a bit of murder. Rachel McMillan breathes life into a cast of characters that defy the clichés of the genre: a rich girl who isn't spoiled, a leading man plagued with anxiety, a mob boss with a heart, and others who bring twists with each turn of the page. McMillan crafts Hamish, Reggie, Luca, and Nate with enough dimension for the reader to inspect each with a slow turn—strengths, flaws, frustrations. Nothing is absolute. The story plays out with the grit and humor of an RKO picture show, with the author's love for the time and place evident with each nod to detail. McMillan gives us a new Nick and Nora, sharing a bicycle and cannoli—and maybe a little bit more."

—ALLISON PITTMAN, AUTHOR OF *LOVING LUTHER*

"Rachel McMillan is a refreshing, talented writer who has created an original and appealing hero in Hamish DeLuca. Enjoy!"

—JULIE KLASSEN, CHRISTY AWARD–WINNING AUTHOR

THE *London* RESTORATION

Also by Rachel McMillan

Van Buren and DeLuca Mysteries

Murder at the Flamingo

Murder in the City of Liberty

Herringford and Watts Mysteries

The Bachelor Girl's Guide to Murder

A Lesson in Love and Murder

The White Feather Murders

Three Quarter Time Series

Love in Three Quarter Time

Rose in Three Quarter Time

Of Mozart and Magi

A Rainer Carol

Nonfiction

Dream, Plan, and Go

A Picture-Perfect Christmas

THE
London
RESTORATION

a novel

RACHEL McMILLAN

THOMAS NELSON
Since 1798

The London Restoration

Published in Nashville, Tennessee, by Thomas Nelson. Thomas Nelson is a registered trademark of HarperCollins Christian Publishing, Inc.

Published in association with William K. Jensen Literary Agency, 119 Bampton Court, Eugene, Oregon 97404.

Lyrics for "A Nightingale Sang in Berkeley Square" were written by Eric Maschwitz in 1939.

Scripture quotations are from the King James Version of the Bible. Public domain.

Thomas Nelson titles may be purchased in bulk for educational, business, fund-raising, or sales promotional use. For information, please email SpecialMarkets@ThomasNelson .com.

Library of Congress Cataloging-in-Publication Data

Names: McMillan, Rachel, 1981- author.
Title: The London restoration : a novel / Rachel McMillan.
Description: [Nashville] : Thomas Nelson, [2020] | Summary: "From author Rachel McMillan comes a richly researched historical romance that takes place in post-World War II London and features a strong female lead"-- Provided by publisher.
Identifiers: LCCN 2020007618 (print) | LCCN 2020007619 (ebook) | ISBN 9780785235026 (trade paperback) | ISBN 9780785235033 (epub) | ISBN 9780785235040 (audio download)
Subjects: LCSH: Cold War--Fiction. | London (England)--Fiction. | GSAFD: Historical fiction.
Classification: LCC PR9199.4.M4555 L66 2020 (print) | LCC PR9199.4.M4555 (ebook) | DDC 813/.6--dc23
LC record available at https://lccn.loc.gov/2020007618
LC ebook record available at https://lccn.loc.gov/2020007619

Printed in the United States of America
HB 09.08.2020

For my opa Thomas Bruce Cann,
who served with the 24th Field Ambulance,
5th Armored Division, Royal Canadian Army

The streets of town were paved with stars
It was such a romantic affair
—"A Nightingale Sang in Berkeley Square"

HISTORICAL NOTE

When you wander Cloth Fair in pursuit of St. Bartholomew the Great in London, you pass through a gatehouse, which is one of the oldest buildings in the city—dating to the time of the Great Fire. As a voracious reader of historical fiction, I often approach books in a similar manner to this gatehouse. As a gateway to the past. Hopefully capturing the essence and sensibility of a time long gone, while promoting further exploration. My most memorable fictional experiences inspire me to read more about the periods, places, and events I have encountered. I am not a scholar, rather a nerdy bookworm and enthusiast who has long wanted to make the London churches—both blitzed and non—a muse.

As a Canadian author writing the history of a foreign city I love, I recognize that my creation of this novel was conceived with historical liberties, often to the advantage of the world I wanted to create while appropriating a history I cannot personally speak to. My limitations, however, should not be a reflection of my deep inspiration or passion for this remarkable city, its people, and its resiliency. I wrote this book with reverence and awe but mostly to inspire you to pursue the history of London (not a hardship, I assure you) on your own terms.

So, let me start with a verifiable fact. My opa, Private Thomas Bruce Cann of Exeter, Ontario, served with the Royal Canadian Army, 24th Field Ambulance, 5th Armoured Division. He volunteered for the role of stretcher bearer because he never wanted to fire a gun. To our knowledge, he never did. I imparted this proud family history onto Brent Somerville. While Brent's division and

European tour during the war are entirely of my own creation, the intensity and horror of his experiences, his postwar PTSD, and his camaraderie are entirely authentic.

THE CHURCHES

Photos of couples marrying amidst rubble and parsons officiating services during the war years are plentiful and captured brilliantly. The parish churches, whole or maimed, were still a mainstay of a community in the midst of the upheaval of war. To add, the determination to rebuild was rampant. If one church had a piece that another did not in the midst of the chaos and destruction, they swapped. The rebuilt churches in London are a complicated and beautiful puzzle piece.

The grading system determining the heritage and preservation of London's history was imparted in 1947; however, long before its implementation, committees were established to consider the atrocities of the Blitz as well as the subsequent plans of action. There was a motion to leave the wrecked churches as monuments to their horrible devastation, but I assure you I am happy that this motion was largely unpassed. While beautiful gardens overrun the ruins of Christ Church Greyfriars and the Priory Church of the Order of St. John, Clerkenwell, in memory of loss, I truly treasure the rebuilt London churches. To the contemporary eye, they may wield the look of a patchwork quilt, bearing the scars of war, but the dedication to the architect's vision centuries later is commendable.

If you spend enough time in London, you wonder how Christopher Wren existed without a Starbucks—for such was his indefatigable drive! He is a true Renaissance man. His influence stretches far beyond London (look to Washington, DC, if you want to see Wren's distinctive architectural influence stateside . . .). After the Great Fire, he was given royal permission to rebuild fifty-one of the churches destroyed. Twenty-three of these churches (as well as St. Paul's Cathedral) remain in the heart of the city's financial center; while many were destroyed during the Blitz, several were demolished in the nineteenth century to make way for modern urban development.

The reconstruction of the churches lasted for decades with many reopening for services as late as the 1960s, but the indomitable work of historians and architects as well as religious leaders and committees to recreate and honor Wren's vision provides a lasting memorial that you will immediately see when you visit the beautiful city.

Though London is a city I have sought several times, I spent ten days last fall specifically exploring the Wren churches (and their friends) and learned closely of the spirit of these remarkable buildings in honoring the intent of their architect while still advancing into the modern era and thus to eternity. I am not, alas, an architecture historian, so all errors in my portrayal of these beautiful structures are mine.

The St. Paul's Watch included volunteers who pledged their lives to a structure under Churchill's orders, and on the Longest Night (often called the Second Great Fire of London in December 1940) Churchill ordered that the cathedral be protected at all costs as integral to the battered city's morale. As such, St. Paul's became an icon of indomitable spirit. Until the 1960s, its un-Blitzed dome was the highest point in the city.

KING'S COLLEGE

I confess wholeheartedly to creating courses, departments, and structures of the Strand campus of this institution to geographically suit the world I was rebuilding. Theology was not a course taught there, but having Brent teach there made a lot of sense for my story. Ah! The malleable wonder of fiction.

THE SOVIET THREAT AND ETERNITY

I love that in the earliest instances of the Cold War (a term coined by George Orwell who, ironically, wrote the tome so central to dystopian fiction), it was a war of "nerds" (as I joked with my editor). Academics and scientists and philosophers. A quiet war, at first, rooted in ideology. While everything (including Simon's very liberal MI6 involvement) is fictional, the Cold War, the discovery of a weapon as brutal and devastating as the atomic bomb, and the rise of Communist sympathy was rampant and often hidden just beneath the surface. The Secret Intelligence Service at 54 Broadway used numerous locations throughout London for the passing of encrypted and top-secret messages. Hotels, the Old Vic Theatre, private clubs as well as churches—such as the Holy Trinity Church, Knightsbridge—became essential for clandestine meetings and drop-offs.

One of the aspects of the Second World War that has always fascinated me is how ordinary people were forced into extra-ordinary roles: often unprepared. Diana's "recruitment" by Simon Barre as well as his method of procuring her for his Eternity hunch are, of course, fictional, but civilians were certainly used to gather intelligence.

In a similar way to Diana and Brent navigating a world of am-ateur espionage, I thought it likely that men swayed by the threat-ening Communist ideology may also try to play an integral role, albeit without knowing a sure way of the ropes.

BLETCHLEY PARK

When I wandered Bletchley Park for research, I attempted to re-create the everyday life of the men and women for whom it became home. While the Government Code and Cipher School was mostly populated by women (a three-to-one ratio), there were men there—

often of academic renown—who were assigned on account of their proficiency in mathematics and chess. The women, too, were often selected based on their educational background and proficiency in languages. It is quite likely that a woman of Diana's talent in languages would have been assigned to Hut 3 in the capacity she was.

Both Gordon Welchman (in *The Hut Six Story*) and the BMP reports developed by the German Air Section at Bletchley speak to signal interceptions and the Y Sections or "ears" of Bletchley Park. While the three-man RAF Y Stations for the listening, decoding, and interception of German radio signals were based at Cheadle, Chicksands, and Kingsdown, I very much needed to keep Diana where she was, though it could be possible for Diana and Fisher to be stationed at the park listening for possible signals, intercepts, and communications over the airwaves. Once I decided that some of these could be interrupted by classical music, I was over the moon.

While I made up the Bletchley traitor that Simon Barre was assigned to find, there was actual traitorous activity within Bletchley Manor. The most famous being John Cairncross: a double agent, late of Cambridge, whose cryptonym was Liszt (after the classical composer). As of 1944, he worked for MI6.

OLEUM MEDICINA

The wonderful thing about fiction is you can create a relic out of thin air. Prior Rahere is very much a real person whose fateful pilgrimage to Rome inspired him to consider the plight of impoverished Londoners and to found a priory and hospital near the Smithfield Market. Yet, I created that artifact and the rumor of his bringing it back to St. Bart's. What is not fictional is the artifacts unintentionally exhumed when Luftwaffe bombs fell. So many priceless treasures from the churches surrounding the oldest gates and areas of Roman-discovered Londinium survive. A visit to London affords this glimpse into the past. I heartily recommend visiting the rebuilt church of All Hallows-by-the-Tower and St. Bride's, Fleet Street, which host some fascinating Roman relics from ancient London.

The London Restoration hopefully reflects my sheer passion for some of the world's most beautiful churches and my awe at the resilience of a nation to ensure that the powers of hell never prevailed against them. Yet, it is not an authoritative text. I encourage readers to visit my Goodreads page (my bibliography was far too extensive to include here) and pursue some of the themes, places, events . . . and churches.

CHAPTER 1

September 1945
Allied-Occupied Vienna

While some adjusted to air-raid sirens and others to the lost light of blackouts, Diana Somerville never recovered from the absence of church bells. The war had taken the bells in London, the home she was impatient to return to, and certainly in Vienna, where she had been for the past five weeks. She'd never hear the resonant peal of the Pummerin, the booming bell cast in the eighteenth century and ruined several months previously at St. Stephen's Cathedral.

En route to a meeting with a man named Gabriel Langer, she looked up at the interrupted cathedral. While the structure was still recognizable, its famed crisscrossed roof had been incinerated. Diana imagined it as it might have been before the war.

As she passed one of the cream Baroque buildings unfelled by Luftwaffe bombs, *Wieder Frei!*—"Free Again!"—was plastered in colorful attribution to the new and mostly Soviet regime in a city quartered by Allied dominance between the British, French, Americans, and Russians. The city was still beautiful despite the propaganda, scars, and craters from the bombs.

How had the Soviets gone from a needed ally into MI6's most imminent threat?

Simon Barre had told her that the loudest voice in a time of devastation could blast through a war-torn city like cannon fire. Or the mournful toll of a church bell. She had been so preoccupied during her time at Bletchley Park and thereafter in this temporary city home that she hadn't paid as much attention to politics. Certainly not with the depth Simon did in his clandestine world. He felt that allowing Communists to assume any power was as large a threat as the war they had just survived. If in a different way.

Diana strode down the sunny streets, occasionally squinting to blur the faces of the buildings so at least for a second her vantage was spared the damage caused by bombs dropped by the Allies, who now promised the city's free and bright future and reconstruction.

Vienna was not quite the city she once had imagined exploring, with cranes modernizing the otherwise historic skyline and the pedestrian thoroughfares of the Graben and Kärtnerstrasse marred by blockades that kept the rubble from tumbling onto the pedestrians. She'd imagined looping arms with her husband, Brent, and peering up at steeples, not waiting for the next directive from her friend and wartime colleague MI6 agent Simon Barre.

Simon said a new war was building: one that would require intelligence and the decryption skills she had honed during her work at Bletchley Park and the Government Code and Cipher School. But mostly he required her intuition and ability to read hidden messages: from the position of a column in a Christopher Wren church to the subtle interruption of a Mozart piece when her ears were attuned to unusual activity in a Luftwaffe flight plan intercepted by radio waves.

His pursuit of a Soviet agent named Eternity led Simon to believe an association existed between churches in Vienna and in London and the spread of the man's Communist influence. Simon needed to find Eternity. The man was rumored to possess a file containing information that could prolong the war. Or catapult the new war he spoke of into a certainty.

A file that men would kill for.

When Diana had protested that the war was over, Simon merely gave her a look she recognized from dozens of times when she asked a question about chess he was surprised she didn't know.

No one, of course, was better suited to search for the concealed clues a church might hold than Diana Somerville, née Foyle. She *loved* churches. Especially those designed by Sir Christopher Wren. And as to recognizing the pattern of Eternity, the man used a signature: the mathematic symbol for infinity. Simon chose the code name when the foreign agent's activity seemed to involve churches. The eternal house of God on earth.

She had seen armed British soldiers overtake their portion of the divided city, had seen a non-Communist foreign minister appointed even as the collars of the Soviet officers bristled.

She had wandered age-old cobblestones in a dark waltz of silenced bells and deserted palaces, wondering what was shadow and what was her imagination. She'd witnessed the drawn faces of men in battered homburgs lined up for a cup of watered coffee at Julius Meinl while women sat with white-knuckled hands crossed in their laps at the Hauptbahnhof, waiting for their emaciated prisoners of war to exit the trains screeching into the station. As the city precariously balanced Hitler's oppressive Anschluss and the Allied indecision regarding next moves, it was a prime breeding ground for the Communist influence Simon was so intent on destroying.

Gabriel Langer, like Diana, was an ally. Simon introduced him as a proud Austrian university professor who had watched his city first captured by Hitler's regime and then divided when liberated by the occupying Allied forces. The last thing Langer wanted was to see his city torn apart again. She wasn't sure how Simon knew him, just that he was as influential as Simon believed she was.

Diana adjusted the brim of her red cartwheel hat, straightened her shoulders, and pursed her lips stained the same shade of crimson as her hat as she neared the heavy wooden door of Peterskirche, tucked between narrow buildings in its eponymous *Platz*. She would find Langer and together they would try to suss out Eternity.

Simon had intercepted a message the night before that linked Eternity—or one of his men—with a concert at Peterskirche. The concert gave her an opportunity to meet the man Simon so relied on in Vienna just before she caught her three-hour flight back to London the following day.

The textbooks, dry lectures, and slides from her studying at King's College couldn't adequately encapsulate the opulent interior, nor could they breathe life into Mozart's Great Mass filling the *hochaltar* amidst gilded marble walls hosting numerous sculptures and inspiring the eye upward to its famed painted dome.

She wouldn't have known as much about music if she hadn't sat across from Fisher Carne for four years in a slatted hut in Bletchley, listening to German signals through the wireless and overhearing daily programs of religious and classical music. None of those experiences could compare to the live musicians who filled the sanctuary now with an explosion of sound. She savored the first bars of the *Grosse Messe* in C Minor as she scanned pews for her contact.

The Kyrie section swelled to the frescoes and tripped over the tile as voices filled every inch of the sanctuary. It was important for her to pay attention to the music. It might be a language beyond each note or phrase.

She spotted white-blond hair and a green collar three pews from the back as per her directive. She slid in beside Langer.

"Are you familiar with Mozart?" he asked.

"I know this piece." Diana cast a surreptitious look at the handbag she had placed beside her at an angle, ensuring the white-handled revolver was tucked away from view.

"A shame we have to hear it scaled back like this. Doubles in each of the vocal sections. Seems everything is rationed these days, even timpani and tenors," Gabriel remarked. She liked his soft Viennese accent and intelligent brown eyes.

"Mercy." He translated the lyrics accompanying the next bar. Diana kept her ears peeled to recognize a code or a message, to seek out a possible key in the architecture of the unbombed sanctuary. Simon had warned her of traitors who looked like friends. Those who balanced two worlds: depressed or destitute by war or unknowing of what good or evil was. Langer, he assured her, was none of those things.

The soprano soloist's rich voice drew her focus.

"A lot about mercy," Langer continued. "Lord have mercy. Christ have mercy." His gaze swept the church's circumference. Perhaps he was trying to hear in lyrics what she was trying to hear in musical phrases: a clue to the identity of the man they were pursuing.

"In the Middle Ages," Diana explained in his language, "men believed if they built the great cathedrals, they would be given mercy. To build a church was to atone for a sin. They were given plenary indulgences and a fast route to heaven. The generations after them were indentured but promised a living. So the men built church after church, knowing they might never see the end. The fruit of their labor as their steeples grew higher and higher to heaven."

"You speak excellent German." Gabriel's gaze took to the fresco in the cupola depicting the *Coronation of Our Lady,* all while his dexterous fingers retrieved a notebook and pen from the inside of his coat. Casually, she opened her compact and smoothed a stray smudge of lip stain with a handkerchief she kept pristine in her handbag.

"My father taught me."

"And who is the architect of this church?" Between them he covertly scribbled something. Mozart swelled and the soloist was joined by the unison of the choir. He passed the note to her.

"Initially the plans were attributed to Montani." Diana didn't miss a beat. "Hildebrandt too. Then Dientzenhofer for the façade." She sought what his note said—*fourth pew on the right*—then crumpled the paper.

A man sat with his hat brim pulled low not two rows over and she shivered. While Simon assured her she was perfectly safe, she never crossed through the city without premonition. Perhaps it was leftover intensity from Bletchley where the Official Secrets Act and the constant warning about an accidental slip of integral information hovered around her daily. Or maybe it was the tug of the Blitz at her heels.

Most likely, it was because of the rumors of what befell spies—both those trained and civilians—and the general sense of morbidity that hung over the city like a shadow. Simon assured her that she had allies. Diana, however, felt completely alone.

The music regained her attention and she recalled all Fisher had told her about the piece.

The gilt high pulpit was a gold and silver representation of the martyrdom of St. John of Nepomuk, the spandrels or triangles around the domed roof portraying the four evangelists.

"And you are returning to London now?"

Diana nodded.

"As you can see, Peterskirche was fortunate to remain intact while so many of our churches were not." His lips slid into a rueful smile. "Perhaps if you tire of the churches in England . . . Who is the fellow, the one named for a bird . . . ?"

"Wren. Christopher Wren."

Glazed with sadness, his brown eyes held hers. "Perhaps someday you will come back and visit our churches."

"Perhaps." Diana reached for her red hat. The Viennese—occupied or not—took great pride in their ability to charm and hold their guests—even amidst bombed churches, even as jagged cracks snaked over the gilt interiors of ivory Baroque buildings.

The conductor held his palm out to the soloist, and the concertmaster bowed. Diana joined the applause. The man with the hat they had been watching rose.

Langer held Diana back a moment with a light hand on her sleeve. "Let me go first." He departed the church while Diana inched toward his pew, peering over the famed cherub carving on its back to see if anything had been left behind.

Finding nothing, she pushed through the heavy door and pressed her back against the curved ivory stone of the church's exterior.

She watched the audience trickle back into wrecked streets that stood in stark contrast to the preserved beauty of the church. The man with the hat was lost to her, though she was already running through a dozen possible reasons to stop and engage him should he appear. Anything to bring back to Simon since the music and the architecture left her without a message.

Several moments later as the throng thinned out and the sun disappeared behind the roof's green dome, Langer appeared.

"Well?"

He held a silver cigarette case out to her and she declined. He lifted one to his lips, struck a match against the side of the church, and lit the end. "Simon Barre loves using civilians. I've known the man several years now."

"As have I."

"You're as much a field agent as I am. Which is to say not at all. Whatever you did to catch Simon's eye during the war must have made a great impression."

"I cannot talk about what I did during the war."

Langer nodded. "And he will want favor after favor and you will know just enough to think you are helping with a greater cause. But mostly you will be . . . what is the English word?"

"Endangered?"

"Baffled. He never works in a cohesive line. He follows his instinct. And sometimes it leads to something like a beautiful concert and sometimes . . ." Langer dropped the cigarette and turned his heel over it. "It leads to nothing at all. So when you go back to your London, remember that whatever you promised him can make you feel heroic. Part of a worthy cause. And other times . . . well . . ."

Langer didn't need to finish the sentence. They shook hands and she walked away. Some things, including Simon Barre's methods, would never need translation.

Diana wove her way back to her temporary flat. Was she being too careful, looking over her shoulder every few steps? Truth was, she had no idea what she should sense as dangerous. And Simon had so little to give her.

An elusive Soviet agent with a penchant for making contacts around churches. Never far from a church. Diana was to tell Simon if she saw anyone at a church. If they set their cases down. If they left anything behind, from a newspaper to a telegram or a note. And to listen. Just as she had when she was at Bletchley in Hut 3, when the airwaves were filled with air raids and intercepted Luftwaffe signals. When anything from a German radio station to the BBC might be worth passing to the code breakers.

Diana had just set down her keys and gloves in the rented flat when the telephone rang. She smiled at Simon's voice on the other end. It called to mind chess and cocoa and late nights when he took her into his confidence. She told him of her current frustration that she hadn't been of much help at all.

"I am going home tomorrow," she said. "I've been here for five weeks and you have called in your favor. And now you're back in London before I am." She clucked her tongue. "So the next time we talk will be on British soil."

"Gabriel Langer is a good man."

"He seems so."

"I appreciate him much as I do you, Diana. Well, maybe not *as* much."

"I'm touched." She wound the telephone cord around her finger. "Not sure if it's helpful, but Fisher always talked about how Mozart's compositions were catalogued. The Köchel Catalogue." She listed the piece they had heard that afternoon. "And there was certainly someone who seemed suspicious to Langer there. But we got nothing out of him. If someone was trying to collect a message, could it be in the catalogue choice?"

"See why I need you?"

"Because we get along? Because I know everything about church architecture and because I am indebted to you and you know I have no choice?"

"There's that. But you also think outside the lines and—"

"Because you're following a trail outside of MI6's jurisdiction?" Diana continued. "It's not like you to go rogue, Simon."

"I'm not going rogue. My team officially has men surveilling the known sympathizers and Soviet supporters in London. But if I can just prove that there's someone else, that this file exists . . ."

"You keep mentioning this file."

"Langer *saw* it, Diana. As did a former Special Operations Executive I work with now and then. I just need to prove it. And I need to find the man who is behind the collected information in it."

"Off the record," Diana translated. "With my help."

Simon was silent for a moment. "Diana, this file is a link to an ideology that could ruin us. It's why I am so determined to do my bit to stop it from spreading."

"We fought *with* the Soviets."

"I know that. But just because you're allied in one line of thought doesn't mean you are aligned in all. Even Hitler hated Communism."

"If you truly think I can help . . ."

"Yes, I do. So let's have a proper tea, shall we?"

"When?"

"The Savoy. Threeish. Day after next."

"A proper tea . . . And then will you let me get back to my life? The war is over, as you well know." But she could still imagine the look of exasperation he would give her. For Simon, there was always another war.

"Let's see, shall we?"

"Simon, you're infuriating." But she couldn't help but smile. Simon was trying to be evasive and professional, but she could hear the grin in his words.

"Am I?"

"You know you are," she said in lieu of good-bye and rang off.

Diana waited before she dialed her husband's number at the flat in Clerkenwell. She supposed it was her flat, too, though she had spent but a handful of time there before he shipped out to Belgium and she chugged to Buckinghamshire on a crowded train. She had been twenty-three then and he had just courted the right side of thirty. So young. Today she felt several centuries old.

While she dialed, she imagined the chiming tower of St. James's next door while Brent set his satchel and fedora on the stand near the corner. Perhaps he would be mentally running through his earlier lecture at King's College after wrapping his wonderful tenor around the courses on New Testament theology. While she had been in Vienna, he had slipped back into their life before the war.

Was he as lonely without her as she was without him? Would he fix himself a cup of tea then take out a sketchbook and work deft lines into dimension, shading churches so they breathed from the page? The prospect of seeing him excited her, which was why she was surprised when her hands wrung in anticipation of their meeting. Of their speaking.

She straightened her shoulders, inhaled, and dialed.

"Hello."

Diana's heart skipped a beat at the sound of his voice. "Brent."

Several heartbeats, then a rigid intake of breath. "Diana."

His voice reverberated through her, even though miles and years stretched between them. Such was their love story that it had to pick up long after other uniformed men and women found each other in long embraces.

While she had initially imagined announcing her return with a joy that made her trip over her words, she merely swallowed and said, "I'm coming home."

CHAPTER 2

London

One would think after surviving the resounding boom of artillery fire, the screams of dying men across the trenches, blaring air-raid sirens, and constant shouted commands, silence would be a reprieve. But to Brent Somerville, it was as deafening as the cacophony of war.

Through the vantage of his window seat on the double-decker bus, on his way to meet his wife at Charing Cross, he made out what was left of the once-majestic churches she loved in streets as familiar to both of them as breathing.

When Brent first fell for Diana Foyle, it was in a city of bell tolls and steeple chimes. Christopher Wren's poetry of plastered columns and distinctive lines defined every street around the old gates of London and beyond. Wren's influence served as a backdrop to their romance. The art entailing the highest point of the city skyline with the dome of St. Paul's on Ludgate Hill, the bells of St. Mary-le-Bow and St. Bride's tolling in friendly rivalry. It spoke to his nerves that he wondered at her reaction when she finally saw them again. Saw him again.

During the war she had been in Buckinghamshire doing translation work from numerous languages, including German, for the Foreign Office while he was hoisting stretchers and wading around murky trenches in Belgium and then Italy. She had spent her leave in the early days with him at arranged locations, saying little about her daily life, which suited him just fine. He didn't want to expose her to what met him daily through the dirt, blood, and artillery fire.

Once the war had ended and everyone else was returning home, she was still needed to continue her work and disappeared for a month. Five weeks, to be exact. No letters from her. No word from her superiors about her situation . . .

Photos didn't capture her smell or the way the wind tickled her hair; telephone calls were just rippled static and took the chime-like wonder from the voice of a girl who, in the earliest years of their acquaintance, never stopped talking.

During those long nights of waiting for the next battle, he would drift into nightmares, imagining the worst, or take out his sketch pad and capture a wounded church or a slice of the horror he experienced as he trudged after his unit. Then, there were the weeks of convalescence when his pain and flashbacks were secondary to his worry for her.

Two fingers on his left hand now melded into one, while a deep gash on his forehead faded into a scar he could just hide with his hair if he combed it right. Once the morphine wore off, he was merely miffed that she was so far away when hadn't they wasted too many years already?

The double-decker swerved around the remains of these churches and the jigsaw puzzle of wrecked Cripplegate. Wounded, scarred, and gutted, with moats of brick and uneven mortar. Signs spoke to the rebuilding efforts, and local politicians bandied about flyers fashioned with a hope as hard to come by as sugar, butter, bread, and tea leaves, which would be strained three times in a morning.

The newspaper headlines dominated by Churchill's certainty of stoic victory when Brent left now announced the triumphs and travails of the Labour Party elected by a landslide while Brent was still in a foreign hospital. He didn't know why the state of their wrecked city shook him as if he were solely responsible for the chaotic peace that stretched before him. Solely responsible for the London Diana would meet after so many years away.

He smiled, remembering how he had dusted and cleaned his flat the night before they were married. But he couldn't scrub away the men with scuffed shoes and wilted homburgs limping from the neighborhood daily in search of jobs that would never be found. He couldn't polish or finesse the women waiting expectantly outside the bakery and butcher shops for hours only to leave defeated, their meager findings slung over their sunken shoulders.

Brent shifted in the bus seat and turned from his reflection in the window. He knew he shouldn't be self-conscious. That she would take London's scars as she took his own—a branding of war. He knew she would love him no matter what. After all, she had vowed as much until death parted them. But the longer he stayed alone in their flat, the more he formulated doubts.

Part of him wanted time to peel back and everything to be the same. Before a miscalculated step and an unexpected blast ignited his hand and marred his forehead. It did more than that, of course. It cost a life. But Brent wouldn't think of that now.

He trained his thoughts on Diana. She had been as certain to him as breathing. If she returned as changed as he was, would he love her in the same way? He felt like a traitor for even allowing those bleak thoughts to fill the space of his overcrowded mind.

Truth was, he wasn't used to being so close to another human, physically or otherwise. Four years of the ravages of war had built up barriers. He could retreat into himself far more deeply than he had before, even when crouched with men in a trench, or while freezing in a tent, or after a long stretch of convalescence. London had seemed a stranger to him the moment he stepped off the train weeks ago before tiredly adjusted the canvas bag on his good shoulder. If he had to readjust to his beloved city, how did that bode for Diana?

He reminded himself, as he had the night before, of how smitten Diana was when he taught her about all seven of the Greek forms of love. He might have to find a way to define each word again, having spent so long alone, but he had seven forms at his disposal. Yes, he returned without having her here to welcome him. But she was here now. He would make sure that was enough.

The long, winding Strand pierced the heart of Westminster's artery. Exiting the bus, Brent took the road to Charing Cross at a quick diagonal. He tried to meet the gaps in the well-known neighborhood's unfamiliar new façade as she might. At least until he saw her.

Diana stood facing away from him, framed by the large statue of an Eleanor Cross. Diana's long fingers tugged the brim of her broadrimmed red hat. He placed his uninjured hand on her shoulder.

She spun on her heel and his heart twisted at her eyes glistening in a beautiful face. "Brent."

Turned out he loved her more than his pride, because for all he had practiced being calm and collected and imagined holding her at arm's length in punishment for her radio silence the last five weeks, the joy on her face obliterated every last instinct for reservation. "Hello." He smiled and adjusted the tie tucked into his vest, thinking of how to kiss her senseless without startling her.

He hadn't kissed her in so long. Memories had taunted him across the Front, particularly on morphine-addled nights in the hospital wing. He could feel her breath on his collarbone and the tips of her fingers at the back of his neck.

Brent leaned in quickly and she leaned back, studying him. He took a step forward and landed on her shoe. She gave a forced laugh, then rose a little on her toes to kiss him just as he turned his head so her nose collided with his cheekbone. When she tried again and met his lips, he barely kept himself in check before melting. But this was not the time. He wouldn't start a physical conversation when he hadn't heard but a word from her lips.

"There's no word, Greek or otherwise, for this awkwardness," he muttered, pulling away.

"Pardon?"

Brent straightened and took her hand. "Diana, how have you

been?" Her blonde hair was half hidden by her red hat and though she was pale, her blue eyes sparkled.

She let out a nervous laugh. "How have I *been*?"

"I'm sorry . . . I just . . ."

"I left my cases in a locker inside the station. I was dying for a cup of tea. And I'm famished. I was determined we could find something to eat before setting off for home. I hope you don't mind."

Brent hated small talk. "Not in the least. The larder is in a rather dismal state."

He wanted to say a thousand things. Ask a thousand questions. Instead, he said, "Tea?"

$\sim\!\!\infty\!\!\sim$

It was always tea. On their wedding night. Tea. At learning he would ship out as the church towers crumbled beneath German bombs unhindered by the searchlights and barrage balloons. Tea. For any insecurity she had about their reconciliation, three letters in a small word and she felt safe. And more tea.

She was almost surprised at how easily he gave in to the suggestion that they return to a common meeting place. To Brent's credit, he didn't wonder why she hadn't taken a taxi from the airport directly home. Then she remembered she hadn't told him *how* she was getting to London, just that she *would* be there. The longer she could put off the flat familiar to her only from a few dinners during their courtship and the first excited hours of their wedding night before the sirens drove them out the door and into a cold Tube station shelter, the better.

She shouldn't be nervous to see her husband. She should be elated. But the years apart had taken away all the well-meaning shoulds and left nothing but mere survival in their stead. She shouldn't have noticed the garish scar he carefully tried to hide, but she did. She shouldn't have let her eyes dart immediately to his damaged left hand either. So much for shoulds and shouldn'ts. There was always tea.

Here now on neutral ground, she couldn't see the flashes of whatever horrors were branded on his mind any more than she could decode a fuzzy radio signal on a stormy Bletchley night.

Diana cleared her throat. "I cannot tell you how wonderful it is to be home. I know that . . . Was it arduous to get back?"

"I was still in hospital, as you know, and then the demobilization efforts took a blasted long time. And you know from my letter that I started back at King's a fortnight ago."

He could command entire lecture halls with that voice, disseminating his perspectives on Scripture. Could command her whole heart.

From across the table in the tea shop, the sun played with Brent's features as a particularly stubborn cloud stole away beyond the pane. A few gray strands at his temples offset his tawny hair, and it rippled reddish gold when the sun struck it a certain way. His green eyes were flecked a little with gold, and amber rimmed their irises. The creases at the corners of his eyes seemed caused by exhaustion rather than laughter.

"I bet the routine is a nice change," Diana said stupidly when no other words formed, turning the end of the sentence up as if in question. But he didn't answer.

She flicked her gaze down at his left hand. He hadn't told her the extent of his injuries. The sight of his index and middle fingers sewn together into one big digit in the middle of his long hand hurt her as if she had felt their pain. He noticed her stare and tucked his hand under the table.

She wanted to close the years between them. To tell him that she had met a man who would outdo even Brent at crossword puzzles. That she had . . . It would be too easy for the secrets to spill out.

The tea arrived with a plate of sandwiches and tarts. Despite her growling stomach she was nervous to pinch a sandwich before he helped himself.

"King's. Yes," he said finally. "I think they're enjoying the classes."

She didn't recognize this strange shell of herself, so why should she expect him to take the reins? Sure, he had served at the Front, bearing stretchers across unthinkable atrocities while she was tucked safely in a hut away from the bombs. Was it the truth about her time away from him that kept her so formal? Diana folded her hands in her lap, unsure of what to say.

For all he knew she merely sat in the Foreign Office and translated. No intercepted Luftwaffe codes. No Vienna. It was the secrets she was forced to keep from him that held her back. In the same way she assumed his scars and experiences kept him from meeting her halfway.

Brent gingerly tilted the plate toward her. She took a sandwich and a tart, then arranged them on her plate. Their eyes met over the tiered tray. For a moment she found the Brent she knew and her heart raced at the familiarity. But he pulled away, reaching for a sandwich.

He seemed more interested in chasing a crumb around his plate than he was in eating. "The students are finding it hard to readjust."

Diana's stomach growled again as a reminder she had been too nervous to eat that morning, or even the night before.

"Do you . . . do you have what you need?" Brent's brow furrowed. "Did you get enough to eat?"

"You know I can't eat when I'm nervous." Diana shoved a triangle of sandwich in her mouth. Who was she to sit here fingering delicacies and taking dainty bites? They were married, for heaven's sake. She spun the tier and selected an egg-and-cress sandwich.

Brent straightened his shoulders and made long work of eating a cheese sandwich. "Strange we should be nervous around each other."

Diana swallowed as a memory formed: his finger brushing her

cheek and over her collarbone, catching the lace collar of her nightgown. She lingered in the past a moment before blinking back to a cold table of strangers enjoying a simple repast. She wanted to curve into his side and sob into his neck and learn every horrible thing he had experienced. They had always fallen so easily into each other. "Talking as if we didn't know each other?"

"I don't know where you were the past five weeks." Brent tried to be stern but sounded merely hurt instead. "And now you're back. I thought you would be here when I returned."

"I was doing a favor for a friend."

"A friend I don't know."

"We lived very different lives the past four years, Brent, and we met new people." Diana sighed. It was one thing for her to present her Simon-assigned role to strangers in Austria, quite another when sitting across from her husband. "There are a few committees—even one formed by the Royal Institute of Architects—now dedicated to ensuring our architectural treasures and history are preserved. They began when the bombs started to fall. There will be a new grading system to classify the importance and heritage of each building, even as some modern adjustments are made. And I thought that, well, with the Wren churches I can provide notes that account for the obvious changes that need to take place but also ensure they are true to Wren's original vision."

"Some will see a crack. A bombed building." The right side of his mouth twitched into a small smile. "You will see a map and imagine the potential in the rubble."

"I have carte blanche access and compensation even to those places blockaded by city work crews because . . . a friend gave me a special letter. So I can provide aesthetic and historical notes to use in the meetings for their new designation." She sipped her tea. "I will take notes and pair them with my knowledge of the churches as they were as well as how they might function in the future. Right now, they're a huge puzzle and it's a monumental undertaking."

She scratched the tablecloth with her thumbnail. "It's what I want to focus on, Brent. Now that I'm back."

"You should be finishing your degree . . . ," Brent started but didn't get far as she warmed to her subject.

"Just like Christopher Wren and his stonemasons after the Great Fire. Walls and windows and pews! All of those tombstones worked into the walls and floors. I've missed my churches, Brent. And if you come with me, you can give me a spiritual perspective! Even the churches that were bombed are still holding services and concerts and weddings."

"You're starting to sound like yourself." His hands clasped the edges of the table.

"Like myself?" She arched her right eyebrow.

"Give the girl a chance to talk about Wren churches and . . ."

She smiled at her plate before she snatched up another sandwich. "You told me that architecture is as sure a form of worship as a hymn, psalm, or prayer."

A smile toyed with his lips. "I clearly have to stop telling you things."

Diana sank into his teasing tone as she might an old cardigan, and her shoulders relaxed. "You know their stories. You know their symbols. You know why the quires are in the shapes of crosses and why the baptismal fonts are near the back doors, and the significance of the high altar catching the eastern sun."

"So do you, Diana. You hammered me with those facts endlessly before your exams. I didn't even know what a quire was before I met you."

"And you the vicar's nephew," Diana said before clearing her throat. "The quire is the area of a church providing seating for the clergy and church choir located between the nave and the chancel," she recited, mimicking her most studious sessions.

"Remember those cards?" Brent said. "I would write a definition on one side . . ."

"And I would write the name of the church on the other." The memory warmed her. "I tried to draw steeples."

"I stopped you, thank heavens. Especially when you insisted that every illustration for our immediate purpose required a parish cat."

Diana laughed. "I never had your artistic talent. It was one of the reasons I fell in love with you."

She watched for his response and exhaled at his softening features. The singe of his lips before at Charing Cross, the slight tremor when their mouths first met, the hitch in his breath when he pulled away, the rest of the kiss lying dormant in his eyes. All the promise she needed was right there.

"Come, let's leave my cases in the locker for a while. We'll go to All Hallows. You pledged your life and soul to me there. It's a perfect place to start rebuilding." She crossed her palm over her heart. "I don't want to go in and take notes just about stone."

"And now with all these dramatic pleas . . ."

"But what's more"—she laid down her trump card—"do you really want me roaming around a bombed church alone at night?" She gazed out the window, the sky gray and heavy with rain clouds. Evening was tugging fast at its heels.

She compelled him with slightly pouting lips and raised eyebrows.

Brent's eyes softened when she covered his forearm with her newly manicured fingernails, leaned over the table, and widened her eyes after seeing the desired effect reflected in his own. "You never could resist that look."

"Turns out I can't resist you after all." He shrugged, his lips creased in a partial smile.

Diana smoothed her skirt. "What does that mean? You *want* to resist me?"

"What other choice did my pride have, Diana? I wondered if you had changed your mind since it took you so long to come back.

See, when you spend enough nights pacing, your mind makes up all sorts of things. Especially after so long apart. About a marriage that took place just before our worlds drove us apart. About a girl you thought you knew and certainly loved until she went missing for five weeks just as you were sorting out how you could possibly return to life again. After where you had been. After all you had seen."

His injured hand was on the table and no longer hidden in his lap. She grabbed his hand and gave it a gentle squeeze, the wedding ring on his fourth, still-whole finger pressing into her palm. "I will never change my mind."

CHAPTER 3

Brent led Diana out the door of the tea shop, keeping his hand at the small of her back. As their teatime had overlapped with the heaviest barrage of early evening traffic, they should have been able to find a taxi, but the sky had opened again in a sudden downpour and they sought shelter under the awning of an adjacent store. Brent suggested they use the opportunity to see to her luggage, but Diana assured him they could collect her cases later.

He turned to study her profile. They used to be so in sync he could anticipate her next breath, sigh, or sentence. A favor for a friend? What favor took five weeks? Translation work? What was left to translate? What friend? He thought he knew all of her friends. She wrote about some of them. A woman named Sophie Villiers who insisted on being called by her surname. A man named Simon Barre who tried to teach her chess. All of the questions Brent had tucked under the café table with his injured hand barreled through his brain.

But he wanted *her*. He wanted to make good on every frantic promise he'd muttered at the first shrill whiz of artillery fire. *If I can just get home. If I can just see her again.* That was before his mind could conjure a silence of five weeks. He tugged at his collar as a car swerved to splash a small wall of rain against the curb.

The tightness in his chest had loosened the longer their conversation echoed who they had been before. That had to count for something. Besides, there was no sense beginning a row as they waited out the rain. "So, these church consultations of yours. We'll just cross through barricades and around city workers and construction and visit churches that have survived the bombings?" He watched another occupied taxi pass.

Diana shrugged. "Perhaps. But we can also attend concerts and Evensong and Communion. They all continued during the war, you know. And I'd like to think they continued even during Wren's time when they were deciding which parishes to rebuild after the Great Fire and which ones to consolidate . . ."

That was his Diana. Fixated on the stamp of Christopher Wren's distinctive vision, his ingenuity and motifs. Her passion for the subject was captivating. Brent's gaze traced the curve of her cheek and wandered to the hourglass curves of her figure against the canvas of a London they both knew well. *Had* known well. Now, it was their blueprint back to each other. They had the same reference points for the shops and street corners around which black taxicabs veered, and the buses like tiered red cakes bumbled around moats and holes of buildings blasted by German bombs.

He flexed his good hand, finding confidence in the consistency: marred but similar, broken yet recognizable. After several ticks of silence, he asked, "What did you imagine saying when you saw me again?"

Diana smiled, wrinkling her nose, not looking straight at him but at a man shaking out his umbrella. "That I wish we would have gone on a honeymoon. A real one. Where would we have gone?"

Brent took a beat. "You would've picked some city with a thousand cathedrals and just dragged me around to churches for days on end."

"And you?" She raised an eyebrow, inclining her head. "What did you imagine saying to me?"

"Do you really want to know?" He waited for her assent, which came in the form of a slight nod. "On good days there was some rather awful poetry. Something about your sparkling blue eyes, the lustrous strands of gold in your hair. The way your curves . . . well . . . *ahem*. We won't get into the pages about moonlight, because by the time I got to the curve of your cheek under a bomb shelter light, my senses returned. Utter rubbish, of course. But romantic rubbish. The sort I excel at." He winked and waited for her smile.

"And on bad days?" she whispered.

Brent cleared his throat. "There were too many bad days, weren't there?" His shoulder brushed hers and a sure flame flickered through the sinews of his arm. On the front in Belgium and later in Italy through treacherous and rainy nights, he found solace in the memory of their last consuming kiss, of enfolding her in his arms.

He looked up, startled, as if his sensual thoughts were so pressing and immediate she might feel the heat through him.

He had imagined so much about their reunion. That they would melt into each other as they had before and pick up where they left off, as if the war were a few ellipses interrupting the sentence of their life together. That the taste and feel and scent of her he had only just grown accustomed to would be a certainty he woke up to every morning. Yet something Holt had told him took Brent aback.

Of course, he shouldn't have listened to his friend when the man set into a tirade about the opposite sex. Holt had recently received a letter from his fiancée, whom he'd met over a previous weekend in a pub. Said fiancée had ended their engagement as quickly as it had begun, and thereafter Holt considered himself a standing authority on all things nuptial.

Holt talked a lot. Too much. And he had several theories that physical conversation in a reunited marriage was not primed to last. His theories were patched up from a few too many with a stranger at a pub, newspaper editorials, letters to the editor, and advice columns. All were laced with his own belief that a hurried tumble after quick vows before one shipped out did not a lasting marriage make.

But that wasn't Brent and Diana's story. They had been together long before that. He certainly had intended to marry her nearly from the moment he saw her. He shoved his injured hand more deeply into his pocket. It was only the insecurity talking.

Five weeks. A favor for a friend.

She hadn't been able to keep the slightest secret from him before. They never made it to Christmas before she excitedly let slip what his present was. Yet the last four years had added a new maturity to her bearing and confidence in the way she held her head. Her chin was turned up to watch the sky break with London's inimitable magic and the sun peer through almost as quickly as the downpour had started.

Diana tugged him out from under the awning. "Oh look! There's a taxi!" She raised her arm to signal.

∽ ᴖ ∽

Sometimes when missing Brent was too much, Diana had focused on every last thing the war had taken from her. A taste of birthday cake, a robust and fully steeped cup of tea, the luxurious feel of silk stockings, the lights in Piccadilly and Leicester Square. If she squeezed her eyes shut tightly enough, she was almost in London again, tracing the familiar route to King's from the flat she shared in Paddington before their wedding or skipping to Foyle's Bookstore on a rainy afternoon.

She would try to keep his memory at bay, but it was never more than a moment or two before her thoughts drifted back to him.

Now as Brent sat beside her in the back of a taxi, her thoughts turned to the breadth of his shoulders, the curve of his chin, and the scent and nearness and feel of him. Their song too. The one she chose for them. Brent hadn't minded not having a say in the selection of "A Nightingale Sang in Berkeley Square." All of her classmates had a song with their boyfriends, to hum absently or to light up to at a dance. Diana had presented Brent with a strong case for a song that was as much about the love between two people as about love for their city.

The city now met Diana in the whole of its complex nursery

rhyme. It sank under the weight of her childhood remembrance and the visits with her professor father from nearby Cambridge. He introduced her to the nursery rhymes firsthand so she could see them before her very eyes. Bridges, posies, and rings, plagues and a devastating fire blazing a destructive path from Pudding Lane, ravaging the beautiful medieval structures before Wren commandeered the whole of the urban sprawl like his personal building block set.

She crooned a few bars of the rhyme that was her father's favorite and then hers too. All about the church bells. She imagined they were talking to each other.

"Oranges and lemons say the bells of St. Clement's."

"You owe me five farthings, say the bells of St. Martin's."

"You still sing like a lark." Brent gave her shoulder a playful nudge with his. Diana couldn't carry a tune. More still, his joshing her about it was a long-established jest between them.

The cab slid to the side of the road and let them off half a block away from the construction around the churchyard. All Hallows-by-the-Tower, or what was left of it, was surrounded by blockades and shrouded in shadow.

A worker approached as they stepped from the curb, shoving his cap back on his head. "You can't be here, luv."

"My name is Diana Somerville, and I am a historian." Diana looked up at her husband. "This is Dr. Brent Somerville." She adjusted the brim of her hat so the worker could fully see her widening smile. "We were married at this church. We just want to take a peek around. You must be almost finished for the night."

"Well . . ." He scratched the back of his neck.

"Please. It's been so long."

The worker scrutinized her two-toned pumps. "It's not very stable. Not safe. You don't want to be roaming around here."

"I'll be careful." Diana was sure if she could just get close enough, she could see the church as it had once been. As it could be again.

The worker shoved his cap back in place. "Make sure she

doesn't trip," he said to Brent. "Not safe. And she's right. I'm done here."

"You have my word." Brent tipped his own hat in thanks as the man set off. "Well, at least we have an entirely full view of the Tower and the bridge."

"In anyone else that would be optimistic. In you, darling, it's just—"

"The sarcasm you fell in love with all of those years ago?" Brent offered Diana his hand to steady her over a particularly uneven plot of ground, and she took it.

She took in the hollow that was once the pipe and wood of the grand organ, the columns overtaken by weeds, the barren arches void of their long-smashed glass panes.

Diana continued to observe the area. The last time she had seen this church it had been in an even worse state of disrepair, and yet she was elated Brent was at her side. "There's still part of a steeple." She picked her way to the surviving shell of an arched window and peered at a few leafless trees. It wasn't just the encroaching chill that caused their bleak barrenness.

Brent inspected the moat of rock and stone rimming the shell of the church. "It's about as cheery as being toted through Traitor's Gate."

Diana followed his gaze to the banks of the Thames, just hidden by the shade of the Tower. "It looks a sight better than the last time we were here." Diana remembered the still-burning embers and shrill police whistles as she and Brent had pressed through after a night that ravaged the city with thousands of dropped Luftwaffe bombs. Half a dozen times he had tried to convince her that getting married in the upheaval and chaos, not to mention even trying to get there, would be impossible. But she wouldn't hear of marrying anywhere else. Then she kissed him to show her determination—and to weaken his resolve until he breathlessly agreed.

Brent ran his good hand up the side of the church wall. She

followed suit, grounded by the cold, sure feel of stone even amidst the skeleton of the church. Diana extracted a small notebook and pen from her handbag and felt the cold handle of the gun Simon had given her underneath. She had almost forgotten it was there. She steadied herself on the side of a brick column. "We can use the Roman influence. The arches! We can easily modernize the church after its reparations while still honoring its Anglo-Saxon history. The crypt, as you know, has always been one of the best in the city."

Diana buttoned the collar of her coat and adjusted her hat for a better view of the city's series of shadows: the familiar Tower and its eponymous bridge, the vantage reminding her of cameos on a postcard from a tourist shop in Carnaby Street. She passed Brent one of the torches from her handbag.

"You know"—she chased a shadow across his face in a sudden swath of light—"I went to St. Bart's and prayed and prayed and bartered with God to take all of the Wren churches but to give me you."

"For anyone else that wouldn't seem much of a sacrifice. But . . ." Brent moved toward something he must have found interesting. He pointed the light at it and, finding nothing but brick and shadow, put the torch down. Then lifted it again.

"But?" she prompted.

"I know how much you love these churches. And I know how rarely you pray." Before she met him, Diana never prayed at all. Her father wasn't particularly religious despite his passion for the architectural beauty of churches. It was only when she fell in love with Brent that his knowledge of theology stirred her to see something beyond beautiful lines, columns, and stained glass.

"I didn't have a lot else to bargain with, did I? And now you're going to remind me that's not how prayer works. That there's no need for bargains and—"

"I don't think one can be expected to remember how prayer does or doesn't work when they're desperate and scared," Brent said solemnly, lowering the light again. "You just rhyme off whatever words your mouth can form and hope they reach the right place."

"Yes. Yes. That's right." She waited for him to elaborate. Hoped he would segue into an example from the Front. From when he was carrying stretchers. Or wounded. The darkness hid the deformity on his left hand while his right turned the torch over and over in his palm.

"Quite the task for the Almighty to consider giving up His house on earth. Even Walbrook?" Brent said with a smile a long moment later.

"Yes."

"Not Garlickhythe?" He raised an eyebrow.

She nodded. "And Garlickhythe."

He gestured toward the rubble and toppled walls. "Seems to have worked."

Diana produced a sketch of All Hallows as it was before the bombing and then several prints of the interior from its various incarnations throughout the years, including a recent rendition showing all of its upheaval, capturing the fire trucks and ambulances, the city workers. Her mind's eye reconciled the church as it was with the church it was going to be. Cracked but with a sure foundation.

Brent wasn't sure what he had expected to find in the nooks and crannies of the remaining wall of All Hallows, but it gave him an occupation other than studying her profile in the moonlight. Diana's elegant lines and bearing were the same and yet . . .

Five weeks. A favor for a friend.

Brent blinked and returned his focus to the building. Sometimes on the battlefield he couldn't remember his middle name. What he had eaten for breakfast. Where he was. St. Paul's words from the letters he taught over and over again to his theology students. But he could always clearly conjure the morning of their wedding.

He had frantically thought of ringing her flat in Paddington after groggily finding his way back to his own flat. With the phone lines down, he had taken five minutes to splash water on his face and change before he set down the steps and out the door, determined to run the not inconsiderable length across town if cabs and buses weren't to be found. He didn't make it beyond Clerkenwell Green before he saw her coming toward him.

Then she passionately kissed away his reticence about continuing with their planned ceremony. They pressed through workers with bribes of beer before his vicar uncle oversaw their vows and signed their certificate. She had been wearing red to offset the devastation of the gray dust and felled stone.

The same red as the hat she was wearing now. He lingered on it before pursuing the shape of something he thought he had seen a moment before. Back when she was telling him she would trade churches for him. It truly was a compliment from her. They were the last link to her father. Their steeples were always the first thing her eye snagged on. When she was nervous or feeling unsafe, they were her sanctuary, and when she didn't know what to say, she filled the silence with facts about them.

Another might have heard this and thought she was measuring a human life against unfeeling stone. But Diana had built up their world as if they were living, breathing things. Friends. More of a home to her than her Paddington flat.

He watched Diana, her back turned to him. What was she seeing? She had an uncanny ability to peel away the modern curtain of their city and peek into the past. He was sure while he was in the twentieth century standing amidst an eruption of stone, she was walking through the hallowed sanctuary of the oldest church in the city, still intact. Still whole.

He took his injured hand out of his pocket and transferred his torch to it. He rippled light over the remnant of a stone wall and peered at a pop of a stem that might eventually flourish into a flower but most likely would just be trampled underfoot.

It was only when a film of dust dispersed and the moon centered on him like a searchlight that he noticed it again. He *thought* he had seen something. Sure enough, a small golden orb was tucked near the base of the brick. Brent leaned down and picked it up. Not an orb, a bottle, besmirched by dust and grime.

Squinting at the bottle, he wondered if he only imagined the outline of a shadow behind him. The portentous feeling was strong enough that he looked up and around. It wasn't Diana. She was several feet away. The worker they met on the way in and a few other stragglers were long gone. "Hello?"

Nothing. Brent continued to examine the small bottle until the glare of headlights washed over the leftover walls in front of him and caused him to blink with their proximity. He slowly rose and turned to see a tall man in a long trench coat whose face was shaded by a homburg.

The man crossed the grassy path from the curb to the church-yard at a purposeful pace. Brent was about to ask the man his business when the silhouette's swift move revealed the outline of a gun.

Brent clicked off the torch, strode toward Diana, grabbed her arm, and took them both behind a glassless window. He shoved her behind him, feeling her oddly even heartbeat as she leaned into his back and shoulder blade. His accelerated something fierce.

Confident they were hidden in a crevice of brick, Brent used the shadows and the sudden shift of the moon away from its cloud cover to quietly pull Diana behind another jutting wall.

The slight shift of a shadow he perceived through his peripheral vision confirmed his suspicion that someone else had been there all along.

Brent made to move and draw the attention of the stranger, but Diana gripped his forearm. She moved closer into his back so there wasn't an inch between them. He thought he had left danger behind him in the trenches.

Making only a slice of himself visible, he concealed them in a corner, waiting for the danger to pass. He'd done much the same during the war. Looking out for his younger and smaller friend Ross, ensuring his hand was always flexed and ready to grab the end of a stretcher. Always wondering if this would be the day that his spot was uncovered and he would stare an enemy gun in the face.

Ross once had compared it to a game of Russian roulette. For try as you might to hide, there was always the off chance that a sniper was above as you watched below, that the moonlight was garish and bold on a night you had prayed for the cloak of cloud and rain. The last thing he wanted was to revisit the feeling with Diana.

Brent reached back and held her protectively still. But she was already settled. The men soon left and Brent slowly moved out, tightly squeezing his waning fear into the small vial.

She smoothed back his hair, and while he couldn't make out the whole of her face in the darkness, her eyes were alert. "All right, darling?"

For some reason he didn't comprehend, she clearly thought the danger had passed. It had barely fazed her at all. The tone in which she used the term of endearment he hadn't heard for months sounded almost apologetic.

Brent straightened beside her. "Who knew churches would be more dangerous *after* Jerry bombed them?" he said dryly.

Five weeks, he thought. *A favor for a friend.*

CHAPTER 4

January 1941
Bletchley Park, Buckinghamshire

T hey prefer unmarried women. The time of those who are married or mothers is better spent tending hearth and home," Professor Silas Henderson had told her when he first mentioned he had a colleague who might be able to find a place where she could serve the war effort in a slightly different way.

When Brent's students had been rallied for King and Country and King's College emptied its men like a tipped-over vessel, Diana was prepared to do what she could for the war effort from London. Her mentor thought about her immediate future away from the Red Cross, munitions factories, and the Mechanised Transport Corps, each employing thousands of British women ready to do their bit.

Diana, unable to shake a foreboding sense of Brent being taken from her, was less inclined to focus on the prospect of continuing her thesis on churches vulnerable under Luftwaffe bombs.

Silas had first mentioned that many young women were going to Wales to continue their education. Diana didn't fancy being so far away while Brent stole into danger. When Silas approached a week later, Diana was cleaning the blackboard of a few mnemonic devices she had created for Silas's students at King's. She tutored those who needed a little more attention, not only in memory of her father, but because she aspired to finish her doctorate and teach someday.

When she turned around, she recognized the light in Silas's eyes from a particularly interesting part of a lecture or a recollection about her father from their time together teaching at Cambridge. He disappeared and returned not ten minutes later with a piece of paper. "I just popped out to make a telephone call. I think I've found something, Diana. Something that will keep you from having to bake or rip bandages."

Silas's contact provided an opportunity for Diana to interview with the Government Code and Cipher School at a mansion in Buckinghamshire. She would give them her maiden name because she wouldn't be married until the day before she left.

Diana arrived at the appointed time for her interview and was asked numerous questions about her research on architectural history, her educational background, what she excelled at in school, her favorite books, and the way she approached problems. The languages she spoke. She was to be given the opportunity to bring Brent back using her brain. She would translate and intercept messages. She would never be able to tell anyone what she did or where she worked.

It wasn't just the nights following her wedding and the incessant bombs that led the newspapers to call the German barrage the Second Great Fire of London that kept her awake. It was that she was stepping into a part of her life that built a wall between her and Brent just as their life was starting.

Diana was briefed about the train trip to Bletchley Station at Milton Keynes and the subsequent walk to the Bletchley Park estate. She was warned that familiar stations were erroneously named to confuse potential enemies, so she best not doze and miss her stop. Further, with the blackout her late evening stop would require a careful path on the short walk from the platform to the elaborate grounds of the mansion turned code-breaking center.

She opened the gift Silas had given her the day she told him she would be leaving for Buckinghamshire: a copy of P. H. Ditchfield's *The Cathedrals of Great Britain: Their History and Architecture*. Since she was a child, the binding, smell, and pages were as familiar to her as the alphabet. Before she could comprehend the separated letters underlined by her father's finger, she studied the sketches and colored with her imagination the transepts and altars the sketches left out.

Diana spent the last morning in London saying good-bye. She ensured Brent's flat—her flat too—was in perfect order. She gave his—*their*—landlady a forwarding address. Her trunk would arrive before her, which left her with merely a suitcase and a hatbox and the sunny morning at her disposal.

Diana could only hope she would do London justice. "I'll save you," she whispered. *I'll come back for you*, she pledged with the same intensity of a soldier stepping farther and farther away from his sweetheart on a train platform.

Wasn't it exactly what Brent had said in so many words? She clutched the handle of her suitcase. He would come back. She was merely stepping into a temporary life without him. Of *course* he would come back. She *needed* him. So why wouldn't he?

She could map her way through a new location and boil an egg, but beyond the rudimentary metrics of day-to-day existence rested the insecurity born of years of having someone care for her—whether her father's housekeeper or the matron in her dorm or, most recently, the woman who frequented her flat near Paddington, caring for every convenience no matter how small or large.

Diana dwelled on the certainty of Brent and his inevitable return until the train chugged away from their new life together.

She endured the crowded train ride: passengers accommodated their fellow travelers within the cramped quarters by sitting atop their luggage. She gazed out the window, fingering the wedding ring that dangled from a chain beneath her collar and admiring the patchwork quilt of fields, sheep, and trees until the sun sank behind the horizon.

She was careful not to doze lest the carefully misnamed stations pass her by. Finally at Milton Keynes, she rose and stretched. She collected her suitcase and hatbox, then maneuvered off the train. She stepped down from the platform, jostled through the crowd, and heaved her luggage at an odd angle before she found herself on sure enough ground to take a breath.

She tried to see herself as Brent did: a smart woman who saw the world in a new way, accustomed to sleeping in Tube shelters, reading papers, and blinking her way through the moats of rubble surrounding her beloved churches. Diana had never been certain of the moment she used the barometer of Brent's opinion to measure herself. She had aged more than her twenty-three years even within the past few days of saying good-bye to her new husband.

Exhausted and frozen, Diana meandered in the pitch black. During London blackouts the familiar street curves and sounds as well as Brent's protective arm and the fact that he knew the city blindfolded served as a makeshift compass.

Here, she stumbled over pathways and roads. A brick gate proclaimed the entrance to the manor grounds and estate, but she tripped just beyond it, landing harshly on her ankle before her eyes adjusted to light and shadows. She drew in a deep breath, a moment's reprieve, as she set her cases on the grass. She took in a yard peppered with trees and sloping toward a glistening pond catching ribbons of moonlight.

Diana retrieved and clutched her cases as a fox or a badger scurried not a yard from her. It was silly to be frightened. Her father always told her the most certain way to find her way back to herself in a moment of uncertainty was to ground herself in who she was. *"Think, think, Diana,"* he would say, *"of what is at the very core of you."*

She could hardly see where she was going. She was tired and overwhelmed. Though only an hour separated her from London, she felt its absence keenly. So she began to sing a nursery rhyme in her painfully off-key voice.

"Oranges and lemons sing the bells of St. Clement's."

She sang as her father had taught her to, when she was scared or confused or merely wanted the sanctuary of a safe, peaceful night.

"You owe me five farthings, sing the bells of St. Martin's."

She was a grown woman, for heaven's sake. She didn't need fairy-tale rhymes. And though the German bombs had obliterated the bells of her nursery rhyme, she would never stop hearing them. Even as she navigated this unfamiliar place, nearly tripping over a patch of uneven ground. Diana stopped, raised her heel, and flicked at the scuffs on her shoes.

She straightened her shoulders, pressing onward, her stride confident, her chin slightly raised. And she sang through the rest of the nursery rhyme. She could sing what she wanted, couldn't she?

A grown woman who clearly wasn't watching where she was going when she bumped into a figure.

"What a voice!" A woman's alto voice cut through the darkness.

Diana exhaled. "I . . . Sometimes when I . . ." She didn't get far in her explanation before the woman looped her arm through hers to steady her. Diana clutched at her cases.

"Let me help you, Little Canary. I know my way around. Even in the dark."

"Thank you." Diana set her cases down, then picked them back up in a surer grip.

"I was trying to make myself feel better and scare away any nighttime bogeymen."

"What's your name, Canary?"

"Diana So—Foyle." She set her shoulders. "Diana Foyle. Like the bookshop on Charing Cross Road."

"Enchanted. I am Sophie Villiers, but Lord help you if you call me Sophie. It's Villiers and Villiers only. Something right uncanny about minding p's and q's in the middle of the night where this bloody bridge has seen girls near to death."

Villiers grabbed Diana's elbow and pulled her across the dark terrain. "So let's cut to the chase. I like you and I don't find it easy to like many people. On account of my father being rich as Midas and my not being able to trust people to like me for me. You'd think in a place like this"—Villiers wobbled before she gripped Diana tighter and steadied her feet—"it wouldn't be like that anymore. But it's a bloody coming-out season the way some of the girls go on. Not most of the wrens. They're just happy not to be in a corner knitting. But I digress. *You*. You seem just the right sort, and you have no idea who I am."

"Villiers. You don't like to be called Sophie."

"Right-o! You're eons ahead. Come! Come!"

Diana and her acquaintance sought out a door and a hallway, warm and preferable to the chill of the outdoors.

"This is where I drop you. But I'll see you around, Little Canary."

"Canary?" Diana stalled in her tracks.

"On account of your unforgettable singing voice," Villers said with a smile and a wink.

Diana pushed on a door that screeched open and led into an unsettling silence. Her heels echoed loudly on the hardwood floor, and she headed into a large, empty drawing room. As she turned to leave, she caught her pale reflection, like a ghost, in the mantel mirror.

She backtracked and found her way down the hall where a uniformed gentleman, his chest full of medals, did little but cock his head at her and present a long pen. "Sign here, please."

Diana was familiar with the next step after her initial training and interview. But *hearing* about something and actually following through with it were two different things. "What am I signing?"

"You know." The man's voice rushed with impatience.

"I merely want to do what I can. My job." She read the Official Secrets Act again.

The verbiage was quite eloquent speaking of King and Country. Diana only saw what kept her from Brent. One word. Another. A barrier. Then another. She couldn't divulge any nature or manner of the work she undertook to anyone. Careless talk would cost lives. Careless talk would be seen as an act of treason.

While her hand shook a little from the cold, a little from

exhaustion, and, of course, a little from the weight of what she was promising, her heart and mind were steady. With sure intent she pressed pen to paper and signed: *Diana Foyle*.

When she finally turned the key and stepped through the door of her billeted house, she watched as the last embers glowed in the hearth in the corner of the room. The branches tapped at the windowpane like fingernails in the wind. Diana opened her suitcase and retrieved a framed picture of Brent. It didn't capture the warmth of his smile or the way his voice could wrap around her like a tight embrace. Couldn't conjure the feel of his deft fingers stroking her cheek and down the slope of her neck to her shoulder while his eyes never left hers.

She had pledged her secrets to Britain as Diana Foyle. But she wrote Diana Somerville over and over and over again on a fresh sheet of paper until dawn peeked through the curtains and her temporary new life began.

~

September 1945
London

"We'll find a cab more easily at Fenchurch Station," Diana said as Brent matched her pace from Byward to Seething Lane. They traversed a street Samuel Pepys often wandered, passing another felled church buried under rubble.

In the yard uneven tombstones like gapped teeth in a slack jaw yawned at trees, shadows blending with skeletons of brick.

"It was Dickens's favorite churchyard in the city." Diana grabbed tightly to Brent's arm.

"What's the style?" Brent's breath was damp at Diana's ear. He was probably just trying to make her feel at ease, much as Gabriel Langer had in Vienna. "Well, what *was* the style?"

Diana looked up and over the remains of St. Olave Hart Street. "Perpendicular Gothic." She could almost find that same happy Diana now through the shadows, over the thrum of her heartbeat, in the whisper of leaves over the stubble of grass even as the church lay in ruins.

"I thought it might be hard for you to see the churches like this. Before we left it was always a source of physical pain for you." His voice, low and certain, rumbled through her. Brent shifted so she could better fit into the slope of his shoulder.

Diana shook her head against his chest. "But St. Paul's dome is the highest in the city. And Great St. Bart's has never been blemished by war. Not in a thousand years."

"Di . . ." He searched her flushed face. "What is going on? I know you don't want to hurt me. I need to know that I can trust you. You're lying to me and have been for quite a while."

"Brent," she whispered.

"Where were you?"

"I needed to do something. For a friend. If I possibly could have been with you, I would have." She gazed up at him imploringly.

Regardless of the secrets imprinted on her heart, the years of separation peeled back. No longer holding on to his elbow, Diana removed her hat, wilted by the length of the unending day, and swung it by her side. "You know, there's some talk of not repairing the churches at all. Just leaving them roofless and gutted as a memorial." She studied his profile. "I'd be sad if that happened." She looked over to the open-walled church where she could see an arch beyond several tumbled planks.

Diana shivered and Brent wrestled out of his long coat and tucked it around her shoulders.

"You'll freeze," she protested. When Brent didn't answer, Diana relished a moment inhaling his spicy scent over the collar. She smoothed out the sides when she felt a bulge in the right pocket.

She slowly extracted it. "What's this?" She stopped walking and held the dusty vial up to him.

Brent leaned over her shoulder to look at it. "Found it by the eastern corner of All Hallows. Seemed old. Maybe that's why those men were skulking around, eh? I read an article in *The Times* about people looting any last treasure from the bomb sites: a bit of a morbid gold rush."

Diana smoothed a bit of the grime away with her finger pad. She reached into the opposite pocket, extracted the torch, and examined the bubbled base of the bottle. A calling card. A Roman artifact. Her heartbeat escalating, Diana cloaked her expression of excitement from her husband.

"I ask you to consult on the spiritual significance of the churches and you, Professor Somerville, may have just stumbled on to something far more valuable."

"A Roman antiquity?"

Diana raised a shoulder, happy for the occupation that momentarily smoothed any animosity between them. "Perhaps a priceless one."

"Priceless enough that someone was searching for it? Would kill for it?"

She reached for the second torch in her handbag. Brent's eyes widened as he spotted the small shine of her handgun. His gaze slid from her handbag to lock with hers.

Here she was closing him out again, yet his eyes weren't filmed with bitterness. Wounded, sure, and clearly as heartbroken as she was by the wall she had built between them. But no resentment.

Part of his look belonged to someone searching for a solution when everything before him was an assortment of lines that didn't add up—like Corinthian columns. She felt something stirring then, as clearly as she did the first time she watched him take a nub of charcoal to paper and smudge a brick and a curve and a line of a church tower.

Diana took the ensuing seconds to frame his face with her hands and draw his mouth to hers under the streetlight. She closed her eyes and fell completely. Deepening the kiss, he matched her growing fervor while tenderly holding the back of her neck with his injured hand.

When he finally, gently, disengaged, his eyes glistened.

The bells of St. James still tolled even as those at St. John's Priory and around the gate were silenced by bomb destruction. Brent had spent so long adjusting to the absence of sound when he was in hospital in Italy. The constant artillery fire, the whistle of grenades, the whir of the battles in the air above him replaced the quiet of an everyday life he had taken for granted. Heavy silence meant now and then a bird's call would startle him with the same intensity as an air-raid siren once had.

The night was calm as they ascended the steps to their flat. Brent turned the key in the door and stepped back to let Diana in.

"Some things never change," Diana said as Brent brushed past her in pursuit of the kettle. He set it on the cooktop to boil. "You immediately rush to put on the tea."

"Habit," he said over his shoulder as he reached for the tea tin. "Even when it got quite terrible, I tried to substitute: treacle, hickory. I never stopped drinking it. I suppose I just like the methodology of it."

Moments later, he watched her clasp the cup he handed her and followed her eyes as they took in the room: the bookshelves containing her tomes on architecture and his on Greek, the worn furniture he had done his best to spruce up and dust before her return, even ironing the sofa cover. Then they settled on the sketchbook he had carelessly left open on the table. The scenes were not Brent's usual depictions of stained glass and turrets, steeples against the London sky. Instead, fragments of the images seared behind his eyes, the ones that were ever present as he drifted off to sleep, had been captured with the same attention to detail but for ragged, tortured faces and fallen buildings.

She sat back without saying anything, though the hand reaching for her saucer shook slightly.

She couldn't know what he had seen unless she entered his mind. And he knew so little from her letters of the part of the war he had left behind: ration books and air-raid sirens, Diana at the Foreign Office. He could imagine her making friends and wrinkling her nose in thought. But he could only imagine.

He looked up and their eyes met. He didn't want her to imagine any of what plagued him at night.

"We got a bit of adventure out of it, wouldn't you say?" Diana said too quickly. She set down her tea and snatched the vial Brent had found to study it in the low lamplight. "And perhaps a nest egg! We should call round Rick Mariner's office when you go to King's tomorrow. Are your offices still in the same corridor?"

Brent sipped his watery tea. Frowned. Wasn't ready to let her into his thoughts yet. "I suppose the grocer will double our tea rations now that you're back."

With the exception of their wedding night and some of the subsequent day, she had yet to live with him. All he had dreamed by way of learning her small habits and quirks and inevitable annoyances could come true. She was right there beside him. And he felt further from her than he had during their separation.

Brent passed buildings every day that had been patched up: a makeshift solution with a quick paint job that hid the cracks. He wondered how long the foundation would last.

"I'll sleep on the sofa, Di. It's been a long time since I shared a bed. Took me long enough to get used to sleeping in one again at all."

"You're not sleeping on the sofa, Brent . . ." Expectation beamed from her face.

He could take advantage of the moment and close the space between them. Her eyes were so wide staring at his face, and her body was leaning forward. "I wake up sometimes, Diana. I have nightmares."

She furtively glanced toward the sketches, then returned her gaze to him. "Then I'll get you water and prop your pillows."

He never thought he would have to guard his heart against her, but he would if it meant he would come out with some self-preservation. "There's a lot between us right now."

Diana blurted a laugh. "This from the man whose first words to me on our wedding night were if I wanted a cup of tea?" She patted his knee. "Your virtue is safe with me." Diana hopped from the sofa and stole his scarred hand.

Brent slowly backed away. "I'm serious, Diana. I'll sleep on the sofa."

A few moments later, pajama clad, Brent stretched out on the sofa and propped his pillow. There was the fear that pricked him whenever night's shade fell. Drifting into unconsciousness often resulted in his waking up thrashing. He had once woken in a fury to find a pillow twisted in his good hand. He wouldn't risk unintentionally hurting Diana.

She had left the door to the bedroom just off of the sitting room open, and he imagined her staring up at the ceiling.

He pressed his arms to his sides. He had never been more comfortably intimate with another human soul. She was a part of him. He certainly didn't anticipate spending the first night of her return on the sofa.

"You're still the most beautiful woman I have ever seen," he said through the open door.

When her voice came a moment later, he could hear the smile in it. "What form of Greek love is this, Professor Somerville? The kind where you chastely sleep on the sofa after reuniting with your estranged spouse and running from danger with a vial that may or may not be a priceless Roman artifact?"

Brent was so unused to smiling that the muscles at the creases of his mouth almost hurt with the wide stretch. "It's beyond definition."

CHAPTER 5

October 1938
St. Bartholomew the Great, West Smithfield

Ham and tomato on rye was more appetizing than it might have been had he not taught three lectures on an empty stomach. Midway through unwrapping the waxed paper, Brent realized he wasn't alone in the churchyard. A curvy woman stood there, her blonde hair under a little green hat set at a jaunty angle on her head. There was a tiny button on the hat as well as a feather to flourish it, offsetting a sun blaring through a lattice of leaves in a cloistered yard off Cloth Fair.

Brent didn't want the woman to turn and find his mouth in mid-bite. So he wrapped the rest of his sandwich, though far from satiated, and slid it into his satchel behind his books to begin sketching again.

Out of his peripheral vision he could see she was transfixed. Her gaze roamed over the contrast of an old, patched gray wall, vibrant leaves, and mossy verdigris kissing the uneven walls. Brent never tired of St. Bartholomew the Great's spell and neither, it seemed, did she.

"You know, you can keep eating your sandwich."

He wasn't expecting her to talk to him. Not that he was nervous talking to beautiful women, though he had rarely seen a woman as perfectly proportioned as this one. Several female students had offered to accompany him on his present excursion, and there was usually a small line outside of his office with what he assumed were a few made-up questions about Paul's friend Timothy. It was a welcome strangeness to be caught so completely off his guard by this newcomer.

"I didn't want to disturb you with the waxed wrapping." She turned and looked straight at him with blue eyes so bright he blinked. "Rahere did a grand old job, didn't he?"

Her recognition of the church's founding prior moved the dial from preliminary attraction to intense interest. She disappeared behind the east side of the church, and Brent focused on his notebook again. He put flourish to the edges and slants of sunlight, finger smudging the corners and leaving a familiar black mark on his fingertip. Soon he would be lecturing to a room of bored first years on Paul. Confirmed bachelor Paul. Maybe that was the elusive thorn in the apostle's side: bachelorhood.

Brent coughed through a growing smile. Sacrilegious. He wouldn't tell his department head that particular theory, even though he wondered at their comparison of Paul to Brent when chiding him. He wasn't even thirty yet, for heaven's sake.

"You're still here then?" Her voice cut through his reverie.

Brent followed her focus over the checkerboard of alternating gray and black near a rooftop patched and repatched since the eighteenth century, capturing the slightest slant of sun.

He wasn't quick enough to tuck his sketches into his folder, though he did leave a trail of black thumbprints over the corner of the page in his hasty attempt just as she approached.

"That's really quite good!" She stood behind the bench, gazing over his shoulder, smelling like roses and the sunlight his sketches never captured.

"Thank you." Brent kept his gaze on her face and not a figure that might inspire monks to scurry to confession.

"May I?" The stranger indicated the empty space beside him on the bench. Brent moved his satchel and she dropped beside him, crossing one shapely leg over the other. "You're an artist then?"

Brent followed her sightline over the charcoal drawing, the

corner smudged by the slip of his forefinger. He smiled. "Just a hobby."

"I love this church and you capture something about it. Something elusive." She squinted, studying the illustration still visible under the shade of his hand before comparing the back of the structure that faced them. It wasn't a prepossessing structure. Not broad like St. Paul's with a distinguished outline that towered over the city and contributed to the grace of its skyline. Not elegant like St. Mary-le-Bow or ornate like St. Stephen Walbrook.

"It's a good subject. What would you say is elusive about this church?" To him, it was partly Prior Rahere: founder not only of Great St. Bart's, as most Londoners called it, but the solemn St. Bartholomew the Less tucked into the grounds of the iconic St. Bart's Hospital, another institution founded following the prior's pilgrimage to Rome and a vision, not unlike that given to Saul of Tarsus, to care for those ill and destitute and at the mercy of London's blind eye.

"It has redefined itself." She sounded like she was defending a thesis in front of a committee. "It escaped the zeppelins of the Great War, sure, but for near a millennium we have been tearing it down and rebuilding it." She peered up at it. "Its outer shell doesn't quite do it justice. Not to the untrained eye."

Was it just him, or did she look at him pointedly then?

"It has seen the whole of England's religious history. Civil War. Henry the Eighth's desecration of the monasteries . . ." She tugged at her green hat. "I talk a mile a minute, don't I? And you just want to enjoy your drawing and your lunch."

"I don't know about that. Maybe hearing you talk about the church will help me see something new in it."

Her blue eyes sparked. "They say Rahere's ghost haunts this place."

Brent put on his professor voice and challenged her. He wanted to know what she would say in response. "Churches are houses of worship. Darkness dispels against the rock of Christ on earth."

She clucked her tongue. "That may be so, but it isn't as fun." She put her finger to her lips. "I swear I sense Christopher Wren at St. Paul's. In the toll of the bells and in those grand columns. They had to hoist him up, you know. To finish the domes. He was seventy-six years old. I sometimes go there to find his ghost."

Brent ducked his chin and thus his wide smile. She neared so their shoulders brushed as she studied his sketchbook.

"I'm Diana." She waited for him to put down his sketch and shake her proffered hand. "Diana Foyle. Like the bookshop on Charing Cross Road."

"Brent Somerville." He loved the softness of her palm against his hand.

Diana inspected a bit of sketching pencil that had transferred from his hand to hers and rubbed at her index finger. "I'm a student of architectural history. And I skipped a rather dull lecture to come here because I wasn't sure how many perfect days we would have left this autumn. It is perfect. Look at all the orange and red leaves. I love it when London has color."

"Where do you study?"

"King's. My true love is Christopher Wren."

"Ah, well he might prove to be a horrible lover, Diana Foyle. For one, you'd have to exhume his skeleton, and after that there's the whole holding him lightly so he doesn't crumble to dust. Not to mention how the kisses might taste. Rather chalky, I should say."

Her eyes smiled and roamed over the Tudor gatehouse and off to Cloth Fair, and he allowed himself a candid moment of inspection before he flicked his eyes away, then back again. They were sitting so closely he couldn't tell where his shoulder ended and hers began, and he was all too aware of the proximity of her kneecap to his. "I'm a professor. Also at King's."

"Oh!" She pursed her lips. "Very serious."

"I teach about the apostles. Paul and Peter. John too. The letters to the Corinthians. That lot."

"I can't say I know much about apostles except that Paul was in Greece, wasn't he? The Greeks had seven forms of love."

"I know." Brent found it rather inconvenient that a few of those forms of love chose that exact moment to parade across his brain.

"Do you speak Greek?"

"Cambridge made sure of that. I burrowed as many tenses as I could in my poor, helpless brain and they stuck."

"I just never knew what the forms of love were."

"You'll need a teacher then." There were few instances when one could truly use the word *enchanting*. He was happy he had tucked it into a safe for this moment. "Yes. Part and parcel of the job, and if I dust off my brain, a workable amount of Hebrew. Why do you ask?"

"My father spoke all of those languages. I was learning from him before he died." She stopped for a moment as if in memory. "I don't usually go off like this. Have you ever just seen someone and talked to them and just known they were meant to be your friend? I know I am awkward and horribly rude, and then there is the matter of your sandwiches . . ."

"My sandwiches?" The corner of his mouth twitched.

"I don't mean anything by the way that I am."

"What way?"

"Droning on to a perfect stranger."

"You're not boring me and we're not strangers. We've been introduced, Diana Foyle like the bookshop in Charing Cross Road. Though I will say that's a bit of a mouthful."

"Move your hand." Diana's red fingernail moved over Brent's sketch, capturing detailed stones and the ancient tower of St. Bart's with his pencil. "You love churches."

This priory-turned-church was more striking to him than it had ever been: far more than a relaxing flit of a muse, distinguished by lines and history distinctive from the hundreds of other churches in London. Sure, the history of William Wallace lingered just behind: the Scottish revolutionary drawn and quartered beyond the stone arch separating the churchyard from the whole of Cloth Fair and out to Smithfield Market. Imagining that gruesome moment always made him shiver, but today those thoughts dispelled.

"I love this one." More now than he had before. "It isn't as grand as St. Paul's or as ornate as Garlickhythe or any of the other Wren churches."

"Wren's Lantern. That's what they call St. James Garlickhythe. On account of all of the windows letting in that beautiful natural light." Her eyes looked over his sketch, then over at Great St. Bart's as if seeking the same natural light.

"Well, this one is a bit of a hodgepodge. I like seeing where all of the different parts have been sewn together." He glanced up at the church, then to his sketch, showing her. "When it was torn and rebuilt and fixed about a bit." He pointed with the nub of charcoal.

She leaned over, studying it, and he blinked to keep himself from staring too intently at her, opting instead for a peek at his watch. He was going to be late for his three o'clock lecture if he didn't walk very quickly and very immediately.

"I must dash." He made a semblance of order out of his sketches and tackled them into his satchel. "It was a pleasure to meet you. And I am not just saying that because it seems like the thing someone should say when they have to rush off. But I truly hope we meet again." He swiped a swath of hair from his forehead. "And I am not just saying that either."

"Let's promise then never to say anything to each other just to say something to each other."

She offered her hand again and he shook it, his own fingers tingling when he turned and walked through the arch in the direction of the Smithfield Market and his chosen shortcut to King's.

Later that night, as the sun mellowed over the brick houses of Clerkenwell and over the bells of the neighboring St. James Church beside his flat, Brent pulled out his sketchbook again.

He peeled off a new sheet of coarse paper and smoothed it before pressing a nub of charcoal to the middle and flourishing out smudged lines. Brent squeezed his eyes shut and let his hand conjure a memory of a woman with high cheekbones and a wonderful figure, turning her head over her shoulder so blonde curls tumbled from their carefully placed green hat with the movement. Behind her he drew the church whose study she had abandoned the moment she noticed Brent on the bench.

He smiled thinking of her, her voice and the easy warmth they had shared. Would he find her quite as irresistible if she hadn't been so surprisingly intelligent? He sketched and smudged and flourished, his heart racing with each new press of the pencil to paper, each shape and curve and line. Once finished, he tucked the illustration into his satchel, unsure of what he would do with it, feeling a little embarrassed to be roaming from lectern to lectern and through corridors and reams of male students with a sketch of a woman captured from a solo occasion.

He felt differently when not a week later, he saw her crossing the Strand in the afternoon. Hatless and clutching a small satchel, oxford shoes scurrying over the pavement. He was happy it wasn't just her physical beauty that allured him. He loved that he shared an affinity for the churchyard with another human. He steadied his drumming heart with this knowledge. This kismet.

Should he approach her? Of course she would remember him. Their meeting wasn't just a few pleasantries exchanged with a stranger in a shared place. She had to have felt the same stirring. She spoke as if she anticipated seeing him again.

He quickened his pace, hoping words would come in the strides it took to reach her.

"Professor Somerville!" Her smile widened as they made to the other side of the street in equal pace. Her cheeks flamed with a beguiling blush. "Is it ham and tomato today?"

Brent was about to speak when Richard Mariner of the history department intercepted them. Mariner scowled at Brent. Brent merely smiled.

Brent reached into his satchel and extracted the folded sketch tucked into a recent translation of Etienne Gilson's work on Thomas Aquinas. "I just wanted to give you this." He pressed it into her palm, letting his fingers linger on her wrist a moment.

He didn't wait for her to open it, rather smiled before he tossed a polite nod at Rick. "Mariner."

"Somerville." Mariner's voice resembled the dead.

Brent turned knowing he had unwittingly made an enemy. And not caring in the least.

CHAPTER 6

October 1945

Four years at the Government Code and Cipher School at Bletchley Park, sometimes known as Station X, under her belt should have more than qualified Diana to seven years of knowing Brent as closely as she assumed one could know another human, and yet their first night together after the war found her alone, recalling the taste of his kiss and wondering as to the depths of the scars on his collarbone.

If she hadn't missed Brent so much or hadn't been reminded daily of the part of her life he would never know, she might have counted those years as some of the best times of her life. She felt confident in her work, she made new friends, and unlike her university life before she'd met Brent, she felt like she belonged. Before Brent, she was a walking encyclopedia, more comfortable with the friends she met in stones and gargoyles, turrets and parapets, than with people.

She gulped a breath and blinked, glancing around the bedroom, momentarily forgetting where she was, then stunned that she was really here. Really home. She could hear Brent through the open bedroom door. He wasn't saying anything intelligible in slumber, but he was speaking. Would waking him in the middle of an intense episode startle or hurt him?

Diana swung her legs over the side of the bed and reached for her robe. She tightened it around her middle and stepped into the chilly sitting room. The vial Brent had discovered—most likely a relic—caught the moonlight through the open window from its position on the tabletop. She tiptoed to retrieve it, then stopped to watch him sleep a moment.

A splice of moonlight through the window offered a view of his face and above the collar of his pajamas. She could just make out a ripple of scars beneath his collarbone on his left side. How deeply and how far did the scars wander over his torso and back?

They had spent so few nights together. Just after their marriage and again on one of his leaves before the letters stopped and her secrets barricaded them.

Brent rolled to his side, but the talking had stopped.

She sat quietly at the kitchen table and played with possible messages that could be derived from the vial, trying to look at it as Simon Barre would. She'd mention it to him when they met the next day. She wouldn't know until she met Rick Mariner what it was, if anything important, and if there was a specific name or description that might lead to another message or cipher. While writing descriptions of a church in her notebook, she looked for messages in stones, patterns on the rubbled ground, anything that might jump out at her.

In her first years at Bletchley, before she and Fisher listened to the incoming and outgoing radio messages every day, she and Simon would study an intercepted message from a neighboring hut, and he played with Soviet and British coding and even sequences of buildings.

The first time Simon mentioned the agent he called Eternity was as far back as the obliteration of Coventry: a blitzed city tortured a mere month before London barely withstood a similar barrage. Some of the cryptanalysts at Bletchley—even Fisher Carne— murmured a theory under their breath regarding Coventry and the possibility that British intelligence and Churchill had wind of the operation before it began and let it happen anyway.

Diana blinked away the notion, the senseless destruction, the newspaper picture of Holy Trinity's steeple breaking through the smoke. She had been devastated that the age-old cathedral had fallen under fire, unable to contribute to Simon's theory.

Even in the midst of devastation, a Special Operations Executive provided a cryptic cipher from the church bearing the infinity sign, which was brought to Simon's attention. Eternity was born.

Simon had admitted to her near the end of the war that he had been planted at Bletchley in pursuit of a traitor. While she was busy ensuring V-E Day and the Nazi demise, Simon was already gearing up for the Soviet war he'd spoken of. Diana couldn't look that far ahead. She'd had enough of war as it was.

Yet for all that the war had taken and all her time apart from Brent, her mind had sharpened like a tool surrounded by the whetstone of powerful brains, whose intellect made her a better analyst. It helped her see that perhaps the mysteries she'd unraveled at her desk were created by people who colored outside of the lines.

Diana learned to color outside of the lines, too, beyond the segmental arches, pediments, and motifs her brain stored in constant measure.

Brent's sketches were still sitting on the table, exposed. She recalled the flash of worry in his eyes when she had noticed them. From the stiffness in his neck and shoulders, it must have taken everything in him not to grab them and store them away. She'd take that as a good sign. She had so little to go on and so many years between them. In that moment he didn't hide from her.

Diana looked to a hatbox still unpacked and sitting near the hat stand by the door. She retrieved it. Under a favorite hat she had tucked Brent's letters, as creased and worn as the accompanying sketches. Of course, her favorite of all—the sketch of Wren's rooftops huddled together and perfectly intact. It was smudged, but the most pristine of the letters and notes. She had treated it as carefully as the wedding ring she had worn on a chain around her neck.

Diana twisted the ring on her finger, tucked her legs under her, and read.

Diana,

Now that we're apart, I feel I should begin addressing you in the terms of endearment that so easily slip from the mouths of my barrack mates—darling, sweetheart, honey. Truth is, I always thought your name was a term of endearment in itself. She was a goddess after all. Forgive me, Diana Foyle like the bookshop on Charing Cross Road, if I thought teaching was horrible. Turns out training is a lot worse, a lot of waiting. Here we all are primed to charge for King and Country and yet the most we have to show for our zeal and patriotism is bad food and half of our pay lost to cards.

A few others in my unit have taken to calling me Padre on account of my profession. They're good lads who will buy you a pint when it's their turn. Sure, they tease me mercilessly on account of being the "vicar's nephew" (their emphasis, not mine), but I can handle it. I fear I've given them more to quip at by my sudden inspiration at sketching the nearby churchyard. The tombstones all tumble into one another, and when the sun steals behind the squat steeple, I can see your face as clearly as I did that first day in St. Bart's.

Then I showed Holt a picture of you—the one snatched at that faculty party. Remember? You'd had enough of Rick Mariner cutting in for the twelfth time and we stole onto the street and you told me all about the steeple at St. Mary le Strand. That shut him up for a while.

She yawned, put the vial down, and laid her head on her folded arms to snatch any sleep the waning night might still yield. It had been years since she had seen Brent, mere weeks since she had seen Simon, and somehow the latter was a bit more of a comfort to her than the former. Because at least with Simon, she would learn her next step.

Diana sat bolt upright at Brent's hand on her shoulder as dawn yawned through the window.

"I'm sorry to startle you." A gentle furrow creased his brow.

"Not used to being here, I suppose." Diana stretched her arms over her head and yawned, sitting in the kitchen chair.

"I have nightmares . . ." He shook his head. "Did I say anything last night?"

"You talked. Muttered. A little. But I couldn't make anything out." Diana rose and kissed the rusty stubble of his jawline. "I'm just happy to see you." She might have been overtired and groggy, but Brent was here. She was home. At last.

So she burnt the toast and made weak tea. The eggs were cold and lumpy but also powdered, so she let herself off the hook for them as she turned over the wooden spoon. She passed Brent outside the bathroom as if they were new roommates at an Edwardian charm school. He turned from her while changing, and Diana flicked a glance at the exposed scar above his undershirt. He was nervous.

Everything I love about you is tucked in your mind, not displayed on your battered body.

She tried to imagine the horrors he had experienced. He had never fired a gun, at least that's what he'd said. She had amassed her own pile of lies. Mightn't he have some to match?

Diana's mind drifted to Eternity: an outline of a man, a supposed traitor who bent both the Communist ideology and British resistance to his will. He had a secret men would kill for and for which Simon Barre would send her away time and again for the purpose of uncovering it.

But enough. She'd meet Simon, give him his lead, and defect, then concentrate on the life before her: Brent scraping butter across toast with his bad hand.

She sensed his eyes on her and lightened into a smile. "Well, if we take the relic to Rick and it's worth a fortune, we can pack up, move to Mayfair, and hire a cook."

She studied Brent as he swallowed the scrambled eggs.

"I think there was a bit of cardboard in there."

"Oh. I'm sorry."

"Gives it character." He winked and she exhaled. "I've tasted far worse."

"You would have. At the Front . . ." Diana took a sip of tea, then smoothed the front of her blouse.

Brent scooped another bite of horrible eggs and met her gaze. "I needed you, Diana."

Her eyes filled with tears. "I needed you, too, Brent."

"Funny how five weeks was nothing when we were first together but an absolute eternity when it stretched out our four years apart."

"Each of those weeks felt like a year."

Brent nodded, swallowed, and coughed. "Cardboard."

"I want . . ."

"What do you want, Di?" The question might have been harsh if his voice wasn't so soft. He truly wanted to know.

"I want it all to be over. I want our lives to actually begin: the way most people do after a wedding. I want routine and early bedtimes and to feel safe."

"I want you to feel safe too."

Diana smiled. "I missed your voice. Just hearing it." She set down her fork and placed her hand over her heart. "There were a thousand things I missed about you, but . . ."

"I want to protect you and you have a gun!" he blurted.

Tears pricked her eyes. He had never raised his voice at her before. When she blinked she saw his eyes were damp.

She sat in silence, her sleeplessness and the scars she had discovered under his collar catching up with her in a knot of panic. "You're not going to leave me, are you?"

His lips slid into a sardonic smile. "And miss your exceptional cooking?"

"Si monumentum requiris, circumspice." Rick Mariner greeted Diana and Brent from his open door, a Piccadilly cigarette between his raised index and middle fingers.

"It's a little early for Latin," Brent said.

While he was handsome with silver at his temples, dimples, and bright gray eyes, Rick's numerous attempts to woo Diana had always failed. At first because she was a student in his seminar and a decade younger than he was, then because her life's path had been intercepted by a red-haired professor of theology who shared her passion for churches and whose deep voice and resounding laugh rumbled through her.

"If you seek his monument, look around." Diana translated Rick's Latin as the inscription from Wren's tomb in the cold crypt of St. Paul's.

"Walking around London you would think his monument is limestone rubble," Rick said.

"And walking around this office you would think Rick was interesting," Brent whispered to Diana as they were motioned into an office resplendent with artifacts and preserved history. Relics and objects and pieces safely tucked away from the bombs.

Richard was only just getting them back from their safe shipment to a colleague in New York. Unlike most, he had the foresight to make arrangements while Chamberlain was still talking about "peace for our time": the peace easily forgotten with Hitler's rising power. Richard said he knew enough about the pattern of war through millennia to anticipate when it would knock on Britain's doorstep.

"So, Somerville, I've seen you in the halls. You're back teaching." Brent and Diana took the offered chairs on the opposite side of Rick's desk. "And you, Diana. Are you going to finish your graduate studies?"

She sensed Brent's intense stare at her profile. They hadn't even had the opportunity to speak about her future plans yet. "I'm making notes on the churches slated for reconstruction. Just like after the fire when Charles the Second welcomed plans for the city. All Hallows, for one. And I suppose I'll be learning to keep house. Didn't get much chance before the war." She flashed Brent a smile. "I'll have a Hoover in my hands in no time."

"Old Barking?"

"She has been known to grace a few churches other than Wren's. Diana just loves churches."

Diana picked at a thread on her collar. "Well, I was married at All Hallows. So I thought it was a lovely place to start. Wren or no Wren."

She reached into her handbag where she had triple-wrapped the vial. She had first placed it in several soft patches of down and cotton and then carefully enclosed it in a drawstring bag that had once housed mismatched buttons. Finally, it was hidden by her monogrammed handkerchief given to her by her friend Sophie Villiers on a night when the lack of Brent and hope had overwhelmed.

"I know there are probably far better ways to do this," Diana said. "But I thought you would get a lot of joy out of seeing it. Brent found it last night." She passed him the bag.

He gently took it, delicately working his long fingers to remove the piece from its crude protection. He made a small gasp before he stood, turned to the window, and held it to the light. When he spoke again, it was as if through a tunnel. "Oh."

"So what is it?" Brent asked.

"You found this?" He stabbed Brent with a look.

"At All Hallows last night." Brent shrugged.

"And it was just the two of you?"

"It's rather odd, isn't it, that someone would have just now discovered it?" Brent added. "But I figure with all the blockades and roadworks . . ."

Rick gave a slow nod, then assumed a stance Diana knew well.

For the only thing Richard Mariner loved more than discovering ancient rarities was having a willing audience to listen to his endless knowledge of said ancient rarities.

Rick sat down and deftly made a nest for the vial on his desk so they all had a clear vantage. "Throughout mythologies as old as Londinium, we read of a vial believed to hold a holy substance." He motioned toward the amber-colored center of the dusty cylinder. "This is now dried-up liquid, of course. Crystallized, as you can see." He pointed to it with a pencil. "The substance would have healing properties. You said you were poking around Old Barking?"

Diana always smiled when someone used the somewhat antiquated name. "Yes."

"A lot of the literature about this specific relic comes from that area, Diana. You know people have excavated there long before old Jerry did it for us."

"What relic, though? What holy substance?" Diana squinted at the vial.

"Saint Somerville, you believe in all this myth and mysticism?"

"More than you, it would seem," Brent said.

"You say potato, I say potahto."

"Rick, Brent has a class in a half hour."

"This vial would contain the vinegar provided at the crucifixion of the Christ."

Diana gripped her chair. "You mean . . . ?"

"In the Gospels, Jesus mentions to a guard that He thirsts . . . I cannot remember which Gospel. They all overlap a tad, don't they?" He looked pointedly at Brent. "Nonetheless, this vial . . . its properties . . . suggest it is indeed a relic long believed to have followed the Roman influence here in our grand cesspool of a city."

"But how can you tell?" Brent leaned in.

Rick stood and retrieved a book from his impressive library. He licked his finger and riffled through transparent pages until he turned the opened chapter to Diana, complete with illustration.

"*Oleum medicina,* 'holy medicine.'" He set the book between them and returned his attention to the vial, using his pencil to circumnavigate the small bottle. "Ovoid here." He gestured to the middle, comparing it to the book, and then around the bobbled bottom of the glass. "A concave bottom. Irregular shape here. And truly this could be any glass or perfume bottle. Bit of iridescence. I am sure we would find several where the old wall was. Come look at it in the light."

He motioned Brent and Diana from their chairs and they followed him, and Rick held it to the window. "Some say that Prior Rahere brought it back from his pilgrimage to Rome."

"The fellow from St. Bart's?" Brent lowered his gaze to meet Diana's.

"You're keeping this?" He handed it to Brent.

Brent nodded. And tucked it in his pocket. "For the time being."

Rick narrowed his eyes at Brent. "Need some of those healing properties?"

Brent shifted. "I held up quite well, thank you."

"Then shouldn't you see it to its rightful place?"

"And where might that be?" Brent glanced at Diana, and she gave a small shake of her head. She wanted to keep it. "I promise not to sell it on the black market," Brent said easily.

"Lovely to see that your office is returning to its same treasure trove." Diana noted Rick's face darken.

She drew his attention with her careful consideration of lined tomes and knickknacks. She stalled at a painting she recalled from an art history class during her undergraduate studies. A portrait of St. Boniface. The infinity symbol was wrapped on the cross, denoting not the mathematical principle and equation known to man, but rather the idea of the Alpha and the Omega, the Beginning and the End. A biblical concept familiar to Brent's lectures but not to Mariner's atheism.

Perhaps it was the prospective meeting with Simon later that day, but Diana couldn't help but think of the Soviet agent Eternity. "This is new."

"Ah! Yes. A gift from a friend as I began recovering my collection." He joined her. "Just because I don't believe in the religious nonsense and the relics, the saints we find in the rubble of churches, doesn't mean I don't appreciate their history."

"Of course."

"Thanks for the help, Mariner." Brent turned and waited for Diana, standing to the side so she could pass.

She followed him through the corridor.

"I got the sense you want to keep our ancient relic, Di." His whisper was soft to compensate for the echoing halls around them.

"I respect Rick."

"But . . ."

"I want to finish a story we've started." She made to loop her arm in his, but he shifted in an infinitesimal movement. She didn't take it personally when she saw the corridor fill with students. He always liked to keep a professional distance at the college, at least during lecture hours. "Is your office the same?"

"Want to see for yourself?"

"Please."

When they finally arrived, her heart was full: a sunny London, a small lecture from Rick on an ancient relic, and now Brent's office. Years peeled back and Diana almost believed bombs hadn't fallen and she hadn't been taken from him for so long.

She knew the smell of his books and the way he lined his pens beside the blotter. She knew he liked to keep short notes for his lesson plans in a line on his windowsill that overlooked a courtyard through puckered, filmy glass.

The hat stand was still in the same corner and the maps of Paul's missions still on the far wall. Antioch. Syria. Jerusalem. Corinth. Even the tip of Spain. Frozen in time like the Clerkenwell flat.

"Do you remember the night we were locked in here?"

Brent raised an eyebrow. "Were we truly locked in here, or did I just come up with a fascinating tale about the night porter's routines?"

Diana flushed. "Brent!"

"Oh, it was hardly clandestine. Before I could even have my way with you, you were asleep near the hat stand."

"I was studying a lot those days."

"Studying? That's one euphemism I haven't heard before."

Yes, the office was the same. Except for two items on Brent's desk. A letter and a silver frame.

Diana reached for the letter, and while Brent almost moved to stop her, he fell back and folded his arms. Then there was the frame on the corner of his desk. She took a step to slowly pick it up. She supposed it was the same picture she kept by her bedside from the moment they separated: from their wedding amidst rubble snapped by the parson. And yet . . .

"I don't recognize this." It was a picture of her. Profile turned upward, peering reverently at a church. "That's Mary-le-Bow." She turned and found his eyes glistening. "When was this?"

"Maybe May or June of '40. You said that Rick had been sending things to America just in case the Germans tried to take it—"

"The day I dragged you around to sketch churches? You were so patient. I wanted to see them all . . . just in case."

"Suppose you were right all along. I had a student's camera. Never got to return it to him when he was called up. I've since sent it to his mother."

Diana returned the picture to his desk.

"What will you do with your day, then?" he asked. "I have a student coming any moment."

"I might check on Great St. Bart's. See if I can't find a dashing young professor eating lunch in the courtyard. Or pawn *oleum medicina*." She said the last bit dramatically. She hadn't anticipated that her ruse for a church consultation would yield a rarity.

Brent removed his notes from his satchel. "Will you be home by tea then?"

"Yes. I'll make it! Didn't get any chance to take care of you before, did I? No longer will you return tired at the end of a long day and have to see to your own tea."

He raised an eyebrow at her. "Can you even make tea, Di?"

"That sounds more like *can* than *will*, Brent Somerville."

At his responding smile Diana almost crossed to his side of the desk to kiss him good-bye, but something in the way his shoulders rose and his arms reached out stalled her. He carefully straightened the picture she had moved.

Diana turned to the door and stopped, hand on the knob. "Brent."

"Yes, Diana?"

"I'm truly sorry. And I think . . . the fact that you are willing to try . . ."

Brent said something she couldn't hear.

"I can't hear you."

A knock sounded. Brent brushed past her to open the door, then ushered in a student with a smile. "This is my wife, Diana."

Diana exchanged pleasantries and shook the young man's hand, only to look back at Brent before she left to find him already engaged in conversation. She didn't close the door completely as she stepped out into the hallway, opting to listen to him. The immediate change in him was apparent. He was engaged, natural. There was no sardonic tone to his voice or false note in his laugh.

Diana was starting to recognize the Brent she knew in small measures. A student he couldn't have known for more than several weeks was getting him in full.

CHAPTER 7

November 1938

Before Diana, there had been other girls, of course. Brent had tasted their lips and stroked the tendrils that tickled their temples and the soft curve of skin under their chins. He had stolen his uncle's car to go into town on a star-spattered night and had proven he was more than just the vicar's nephew. Had done his fair share of wandering in and out of Keats's sonnets and pining under the long span of the orchard near the manse. Had broken a few hearts and tucked the splinters of his own deep into his pocket next to a folded sketch.

Then he was with Diana and all the sonnets and pining were replaced with something far deeper. Something that occupied his mind far too often. And at the most inconvenient times. Such as the middle of a serious lecture at King's.

Diana stepped into a path that lit the focus of his sketch of Great St. Bart's and stayed there: her silhouette inspiring the swift movement of his pencil, even if his drawings would never capture her eyes and lips.

He had scribbled his office hours and lecture times on the back of the drawing he handed her after their meeting in the churchyard in hopes of seeing her again. As much as another unexpected meeting off of Fleet Street or Cloth Fair would have delighted him, it was too often raining and chilly as autumn set in and something sparked in him.

Though he turned every corner with a slight leap of his heart that she might be just beyond, under the toll of a bell or the shadow of a steeple, he was surprised when he looked up from his lectern to see her. The attention of thirty-five students shifted from the sound of his voice at the front of the room to whisper quietly as Diana appeared in a tartan-patterned wool dress that might have been commonplace if not for a red belt that drew his attention to her perfect proportions. Proportions clearly not lost on the wandering eyes of his students.

Her attempt to gracefully settle at the back of the classroom was thwarted when one shoe crossed at an awkward angle over another and she fell sideways into a chair.

Brent cleared his throat to stifle his smile. "Paul's letters to the Corinthians." He resumed the lecture, tugging at his collar. Why was the room suddenly warm? And how could his proficiency in the Greek tongue wander absently and settle near the window out of reach? "The Greeks described this as . . . as . . ." Brent shuffled his notes. He was a renowned Pauline scholar, for heaven's sake, in an envied and prestigious tenure position at King's College.

He trained his eyes away from Diana Foyle and returned to the lecture with straightened shoulders and renewed resolve. Shrugging off the attention of female students keen to have him explain the Greek words of love he referred to in his lectures was an almost daily part of his life. But the youngest professor in the department with red hair, handsome features, broad shoulders, and crooked smile inspired more than a few second looks.

He finally stared directly at her, and she ducked her head. His one-track mind derailed.

Eventually Brent dismissed the class and gathered his notes. Usually a student or two loitered after class, approaching the blackboard and asking about a term paper or scheduling an appointment, but something about Diana's presence deterred them and they filed out. But not before a few furtive glances—most from female students— slid in her direction.

He slowly approached her as she was picking at the skirt of her tartan wool dress.

"You really are a beautiful artist," she said by way of greeting.

Brent smiled, shoving his notes in his satchel. "I was hoping you might stop by my office. Wasn't expecting the middle of a lecture."

"I'm sorry."

He had imagined her eyes several times from their first meeting. He hadn't anticipated that a change in clothing might change their color. Still blue but with a grayish tint. "What did you think?"

"You're wonderful up there. I could listen to you for hours. I came here because I . . ."

"Have a question about Paul's Grecian correspondence to the Thessalonians?" He raised an eyebrow.

"Not as such."

"Have a burning desire to learn the correct pronunciation of Sosthenes?"

"I'm not a very religious person," she blurted. "I suppose Paul wouldn't have nice things to say about that. It's not that I have anything against religion. It's just that it's so big and I like things I can see. Like churches. Just there in front of me. In words and history I know. Otherwise it is just a big concept I can't quite grasp." Her eyes widened. "I suppose I thought this might be something like asking if you would like tea."

"Something like tea?"

"Tea. You like tea?"

Brent grinned. "Yes. Tea with you sounds . . . well, I don't believe my Greek vocabulary extends *that* far."

He led her to the hallway and closed the lecture hall door. Then the clack of her Spanish heels fell in step beside him. He led her by way of his office where he deposited his books and gathered his hat before they met, shafts of sunlight ribboning over the midday traffic of the Strand.

Diana kept them at a frantic jog rather than a simple pace. "Can I take you somewhere?"

"You're already half dragging me down Fleet Street."

"You won't regret it."

Brent's peripheral vision offered her profile in full view. "No. I doubt I would regret it."

She tugged on his sleeve several strides from Ludgate Circus, affording the view of three Wren steeples: St. Bride's; St. Martin, Ludgate; and just ahead, the Baroque dome and golden cross designating St. Paul's Cathedral at Ludgate Hill.

Brent said, "I confess I'm a tad familiar with it already."

"You've never seen it with me."

"True."

"So have you really seen it at all?"

⸎

Diana's father had once told her the cathedral was at the location where, centuries ago, a temple of Diana stood. She loved hearing more about her name.

"Since I was a little girl, I think I have seen the world through churches. My mother died when I was born. She loved churches. I wanted to see more relics and lady chapels." Diana stopped. "Cathedrals have libraries, you know. They have stories built into them."

"Endless stories." Brent nodded.

"My father told me the churches are my friends . . . That when I heard a church bell or was wandering in a field or meadow or just lost, that the heart of every city and town was a church. If I was somewhere new and had lost my way, I could look for a steeple to guide me."

Her eyes studied her shoes while her smile widened. "He told me to look for people who appreciated churches just as he and my mother did: as if they were the true north of every compass."

Diana's heart thudded. She hadn't talked about her father to anyone but Silas Henderson before. She loved the sensation of Brent's arm brushing hers as they neared the cathedral. The bells warmed to a chime and the sun blasted through the windows. Everything in her life had felt heightened and exciting knowing that she might intersect Brent's path at any moment. She hadn't been sleeping and had little appetite. Her father had told her love at first sight was improbable.

Besides, it wasn't love at first sight—though the sun emblazing his auburn hair and the intelligent spark in his gold-flecked eyes stirred something—as much as love at first *sound*. He had the most wonderful voice. It reverberated deep through, and the few times she had heard him chuckle, her heart fluttered.

"You've heard of Paul's walk?" she asked as they approached the steps of the Baroque cathedral: columned and white, bulbous roof supporting the tall steeple. It was the highest building in the city flourishing into a cross and a small cylinder soaring above the skyline, denoting God's ownership of the world and, of course, the cathedral consecrated in His name. Two marble angels with swords bordered the gate. The hour was struck and marked by the bells, and Diana thought of Great Tom and Great Paul. Both cast in Whitechapel. The former one of the largest on the planet.

"I haven't."

Diana beamed with the prospect of teaching him something. "Hundreds of years ago in Stuart and Elizabethan times, lords and courtiers and every man from the gentry would meet here just before lunch and wield the news and gossip of the day from news-mongers." She smiled at him. "They walked back and forth, probably grumbling about whatever the gentry grumbled about and—"

"And what would that be?"

"Maybe the price of wheat or politics or who had the best sheep or the best chandler. Then they would break to eat—probably potted pies and ale—then come back and grumble some more."

They entered across the checkered tile from the baptistery to the fresco, Wren's consummate craftsmanship apparent from every balustrade to the high altar, windows, and spiral staircases.

"The Crossing." Diana pointed as they made their way through the echoing sanctuary, starting at the nave through the dome: the quire before them hugged by the north and south transepts on either side. "Funny, eh? The entire building is in the shape of a cross. But even inside it keeps with the theme."

Her words sped: talking of pilasters, corner bastions, and circular chapels. She slowed to look up at him. She had stepped out with men who said she talked too much. She always did when she was nervous. Men who thought she was too pretty to be talking so much, to convince them of topics they had no interest in. They never said as much, but she could hear it. *"Ever go to the pictures, darling?" "Why not take a night off from all of that, eh?"*

Her words rushed out, filling the hallowed, high corridors of St. Paul's, not the result of nerves but of excitement. "Wren presented design after design." Diana's gaze wandered from the homburg brushing Brent's pant leg in his loose grip and up to his profile. He was truly taking it in, focused intently on sights he must have seen before.

"And he was proud of them. He wanted to work on them whether or not Charles the Second approved. It went through many phases, even before the Great Fire. It had to be worthy of the reputation of the city and the nation." She wasn't sure why the spell of these buildings held her so tightly. They were brick and mortar and artistry, pleasing to the eye but not flesh and blood. "Sometimes I can't tell whether the emotion I feel in these places is from something emotional or spiritual. But I feel like I've known these churches all of my life."

Brent slowed before the organ case, flanked by pipes as gold as the carved cherubim above the choir stalls. She followed his studious gaze until it turned and rested on her. "You weren't kidding about Wren being your true love."

She ducked her head a little. "I'm dreadfully boring to you."

He cocked his head. "Not quite *dreadfully.*"

She felt something click in place. "Truly?"

His smile was gentle. "Truly."

"I wanted to see you again. I worked it out in my head. Especially after you gave me that sketch." She kept her voice low so it wouldn't echo up to the rafters and ricochet over the rooftop mosaics. "That you might want tea. And I would have liked tea. But then I was in your lecture and I thought I'd take you here. Though I did take some notes. And I signed out a book on Paul. And the Greek forms of love. Oh, why am I talking so fast?" She flustered a sigh before she continued in a louder whisper. "I just really wanted us to have something to talk about."

"If you took me to St. Paul's, then maybe we would have something to talk about?" He turned from her and resumed strolling around the floor, peering up and over the Baroque columns and sculpted edges, the light from the windows accentuating the smile creasing his eyes.

"I never saw anyone but myself interpret a church the way you did. The way you sketched it."

Brent Somerville leaned over. His breath flowed in her ear, and she felt the warmth down her neck and through her completely. "Do you have a favorite part of this church?"

"Y-yes." Though she momentarily forgot what it was. Couldn't be helped, though. She had also momentarily forgotten how to breathe.

"Then why don't you take me there? So we can have something to talk about. Though I feel we would have something to talk about anyway."

Diana nodded, took a deep inhale, and leveled herself. "Wren used the Catholic Baroque style to his whim and will." Diana's voice picked up speed as she led him toward the ascending stairs. She could feel him so close behind her. "He imparted his Protestant convictions by opening the quire so confessional boxes were replaced by a broad, open sanctuary, a high pulpit. The space encouraged preaching." She flicked a look at him. "You'd know all about preaching."

"Would I?"

"Paul was a preacher."

"He was also a fussy bachelor who got his head chopped off." He chuckled. "But enough about Paul."

There were three galleries atop the grandeur of the cathedral, layered up to the highest point of the dome. The Whispering Gallery, the Stone Gallery, and the Golden Gallery. It was to the first Diana took Brent, surprised at her boldness when she reached out and grabbed his forearm, feeling the sinewy muscles beneath the layers of his jacket and cotton shirt.

"The Whispering Gallery." She led him to the staircase. After a narrow ascension of almost two hundred steps, Brent steady behind her, she showed him the circumference punctuated by perfectly measured windows and columns. The nave below and the high dome above watched as she coaxed him to the other side of the railed dome. Soon they were facing each other across the great void.

She explained he would be able to hear her through sound waves that rippled through the circular circumference. "Say something!" she mouthed, heart thrumming, delighted they had the gallery to themselves.

Brent turned his ginger head toward the wall. Diana waited with bated breath for the reverberation of his words to join her on the other side, her ear pressed to the cold stone.

"Your name is Diana Foyle. Like the bookshop in Charing Cross Road."

A smile tickled her mouth. She couldn't see his eyes, but his body language was relaxed. The same shoulders that squared to command a lecture hall, the same voice that expounded Paul's letters to the Thessalonians. "Yes," she said to the wall, turned from Brent but feeling his eyes on her anyway.

"And I think you are the most beautiful woman I have ever seen."

Diana held her hand up to the wall and pressed her palm on it. Maybe she could feel the words through her veins and keep them. And she knew then she would love Brent until the day she died. As long as St. Paul's stood, she would be his.

CHAPTER 8

October 1945
London

Diana straightened her shoulders and set out from King's College. Devastation shadowed every corner, not to mention the slight signs of defeat in sunken shoulders or the pain in a stranger's eye when you passed to cross the road.

Uniformed servicemen swerved to avoid the sharp turn of a bus, schoolchildren responded to a whistle, and construction workers hoisted long planks over their shoulders. The cerulean sky matched the bright paint whose fresh tang wafted to her nostrils with a puff of breeze that stirred leaves around her heels. A woman's bright-green coat when seen at closer view had been rehemmed. Clothing was still rationed and stockings still impossible to find. A bobby's handsome aquiline profile when turned fully revealed a patch in lieu of an eye.

She focused her approach to The Savoy's rich deco sign. Brent had talked of taking her to The Savoy before they married: to a world of pressed ivory linens and polished silver. Some of his faculty parties and postlecture dinners were held at elegant venues across the city, and she loved watching him attempt to straighten his bow tie that, rather like his smile, was always delightfully uneven. She wished she were with him now, that his arm was steadying hers, his rich voice rumbling through her with a word of encouragement.

The doorman stood sentry to let her in. She wasn't two steps in the direction of the ornate tearoom before she was intercepted by a tall man with carefully pomaded black hair, almost purple under the bright lights of the lavish foyer.

"Diana." Simon Barre offered her both hands.

"It's good to see you, Simon."

He represented chapters of a life she couldn't share with Brent. The person who—even more than her friend Sophie Villiers—understood exactly what she had seen and thought since she watched her husband disappear into a khaki throng of soldiers at the train station. For while Villiers had occupied a long wooden hut nearby, Simon worked with Diana in Hut 3.

She mused on its squat perimeter and rickety radiator before the pleasant curtain of the present pulled her attention back to a waiter ushering them to where tea would be served. There, amidst crystal glasses catching prisms of chandeliers, tiered trays of sandwiches and delicacies putting the previous day's repast to shame, and elaborate floral centerpieces, they would sit and forget the part of the past collected in cups of weak cocoa and burnt toast.

Simon pulled out Diana's chair and she settled, folding her hands in front of her.

"Full-cream tea." Simon ordered, blue eyes appraising her with a twinkle. "And champagne." The waiter bowed and retreated. "When is the last time you had a decent glass of champagne?" Simon said in response to her snicker.

"Not even at my wedding."

"Ah. Listen." He held up his index finger as a swell of strings from the chamber quartet in the corner was joined by the soft line of an oboe. "I don't know if I would have been as aware of Mozart had it not been for old Fisher."

Diana smiled. "With all the subtlety of a peacock." She gave Simon a keen look. "Fisher would have thought he had the ability to blend in with a crowd, but he didn't. Not quite. The moment he set those big brown eyes on someone, something shifted."

She had been able to interpret moments of Simon's vulnerability with the same sheer precision as the German phrases she was asked to translate during her first months at Bletchley. Simon presented one aspect of himself in hopes he could make the world better by being stern and professional and always on task. But deep down she knew he was kind. While it was true he was using her in exchange for something he had done for her during the war, the favor and the weeks in Vienna were small exchange for the gift he had given her.

The waiter appeared with a bottle of champagne and two flutes. With their glasses filled, Simon inclined his to her. "Now what shall we toast to?"

Diana never wanted to waste a toast again. "The war is here, Little Canary." Diana conjured her best Sophie Villiers voice for Simon. "Sherry is in near drought. Don't sip until you've acknowledged the moment! There are so few of them, darling. Here. *Sláinte!*"

Many of those moments Diana had noticed how Simon looked at her tall brunette friend and Sophie at Simon the same. "To Villiers!" Diana raised her glass.

To Simon's credit, he didn't falter beyond a slight flash in his blue eyes. "To . . . friendship." They clinked their glasses. Sipped. Diana's heartbeat accelerated. Here she was, delighted to be back in Brent's arms and yet feeling the safety in a familiar face.

To the untrained eye Simon's transformation was not apparent. It wasn't just in the removal of the gold-rimmed glasses he had always shoved to the bridge of his nose, the knit vests and shirts replaced with creased cotton under a double-breasted pinstriped suit. It was in his carriage. His shoulders were straight and his eyes focused on everything with shrewd intelligence. The elegance of The Savoy fit Simon with the careful measurements of a bespoke suit.

Diana set her glass down. "Better than cocoa."

"We never lacked for cocoa."

The tea arrived. Diana reached for a muffin and slathered on strawberry jam so it settled into the grooves and puckers of the toasted pastry. She tucked in, feeling almost guilty at her ease of appetite with Simon when her stomach had been in knots with Brent the day before.

The posh atmosphere and high society settled over Simon like a cavalier embrace.

"We went to All Hallows last night."

"*We?*" Simon arched an eyebrow.

"What was I supposed to do, Simon?" Her exasperated tone drew a look from a nearby table. She lowered her voice. "I hadn't seen him in years and our first day back together I leave him with my luggage?"

"So he bought your story?"

"He isn't buying any of my stories. Certainly not my consultations on the churches, and that is what hurts me even more than merely lying to him." Diana swallowed too quickly. Choked. "I want this war to be over. Your war. Their war. The war."

"Who interrupted you?"

"A man with a gun."

Simon subtly assessed his surroundings without looking over his shoulder. He carefully surveyed the other diners. She tensed with awareness: a dropped fork, a clinked glass, the pop of a champagne cork. He straightened. "A gun?"

"Was it one of your men?" She searched his face. "Was someone anticipating . . . ?" Diana didn't know how to phrase the end of her sentence.

Simon didn't answer either way, just shook his head. "But the new war is boiling under the surface. It won't be the one we just saw with guns and artillery fire and bombs desecrating our city. It will be a quieter one of propaganda and intelligence." Everyone else's confidence faded under the weight of Jerry bombs and rations, but not Simon Barre's. It was forged and finessed in crisis. He sipped his champagne. "I still need your help."

Diana exhaled her frustration. "I did what you asked. I made good on our exchange."

"I know. But I still need you. Langer has another lead on Eternity from Vienna today."

"Churches. Bombed churches in rubble." Diana smoothed the napkin on her lap. "There is an *actual* committee of architects from the Royal Society consulting on them."

Simon nodded. "So perhaps you need to try to be at the churches for community events. I thought of this."

"Simon. Isn't there someone at MI6 . . . someone *qualified*?"

"Oh please, Diana. Anyone can list off facts. Who can put in their heart?"

"Romanticism doesn't become you."

Simon reached into the inner pocket of his jacket to retrieve a few sheets of paper. "Pamphlets. Charity concert. Evensong. Weddings. Sunday services. Charity drives." He spread his hands. "Everything. You just need to know where to start. To find a pattern. You love patterns. You'll see something. I just know it."

Diana reached for the papers occupying the pristine white tablecloth as Simon continued to speak. "I cannot see how you would be able to keep yourself three feet from any Wren—bombed or not. They are your certainty. Maybe start there. Just the Wren churches?"

Simon leaned forward. "My certainty is Eternity. MI6 has been able to intercept Soviet rings here. But none with any tie to churches. But I have a hunch, Diana. And you know my hunches."

She tilted her head. "Well, Eternity certainly wasn't there last night. Just some man with a gun. You said he never carries one." Diana shrugged. "But he may just be a ghost. So . . ." She plucked a petit four from the tray. "I don't even know what to look for, and don't you think you have spent enough time for King and Country? Simon, aren't you *tired*? Especially because this is not an *actual* assignment, rather a theory?"

He shifted in his seat. If he had been wearing his gold-rimmed spectacles, he would have taken them off and cleaned them. "Of course, a million and one loose threads were left by V-E Day. Why would anyone care about unfiled paperwork or an unresolved mission? It's *all* over. But I didn't finish what I set out to do. I told you that MI6 had me at Bletchley to seek out any traitorous activity. And they did find a traitor . . . Yes, you can gasp. But he wasn't found by me, and I carry this sense of unfulfillment. But the traitor they found isn't Eternity. I've had this hunch about him since Coventry, and war or no war . . ." Simon turned over the spoon by his plate so the silver caught the gleam of the chandeliers.

She sighed. "I don't believe you. You wouldn't risk my life for a sense of unfulfillment."

"This is bigger than you know, Diana. The scary thing about loud ideologies at a time when a country is broken is that the loudest and most assured ones dominate until they seem *right*, they seem conscionable. Look at Hitler. Once he was a poor artist. Then he stood up in a beer hall against a problematic republic. You said the Soviets were our allies, yes. Against a *common* threat. Doesn't mean they *aren't* a threat."

"We're too tired for another war."

"And this ideology will prey on that. Because it isn't warfare. It isn't something people can see or be physically scarred from in combat. It sinks deep until you're not sure where your belief system ends and it begins. It will seep through quietly with respected men with titles and political ambitions and diplomas. Men we should respect. When people are vulnerable, they look for any rock to hold on to. Everyone wants to know what the past six years were for. When I came back, I couldn't walk two steps without one of those Labour pamphlets landing on my shoe. It was like manna to people because it appears to set to right what was wrong."

"And you think you can contain it? With this file?"

"You and I never fought a war on a grand level, Diana. Not like your husband did at the Front, even. We took it one code at a time. One radio interception at a time. One file and one church at a time." He sipped his tea. Shook his head. "I won't lose my country to this. Not to this war of thought as scary as warfare or the American bombs.

Scarier because it grips the very soul of a man. It will burrow deep in our nation's consciousness if we're not careful, and before we know it, we will be trapped. This is the type of silent war that leads to the one we just lived through. You don't want that for your future children. I don't want it for mine."

Diana chewed her lip and fingered a petit four. "It seems too important for one of your hunches."

He chuckled and averted his eyes. "Everyone in my line of work relies on hunches. But don't go spreading that around."

"I don't want to be one of your hunches, Simon. We're friends."

He nodded. "Friends."

"Yes. Why not get another agent to help you?"

"Because another *agent* doesn't love churches the way you do. And no one in the London office is listening to me. My supervisor is this close to putting me on probation. I have to get back to my actual assignments. This is—how shall we put it?—*extracurricular*."

"As you said, this entire reliance on churches is a whim, a hunch."

"Since Coventry . . ."

"Spare me. Since Coventry you think you found a man who is using churches as an easy-to-find and public place to exchange information. Only you could peel back that devastation and national disaster and focus on what you thought was a Soviet sympathizer."

Simon leaned across the tablecloth. "Everything must mean something. If we throw something out or dismiss it, we might *miss* it, Diana. Don't you see? Coventry was bombed while the Soviets were still our allies. Our friends. I was starting to see dissonance and no one believed me." He took a moment. "You went to All Hallows last night?"

"A sentimental trip. You know I was married there."

"Did you tell your husband—?"

Diana stepped on his question. "What? What could I possibly tell him? I was working far away for five weeks on one of your hunches!"

"Ah." Simon smiled. "Do you see why I need you? You're thinking even with nothing to go on. Like that Mozart catalogue back at Peterskirche."

Diana wanted to seethe and rail. The opulent interior surrounding their tea stalled her. "I don't know if the relic means anything at all. It seems odd that something so priceless would have been so easily found, of course. And it didn't help my cause with Brent." Diana sipped her champagne. Instead of bubbling her nose delightfully, it soured her stomach. "Why do I have to play inside your lines when you color outside MI6's?"

"Diana."

"You hire civilians without official paperwork. Yes, I am one of those civilians, Simon. You have this grand idea that Eternity is a spy connected with churches since Coventry Cathedral even though there is no proof that we knew about that devastation. You work in theories you uncover with your smart demeanor and intelligence."

"I just want to see this through to the end. You cannot forget what I did for you."

"A true friend, Simon, does things for a friend without exacting quid pro quo and . . ." Diana stopped when she noticed a slight shadow cross his eyes. "I know you mean well," she said in a softer tone. "I am going to follow it to another Roman church anyway." Diana played with the stem of her champagne glass. "Stephen Walbrook. Built over an old river. There was no message, so I am making up my own hunches."

"Walbrook . . . Walbrook . . ." He tilted his head. "*Oeil-de-boeuf*?"

"You remembered." Diana smiled. She had taught him a lot of architectural terms during their time together.

Simon straightened his tie. "That's when I realized that you were exactly what I was looking for."

"And is your quarry still a rumored file?"

He waved his hand, but the gesture was belied by the seriousness in his tone when he said, "A rumored file to you, perhaps. But to me? Everything. Diana, this new war and the rise of Soviet

Communism depend on men . . . *smart* men who will buy into its message. But it also relies on men of influence and means to wield the weapons at their disposal. Not just guns, but ideologies. I told you before Vienna about the file."

"The Eternity file. The one that contains a list."

"Not just a list of almost guaranteed supporters of grave financial, philosophical, and reputable influence, but of those who have access to everything one might need to start a new war. Scientific ideas for warfare. These are smart people, Diana. Academics like you. Not just here, but in America."

Simon took a sip of champagne. "Don't you see? America entered the war, albeit late, and things turned around. They bombed Japan and sent a message. Now the war is over . . . temporarily. Do you think the Soviets didn't notice how with one explosive the Americans obliterated nearly an entire city? What if the same physics, the same recipe for destruction, ended up in the wrong hands? Can you imagine where Britain might be?"

"But you only have a hunch."

"Eternity has this file. His associates contribute to it through messages. My SOE agent decoded a cipher that placed it in London. It's why I let you leave Vienna."

"You *let* me?"

"And if messages are going to be passed off during some clandestine meeting in the shadow of a pew at a bloody church, then we will be there. Hence, if I must stress it again . . . the need for you."

She almost missed the intrigue. She supposed because it felt far safer and normal than sitting with Simon Barre sipping champagne and talking about spies.

"Please, may I tell Brent?"

"Pardon me?"

"You owe me, Simon."

"For what?"

"I went above and beyond our agreement and you owe me out

of friendship. In Brent's letters he talked about his fellow soldiers at the Front who had an immediate unshakable bond." She waved between them. "That's us. You and I. Shouldn't we have someone else in our corner?"

"For this immediate unshakable bond?"

"Don't be sarcastic. But, yes. And perhaps we weren't in the thick of it, but we are now. Again. *Still.* You put me here. You made me spend five more weeks without him. I can't get around what I signed in Commander Denniston's office at Bletchley without being drawn and quartered, but I can get around you."

"Do you really want to put him in danger?"

"If I'm in danger, he already is. He will just follow me everywhere. And how dangerous are a few nights of music? Evensongs? Choral performances?"

"Diana . . ."

"You don't expect him to sit at home and smoke his pipe while I go to churches at night, do you? I told him to supply the spiritual perspective, but that was about as convincing to him as my working for the committees. You know the workers there during the day are the actual committees surveying them. At best, I hope we will just be seen as two odd relic hunters while we sniff out what you need."

Simon studied his fork. "You can't tell him."

"I won't ruin my marriage for you. I am already so precariously . . ." She stopped. She didn't want to cry, but her lip was trembling and the napkin she had begun wringing in her hands was in a tight knot.

"I am calling in a favor," Simon said, though his voice was soft and his eyes warm on hers.

"You already called it in."

"You promised me, Diana."

"And I promised *him.* I promised him a million and one things the day I married him at All Hallows. I don't have to choose between you. I just need to tell him. Just this one thing. That you need civilian aid and . . ."

Simon's unfathomable bright-blue eyes blinked but didn't waver. Well, at least for one long moment. Then he motioned the waiter over with a fluid movement. "Hunches are not bad things. Sometimes one clue can ripple into another, and you of *all* people know that a wave of sound or a misplaced comma can determine anything."

"Please, Simon. I didn't see him in hospital. I didn't return when he did. I hate lying to him."

Simon folded his napkin gracefully on the table. "You're not lying about your desire to see those churches again." He studied her. "A man would want a woman who shared his . . ."

"Interests and passions?"

"Exactly."

She frowned. "There you go acting so cool and collected. Do you know where she is?"

"Who?"

"Simon . . ."

"Evensong. Vespers. Sunday services. If there are people around, then the city workers won't be suspicious and neither will Eternity. And while you're there, you can find a way . . . You can . . ."

"I can find a way to reconcile my love for bombed churches with this invisible string you are following?"

"Precisely." His smile indented attractive lines like commas on either side of his mouth. "When you're going on *nothing*, you have *everything* to work with."

"We're not back in Hut 3 with you telling Fisher and me what to do."

"You'll have time to spend in the churches you love, Diana. You can blend in with the other parishioners moved by beautiful pieces of music."

"I'll have one more secret to keep. It wasn't enough that there were four years of my life and an official parliamentary act. Now I'll have you too."

"But what a secret." He adjusted his tie.

Diana rolled her eyes. "Fine. If you're going to work off a hunch, then so am I. Brent found a priceless vial last night at All Hallows. Dating to the time of the Roman period here. There are several churches within the city center that have some Roman influence. It's a hunch, but it's a start."

"I like this. In any of the intelligence I have collected on Eternity—"

"On your ghost . . ."

"—it was within the center of cities. It's why I had you and Langer at Stephansdom and Peterskirche. Central."

"And what about your former SOE agent? Do I get to meet him?"

Simon peeled a few pound notes from a silver clip and set them on the tablecloth. "I'll ring tomorrow. No, don't get up. Finish your tea."

Diana watched him walk away, shoulders straight and stride purposeful. As if he owned the world. He did own one world, she thought ruefully, watching the last bubbles fizzle in her now-flat champagne—hers.

CHAPTER 9

Brent assumed he would fall into the ease of lecturing again. After all, he had craved the normalcy of it so often at the Front. After his student meeting and subsequent lecture, he shuffled his notes and closed the door of his office where Diana's scent still lingered. He straightened his shoulders and recited a lecture he had given multiple times while his brain drifted to the day before. Diana was back. She had a secret. Someone had a gun in a churchyard.

Perhaps whatever secret she hid was so dangerous she didn't feel she could tell anyone, not even him, and she might have buried herself so deeply that she felt at odds with digging her way out. He'd play it quiet: mention the artifact and a man with a gun, assume the police would know if this was a pattern of looting. Maybe get them to tell him what Diana would not.

She was secret after secret, and he hated getting foolishly played to trip into churches with her. But some semblance of his pride made way for the fact that she wouldn't be deceiving him unless she truly had to. If she was in danger, he needed to know. He also needed to be smarter than to lug a priceless relic around the city with him.

He turned the relic over in his hand. *Oleum medicina*: holy medicine. He could use some medicine right now. Preferably the kind that would switch off the part of his brain that painted the entirety of King's College with Diana's memory. All of the churches too.

In front of St. Martin Church, Ludgate, Brent had realized he wanted her for the rest of his life. While light had flickered through the dozens of windows in Wren's Lantern—St. James Garlickhythe—Brent first reached for her hand. At All Hallows-by-the-Tower, the crypt below the cold stones witnessed the first time he had pressed his lips to the soft skin of her wrist. He had learned that her mother had died at her birth and her father was a professor at Cambridge as the mournful chords of Stephen Walbrook's organ ascended to the famous coffered dome. Under the great bell of Mary-le-Bow she had told him she loved him. She said it first. It spilled out just as rain pounded the arched windows and he tucked his sketching pencil behind his ear.

They also talked about languages. The romantic ones she spoke on account of her boarding school background and her determined father had roots so different from those in the languages familiar to him. While there was poetry in ancient rhythm, she found it difficult to wrap her head around some of the characters Brent showed her. But he promised her that every word he pointed out in a dictionary she could not read was one of the Greek words of love, and she adored him for it.

She had become a fixture at King's beyond the faculty parties she accompanied him to.

Silas Henderson had hired her as a tutor in a part-time position. Had counseled her on finding a tenure track. "It was Rick's recommendation, of course." Neither mentioned it was also because young men in their early twenties were being served their orders far from the laurels and halls of King's.

There was a lot of Rick in those days. Even if Brent didn't count him a true rival, Mariner was continually persistent. Brent smoothed his finger over the artifact. The man was a cad, but he never had Diana's heart. Still didn't. Brent did. He *hoped* he did.

Five weeks. A favor for a friend.

Brent shook his head. He couldn't shake the feeling that it was more than a little odd that it was just sitting out there in the open. Workers tramped in and out of the grounds at All Hallows almost daily. That it was priceless enough that someone might kill for it. That it must have been noticed by the many archaeologists and planners circling the grounds.

Brent rubbed his bleary eyes, grabbed the vial, and headed to Rick Mariner's office a short stroll down the corridor. *Desperate times.* He growled as he knocked on Mariner's door.

"Two days in a row, Somerville. You must have missed me something fierce. Still planning on keeping that relic?"

"I was wondering if you knew an archaeologist. One who might work with the wrecked churches who might know why a civilian could so easily find a valuable artifact."

Rick didn't meet Brent's eyes. "You want a second opinion?"

"No. I don't doubt your assessment. But I want to know what is the best course of action."

"A compliment. I'm flattered." Mariner shrugged. "Try Margaret Reed. She's been heading some digs around the old walls."

Brent smiled briefly at the telephone number Mariner gave him and turned toward the door.

"Diana sure took her time getting back to you, Somerville."

Brent stalled in the doorway. "Well, it took all of us time to get back. Those who served." They both knew Rick hadn't on account of his eyesight. Brent thought of adding another jab that pointed to what was surely his rich father's influence but decided against it. "Chaos, wasn't it? For everyone."

Brent returned to his office to find a letter under the door advising him to begin publishing again. Treatises and books and guest lecturing. They'd press on as if nothing had happened. He had always been a bright mind and an asset to the scholarship and affluent reputation of the college. He shuffled a few papers, opened a nearby book, and closed it again.

Brent's relationship to his field of study had changed drastically. Little help his mate Ross had been when he and the bloke pushed blindly through a maze of mud, smoke, and consistent artillery, not hearing Ross's directions over his own yelled responses. The hope Brent found in the enthusiasm in Paul's letters, the surrounding culture, the apostle's ability to speak in the languages of the countries and regions he was visiting to be best understood had waned with the death Brent saw daily. Sometimes he felt so different—especially since his weeks back behind the podium—speaking on topics as familiar as breathing but weighted with the history of his new perception.

A new perception now shadowed by Diana's return.

He closed his folder, rolled his pen over the blotter, and made up his mind on two immediate courses of action that had little to do with his professorial job and all to do with his personal life. First he would call Margaret Reed, then he would go to the police. A man with a gun had been roaming a churchyard. Brent at least deserved to know if this was a pattern or the center of a larger investigation. He had heard of looters during the war. Perhaps this was something he and Diana would encounter again if she continued to consult on churches. He wouldn't risk it. He had lost too much already.

Brent took a deep breath and dialed Margaret Reed's number.

They exchanged pleasantries and he mentioned Rick Mariner's referral.

"Smart man, Mariner."

"Yes," Brent said. *Among other things.*

Margaret continued to list zones and blockades, a background on the work that had already been done and that was in process. Brent provided the necessary "mm-hmms" and "rights" in agreement, even as his mind trailed.

What had Diana been looking for? Or was it possible she anticipated meeting someone? Then why take him with her? He knew her interest in the churches was genuine and beginning at All Hallows made sentimental sense, but he couldn't shake the feeling that she was far calmer than he had been at the sight of a gun.

Was there a pattern in the churches she took him to? Walbrook was a Wren. Diana was a Wren scholar. Why not find an architectural historian with a stronger knowledge of Roman London to see to the former?

"What I have is a fairly priceless artifact according to Dr. Mariner's assessment," Brent said.

"People were looting churches even while the bombs went off. Just as they were houses. Though I don't recall pillaging churches being slated a capital offense. A good treasure hunter would have gone through immediately. Especially the buildings in and around the gates where items would arguably hold more value. That and the riverside where the Romans would first have docked on the banks. A team of archaeologists has been quite dedicated and quite careful. You never know when there is an undetonated explosive. They rained like Noah's flood itself, did they not?" Margaret stopped a moment. "Most of what we found is around the wall. Cripplegate. That neighborhood will never look the same."

Brent grimaced. Clerkenwell's priories and arches were equally desecrated. Christ Church Greyfriars was overrun with rubble in nearby High Holborn. The city had released a series of commemorative postcards, owning their losses and capturing the world they intended to rebuild.

Brent sighed. "So the most valuable artifacts? At All Hallows perhaps? Stephen Walbrook?"

"It's been a hard balance as the city crews have had to clear the rubble without destroying anything of great significance."

"So I couldn't just wander into a bombed churchyard like the amateur I am and stumble onto something?"

"I suppose you could, but it is unlikely. Men have been working for several years now, ever since the Blitz started. Tell me more about your found artifact."

"Rick Mariner said it's *oleum medicina*. But why would All Hallows have a relic? I thought relics were interred only in cathedrals."

"There is some scholarship, though not widely known, that says this returned to London with Prior Rahere."

"The fellow who built Great St. Bart's? The hospital?"

"Yes, he went on a pilgrimage. He had a regular Saul of Tarsus moment. If true, it would account for how it got to St. Bart's. There are a lot of black-market relics around. If it is what you say, it is worth a fortune. Sure you're not going to pawn it?"

"I guarantee you I am not. It is just one clue leading to something far more valuable." Brent gingerly put the vial back in his pocket. "And it's rather odd I have it at all."

"And where at All Hallows did you find it?"

"By the wall. Well, what remained of the wall." How had the workers missed the vial he found? Was it a mistake or an oversight or something contributing to every mystery following Diana? Could it be bait?

The long static silence on the line and Margaret's asking if he was still there drew him back. "You love history, like my wife. And the Germans did their best to erase ours from right under us."

"History without fallen kingdoms is just a fairy tale, Professor Somerville. The true beauty is in resilience. We'll see the cracks in our façades, but we will know what went into their creation. London will be more beautiful because it was torn apart but didn't stay so." She paused a moment. "If you like, I can give you a contact at Scotland Yard. They've been very helpful at distributing artifacts as best as possible. His name is Wright. Martin Wright."

Two birds with one stone. "That would be very helpful. Thank you." Brent scribbled the man's name before he thanked her again and hung up.

Brent collected a breath. *You're calling Scotland Yard. About your wife. And she doesn't know.* His hand hovered over the receiver. He could so easily ring Diana and tell her exactly what he was doing. Involve her. The danger was equally hers.

But before he could think or stop himself, the operator transferred him to Martin Wright's secretary and Brent was answering a list of questions and arranging a meeting time less than an hour hence.

The cab ride to Westminster and Scotland Yard seemed too long and too short in turn. When he stepped through the doors, the same young woman who spoke to him on the phone met him in a long corridor and ushered him into Inspector Martin Wright's office on the second floor.

"A Professor Somerville to see you, sir," the secretary said after a rap on the door and a gruff, "Come in."

Brent smiled at her and removed his hat.

"Don't see a lot of civilians here, especially not with missing trinkets," Wright said by way of greeting. He took a long drag of his cigarette without rising to shake Brent's hand. He motioned for Brent to sit. "But it's slow going and since you sounded so earnest on the phone, my secretary wanted me to help you."

"You mean crime has decreased since the war?"

"Oh no. Not at all. I just can't do a lot about it." Wright stretched one leg out from behind his desk and tapped it. "It's aluminum now. Can't exactly cat-and-mouse baddies through Islington."

"I suppose not."

"Lucky to have work at all. Mostly paperwork. But I had some time and Nancy said something about a professor and a relic and I thought I needed a little culture, Somerville."

"Yes."

"And you say that someone pursued you with a gun at All Hallows?"

"Yes."

"And you were followed at All Hallows?"

"I don't know if I was followed, but a man had a gun."

"Or if I could look into who might want something of your wife?"

"Oh heavens, yes."

"But I can't."

Brent shook his head. "I don't understand."

Wright butted out his cigarette and lit another one. "I can't look into your wife's files without military clearance."

Brent startled. "What do you mean?"

"I don't have the level of clearance to work on files of that level. What did your wife do during the war?"

How did Brent fashion what he knew was a lie into something enough for the policeman? "She wrote me about her translation work with the Foreign Office. You're sure you have the right Diana Somerville?" His heart thrummed loudly. "Try Foyle. We had just married before I shipped off."

Wright shifted a few papers, but Brent knew this was just for show. "I'm sorry."

"You could check out Sophie Villiers." He warmed to this idea. "Diana had a friend. She wrote me about her. Her father had some sort of title."

"I did," Wright said. "Mentioned in association with your wife. Villiers. Military classified. Is it possible this has nothing to do with a stolen artifact? This is out of my jurisdiction, Professor."

They both knew the question was rhetorical, but even so, Wright looked concerned when Brent didn't answer. He couldn't make his mouth move. Frozen to his chair, Brent tried to imagine four years of Diana's life a blank slate.

"It's clear you had no idea." Wright's brow furrowed. "We underestimate them, don't we? Think they'll come home and just blab everything like a church social. But it is clear they have secrets too. And your wife is a locked vault. A good secret keeper."

Diana, who muttered all of the gates over and over and who woke up with a new slice of information about Wren. Who was never really comfortable in groups but chatted incessantly with him. Who had all the grace of a pigeon at their first dance. Who couldn't hold a tune to save her life.

"So . . . you can't help us, then." Brent matted his hair down over the scar on his temple.

"There's a lot about this situation that is out of my hands, Professor Somerville. Not a lot you can do either. In cases like these if a file requires military clearance, it is almost certain the subject signed the Official Secrets Act. In which case there is a severe chance that if your wife did divulge her wartime activities, she could be penalized by imprisonment or, worse yet, tried for treason."

Brent felt the room swim. It was too hot and close all of a sudden. He couldn't sit here and think about Diana and treason in the same sentence.

Brent held out the vial to Wright, who waved it away. "I have no evidence that this was connected to a crime."

Brent turned it ruefully. Maybe it would turn out to be a hint. A clue.

"Where did you serve?" Wright asked.

"Ortona. Ghent. A lot of small villages in Belgium."

"If you decide to pawn that dusty thing for a small fortune, you've earned it."

Brent pressed his lips together in a sad smile. "You're sure the file is Di . . . is my wife's?"

"Couldn't get anywhere with it. Even if I wanted to. I'm sorry."

"Well, thank you for your time." Brent collected his hat and made for the doorway.

"Hold on one moment," Wright said and Brent halted. "It's likely not her fault."

"I know that."

He patted his prosthetic leg. "We were all asked to do something or other, weren't we? For the war effort."

Brent focused on the door handle. "For the war effort."

He strode from Westminster along the Thames, the boats bopping over murky water rippling in the sun. He couldn't catch his breath, and as soon as he found it, it left again in a ragged gulp. He was living with a stranger. She had rescinded her married name. Brent couldn't fathom the apparent love in her eyes was a ruse. She'd fallen into him with such relief as if a four-year-long exhale rushed through her the moment he came into view. She couldn't be such a wonderful actress. He had held her. Touched her. Loved her. Laughed with her and told secrets in the dark with her. They had plotted a future and now, living it, they were passing by each other.

Brent felt nauseous. He waved away the kind ministrations of a stopping passerby and straightened his shoulders while he shoved his injured hand into his trouser pocket. As if in mockery, St. Paul's began to chime. The bell friends Diana so loved. Great Tom and Great Paul cast in Whitechapel.

Once Brent reached Fleet Street, he changed his course and walked not to Farringdon and Cowcross in the direction home but to the opposite side of Smithfield Market . . . or what remained of it. He paced quickly through Cloth Fair and set into the church courtyard where he had first seen Diana: green hat askew, smile wide, talking about Prior Rahere. His heart had turned over and then been new that day. All hers forevermore. But all whose?

Inside the dark, echoing stones of Great St. Bart's, he found a chair and scraped it over the cracked tile, removing his hat. A lone congregant lit a candle in the chapel behind him, the sunlight catching the few medieval prisms of glass that had withstood the fire and the Great War. Funny, Great St. Bart's was untouched by the recent one. Still intact. Looked about the same. Unscarred.

How could he face her now? What would he say?

There was something in the din and acoustics of a hollow church of rock and brick that welcomed an exhale. You could hide yourself in here. Safe in its boundaries. He let his gaze roam over the room. Inlaid checkered tiles and thousand-year-old stone had been blighted by footprints. Candelabras flickered unevenly, wax melted into blob statues where they met their pewter holders, nearly snuffed out by prayers.

He and Diana were just beginning to find their footing again. Just beginning to sew up the rift that separated them. But at the moment, the entirety of their foundation was losing its stability. She was holding back.

But she wouldn't without a reason. His brain knew that even as his heart was in knots. She would never be unfaithful to him and he couldn't fathom her doing anything dishonest for any but a good reason. He loved her. He owed her his own stories, too, the ones he held cloistered inside.

Deflated, he could barely find the energy to sit upright in the quire. Footsteps sounded from the north transept, then retreated. The door latched with an echo. Brent was alone. But not truly alone. The Voice that kept intercepting his thoughts in the stillness negated that. Brent knew that voice. It had met Paul on the road to Damascus and had comforted Brent numerous times on the field. Even when he didn't want to acknowledge it.

It reminded him she needed *his* protection. But Brent needed her *honesty*. What if . . . ? What might she have seen behind a signature that swore her to secrecy? He carried his own rucksack of secrets, the weight of Ross's memory sinking him again and again.

He could make it up to Diana by trusting her. Either that or let her slip away from him. The latter was impossible.

Brent kneaded his injured hand across his knee, the wool of his trousers scratching uncomfortably with his movement. And if she had signed an official act serious enough to hold the threat of imprisonment or treason, what secrets might she be bearing?

So his hurt at her betrayal, his mistrust, his own insecurities needed to stay behind, tucked into the ancient abbey walls, safely hidden by the carved stone, Prior Rahere's everlasting tomb. A church that had withstood the fire and the firebombs and the zeppelins of the previous war.

"Well, poor Old Barking here won't toll its bells for a while. It's all rubble," she had said on their wedding day at All Hallows. *"But it still has a foundation, Brent."* She fell into him, strong and sweet. *"Architecture aims at eternity."* She quoted Wren before leaning up with a butterfly touch over his lips. *"And that's what we'll aim for too."*

He looked at the walls around him and the tile underfoot interrupted by gravestones centuries old whose names and dates were nearly unreadable with wear. It wasn't a Wren church but had fared far better. He had always loved this church. Never more so than when he saw a woman with a green hat turning to take it fully in.

Brent swept his hat up from the empty chair and tugged it over his hair as he stepped into the sunlight.

CHAPTER 10

The only other time Diana had been at Brent's flat—*her flat*—in Clerkenwell alone was when she was packing her suitcase to leave for Buckinghamshire. After returning from her meeting with Simon, every tick of the clock or hum of the radiator startled her. Footsteps on the ceiling overhead almost made her spill her tea. Diana took a long breath and turned on the wireless. Classical music funneled out. The kind she heard when she and Fisher had been assigned long nights of listening to radio signals.

She quickly turned the knob until Glen Miller and his orchestra sped the tempo of Cole Porter's "Begin the Beguine" so that its wistful chords and mournful words seemed almost happy.

She and Brent had danced to this once. Well, *tried* to dance to it. No matter how hard he tried to teach her and pull her in step, she could never help but trip over her two left feet. Unless it was their song, of course. She could always find the rhythm to match his when "A Nightingale Sang in Berkeley Square" began to play.

She hummed off-key, sat at the kitchen table, and perused the list of church events Simon had given her at tea. There were *so* many churches. Many just shells now, but others continued their parish events and some merged with other churches.

Eighty-eight parish churches were destroyed in the Great Fire of London, of which Christopher Wren rebuilt fifty-two. It was not even ten days before he brought his plans to the king. The barely standing steeples could be a place to start. Simon had mentioned the patterns Langer found in Vienna and Prague.

"If I were a Soviet agent with a file people would kill for and I needed to meet with men clandestinely . . ." Diana set her pen to paper. She thought of the churches within the London gates as a possibility. Then of the possibility of Roman churches as she had mentioned to Simon. Anything with a pattern or a theme. Simon said Eternity was suspected to be a man of intelligence and academic background. It could have been a coincidence that they found the relic the night before, of course, or it could have been a sign. She had read articles throughout the war about how bombs had exhumed archaeologists' treasure troves. So much of the oldest Roman influences intersected the churches.

She just needed to know where to start. She settled on asking Brent to accompany her to St. Stephen Walbrook this evening.

This evening. She had to feed him! He'd have been working all day. Diana hopped up from the table, tucked the sheets inside an oversized book of Wren sketches, and set it on the bookshelf.

Brent just hoped Diana didn't look out the second-floor window. Or she would see him. Hand on the door to the entrance of their building, then off of it. Key turned in the lock and then retracted again. What would he say? "Hi, Di. Good day? So, I went to Scotland Yard and apparently your file is classified. What's for tea?"

He straightened his shoulders and finally pushed the door open, then ascended the short flight of stairs to their flat. "Di?"

She stepped out of the kitchen, running her hands over an apron. "How was your day?"

Brent slid off his shoes and set his hat on the hat stand. He wriggled out of his coat and hung it on the hook beside it. Then he turned and noticed her coat draped over the arm of a wing-back chair.

"You're not leaving this here?" Brent looked at her coat.

"I must have forgotten when I got home."

"The coat stand is right there!"

"I'm sorry. I must have forgotten."

"Is this going to be a habit?"

She didn't answer. He didn't blame her. He was being a cad. But he couldn't think of one safe sentence, no matter how he had practiced on his way home, without calling her out on what he'd learned. It was one thing for his heart to promise he would believe her and trust her. It was quite another when she was standing in front of him as a smoky scent wafted from the kitchen.

"Drats!" she muttered, dashing to the oven.

Brent pretended to read the paper while she saw to the table. He watched her through the open partition separating the kitchen from the living room. Her blonde hair had escaped from its careful updo and her tongue crept out the side of her mouth in concentration.

This was the Diana he knew. He had to try harder. It was cowardly to resent her. To be jealous of the time they were apart. The war turned everyone into secret keepers.

Diana's attempt at tea was a half-burnt can of soup and scrambled eggs with a few tomatoes grilled to a burn. He fancied himself the type of man who would never demand that his prospective wife know her way around a kitchen, but Diana was almost impressive in her sheer lack of culinary skill.

He shouldn't have found it endearing, but he did. Especially since she was clearly walking on eggshells.

"I'm sorry about my coat." She cleared the dishes from a meal shared in near silence.

"Long day. I am sorry I snapped at you."

Diana smiled. "I'm headed to Walbrook. Fancy coming?"

"Right now?" Brent folded his napkin on the table.

"Do you have a lot of preparation for your classes?"

"No. But ..."

"Well, you don't want me going alone in the dark, do you?"

"No. I certainly don't want that."

"Then let's make sure it's still standing."

"You *know* it's still standing, Diana."

"I want to see it with my own eyes."

~

Not ten minutes later, Diana tugged him out of the flat and waited while Brent turned the key in the lock.

London was still beautiful in its upheaval. Its scars and its wear, its streets with patched holes and scarred buildings still standing. For every tower of brick there was a crane and a construction worker exiting a lorry, and the staccato sound of a hammer rang over the silence where church bells had once chimed. She brightened as they roamed ruined roads and leaned into him.

Over a million homes had been destroyed, and the prefab houses established in answer to the housing crisis occupied their space, slapped together like matchbox-sized building blocks—enough to make an architect quake. A slow, certain spark like the burning detonation cord to a bomb in a cartoon snaked through a populous who still shuddered and jumped at the things that went bump in the dim-lit half-blacked-out nights. As if it could happen again and again in their heavily rationed and bruised city.

Brent and Diana found their way through a stream of students protesting Francisco Franco and holding anti-Communism signs and strolled past a shop window adorned not with the latest dress patterns but with artificial limbs, perfectly suited for the men with amputations settling back in after life at the Front.

Diana clutched Brent's arm tightly. Her eyes flicked to his injured hand. It was nothing. A pittance, really, when compared to the mangled men he had lifted onto stretchers crying for their mothers or their sweethearts and demanding they be left whole. For the most part, Brent never turned another chapter of their story.

He turned from the window display with a surge of gratitude. His wife was keeping several things from him, not the least of which her whereabouts the past four years, but she was still beside him just as he had prayed every night or morning and before every skirmish or battle. And he, with the exception of a few scars and a maimed hand—providentially *not* his sketching hand—was alive. And here. The knowledge bowled him over a moment and he looked down at her in the moonlight.

St. Stephen Walbrook stood not a few blocks from Wren's Monument to the Great Fire. When they passed the high Palladian-style Mansion House, its portico rich with columns Diana had pointed out as Corinthian, her smile lit up her face, compensating for streetlights still on half blackout.

"Happy, Di?"

Her smile was broad and just for him. He knew in his core that she loved him. No one could act at looking at another as if he hung the moon in the sky. It was part of why their severed years pricked so deeply at him.

He placed a steadying hand on her back and they entered St. Stephen Walbrook through a deceptively small doorway in a deceptively unassuming stone tower with a steeple Diana told him was trademark Wren. She motioned to features similar to St. James Garlickhythe and St. Michael Paternoster Royal. The casual passerby wouldn't know the door opened to a grand sanctuary. Columns stood sentry and flourished into lath and plaster, ornate figures and sculptures. During the daylight, sunlight spilled through the arched windows and prismed the mosaic floor.

"Wren would hate the floor." Diana followed Brent's gaze around the space. It was a church you could stretch and sigh in, and his wife was in her element. "There used to be boxed pews here. In the Victorian era. Wren wouldn't like the arrangement." She scribbled in her notebook. "They might have better luck returning it to his open vision. No boxed pews." She underlined with a vehement stroke.

"He put a lot of theological weight into the balance of the pulpit and the high altar. Maybe you'll find another relic here."

"Oh?"

"It's said that St. Stephen's was built over a Mithraic temple from the Roman times. Just on the river. There's still a river beneath here."

Brent found it hard to imagine rippling water underneath the bombed rubble surrounding him, but he looked to his shoes just the same before his gaze roamed over the columns, and soon they peeled away. His mind was transported. He recalled leaning against the side of a church with Ross while the sonorous sounds of Mozart's "Ave Verum Corpus" trickled through glassless windows. Before everything fell apart. When his left hand spread its whole fingers on his sketch pad and his mate Ross was beside him.

"Brent?" Diana's voice was at his ear.

"Sorry, I . . ." Brent took two frantic paces away from her, turning so he would miss the inevitable questions at the sudden eruption of tears in his eyes. He could feel her behind him even with the space between them. She flipped through her little notebook. The stream of torchlight on its pages cast the same shadows of similar light hitting his *Boys' Own Adventure Stories* as a kid. She was picking up, he supposed, where she had left off the night before.

"This church's frame has held up well," she remarked softly, facing where the wall-length organ formerly sat on the west side, wooden pipes piercing the ceiling. Brent could almost imagine the church as it was. Gone now, like the smile in her voice. The only light was from their torches, hers smothering the ceiling to where the *oeil-de-boeuf* window had been. "The dome was his original sketch for St. Paul's." She looked up through the ruined roof.

"It was here, wasn't it?" Brent said hoarsely after a moment. "That I told you I had my orders."

"Yes." Diana pressed a smile. "You said that Wren was a barrier. That I could handle bad news a little better in a beautiful place."

The damage was minimal given the glorious surroundings.

At least in comparison to poor All Hallows and some of the Wren churches along Fleet Street. He stopped before the font and narrowed his gaze. Perhaps another shiny artifact would catch his eye as the vial had. "And what is the spiritual significance?" Brent muttered, kicking at a loose stone on the tile, wondering if she would listen. *"'And I say also unto thee, That thou art Peter, and upon this rock I will build my church . . .'"* Brent kicked at another wayward stone, the starlight spilling through the grand, ruined Wren dome. *"'And the gates of hell shall not prevail against it.'* Well, seems the gates of hell did quite a—"

Brent stopped in his tracks. He flicked a look up at Diana leaning over something in the opposite corner. She picked it up as Brent noticed a shadow draw near her.

He watched and waited a moment.

"Good evening." The man's accented voice matched his sharply cut suit. *Czech? Russian? Polish?* Brent wished he had brushed up on more dialects.

Diana's smile outdid the dim streetlights swimming over the walls. "Good evening." Her shoulders straightened as her hand reached into her bag, most likely for her permit, maybe for her gun. Or maybe to deposit something inside.

"What's a beautiful woman doing skulking around a church at night?"

"I'm not skulking," Diana said easily. There wasn't a trace of the woman who stumbled into his lecture those many years ago. "I'm consulting."

The man leered. Brent thought of stepping forward, but he wanted to see how it played out. How she handled it. What she said. If she would hide behind the same front she put on for him. The last time she consulted in a church, a man with a gun turned up.

"Consulting?" One step and another, the shadow slid forward, seemingly positioned to look straight past Diana until he stopped.

"Yes." She held up her notebook. Began the spiel about grading and reconstruction, her voice even as she pandered to the altar of Christopher Wren.

Diana's shoulders were straight as the man stepped in. A jolt of nerves sparked through Brent's arm and settled in his fingers.

The man stepped closer to Diana and grabbed her notebook from her, wringing her arm before Brent reflexively pounced. He grabbed the man from behind, wrenched his hand from Diana's arm, and hooked his arm around the man's neck in a tight grip. "Touch her again . . . ," he hissed.

"Brent!" Diana pleaded when it was clear to her, if not to Brent, that the man was seconds away from strangulation.

The man choked, wheezed air. Brent slowly let go. Too slowly. He'd always been strong, but hoisting men over battlefields for four years clearly contributed to his force. The man coughed as he tripped backward. "I . . . I . . ."

But the man didn't speak. Not that Brent was anticipating an answer. He was in challenge mode. Brent's nerves and heartbeat were so highly elevated that when the man left the way he came, Brent was still on edge. Leftover tension spiraled through him, the stones closing in and the night sky clear through the space where a dome had once sheltered the wrecked mosaics, altar, and organ.

Diana slowly retrieved her notebook from the dusty ground.

"Your gun is in your handbag, isn't it?"

Diana nodded.

"Because what you're doing is dangerous." He waited through several ticks of silence.

"Brent . . . please trust me."

He nodded. "I *will* protect you. You will not come to any church without me. Do you understand?"

"That's what I suggested. You could give me a spiritual perspective and—"

"My spiritual perspective is that I am following my wife around at night with no clue as to why."

"I don't want to be alone." She shuddered and fear flashed in her eyes. Diana was rubbing her arms as if to scrub them clean of a stranger's touch.

He inched closer. "I won't let you." He wouldn't let her be associated with anything that could lead to danger. He would return the vial to Rick Mariner the next day.

Her eyes glistened. She nodded, then fell into him completely and pressed her lips to his.

Brent Somerville, despite his best intentions to demand that she tell him what they were into, was only human. So amidst the dust and cracks of yet another devastated church, he kissed her back.

CHAPTER 11

December 1940
London

"P art of me wants it to start," Tibbs said to Brent as they sat through another long and uneventful day of what *The Times* described as the Phoney War at their barracks near Oxfordshire.

After their daily drills and training, terrible canteen food and endless rounds of cards, Brent had found a few neighboring churches to sketch for Diana with golden bricks and toppled little adjacent cemeteries that loaned themselves well to the curve and shade of his pencil.

Alex Tibbs was blond and what most women would consider handsome, with the exception of slightly crooked bottom teeth and a cauliflower ear from years of varsity boxing at Manchester. "I know that when we're in the thick of it I will regret saying that, but sometimes just sitting waiting for something to boil is worse."

Holt agreed with him. He was tall with deep-black hair and an overbite. When he wasn't boring them to tears about how he would rather have been a pilot, he was talking about a girlfriend back home.

Brent tugged at the pressed shirt beneath his green woolen serge coat and straightened his tie. His leave was to be from Christmas to New Year's. Usually a time he would spend with his vicar uncle, who had cabled him more than once. But Brent had something else in mind. The Jerry bombs were terrorizing London in what journalists coined a blitzkrieg—some German word for "lightning war."

When he had spoken to Diana, the telephone static did little but exacerbate her tears. Her churches were toppling and she felt each like a personal wound. Christ Church Greyfriars cracked her heart and St. Mary Aldermanbury set her sobbing. "It's like I can feel their loss. Way down deep inside. It's like . . ." *It was like her father dying all over again,* he filled in.

There was nothing like hearing her shaking voice at the prospect of fallen Wren churches to stir him to eternity. He wanted to belong to her. But he also didn't want to take advantage of her without a lifetime commitment. He had seen too many men in his barracks in Tipton cashing in on the possibility of one last chance in the fervor of too much ale and too few tomorrows.

"I suppose you'll be seeing that goddess Diana," Holt said, more than once casting a look over Brent's shoulder when he was sketching her or taking out a picture he kept with him. In it, she was in her natural habitat, staring up at a church, the light catching her high cheekbones and the curve of her chin. He could never quite capture the fluid lines of her face. She couldn't be contained by charcoal.

"I suppose I will." Brent had kept Diana from them for a long time. He had no use for the men in the barracks hoisting up their latest conquests alongside ale slopping over the side of their mugs. He wanted a part of himself that wasn't khaki, mud, and early roll calls.

But with Holt, Tibbs, and Ross trying to forge a sense of camaraderie, he finally gave in. Proud, of course, at their assessment and low whistles.

"She's gorgeous," Holt said.

"That figure." Tibbs did an impressive double take. "You're sure this is not just a cutout of Veronica Lake?" He held the photograph to its side and against the sun.

Ross snatched the photograph. "I can't believe our tweed-wearing padre here landed this goddess. Diana, you say? You're sure she's not out of *Photoplay*?"

The *padre* moniker had started when Brent told them his profession and about his uncle.

"When have you ever seen me wear tweed?" Brent tucked the photo into his sketch pad. "She's intelligent."

"Intelligent." Holt chuckled. "Brent Somerville's in love with the girl's *intelligence.*"

Tibbs added, "She has such an exceptionally shaped . . . brain."

Brent ignored them, but when the idea of proposing had first popped into his head, he waited until he found Ross on his own. Matthew Ross annoyed Brent to the point of distraction their first week of training camp. He was a perfectionist, and he asked incessant questions. He was at least five years younger than Brent, and while Brent's hair was a dark, serviceable red that could look almost brown when wet or in the shade, Matthew Ross was a carrot top. With a snub nose. But despite his scrawny stature he was deceptively strong, and his Quaker background meant that he appreciated Brent's profession.

"Propose, Padre!" Ross had said. He was always excited when Brent spoke of a member of the opposite sex: a language thoroughly foreign to him. "Or Holt was saying that he didn't even need to go that far with his fiancée. If you go and spend a weekend with her at a hotel, give her a real wedding after the war. Give her something to live for if we don't make it through." Ross whistled. "And a little something for yourself too."

"Stop twisting your appalling lack of romantic instincts into a philosophical mantra." Brent kicked the boot Ross had just polished so he had to descuff it again.

"I'm sorry."

When Brent packed his belongings for his weekend in London, Ross watched him carefully. "I think she must be the most beautiful lady in the world."

Brent squeezed his shoulder. "You're a good lad, Ross. If you promise not to follow these two louts around at the weekend I'll give her your wishes."

Train rides seemed longer now that he had someone waiting at the platform. Behind him, a rather ribald rendition of "Jingle Bells" occupied several servicemen who had clearly tipped into the festive cheer before boarding.

Brent smiled through his annoyance. It was loud and raucous and he couldn't get two pages sketched in his book, but he didn't mind. He pressed his face to the glass pane and ignored the mothball scent of the woman snoring loudly beside him. He smiled because he could smell and taste Diana already. Could imagine the way her blue eyes would light as he came into view and she'd immediately trip over herself to tell him about her week.

The train screeched into the station and, of course, Diana was there with her red lips and perfect figure. Before he could swallow or think or take a breath, he blurted: "I think we should get married."

Diana spluttered, "N-not even a hello first. Straight into the proposal."

"I would have proposed to you the second I met you, but it seemed a little too Heloise and Abelard. And I didn't want you to think I was merely interested in your looks." He slid her a side glance. "Though . . ."

Diana blinked. "Before you go?"

Brent nodded. "Partly so I don't give in to my baser instincts and take you to a hotel in Paddington. Oh, don't blush. Heck, everyone is willing to give their contribution to the war effort." Brent looked at her a moment. A long moment. "Mostly"—he ironed out his playful tone—"because I love you with my whole heart and mind, body, spirit, soul. All of it. All seven Greek words for it and more and I always will. Seven is really a trifle of a number when you think about it." He kissed her softly. "Not nearly enough." He pressed his lips to hers again.

"I always wanted to get married at . . ."

"All Hallows-by-the-Tower."

"You remembered."

"Shh! Don't tell the Luftwaffe."

"But . . ."

"Jerry keeps bombing steeples. Terribly inconvenient, Di. And, of course, frightfully rude."

"Brent . . ."

"We'll have to be quick about it then, won't we? So we don't get singed."

———— ❧ ————

The moment he had stepped off the train, Diana beamed at the sight of Brent in his smart uniform with buttons that caught the gold flecks in his eyes and matched the sheen of red hair gleaming under the station lights. Her heart couldn't say yes fast enough. She blinked to make sure she was actually awake and walking beside him.

"I've been to see Silas Henderson."

He looped his arm around her and pulled her close. Pressed a kiss to her hair. "Shocking." He straightened his shoulders. "And what fascinating and previously uncovered fact about Christopher Wren are you about to talk to me for hours about?"

"Actually." Diana focused her eyes ahead. She couldn't look at him and speak the words she rehearsed on the Tube. "I think he's found something for me to do when you leave." She swallowed. "I'll be far away from here. Safe as houses." *"You can win the war while using your brain,"* she remembered Silas saying before she left for her interview.

Brent, green eyes lit with what she imagined was the prospect of her forging herself to him and in a blasted hurry to send off a telegram to his uncle to take the next morning's train to oversee the whole thing, merely beamed at her. Half listening, eyes all desire.

And she loved him so completely it startled her.

They wouldn't marry before New Year's, fudging Christmas as all Londoners did with carols on the staticky wireless and rationed versions of plum pudding while the blackout dimmed Oxford Street and Piccadilly Circus, the holidays taking the German threat in stride.

The new year approached a city at the end of its rope when Jerry blasted it with thousands and thousands of explosives in an unending assault. Londoners frayed by terror and exhaustion called it the Second Great Fire. Bells were silenced with the attempt at complete annihilation through a ceaseless barrage of explosive destruction. Priceless architectural treasures fell victim to the German inferno. Newspaper headlines blared with statistics of lives lost, but somehow Brent's uncle had made it to the guesthouse the night before.

～♏～

A small red pillbox hat clashed deliciously against her blonde hair. It had a tiny veil that covered her forehead and skimmed her blue eyes. But her lips were on full display and slightly turned up. "What are you thinking?"

"I was thinking I could kiss you, but it would be a shame to ruin your lipstick."

"I have more in my handbag." She laughed. "But it might be bad luck to kiss before we say our vows."

Brent looked pointedly at the pigeons molting over the remains of the altar and a stray tabby that hovered, tail in straight salute, near the vestry before it scurried away at the sight of a fire hose. "Yes, clearly our *kissing* would be bad luck."

"Should it be a bad omen?" Diana said while Brent kept a tight hold on her hand. "A church relegated to rubble?" Her gaze took in the four corners, the remnants of the walls.

"But it's still here." He followed her gaze. "Almost." He had a relatively clear view of the still-standing Tower and the bridge beyond to the banks of Southwark. It was a little murky with leftover smoke, the Thames catching the barrage balloons in bulged shadow. Diana seemed eager to see what it could become again.

"Don't twist your ankle, Di. Would be a rotten thing to do on our wedding day."

"Your wedding day?" A worker took in the floral bouquet draped by Diana's hip and Brent's pressed uniform. "You don't want to get married here, miss. We can barely put out the remaining fires. There's a shortage of water. It's not safe."

"Oh yes, I do!" Diana said brightly, without missing a beat. She charmed him with a dazzling smile, and he doffed his hat. "He's shipping out tomorrow and we only have this. Please. We'll be quick about it and we've brought our own vicar."

Brent assumed Diana had a million and one childhood dreams about her wedding, in which smoke snaking like thin rope from a vestry and sanctuary indistinguishable amidst an eruption of rock didn't play a central role. Centuries of brick had toppled in an instant, a steeple lying vulnerable at Brent's and Diana's feet, yet she was willing to forge her faith and her heart with his amidst the desecration of the rocks surrounding them.

But she loved him for some strange and incomprehensible reason. He felt it with every pulse in his fingertips. And while she so easily recited her vows, he tucked them into his heartbeat. He was a little sarcastic and a lot unworthy. He had a past and had made several horrible attempts at emotional connection with women he wouldn't have cast a second glance at had he known that life would procure a Diana.

"It has a strong foundation," Brent's uncle said.

The firefighters and city workers popped the caps off bottles of ale in spontaneous celebration. Two of whom had acted as quick witnesses, keeping eyes and ears peeled for the figure and bellow of the foreman.

Diana gripped his arm. There would be no blurred line between where he ended and she began. "I wanted this moment since I first sat next to you on that bench."

Brent snickered. "Ah yes, nothing quite sets off my ardor like ham and tomato in a medieval church lot." He squeezed her hand. "Which devastatingly charming line, Di?"

"I told you the Greeks had seven forms of love. And you said I'd need a teacher."

Brent sobered a moment. "I did. Didn't I?"

"I always wanted that teacher to be you."

———— ✺ ————

Diana's wedding was rushed and far from perfect. Her lipstick was smudged and her best pumps scuffed, but she plumb forgot the moment Brent swept her up to carry her over the threshold—at least he tried to carry her over the threshold—her knees a swath of fabric and nylon over the crook of his arm as he ascended the steps to their second-floor flat, not compensating for the narrow turn on the landing and swerving her into the wall.

"Ow," Diana said.

"Oh." Brent recalibrated.

The sweeping gesture resulted in Diana poorly balancing and almost breaking the bottle of wine Brent's uncle had given them as they approached the door. "You're very strong."

"Years of rowing, as you know. And easy when I have a goddess in my arms. You feel weightless." He clasped her to him while attempting to finagle the key into the lock. The awkward angle put her at odds with the wall again with a loud clamor that prompted a slammed door overhead.

Diana giggled. "Ow." She buried her nose in his neck, feeling the freshly cut bristles from his recent regulation cut at his hairline.

Brent set her down and she saw that the flat had been scrubbed to within an inch of its life. It smelled like disinfectant and something floral, and then she spied the large bouquet of two-day-old roses erupting on the coffee table in the front room. Diana smiled at his efforts. It almost made her forget the smoke and the buildings they had passed bearing the scars of a Clerkenwell not completely immune from the bomb assault of the last few days.

Not standing on ceremony, Diana looked around Brent's sitting room. Books, like waiting friends, filled every corner. Uneven in toppling towers and unassuming in perfect chaos. "Our books can finally meet each other and live together on the shelves! The best part about being married, wouldn't you say?"

"Darling, if you think the best part about being married is doubling up dusty old tomes in my dodgy flat, then your education is sorely lacking."

"I suppose that's where you come in."

He lifted a curl from above her right ear. "I suppose."

This was her home now. Even as he spirited off to war and she to Buckinghamshire. Even as the uncertainty of their future spread. She must familiarize herself with the mismatched carpet, the sofa, the chipped teacups, the crevices and shelves and table space laden with books while he fought far away and she attempted to survive without him.

"You're a smart man." Diana grazed her lips over the stubble at his chin, and his Adam's apple bobbed in response to the trail of her lips down his neck and into the space of his shirt offering the slightest view of collarbone.

They were close enough for her to feel the slightest intake of breath reverberate. For her to see the peak of his eyebrows and read every last freckle, every last crease at his mouth and eyes, the little flecks of gold overtaking the green of his eyes.

"Would you like tea?" His voice sounded as if it had been railed over several tracks.

"Tea?" She raised an eyebrow. "Am I to understand that you swept me over the doorway in your arms on the night of our wedding and your first thought is if I want tea?"

"Di, darling, give a man some credit for at least feigning a semblance of self-control." He slowly closed his eyes, then lowered his mouth to hers.

They explored and finessed. They experimented. They formed

words their tongues had never previously found a way to verbally express. They continued.

Tea forgotten.

"You'll teach me all the Greek words for love?" she asked much later, feeling a little like Diana but also a lot like a woman she was just meeting for the first time.

"Did I teach you *agape*?" His voice was a little thick and unfamiliar in the shadows.

"Yes. You did. But don't tell me all of the rest of them at once," she said into his collarbone. "I just want one more."

"You could just go and open any of my books . . ."

She didn't want to leave his side. "I don't want what the books would say. Isn't it true that you changed your mind about them when you met me? You said that once."

"Yes. And every day after that." He interlaced their fingers. "I think if I had to choose just one. Right now. *Philia*."

"*Philia*," she repeated, trying it on for size, lifting onto her elbow to watch the shadows of moonlight unsullied by streetlights stealing through the blinds to dance across his face.

"Deep friendship," he explained.

Diana laughed. "Friendship? Seems a little ironic . . ."

Brent lay still a moment, staring silently at the ceiling. Was he considering the expectation of his time on the Front? Was he recalling the hastiness of their vows? She wondered . . .

She turned over until she was crooked into his side. He sighed and pulled her against his rib cage where no line could distinguish where he ended and she began.

"What are you thinking?" she whispered.

"That this is the longest you've ever gone without talking about Christopher Wren."

When the searchlights blared their warning as loud as the air-raid sirens, Brent cursed. "Jerry couldn't have just given us one night?"

Diana woke with a start, pushing back her blonde hair. She was so beautiful through the striped blinds it hurt his heart.

Brent dressed quickly in the dark. "I can't possibly resume all of the many biblically ordained moments I had prepared for intervals throughout our wedding night if we're squished like sardines on the bloody Farringdon platform overlooking the Hammersmith Line!"

The sirens rumbled through him in a discordant clash with the low engines of the dipping airplanes. Brent's chest hitched. Before, he would adhere to his own routine and spill out into the street with the throngs, satchel slung over his shoulder. He had to put Diana first. He had to protect her. The wave of the new responsibility shook him. She wriggled into a skirt and sweater. He looked for her coat and a scarf with the torch he kept on the bedside table.

"What are you doing?"

"You need to be warm enough."

"Brent, get that light out of my face." She laughed as the torch roamed over her, grabbing her coat and scarf, sliding into her boots.

Brent made a beeline for his closet and pulled out extra clothes: cardigans and a few scarves of his own. An extra pair of mittens. A rather odd-looking deerstalker with flaps like a basset hound's ears. He shoved them at her before he dashed to the kitchen and pulled things randomly out of the cupboard, shoving them in his bag. He filled a canteen with water and blindly grabbed a few books, including one set beside her unpacked case. He tucked in a few pencils and a newspaper with an incomplete crossword.

They made it out of the Clerkenwell flat and into a night deeply cold considering the time of year. Perhaps on account of Brent's having to disentangle himself from his new bride and their fleeting few moments. More laden with provisions than usual too. And finally they descended the steps to the Tube station.

Brent jangled the copper coins in his pocket, fed the toll into the machine, and ushered Diana ahead, the night sky a distant memory. The city didn't want them down there, hovered over the track lines, but Londoners hovered anyway. Transient moles for whom civic rules paled in the moment of life or death.

Brent usually kept these crammed nighttime vigils alone: reading or sketching people, dozing with his chin on his chest. Now she was here. Try as he might—despite the smell and crowd, the whimpers and the terror overhead—he couldn't keep the smile from his face. He took her hand, the gold band he'd slid on her finger winking in the muddled light. She was truly his.

Brent led her to a slice of open space on the platform, the escalator and tracks packed with people. Unfolded bedrolls, radios emitting staticky music, flasks of tea and sandwiches spread in morbid picnics, a woman feeding her baby, children playing jacks on a small square of tile.

Diana retrieved a book on the cathedrals of England from the satchel. He followed her finger over the outlines of sketches. "Ditchfield." Brent noted the author's name.

"It's one of my favorites. Silas gave it to me a few days before you came back. It's my father's copy." She turned to the chapter on Westminster. Brent peered at the ornate sketch of the age-old abbey. "Wren had designs for the steeples here," she whispered.

"Wren never slept, did he?"

Diana yawned. She let her head fall to his shoulder and he smiled at the feel of her. At the few stray strands of hair that tickled his nose and mouth.

"Poet's Corner," she murmured.

"Everyone buried there has the most wonderful names." He looked over them, grabbing Diana's hand and holding her plain wedding band up to the light.

Diana nodded and he felt the movement through his windpipe and neck. "We'll name our children from Poet's Corner." Her voice was dreamy, and though he couldn't see her eyes, he wondered if her lids were flickering, if she was close to sleep.

"How many will we have?" He lowered his lips to the top of her head.

"Lots." Her voice was sleepy. "And they'll all be names from Poet's Corner. Mary and Fanny and Eva."

"And boys?"

"Isaac. John. We'll have lots of time to choose." She yawned.

"*Storge*. The natural love a mother has for a child. Selfless love. You have it in spades." Brent smiled, waiting for her response. "You'll be a wonderful mother, Di."

Diana must have drifted. He gently closed the book and moved it away. She shivered a little and he wrapped her closer, maneuvering an arm that was likely to fall asleep under her lovely weight and grabbing a sweater from the hastily packed satchel. He laid it atop of her coat and scarf and tucked it up to her chin. She didn't stir, his shoulder her pillow.

Brent finagled his sketch pad from beneath the Ditchfield book and retrieved a slice of charcoal from his pocket. With his free hand he swiped black in the slopes of an arch, segmenting the tiles of the subterranean world, smudging faces in intentional blemish and shadow, crisscrossing the rail lines, capturing everything in his periphery. Then her. Diana: blonde hair disheveled and unpinned, lipstick she had refreshed only to have it smudged by his own lips just before they crossed into the station.

─────── ✿ ───────

December 1940
Clerkenwell, London

In the Clerkenwell flat on their last morning together, Brent intertwined his fingers with hers, holding so tightly his wedding band pressed into her palm. She loved the sensation. He spoke of all the plans he had for when he was on leave.

She watched him fold clothes and place them in a rucksack. He wasn't packing for more training or to head to a base only a few hours away. He was going to war. Diana swallowed hard. She tried to memorize the slope of his shoulder, the curve of his neck, the way his long fingers turned fabric into itself. "What are you thinking, Brent?"

"That these collars will be wrinkled the moment I step off the train and I hope someone has an iron."

"Oh."

Brent looked over his shoulder. "Perhaps also that you're my favorite part of myself."

Diana smiled. "You're my favorite part of who I am too."

They didn't have much time, but they had used up all of their words. So Brent traced his finger over her hair and down her collarbone and slowly perused her.

Wren's first blueprints for the reconstruction of St. Paul's were created at a relatively accelerated pace. Later drafts were undertaken with slower intention. Diana almost laughed that the fleeting thoughts her emotions allowed drifted to Wren even as Brent was carefully and intentionally memorizing her.

For a woman who usually took the whole of London in stride to greet as many bells and steeples as possible, she set a gallows pace to the train station. He allowed her to see him as far as Farringdon. He wanted to have time to settle into himself before the transfer at King's Cross.

"You're not allowed to cry." Diana's voice trembled as the gated entrance appeared.

"And you are?" He raised an eyebrow.

Her mouth hovered over his. "Yes."

"I know how hard it is for you to lose people. You've lost so much. I never want you to be alone." He tucked a strand of hair behind her ear. "I want you to roam through a city and not feel that you have to find a steeple to feel safe. I want you to want to find me instead. But . . . I can't promise that right now and it hurts me deeply."

"Brent . . ."

He touched his finger to her lips. "I know you, Diana Foyle like the bookshop on Charing Cross Road. I know that you ramble about Christopher Wren as a defense mechanism when you feel like the world is big and you are small. I know you are worried that you don't fit so you straighten your shoulders and look gorgeous and paint your nails and line those perfect lips so you can play pretend at not being afraid."

"Y-you've . . . you've never said that, and—"

"Hush! I believe in you more than you ever will yourself. So when I'm gone and you're wrinkling your nose in that adorable way and not fitting in, know that you suit me, Di. Even if no one else in your world ever understands the brilliant and special and strong and extraordinary woman you are, know that I do." He kissed her gently. "It's what I'm coming back for. *You're* what I'm coming back for."

His mouth was on hers in an instant and she fell into the rhythm of a different variation. A different page of a new chapter. Frantic and urgent at once, Brent dipped her slightly, grasping her closely as inconvenient elements like air and gravity turned against her in the conductor's shrill whistle and the too-fast ticking of the overhead station clock.

A conductor whistled again. Brent closed his eyes and met her mouth again. "I should go."

"Don't." Her lip trembled.

"Here." He reached past the smart, polished buttons of his uniform and into the breast pocket. "Take this."

Diana turned the paper over in her hand, unfolded the creased sheet, and gasped. "It's all of them." She beamed at him. "All of them."

He blinked a tear as she ran her finger over every dome and

steeple captured by his sketches to every crevice, brick, and curve. The great bell of Mary-le-Bow, the turrets at Sepulchre-without-Newgate, St. Bride's in Fleet Street—still whole. St. Clement Danes. The dome and Baroque grandeur of St. Paul's: finessed to every column. St. James Garlickhythe and Magnus the Martyr and Christ Church Greyfriars. The whole of Wren's canvas.

The train whistled and Brent shifted. "I really must go."

Diana nodded and pressed the sketch to her heart. "Thank you." Her churches. In perfect precision all in a row like a line of chess pieces, as intricately beautiful as the skyline from Southwark over the Thames catching the whole of London like a masterpiece.

She'd miss his lips and his touch, the surety of the world she had discovered with him at the helm. But the alternative was the Diana who hadn't stolen across Cowcross Road to Smithfield Market to say hello to Great St. Bart's one fateful autumn afternoon.

The alternative was a woman who hadn't known she could step beyond herself and trust someone to see who she truly was. The alternative was unimaginable.

CHAPTER 12

October 1945
London

When they finally returned home, Diana was still shivering and Brent was still on edge. Despite the threat to their safety and the force the stranger had used, she smiled thinking of how immediately protective Brent became the moment he sensed she was in danger.

She reached into her pocket and felt at the cigarette package she had seen in the corner of the church. It could mean nothing, but hadn't Simon told her to look for anything? And before the man appeared at the back of the church, she hadn't seen anything else out of the ordinary. Most likely it was leftover litter.

Brent turned the key in the lock, then bent over a moment to retrieve something tucked under the door. "For you." He rose to hand her a plain white envelope.

Her name was written on the front in Simon Barre's hand. Diana took it. "Thank you."

"I'll make tea, shall I?" He helped her out of her coat, eyes more than once moving to the envelope dangling in one hand, then the other as she wriggled out of her sleeves.

"Please."

Brent walked to the kitchen, flicking the wireless on along the way.

"*For London to rebuild,*" a voice was saying through the speaker, "*it will require every man, woman, and child to be amenable to change. Our new zoning laws will find more of us outside of the city proper on properties built for families and...*"

Diana crossed to the radio and turned the dial until Edith Piaf's earthy voice filled the flat, then she sat on the sofa. Brent was purposely taking his time in the kitchen so she could read her note.

She slowly opened it to find a warning from Simon. She should only see to the churches during the daylight hours or the activities he mentioned during their tea at The Savoy. A colleague of Simon's had been killed in London. MI6 thought it was an accident. A wrong target. But Simon was certain it was Eternity.

Diana folded the note quickly with a shaking hand and tucked it in her pocket, looking furtively at the coat pocket bearing the cigarette packet as Brent handed her a cup of tea.

"You're still trembling." He frowned and sat beside her.

She sloshed a little tea over the side as she set it down. "It's cold."

He looked at the wireless. "You turned the dial before I could hear more about that fellow and his zoning."

She ran her hand over her arm the man had touched. Then she focused on forgetting Simon for a moment. His letter. The cigarette packet.

She glanced around the small living room. "For one night I would love to pretend that it is years ago. And I am here far later than I should be, considering I am a proper young lady and you a bachelor professor. And I beg you to let me sleep on the sofa . . ."

"Ironic." Brent looked good-naturedly at his temporary bed.

"You never let me."

"I couldn't trust myself. You were safer away from me."

Piaf's yearning French melted into the opening chords of a song Diana knew as well as breathing.

"Not the Vera Lynn version we first danced to," he said wistfully as Bing Crosby crooned the first bars of "A Nightingale Sang in Berkeley Square."

She wanted Brent. More than the kiss they had shared in the domeless sanctuary at Walbrook. But he was slowly letting down his guard. The longer the song played, the more her mind blotted out everything about the evening but his lips on hers in a broken church.

Every night she moved to cash in on the thousand and one daydreams that had seen her through bleak days, weak tea, and fingerless gloves in a bleak Bletchley hut. But Brent was rigid and silent tonight. The tea sat untouched, and he didn't bring up the subject of her gun or the assailant. She didn't want him to retreat into his lesson plans or a book. Didn't want to lose him when he was so close.

She yawned and he looked at her tenderly and his wordless communication inspired her to think he might obliterate the last barriers between them. She moved to touch his face, to close in. She fingered his collar and unfastened the top button.

"Good night, Di," he said kindly, then kissed her softly and retreated.

"No." She gripped his arm. "You can't honestly make me sleep alone tonight. Not after what happened." She hugged her arms over her chest. "You said it yourself, I'm still frightened."

"I don't think . . ."

"A man grabbed me, Brent. It hurt. And I keep thinking about what might have happened if you hadn't been there." She could see he was *this* close to giving in. He swallowed and his eyes softened. "Please."

His assent was several moments in coming. "Alright." He nodded. "I hope I don't regret it."

"I'm your *wife*."

"I know. That's what frightens me."

She heard him perform his nightly routine and followed him thereafter. His even breathing denoted sleep. So Diana stared at the ceiling, inhaling the smell of Brent's tooth cream and soap. She watched him settle into slumber, his repose smoothing out the lines on his face

She smiled at his sleeping profile before she closed her eyes.

As had happened the night before, in the early hours of morning

Brent shifted and thrashed. Diana woke with the movement. She lowered his arms to his sides and held them firmly until he twitched and settled somewhat. Would this be a nightly occurrence?

She hated that he had woken without her for months. Hated that a stranger—a nurse—was the face he had seen while he was in hospital. She wished the face that met him in the midst of his agony and uncertainty had been hers. Of course she had no idea what reeled behind his fluttering eyelids. Just that there was an entire world of his life she would never inhabit.

Diana smoothed strands of damp, dark-red hair from his forehead and watched him for a moment. He went still and she leaned back a little bit. Waited. Counted. He seemed calm enough, if a little agitated. She leaned over to kiss him on the forehead and his eyes snapped open.

Brent shot up and took her wrists in an iron grip and shoved her back against the headboard. Diana gulped what breath she could with the shock of the sudden movement. She flinched and struggled as his grip tightened. "Brent . . ."

But it wasn't Brent she was looking at: those intense, hard eyes—seeing her but not quite seeing her—and splotched cheeks.

His hands were iron clamps on her wrists.

Diana spluttered a sob. "Brent . . . Brent! Please let go—you're hurting me!" she yelped.

His eyes lost their glassy faraway look and focused on her: first with shock, then with sheer anguish. He gasped and fell back a little, looked down at his white-knuckled grip on her wrists, eyes widening as he loosened his hold. She gaped at him.

"Di . . ." He panted, scanning her face frantically.

"Y-you're frightening me." She stayed perfectly still against the headboard, catching her breath, tucking her now free arms against her sides.

"Di . . ." His voice was strangled. "No. Did I . . . ? Diana, did I hurt you?"

She shook her head vehemently. "You didn't mean to."

Brent looked her over tiredly, eyes never focusing. She registered the stark agony on his face, winced at his voice attempting to form words.

"Go away," he said starkly.

Diana froze, then shivered and rubbed at her arms. Should she reach out to him? Should she think of something to patch their silence and sew it into something comforting? "You don't mean that."

"Go. Away...," he repeated with a hint of desperation. "I need... I need to just... Go away."

"I want to help you."

"Please go away." His words fought through harshly.

Diana swung her legs over the bed and retreated, then clicked the door behind her. Her breath was on a fast track the moment she sat on the sofa and was quickening by the moment. She took a few deep breaths, rubbed her forearms, and pulled the sleeves of her nightgown over her still-stinging wrists.

Just before closing the bedroom door she'd swiftly swiped the cigarette pack she had retrieved at Walbrook. Now she tucked her legs underneath her and held the pack to the light. She hadn't realized she was crying so intensely until the letters on the carton blurred.

If Brent talked about what was plaguing him, maybe it wouldn't build into his dreams until he lashed out at her. If only she could have held her tongue. She knew her words telling him he frightened her would winnow their way into his mind and be stored there like coal in winter. She would worry about him and he for her, and together they would tie their secrets and insecurities into a ball of knotted yarn and never make it through.

She bunched her fist and pounded it on the table. Two steps forward. Eight steps back. She wasn't frightened of him. How could she be?

She wiped her eyes and focused on the cigarettes. Sure enough, in the flap, the eternity symbol was etched in light pencil.

The logo on the dark-green box read Pall Mall. Diana opened the lid and retrieved a cigarette. Odd. The cigarette itself was a completely different brand. There were sixteen cigarettes in the pack. All the other brand. Two Brymay matchbooks were squeezed behind the row of cigarettes.

She bit her lip when she heard the bedroom door open and tucked the packet beneath a fold in her nightgown. Brent raked his fingers through his hair into disruption and his face was ghost white. He tied the belt on his robe and surveyed her.

"Have I . . . has that happened since you've been home?" His voice was so low she almost didn't hear him.

"You didn't wake up before. Sit here." Diana rose. "I'll make tea. Brent, sit down." She took the opportunity to put the cigarette packet at the back of a canister on top of the Frigidaire away from his sight and waited for the kettle's shrill whistle. Neither Brent nor Diana smoked. Moments later she joined him.

"You're exhausted." She studied his face. "I was so hoping you would fall back to sleep. You seemed to calm down after those . . . nightmares."

Brent ruefully studied his tea mug, then slowly sipped. His hand shook as he set the cup on the table. She stopped tugging nervously at the sleeves of her nightgown when she followed his sight line.

"Let me see," he said gently.

"I don't want you to be upset. This is far worse for you than it is for me."

"And I don't want to hurt my wife," he said bitterly. "But such is our lot."

Diana held out her wrists and Brent slowly peeled back the fabric and winced, fingers light as feathers at the heel of her palm, barely touching her. He shuddered at the bands of red around her wrists. They would certainly darken to bruising by the next day.

He raised his eyes to hers and she blinked a tear away. "You're very strong."

"I'll sleep on the sofa again." He ran his hand over his face. "I said I would and I should have stayed there."

"Brent. Not this again."

"I'm so sorry, Diana." He set her wrists in her lap and touched her face. "You must know that I would never . . . I would . . . ," he choked out.

"Of course I know. You didn't mean to. You didn't know what you were doing. I wish you would tell me what you see in your dreams. Is it one specific moment, or is it just . . . everything? If you talk about it, then maybe it won't haunt you anymore."

Brent stared at her deeply, then dropped his gaze to her wrists. Any temporary physical pain paled against Diana's recognition that they weren't advancing as she wanted. She wanted to be nestled in his arms, to taste his lips, to be back to where they were—so familiar with each other.

Diana took a somber sip of tea. The night was catching up with her and she yawned.

"Go back to bed, Di."

"Not without you."

"I won't sleep. Not after . . ."

"It's not your fault."

Brent's cup clanged with the saucer. "You were scared of me."

"I was a little startled. I'm not now. Shift over." She waited several seconds before he reluctantly closed the space between them. Diana grabbed his arm and moved it over her shoulder, tucked her legs up under her knees on the sofa, and rested her head in the crook of his neck and collarbone. "There." Her voice was drowsy, eyelids fluttering.

"If I hurt you again—"

"I'll recover."

Brent shook his head, ran his good hand from her hair to her cheek into the curve of her neck. "I wouldn't."

Diana's smile spoke to the life she had dreamed of before the direction the war had spun her. The life that brought him back. A ruined church. Buttered sun melting over the Thames. Brent carrying her sloppily over their threshold. Never once setting a pace she couldn't find a rhythm to. Not as long as he was leading and turning her: one hand at the curve of her back, the other hand in hers.

Diana yawned and fell into him. "I'm fine."

Brent's voice faltered. He stalled and attempted, then attempted again. After several moments and several beats, he whispered, "I love you."

Diana felt it through her fingers and her toes, through the startle of their night together and the uncertainty of tomorrow. She relaxed into him and the words.

CHAPTER 13

January 1941
Bletchley Park

Diana read and reread Brent's letters, finding that if she stared long enough, the sentences she thought she had understood could mean several different things, and the placement of a comma or arrangement of a phrase could change the entire tone. The longer she intercepted messages and searched for possible patterns and words, the easier it was to see any correspondence through the same filter.

The green hills nearby divided Bletchley in equal distance from London, Oxford, and Cambridge, making it the intellectual center of the three. Diana translated messages for an operation inside the huts and stuck closely to Fisher Carne and Simon Barre.

"Do you know the myth of Sisyphus?" Fisher had said her first day. "Who pushes the rock to the top of a hill only to have it fall to the bottom again?"

"Yes."

"Sort of what it feels like here."

Diana shivered and felt at the chain around her neck holding her wedding ring. She was put straight to work with weak tea and cold fingers shoved into fingerless gloves and put her German to good use.

"You just take it a day at a time. If you don't, you'll go mad thinking of all of your limitations and the magnitude of what we're up against." Simon rolled his pencil up and down the desktop. "You have to be able to section your brain and keep things in compartments so they don't all spill into one another. And you can't focus on what you cannot control."

"What do you mean?"

"We are one cog in the wheel that cannot know what the other cogs are doing. Which is why we see Villiers but we have no clue what she does."

While some girls kept pictures of their boyfriends or postcards from home at their workstations, Diana kept the sketch of all of the Wren steeples Brent had given her on their wedding day. She liked feeling something so familiar near to her.

The messages were received through a sort of makeshift and rudimentary system involving a tunnel and a tea tray connecting Diana's Hut 3 with the eastward Hut 6. The latter would receive intelligence, messages, and telegrams as well as process the German army and air force messages using the Enigma machine, encrypted by the Germans and constantly scrambling messages. The decrypted messages were passed to Diana's hut for reporting and translation.

It was always bustling. Diana used her German to the best of her advantage, thankful her academic father had ensured she had as many languages as possible under her belt. Did the messages she translated and processed about locations, artillery, and regimental movement have something to do with Brent? She felt closest to him when he included a sketch of a church or a countryside with his letters.

At first she would leave her shift to catch the night bus to Leighton Buzzard where she billeted with the vicar's family. They were kind and even had a radiator in her room. But Villiers wasn't satisfied with the arrangement, especially when it cut her time short at the pub with Simon, Fisher, and Diana.

"Leighton Buzzard of all places!" Villiers clucked her tongue and with her inimitable magic snapped her fingers, and soon Diana was housing with her in a shared flat a five-minute walk from Bletchley Manor. She asked Simon about Villiers's influence, having early on deciphered that the two were either close from their time together or more likely had been acquainted before the war.

At bedtime Diana turned off the constant noise and files and slipped into a memory like a sweater. To try to sleep she didn't count sheep but rather listed London gates and Wren churches and Greek forms of love. Pragma. Philia. Ludus. Storge. Agape. Aldersgate. Bishopsgate. Newgate. Ludgate. Garlickhythe. Walbrook. St. Martin, Ludgate. St. Andrew Holborn.

Diana crossed her arms over herself and tried to hear Brent's voice, to feel his breath rumbling through her. But a picture was a poor substitute, and even the patched-through telephone calls made him sound as if he were meeting her through a tunnel. Nothing in his letters and sketches, rusty calls or memory, would bring him closer. Sometimes contact made him seem farther away.

One night Sophie Villiers came home from a night shift to find Diana crying on the sofa. "I'm s-sorry." She hiccupped. "I-I haven't been able to stop."

"Really. Stiff upper lip. It'll seem better in the morning. And so on and so forth." Villiers rocked on her heels, her tone and flippant words belied by the sparkle in her eyes. "What? I am not good at this sort of thing. You're missing your young man and I have little to do with the opposite sex. Unless they'll buy me a drink." She cracked a smile, which Diana slowly returned.

Villiers was a woman Diana wasn't sure would become an easy friend had they not been thrown together by circumstance. Many debutantes were at Bletchley Park: women with the same history and pedigree as Villiers, who came from a long line of dukes, duchesses, and titles that made Diana's head spin. Just as the Government Code and Cipher School preferred unmarried woman, so it preferred to recruit women from good families believed to be innately trustworthy.

Sophie, despite her name and her habit of drawing every gaze as she entered a room with her height and erected shoulders and signature lipstick, never connected with the other women from similar affluent backgrounds.

More often than not, she merely intimidated them.

"I suppose you think I am silly." Diana rubbed at her nose.

"I mostly think you're silly when I hear you whispering all manner of strange church names under your breath and—"

"They're a safety net. I told you."

"You're a funny one." Villiers stretched her arms. "But this is more than just your missing him. This is a new level of melancholy." Villiers put her hand to her chest. "You didn't get a telegram, did you?"

Diana shook her head. "No. More just feeling sorry for myself."

"Well, it's your day off. We should do something."

"I wanted to catch up on my wash and take a nap. Listen to the wireless."

"Dull. Dull. Dull." Villiers clucked her tongue, settled beside Diana on the sofa, and crossed her legs. "You'll worry less about your young man if we're thrown in with a lot of rowdy people. And there's some sort of pantomime. Come."

They entered Hut 2 at a fast pace to find it, as usual, filled with uniformed men and women sipping tea and the dark pints of ale whose inclusion firmly established it as a daytime social hub. Men and women were chatting in groups or slumped exhaustedly over tables, trying to turn off their brains for a few hours without getting inebriated enough to mar their performance or, worse, spill any secrets.

"Simon Barre!" Villiers saw him before Diana did.

"You seem to have a sort of radar for finding him, Villiers. This is not the first time this week that—"

"Hush, Canary."

Villiers parted men and women like the Red Sea to approach Simon's table and cut through his conversation with a pretty young woman.

Simon looked up at her casually and slowly flicked ashes from his cigarette. "By all means, Villiers, don't stand on ceremony."

"I need you a moment."

Simon responded with a smooth smile, though it never reached his eyes. He dismissed the young woman before him. "Mary, a pleasure."

Mary shot Villiers an incensed look as if to say, "How dare you take me from this handsome man and not recognize how under your spell he is!"

Villiers straightened her trousers and crossed her legs with a fluid movement before Diana dropped beside her.

"Yes, Villiers. What do you need me for?"

She took up the half cigarette Simon had discarded and lifted it to her lips. Its effect was subtle to Diana but an absolute bell clang to Simon. She took a quick draw. Blew it out easily. Villiers offered the cigarette back to him through her pinched fingers.

Diana opened her mouth to say something, but the silence was too palpable. Watching these two face off was dizzying.

"We're bored."

"Very well." Simon made a long show of pressing the cigarette to his lips. "I was on a date."

"That was *not* a date."

"How would you know?" Simon asked.

Diana twinkled. "Yes, Villiers, how would *you* know?"

"Because I've been on a date with Simon."

Diana sputtered at how blatantly she offered this information.

"And it was an unmitigated disaster, wasn't it?" Villiers arched an eyebrow at Simon.

"This was not an unmitigated disaster, Villiers. We were having a nice drink and—"

"Exactly." Villiers tapped her nails on the table. "Which is how I know it wasn't a date."

March 1943

Diana was moved from translating to listening to air signals. The Air Section produced intelligence based on the patterns of day and night fighter reactions. The intelligence and information gleaned from listening for German interception through the airwaves was at once redundant and fascinating. In an age of innovative communication, Diana was never sure what signal she would pick up.

A daily analysis of activity and patterns would often reveal how much time a bomber would spend over a target or even the sequence in which pilots would complete their missions. Diana became familiar with call signs, patrols, and traffic characteristics. She was attuned to how the weather could change an operation and how the slightest mission might be unsuccessful if a message was interrupted by a warring sequence.

Fisher Carne was also assigned on account of his pitch-perfect hearing. They shared smiles every time the scrambles, shrill signals, and static wavered at the interference of a daily musical program from a radio station in France. Some nights it was clear over the channel and others not. She was sure he got a near-honorary degree in the architectural facts she gave him as she did in music. He was a mathematician as a course of research, but music was his passion. It just happened to overlap.

"The same part of my brain that solves complicated equations takes into consideration the measures and beats," Fisher had told her. "The same part of my mind that enjoys a particularly complicated measure of Mozart is the same that tackles a nearly unsolvable line of algebra. So my passion and my work are neighbors. But I cannot spend my whole life in research, Diana. Neither can you. Your brain has a wonderful capacity for patterns, given your education and your passion. But step outside of yourself. Listen. *Truly* listen."

Fisher's workstation didn't host the usual knickknacks. Instead of a portrait of a sweetheart or a wife or a sister, there was a framed portrait of Mozart. There was also a favorite piece of tackle and a carved insignia of a mathematical symbol.

Diana loved the romantic notion that arduous hours of straining her ears for any modicum of intelligence might be worthwhile and the daily analyses and logs that Strauss might funnel through. Or Bach. And Fisher's favorite: Mozart. He had told her about the Köchel Catalogue. The more Diana listened, the more she appreciated it. There was a pattern in music just as he said. She began to anticipate where a movement would begin and where sequences would repeat until she could hum along and anticipate a phrase.

"There." She looked up to find Fisher watching her closely.

"What?"

"Your face. It changes now. You're a Mozart lover, Diana," he said proudly.

⸺ ꝏ ⸺

The more she spent time with Simon, Villiers, and Fisher, the more her mind stretched and the further she felt from her old world.

She was fighting to get back to it, of course, just as they all were. But part of her knew she would never forget that the war had taken her beyond herself—just as it had taken her from Brent. The hardest was recognizing that the longer she spent away and the more she learned, the bigger the barrier she was building between them.

"Secrets seem easy, don't they, Diana?" Simon said. "You tell a few like we do here. Say we make radios. Lie to those billeting us. Refuse to let our family know the extent of our work here. It seems easier to just keep a secret. To tell the lie. But secrets often overstay their welcome. You tell one lie for the right reason and then another and you layer them one on top of the other and soon you cannot tell where the secrets and lies begin and the truth ends." Simon lit a cigarette and took a long inhale.

At first Fisher hated his job. But somehow Simon worked his

magic and continued to convince him he could treat it as a hard-to-solve equation or a complicated line of music, and soon Fisher Carne was willing to do the best he could. He also evidently started to enjoy Diana's company.

"Farthing for your thoughts, Diana?" he had said on more than one occasion. Sometimes accompanied with a toss of the coin. "You're a smart girl."

"Everything in my life is Christopher Wren," Diana told Fisher on one of their many nights at the pub. Fisher was a bit of a mystery to her. His demeanor wasn't as suave as Simon's, and even Villiers's proud façade could be penetrated by the promise of true friendship. She assumed his standoffish manner was one of his oddities. He was pretty much a genius, handpicked by Denniston himself on account of his winning several nationwide chess championships, though Simon could give him a run for his money, and often did, and Fisher's mathematic proficiency broke many previously uncontested theorems.

"You were studying at King's, weren't you, Diana?" Fisher asked as she set her pencil aside. "I was mates with a chap named Mariner back in the day."

"I took several of his classes." Diana brightened. She hadn't had much time for Rick after she began seeing Brent, but a familiar name from a world she missed brought a smile to her face.

They were doing important work, but that didn't mean there weren't unending days of doldrums. When the messages they intercepted and archived were constant, her brain spiraled. But she could always rein it back in during nights with Fisher, Simon, and Villiers at the local public house that showed her the life she had missed by keeping to herself during undergraduate studies.

"You're nowhere near King's and still defending a thesis," Simon would josh to Diana when she fell into another Wren spiel.

"Get us another pint, would you, darling?" Fisher didn't look up from his next move, more interested in chess and clearly wanting to keep Simon's attention on the board and not Diana's architectural facts.

"Get your own, Carne," Simon retorted.

"It's alright. I was going anyway."

The Bletchley men were always in the mood for debate, especially when two or three sheets to the wind. Diana needed little but a loud voice and a few glasses of lemonade to rouse her into extolling the virtues of her favorite architect. She missed Brent. She missed London, but the community at Bletchley contained a spark and intelligence that mimicked what she was sure she had missed during her freshman years at King's. It wasn't unlike college with late-night pub nights, couples using the bench near the pond for a midnight rendezvous, horrible canteen food, and even badminton on the lawn.

In some ways Diana had been given a second chance to live her life as it was always meant to be.

Villiers heralded a loud, "Hear! Hear!" and raised her sherry glass, as if to stir the whole of an unhearing crowd of card players and dancers just finding the beat of a tune spilling from the nearby and static-riddled wireless. Villiers never talked about what she did, of course, but she had infiltrated every space of the Park. She was striking to look at and opinionated. Yet unwaveringly professional. Though it seemed she was speaking fast and loose given her passion and strong gaze, Diana recognized her talent lay in her ability to inspire others to believe that she had welcomed them into her confidence. Whereas, in actuality, she displayed a carefully calculated suit of armor.

"They say war is a man's job. But there are three to one of us here. If war is *just* a man's job and they all leave for North Africa and the Sudan and heaven knows where else, then is the country just to fall apart in their absence?" Villiers shook her head. "It is because we are the seams, Diana. Here, there are two possible outcomes to every problem: the right or wrong one solved the traditional way and the right or wrong one solved in such an interesting and non-conforming way that the solution will echo decades after."

Villiers tapped the ashes from her cigarette. "We are in the latter, Little Canary." She smiled for Fisher and Simon. "And because we are women, we are a far sight better than you lot at it. Women know how to look at something and think about it, not only for its objective solution but one that thinks of the emotional consequences."

"Are you admitting that you are a woman?" Diana laughed. She didn't want Villiers to suspect she saw the dart of her glance in Simon's direction in that exact moment she spoke of emotional consequences.

But Sophie Villiers was right: Bletchley Park was a female domain. Women drinking pink gin and painting the illusion of stockings from bottles when nylons were hard to come by. Many tried to draw the attention of men. Smart men: for the most part the workers were culled from academia. And some of these men were as accustomed to social situations as a duck in Antarctica.

Devoid of her own romance, Diana focused on the potential of others. When you fell in love, she supposed, you were predisposed to notice its signs in other people. Simon's features softened when Sophie Villiers was near.

At Diana's jest, the dimple that always formed during Simon's witty banter with Villiers smoothed away. He turned and their eyes met. For a moment something crossed his face, a little like a plea, a little like embarrassment. Villiers and Simon were connected.

Fisher chose that moment for another customary grilling. "How did you meet your boyfriend, Diana?"

"Bit of a swerve in subject, Fish." Simon took a swig of lager.

"At Great St. Bart's." Diana flushed a little at her ear tips. A memory tugged of russet oranges and yellows before London was swirled in unending gray. "In the churchyard. It was so perfect that autumn. Everything was perfect. He was sketching the churchyard. It's one of my favorite spots in the city, and inside is a gorgeous Lady Chapel.

It's tucked in Cloth Fair so you don't immediately see it, but it's close enough to the hospital. It's one of Prior Rahere's buildings. He went on a pilgrimage to Rome and had a Saul of Tarsus moment. Just like the story of St. Paul in the Bible."

"Calm down there, Canary," Villiers said kindly. "The faster you talk, the more it looks like you are going to spin yourself into a dither and off your chair."

"London, as we knew it, is one big dust pile. Tipped-over building blocks." Simon tapped the ashes of his cigarette.

But Diana refused to see London as it was in their conversations and the newspapers. She continued to see it as it could be.

"Cocoa, Diana?" Simon asked one afternoon when her eyes were crossing over her work. She nodded and followed him.

"Cheers." He tinked his mug with her own. Mugs were hard to come by in the huts, and Simon and Diana were fastidious with theirs. It was said Professor Turing over in Hut 8—Villiers's side of the Park—chained his to the radiator so no one would nick it.

Diana rolled her shoulders. There seemed to be a constant crick in her neck these days from leaning over her typewriter.

Simon had a kind smile that reached his eyes and crinkled them a little—rather like Brent's. "Very pious of you." He fingered the rim of his mug.

After a day of listening to the click of heels across the floor, the reverberations of slamming doors, the clack of typewriter keys and transmissions, the constant low of a wireless, and the snaked beep of incoming signals, the hum of the pub was a reprieve. A different kind of noise. The Bletchley huts were persistently noisy, every slight sound an echo in the perimeter of a stuffed, windowless room.

The nurses had started jolting people with ultraviolet experiments because of the workers' lack of exposure to sunlight. Trapped like sardines in a can with nothing but winter black when they shuffled out exhausted after the night watch. She supposed the pub entrapped them too. But at least on their own terms.

"I miss the light. The natural light. In the nave churches." Diana turned her cheek as if to feel the sun. "Like Stephen Walbrook. You've been? It's all curved and vaulted. But that light through the clerestory windows. The spaces you have to look up to see." She breathed in sharply. "Just lower than the oculus or that top window that gives it the look of a sort of lantern." She sipped her cocoa and checked to see if she was boring Simon.

"Oculus?"

Diana nodded. "In French the term is *oeil-de-boeuf*."

"Bull's-eye," Simon translated. "I suspect you have a perspective of the world that no one else does. Being able to be so passionate just about light. You're an interesting woman, Diana."

"I would almost think you fancy me, Simon." She laughed nervously. She knew better. So did he.

Simon straightened, adjusted his glasses. "What does that . . . ? Never mind. We're stuck in this rummy tin can for heaven knows how many hours a day, and I realize there is a whole side to you that I don't know."

"That goes both ways. Tell me something you're passionate about."

"Other than chess?"

"Yes, other than chess."

"Right now I am passionate about seeing beyond the war. It won't last forever and we won't always be in this bleak tin can with rubbish tea and unlimited rubbish cocoa. It will be a new world. And we will need to change it."

"Change it?"

"Well, for one, we'll have to rebuild all the churches Jerry keeps blasting." But there was a slight tonal shift in his voice she hadn't heard before. "You, of course, remember when Coventry was bombed?"

"The loss of a beautiful cathedral."

Thereafter, she told Simon all about the churches. The protruding chancel and tower porch at Magnus the Martyr, that St. Mary-le-Bow was the first city church built in the reconstruction after the fire. That Wren married math and imagination together so the whole of London was his complicated symphony. *Numero pondere et mensura:* by number, weight, and measure was what he ascribed to. All the while believing the absolute truths of geometry and arithmetic.

"I hadn't realized you were so interested in all of this. You made fun of me. You and Fisher when I first came here."

Sometimes she would see something change slightly in Simon, a sort of invisible mask that would close him off from her.

"We see each other more than anyone else in our lives," he said easily. "I am merely taking an interest."

Yet, with the exception of his favorite chess moves and his teasing of Villiers, she knew little about him. He remained a closed book.

Turning the next chapter on Fisher, however, came more easily the closer they worked together. For one, she could tell by the slightest shift in his body language when he was bored. After his day's transcriptions were done, his brown eyes opened on her with an almost lethargic glint. "You want to learn more about patterns?"

"Yes!"

Fisher took out a pencil and fresh piece of paper. "Well, now we have machines and keys. In the Boer War and the Great War, a type of cipher was popularized. Some posh gent it is named for. A Playfair cipher. It is like an elaborate crossword puzzle."

"I like crossword puzzles." Diana massaged her fatigued neck muscles.

"Then let's play. Come here."

Diana carried her metal chair to his side of the desk and leaned in.

He drew a grid and then another and walked her through every step of filling each square with a sequence of letters. She had to combine the sequence from opposite corners.

"But you need a key," Fisher said. "Some use a Bible, a dictionary, a book that anyone might have in their library. Others are far smarter. If it were me, I would play with people's perceptions. I would lean into the psychology of it all. How many times have you been able to decrypt a message just on feeling?"

"Several times. I just will the letters to mean something." She smiled. "Must seem silly."

"No. It seems like human nature. Not my favorite subject but undoubtedly something that needs to be accounted for when engaging an enemy."

Diana pressed her index finger to her lips. "Do you have any enemies, Fisher?" She couldn't imagine this introspective and bright young man having offended anyone for any reason.

"Everyone has enemies, Diana. Even if one cannot see them."

"You don't mean me?"

Fisher gave a lopsided grin. "You might be an exception." He paused, pressing his pencil to a new sheet of paper divided by the squares outlining a potential cipher. Together, they played for another hour at least. Then he rose and brushed his cold lips against her cheek. "You, Diana Foyle, are a doll. An absolute doll."

She blushed at the compliment. Something in Fisher's rigid stance and the dry, chalky press of his lips beneath her cheekbone explained so much about him. The man was a foreign zone when it came to human touch. While Diana had been shy and preoccupied by the degree and research she meant to conquer in honor of her father, Brent Somerville had intercepted her path so that touch and connection became second nature to her. But Fisher . . .

Diana smiled. "And you, Fisher Carne, are one of the smartest men I have ever met."

She relayed all of this to Brent when her call was patched through with as many staticky signals and connections as a telephone Frankenstein.

"You're like sunshine. I bet they all line up for a bit of it. Don't be scared, Diana. Make new friends. Christopher Wren, for all of his charms, is a poor date to the cinema."

"Make new friends." And she had. Fisher, Simon, and Villiers. *Real* friends. Friends who didn't misinterpret her sharing of favorite facts as an opportunity to show off. Friends whose company she looked forward to sharing at the end of a long day.

Diana realized she was carving out a new part of herself that had been previously hidden. Brent didn't realize it had taken everything within her to approach him at Great St. Bart's. He didn't see her straighten her shoulders or register the even breaths that smoothed her voice into something in the vicinity of confidence. He didn't see . . .

Or did he?

CHAPTER 14

October 1945
London

Y̶ou can't come round the flat, Simon, while my husband is at
work. If the landlady saw me admitting a single man who is
not a redheaded professor . . ." Diana tugged her sleeves over her
bruised wrists. She set her mop down and tugged at the kerchief tied
in her hair.

"You're doing a rather horrible job of pretending to keep house.
What is burning?"

"Drats!" Diana dashed to the kitchen and opened the oven door.
Enveloped in smoke, she coughed, grabbed a dish towel, and waved
away the black cloud until confronted with a ruined rectangle.

Simon watched, amused, from the door. "Smells wonderful."

"Oh, shut up!" She tossed the dish towel onto the counter. "Well,
my flour rations have spread far."

"Where's this relic?" He motioned her back into the sitting room.

"Brent has it at the office."

"Langer rang from Vienna. A similar artifact was found on an
arrested double agent. Not as old as this one but from the Habsburg
Empire."

"What are Soviet agents doing with artifacts?"

"Nest egg maybe? Who knows." He removed a folded piece of
paper from his pocket and passed it to her.

The infinity symbol, then:

птица

шпиль

"Russian?"

Simon nodded. "The words for *bird* and *steeple*."

"Wren churches?"

Simon raised a shoulder. "Could be."

"That's so ironic, isn't it? A Soviet agent using Wren churches?"

"Or a double agent," he supplied.

"Who just happens to use the thing I love most in the world?"

"Well, at least you'll enjoy yourself. An agent was apprehended near Piccadilly Circus last night. That's where the note was found. Another suspected agent was found dead in his apartment building. Strangulation."

Diana shuddered. "When you said this was dangerous—" She stopped. "But this is putting a pretty big hole in your church theory."

"Except for that note. I still have my hunch, Diana. That the two are related. But I don't like where it is leading. So keep your gun close at all times."

The clock above the mantel began to chime. "You have to go. Brent will be home soon and he can't see you here." She began to assure him that she would take Brent to a church that night but recalled how he had advised her against it. Better to just go ahead and report to him afterward.

"Hold on to that relic. Don't go donating it to a museum just yet."

She nodded. "I won't.

"Take care, Diana."

She was attempting to salvage what was left of dinner when Brent appeared. He brushed his hair from his forehead, his glance hovering between curious fondness and annoyance as he took in the mop and the unmopped floor. The duster on the undusted table.

"You've been busy," he said with an affectionate smile.

"I know…" Diana stopped and started. "I know that you like things in a precise line. I know that you want things in order and I know that I… The kitchen…" It wasn't just the kitchen. It was the entire flat. Brent took in the scraps and scrapes and spills, satchel still over his shoulder, hat still on his head.

Diana's hair was tied with a kerchief, a slipshod bow at the front of her forehead. Her soiled apron was splashed with flour. The squares of hard biscuits in her tin could not have fully appreciated her sacrifice in rolling the hard dough. She had worsened the stain on one of his best shirts and ironed a hole into a tweed vest. The larder was a hodgepodge, the Frigidaire a strange, solitary home for baking soda and a solitary egg. She was a terrible housekeeper.

He should want a woman who could darn socks and boil an egg. Instead, he chose the woman who would sabotage a bowl of oatmeal, who would somehow—illogically—turn toasted bread into a war zone. Dishes a small child would feel natural at creating, she ruined. Her heart was in her eyes, lips tightened expectantly. Offering nothing but barely passable fare and wrought-iron pans overstaying their welcome on rusted elements.

"Di, this is quite… quite…" Diana was a stranger to measuring cups, but he loved her beyond equation. He stepped closer. This was what he dreamed of. To come home from a long day and find her here. Sure, the flat was a disaster, but his heart flipped at the sight of her efforts.

"I'll learn." Diana's fingers wandered across his shoulder blades as his mouth lowered to her ear. "Did you have a good day?"

"Brought up Luther. Unintentionally started a debate on the justification of works and grace." He stalled. "I also gave Rick Mariner the relic, Diana."

"Without consulting me?"

"I think we both had enough danger the other night. It's safer with him. What do we possibly need it for?"

"But you said we were keeping it. That first night."

"And then I saw you had a gun and then we went to Walbrook where you were assaulted. What were you planning on doing with it anyway? Pawning it?"

"No, of course not. I just . . ."

"It's not a rabbit's foot or a penny farthing. We have to give back a priceless treasure. I trust Rick to do what's right with it. Come sit down." With the exchange of the relic, Brent was more determined than ever to erase every last secret between them. Diana moved the mop. She helped him out of his coat and took his hat and case. He occupied the couch, watching her deposit his things near the hat stand.

"Always fancied doing that when you returned from work every day. All the simple little things I dreamed about that are just routine and real life. Oh! But I haven't offered you tea. I'll see to the kettle."

"Don't see to the kettle just yet. Come sit a moment."

Diana lowered to the sofa and turned toward him. He looked at her hands folded in her lap.

"It's quite alright. Truly." Brent studied her a long moment: blue eyes wide on him, blonde wisps escaping from the kerchief, her teeth worrying her bottom lip. He wanted to kiss her deeply. Untie the knot of her hairpiece. "Where were you, Diana? When you were away? Those five long weeks. That favor for your friend."

"Brent . . . More than anything I want . . ." She wrung her hands. "I can't tell you."

He nodded. Exhaled. "I am choosing to trust you because I do love you and I want this to work." *And because Ross told me I had something to go home for. You have to be worth it. This has to be worth what Ross did.* "But I need to know a few things."

"Anything I can, I will tell you. None of this has anything to do with you."

"Are you lying about how you feel about me?"

"How can you possibly ask me that?"

"Because there are so many contradictions. I need to know that you still love me."

"Of course I still love you."

"Or your vows to me?"

"I would never lie about that." Diana followed his gaze to the white splotches on the kitchen linoleum.

"Did you use your maiden name during the war?"

"Yes. But I didn't want to. You have to understand. I never even got a chance to be a Somerville. After the wedding. Not to anyone but—"

"But me, Diana. I was off in the trenches assuming you took the name I gave you."

"I know." Her voice was sad, solemn. Her eyes devastated.

"Did the Royal Society of Architects ask you to consult on churches?"

"No. Someone else did."

Brent raked his fingers through his hair. "It's a good thing you're *you*, Diana. Because I might be a fool, but I certainly wouldn't be a fool for anyone else."

"It's a good thing you lectured on grace today." She smiled. "Because you're doling out a lot to me and it's worth more to me than you know."

Brent let out a long breath. "That will have to be enough."

"I will answer you as many times as you need. But just remember, Brent." She looked pointedly at his carefully creased and buttoned collar hiding the scars underneath. Brent shifted and tugged at his shirt. "I'm not the only one keeping a secret."

———— ❧ ————

London had its own secrets. Brent tried to read them as they ventured out that evening. It was the first day, he supposed, of an established routine. He would teach, she would attempt to house-keep, and after a burnt dinner they would set out into the city to visit her churches.

As they continued on their way, the affinity they enjoyed before the war returned until they easily fell into matching steps, Diana's shoulder brushing his own.

"Do you know on the very worst day of my entire life, I couldn't even recall the little part of myself I had built my entire life around? The apostle Paul." Brent studied his shoes. "All that my uncle taught me. All that I found in Cambridge and in books and in my uncle's library. It was like a curtain closed and I couldn't remember anything. Corinthians. Galatians. All those blasted letters. The things I had memorized, and now I stand in front of that lectern and feel like I am an actor. Like I am just reciting something I have no right to."

Then, silently, they strolled Westminster. They stopped at the fountain in the chaotic circus of Piccadilly, rambled under the dimmed lights of Leicester Square adhering to the slow creep from blackout back to full light in the wake of war. They passed beneath familiar golden gothic structures as the lights of Parliament winked and Big Ben tolled for the boats and ferries bobbing in the Thames and people scraping back to a semblance of normal life.

Brent hadn't assumed the churches would be dangerous spaces. Rather, exciting prospects for a few hobos in need of temporary shelter and prowlers who wanted to sketch or take photographs or loot.

He had dragged his sketchbook along, guessing Diana's pilgrimage could last a few hours. He knew the curve of her neck and the flash of her eyes well enough to detect when she was truly taking in the potential of a church's reconstruction or merely absorbing its loss.

"There is something beautiful in sacrifice, isn't there?" she said in a low voice. "Something liturgical in rebuilding. In reconstruction."

But it was a dark beauty and one distilled in shadow, stone, and exhumed graves. Diana routinely reflected on the woodcarvers and stonemasons who never lived to see the whole of their work.

Brent soon realized the unsettled feeling that stretched over his shoulders and pricked at his stomach was not just left over from his time in the war, nor from their first fateful visit to All Hallows-by-the-Tower. Diana was being followed. The entire world was on edge, sure. Brent more so for the years of artillery fire and stretchers to bear while the fear of explosives, of outdoor elements, and of surprise sank the sky low and pulsed the injury in his left hand.

Every footfall and silhouette. Every slight noise or scurry. He found it hard to believe that for even an infinitesimal moment upon their reconciliation, he would deny Diana his presence.

As their nightly excursions continued, Brent tried to find some meaning in the sequence of churches they visited. The first few were clearly of the Roman era, whose history tugged at the city's heels. Then a random sequence of ones that hosted either a sermon or a concert or wedding. Some, he assumed, were to her whim. Others, he might have figured for nostalgia.

St. Clement Danes, a church she had pulled him to when they were dating, for example. It was whole and unscarred. A building Brent had taken for granted a million and one times when he passed it during his tenure at King's. It was one of two structures known as the island churches that punctuated the otherwise fluid succession of structures from Fleet Street swerving into the Strand.

Before Brent registered shadows and Diana disappeared into a silent self that detached from him to meet careful lines and Doric or Corinthian columns or the whole of Wren's sculpted poetry, he was hers.

Her notebook lay in repose in her open, languid fingers and her eyes flitted from a church sanctuary she knew and loved to him again and again.

Moments later, beyond Wren and himself, a shadow appeared in the open doorway. Diana grabbed at her permit and Brent stilled his shoulders beside her, edging so she was slightly behind him.

A man entered, removed his hat, and looked around from roof to chancel. His eyes settled on Diana a moment, Brent's erect shoulders still as stone.

He and Diana ignored the man. Brent hoped he would dissolve into the night, but he lingered.

If she noticed, Diana was unfazed. Instead, she scribbled in her notebook and cast Brent a glance now and then. When they left, their footfalls fell in step as they often did with familiarity, the past in their stride.

They weren't two blocks down Fleet Street, rimming the obvious Tudor grandeur of Prince Henry's Room and heading beyond the Temple, when Brent sensed they were being followed. It was something he had honed on the Front, a sense that was sometimes unfounded and in other instances lifesaving.

He leaned into Diana so they were aligned.

The man, however, was interested. Intent. Brent met Diana's expectant gaze.

Brent tugged her on a diagonal across the street. He familiarized himself with their surroundings: the nearest taxi driving by, the nearest public house, restaurant, or tea shop where they could duck in at a second's notice.

But Brent Somerville, at his core, was also stubborn. He wanted Diana to be able to trip over London and take it under her wing. He resented the slightest prickle on his neck and her gentle shiver. So he switched into confrontation mode. Sure, his weapons of choice were an umbrella and a satchel. And her revolver. He slid his arm around her back and retrieved it from its resting place tucked into the waist of her trousers.

"Are you following us?" Brent demanded.

"Why would I be following you?" His heavy accent belied his

rather English sweater vest and poorly flourished bow tie before he began speaking in Russian.

Brent continued their route, tugging Diana along at a frantic pace. While she was silent, he made out her heavy breath. Cabs passed, sleek and black, under the streetlights. His mind was created to connect the dots and read more deeply into a moment or a sentence or a translation of Scripture. Shadows spouting Russian were something new, but he would take it in stride. But Wren churches couldn't account for the shadows and the danger he sensed rather than experienced.

The footfalls didn't stop, however. They pounded a rhythm matching Brent's mounting heartbeat.

"I know that man is following us and I wish I could tell you why." Her words whistled through clenched teeth. "Brent, we need to follow him."

"He's following *us*."

"I know that, but we need to find a way so that we're pursuing him."

"Pursuing a stranger in a trench coat like something in a James Cagney film! Diana!"

Beyond thought, pride, or purpose, Brent shed the skin of logic and defied reason in exchange for Diana's unruly hair and ineffable determination.

So while the footfalls were a heavy percussion behind them beyond St. Martin's, he pulled her down a side street that left St. Paul's in their wake. And soon he no longer felt the pulse of the shadow or the fear that he would be overtaken. Calming himself, he waited several breaths, Diana curved to his side like a comma. She was a barrel of secrets and yet she was vulnerable. Unsure.

The moon slowly rose and the stars pricked the night sky. He wielded London in the palm of his hand, with every alley, nook, and crevice his for the taking. He grabbed her hand and towed her through a crisscross of routes that would try even the most seasoned Londoner.

The Russian man was certainly startled the moment the tables had turned, and by the time they reached the bridge over Holborn Viaduct, Brent could hear the man's heavy and exerted breathing. The man continued at a rather fast pace, leading them through a sloppy maze.

Brent kept a death grip on the gun and held Diana beside him. The man strolled across the street, hands in pockets, and Brent waited for a taxi to pass before crossing the street behind him. They neared the man, who led them through Smithfield Market.

He finally stopped and swerved. He said something in his native language with an exclamation Brent could only assume was an expletive. "What do you want?" he demanded in poor English.

Brent held the gun in front of him. "I don't fancy being followed. So what do *you* want?"

The man looked at Diana. "You are causing trouble."

Brent tucked Diana behind him and held her with a restraining arm. "I have my sketching and she has her church consultations. The only trouble I see is a man pursuing us unnecessarily."

"You are causing trouble. We know about you." He addressed Diana again. "This is a warning."

Brent waved the gun. "A warning? I'm the one armed. I am giving *you* a warning. Turn around and leave."

"Do you work for him?"

"I'm a theology professor," Brent enunciated. "And this is where we part. Carry on."

The man turned and left.

"Where is he going?" Diana whispered. "We have to see where he's going!"

"Diana, he knows we're behind him. He won't just lead us to his destination—we'll just be looping London all night."

Her shoulders stiffened. "Then let's loop London."

Brent dropped the gun to his side. The man retreated, looking behind him again and again, then headed back toward the route he had just taken. Wherever he had been going, he clearly decided against it.

Brent steered her elbow in the direction of home. Clerkenwell had always been a lopsided affair. But when he pulled Diana into its uneven tumble of buildings, he knew its walls and brick surroundings were a measure of safety. He resisted the urge to cast a glance over his shoulder, but she stole a look all the same.

Brent fiddled with the stove and the kettle. Diana's figure was cast in a perfect silhouette of shadow, framed by the blinds and the living room lamps. She was almost ethereally beautiful. Maybe even more so now, not studying Wren churches or shrugging into life like a sweater that was too big for her. Rather like a confident woman, she tilted her chin a little defiantly, all of her secrets straightening her back.

"It took the war ending for me to point a gun at someone," Brent said ironically as he handed a cup of tea to her before he transferred the gun from his coat on the hook to her handbag.

CHAPTER 15

May 1944
Bletchley Park

"This war will be won by those who see the world a little differently than most," Simon had told her when first they met.

War or no war, Fisher, Simon, and Villiers daily taught Diana to see her world differently. Simon tried to teach her chess, a game that, despite her proficiency in so many other problems, evaded her. Fisher was on hand to teach her about music. She had once watched him cast a line to the pond in the yard on the rare occasion he had the opportunity to practice the activity contributing to his nickname. Later at the pub, he told her fishing helped his logical focus.

"I work out all sorts of problems in my mind. Math problems. Logic problems. Problems about the world. You know, in equations, things turn out equally with measured reason. When I see the state of our world, even the chaos of our lives here sometimes, I cannot help but think we could borrow from the field of mathematics."

Simon, evidently trying not to notice Villiers flirting with an airman at a nearby table, soured. "If everyone saw the world through your eyes, Fisher, we'd all be automatons. It leaves no room for human emotion."

Fisher took a long sip of lager. "I'm sorry. I believe that Simon Barre is trying to lecture me on human emotion."

"Sometimes on my birthday," Diana said to placate them, "my father would lay out a bit of a game where one clue led to another—all little presents until my big present. Like a bike or a music box or a trip to Paris. I know he meant the exercise to sharpen my mind, but the time and effort behind it were all emotion."

Simon's smile was shrewd as he collected his empty glass from the stained table and rose for a refill. "That's why we need you, Diana. You meet us at the intersection of logic and emotion." He extended his empty hand for Fisher's glass. Then he walked to the bar, taking a stroll by Villiers's table.

What was between them? She always thought Brent was a better student of human nature, but what would he make of them?

From the start Diana thought Brent and Simon would get along. Simon was introspective and thoughtful. Exhaustion never crept into his voice, and his mind was consistently sharp. He was a bookish fellow who mostly kept to himself, save for Fisher Carne and Villiers. The latter at one end of a current charging through the two of them whenever they occupied the same space.

"You sure you don't want another wine, Diana?"

She yawned and shook her head.

Fisher took a long sip of ale. "This helps me sleep at night."

"How do you sleep at night?" Simon asked Diana as he approached their table, fresh drinks in his hands. "Shut your brain off? You must worry about your young man."

Diana knew full well that worry was as physical an ailment as a winter cold. She lay awake at night imagining every scenario, worrying until perspiration beaded on her forehead and her throat was sore. Wondering how she had been accustomed to being alone for so long, only to become so emotionally tethered to someone that the thought of him being injured or crippled or tired or hungry pierced straight through her.

"I know how she sleeps," Fisher contributed. "She counts churches as some would count sheep." Diana laughed and he continued. "I grew up in Canterbury. Did you know that? City of pilgrims. And relics."

"A cathedral can only be such if there's a relic," Diana said.

"Is that true?" Fisher said. "Never thought of it before."

"Because a relic was what the pilgrims would come and see. And it was good for the town's business. They would have market days and feasts for the saints and fairs."

"For your sake, Diana, I hope your young man makes it through."

But then she would open one of Brent's letters—or, more often, steal a look at one of the many churches he had sketched her—and feel as if every thread of her life was interwoven tightly with him. How often did one just understand someone . . . from the very first moment?

It was Fisher who noticed that Simon was ill a few weeks later. The close quarters and poor ventilation meant that illnesses seemed to bounce from one person to another. Fisher got word from the infirmary that Simon had pneumonia and was transferred to the town hospital.

Villiers was a study in composure. She touched the curled slope of her perfect, shiny brown hair as she stepped into their flat the following evening.

"Fisher said he would tell us about Simon," Diana said. "I'll make you a cup of tea and we can ring and see if there's any update."

"Why would I need an update?"

Diana shook her head. "Because there's no use wringing our hands about Simon separately when we can worry about him together."

"Worry about Simon?" Sophie made a sound that was almost a word.

"You can admit that you're worried about your friend. It's not a weakness to care for someone."

"It is when it's you. All moon-eyed over Brent Somerville's sketches. All worried he won't return. If I don't care, there's no chance of loss."

"That makes *no* sense. You can't stop yourself from caring for someone. Because your brain can tell you all it needs to, but your heart . . ."

"Not all women are the same as you." Sophie wriggled her gloves off her fingers and set them on the counter.

"I am not saying we all *love* in the same way . . ."

Sophie stopped midstep en route to the stairwell. "Love? Who said anything about love?"

＿＿＿＿＿＿ ❧ ＿＿＿＿＿＿

Simon had recovered and entered the pub pale but animated. Diana assessed him with her chin slightly raised. She noticed the slightest quiver of Villiers's lip and the slightest exhale moving the smartly tied scarf at her collar. Villiers lit a cigarette for Simon and one for herself, and they communicated in long lines of passive smoke.

After Fisher had disappeared for chess at another table and Sophie had gone home, Simon took Diana into his confidence.

"Maybe it's just my near-death experience talking, but do you know I think I'll spend most of my life trying to impress her? Without her knowing I am trying to impress her?"

"So I was right. You knew her before."

"Of course I did." Simon studied the last gleam of amber in his pint glass. "She refused me."

"Refused?"

"I asked her to marry me once and she said no. She said that we were too similar and that we would stand off forever. That people like us are independent and we need to be able to . . ." Simon swilled the ale a moment and finally drained the glass. She knew there was more but didn't press.

Diana had rarely seen him finish a second pint as he had just done. Usually he wanted to be in complete control, and often he and Villiers would engage in a conversation that would drive his attention anyway.

Later that night, Diana drew her knees to her chest on her bed and read one of Brent's most recent letters. They weren't dripping with love language and he didn't shower her with nicknames, but she didn't need that to recognize the surety of having someone so deeply attuned to her. He was in her very fabric.

Her love story had fallen so easily into place, it seemed. She had never doubted it, had always wanted it, and the only true work and turmoil it had taken her hadn't been on account of confusion or emotion, but the war and distance and the lie she would have to formulate every day of her life. The barrier that the piece of paper she'd signed had built between them.

For as much as she wanted to return to Brent and begin their life and fulfill every last dream they whispered in the dark in their fleeting married days together, she also knew that the end of the war clicked everything back into place. She would be back at King's and her studies and away from her new friends. Would it be enough? If years down the road should the conflict end and she return safely to his side, would she blink and wonder if it had happened at all? Would it become something she almost remembered, an echo like a story almost told until it faded into something nonexistent?

Simon was quiet at his desk the next day, and while the rhythm of their world clicked on with typewriters and telegrams, reports and shuffles, Diana could sense that the others were treating him more attentively and kindly. Getting him tea, asking if the radiator was too loud or if he wanted to work away from the window. Simon had earned a deep sense of respect and loyalty.

Diana tried to focus on the feed from her German signals. She realized the importance of always being alert and aware. Radio waves could crackle through unintentional feeds and pick up all manner of messages. At times a strong reception would crackle or a shrill sound would pierce her ear until she held the earpiece away a moment and looked up at Fisher.

The next night, the beautiful musical programs at eighteen hundred hours when they were on the night shift were a welcome reprieve. She was so used to some of the composers now. When an incoming signal from the Germans interrupted any part of a symphony, she felt it a loss, even though the signals were what kept their ears pressed for hours a day.

Fisher and Diana noted the route of German air force bombers over their target and a report on the weather.

Later, after the shift, music carried into their conversation in a language she shared with Fisher, who more than ever was willing to barter his knowledge of the composers as she told him of Prior Rahere and the courtyard of a medieval church where she had fallen in love.

"I almost envy you." Fisher collected his hat and walked her out of the building. "Because everything in your love story is set up in a perfect line, isn't it? Like a composition or a problem."

"I wouldn't say that."

"And you know it will end well."

"How? How do you know?"

"Because all the variables are there. Perfect meeting. Perfect love story. He'll come back and you'll live a boring and happy life."

"Maybe you will too. A perfectly boring and happy life."

Fisher took a long time in responding. "I can't imagine going back to teaching after this. Day in and day out at a blackboard. And can you imagine me back in Canterbury? Attending Evensong? Tutoring? Having tea with my mother on Sundays? I've seen too much of the limitations of our world, Diana. And I want to make it right."

"How?"

Fisher shrugged. "It's a problem I'll solve." They neared the path she would take toward her house and she bade him good night.

"Maybe I'll go sit in the yard at Great St. Bart's," Fisher said. "See if a pretty girl shows up."

Diana looked over her shoulder and gave a quick wave. "A perfectly boring life."

CHAPTER 16

October 1945
London

Diana looked around the empty bedroom, to the vacant space beside her on the bed and then to the closet where a hatbox full of Brent's letters sat. During his training and then after he shipped out, he wrote about his daily life and his new friends. That Tibbs and Holt fancied themselves playboys, and Matthew Ross was a quiet chap from a Quaker background. Brent had expanded on each during the few times they met while she took leave and he was able to escape his life.

What am I doing?

Brent would sleep on the sofa forevermore now. She rubbed at the faded bruises on her wrists. Through the open bedroom door she strained to hear the slightest indication that he was awake over the ticking clock on the mantel. She rolled onto her side and then her stomach. Then onto her back again, flinging her arm over her eyes. She supposed she could count sheep. Or churches, as she did during the war.

Perhaps she couldn't topple every barrier between Brent and herself, but she knew she'd sleep easier the moment he was involved. Simon had told her she was incognito, but this was the third time they were not alone at a church and the pattern certainly stood out.

She'd give Simon an ultimatum. Especially if her work was becoming as dangerous as his note had said. He had telegrammed from Vienna where he was meeting with his SOE agent, saying that he could be reached by telephone.

She squeezed her eyes shut, then risked waking Brent up by tiptoeing out of the bedroom for a glass of water.

"Can't sleep?" His very awake voice cut through the dark.

"No. Can you?"

"No."

She turned on the light on the side table and sank onto the edge of the sofa by his feet. He sat up and swung his legs down to the floor to give her room. She closed the space between them and kissed him softly. "I know what might help."

His thumb ran over her arm to her shoulder blade in a customary move familiar to her from when they had lived out their marriage vows to every last letter after their wedding and on the few subsequent occasions of Brent's leave. "Are we going to talk about tonight?" he said quietly.

"Not yet. I wish I could, though. You have no idea how much."

Brent released a loud exhale. "Well. If we're not going to talk about that," he said, shifting away slightly, "you need to think about when you're going to start your graduate studies, Diana."

"Oh."

"Tell me you've thought about it. The war took away your pursuit of your degree, and who's to say you might *actually* be needed at some point when they start their restoration."

"I've been so preoccupied."

"I am well aware." His tone darkened a moment, but he quickly lightened it. She knew he recalled his promise that he would trust her. "You need to speak to Silas. He can help you find a suitable supervisor and we need to get you enrolled. I'll tell him to expect you tomorrow."

"Brent, there's so much going on right now. There's the church consultation and I am resettling."

"When . . . whatever it is you're doing is over, you need to have a plan. I'm not letting you waste your brain tending house."

"I'm rather terrible at it."

He smiled. "I'm likely to starve, but I don't care. But I do care about your future." She could hear the smile in his voice. "I married you for your brain, Diana. So keep it sharp."

"Not for my looks?"

"Heavens, no. Can hardly bear looking at you, unfortunate creature."

Diana giggled. "Well, it's equally difficult for me, you know."

"How so?"

She turned her face toward his. "You're a ginger."

"Horrible, is it?"

"The worst." She kissed his nose.

"Come with me tomorrow and at least talk to Silas?"

Diana nodded. Brent made to settle in again, but she stopped him. "I'm wide awake now. Why don't you take the bed? It's not been a fair balance so far. Get a decent sleep." Brent opened his mouth in protest, but she said, "Please. I'll just read myself to sleep." She squeezed his hand. "Take the bed."

He slowly rose with a nod and patted the empty side of the sofa. "Kept it warm for you."

She smiled in the darkness as he creaked the bedroom door shut. Diana pulled her knees to her chest and sat for several moments before she rose in the direction of the telephone and stretched the cord as far as it would go so she could whisper into the receiver.

When finally she was patched through to Vienna, Simon said, "You alright, Diana?"

"I will be when you let me tell Brent what's going on."

Simon's curse through the receiver was muffled. "We talked about this."

"Or else I stop."

"He can't be involved. Especially with your faulty cover story."

"Faulty cover story?" Diana laughed.

"Diana, this is about you and your unfortunate marriage."

She'd have been upset if his tone hadn't been so teasing. "My marriage is not unfortunate. Brent's helpful. We were followed from Clement Danes and Brent turned the tables."

"Followed."

"Now you're standing at attention. A Soviet. He threatened me. Well, he *warned* me."

"Where did he go?"

"He was heading in the direction of Smithfield Market. It was clear he didn't know London. But Brent scared him off, and barring us leading him on a wild-goose chase all night, we let him go."

"This is why Brent—"

"I am not a trained field operative, Simon. I don't have all of your gadgets and weapons. I am a woman of medium height who startles at her neighbor's pet badger. Brent is strong and he would die for me. He also can hold that gun without his hand shaking, which is more than I can do. I need him."

"I don't want my involving you to be a mistake."

"I can very much assure you that it *is* a mistake. I've found no messages. I have encountered a few mysterious men, but they've stumbled in and out. Oh, and I did find a pack of cigarettes. The brand on the rim is Piccadilly but the carton is Pall Mall." She could hear Simon's brain processing on the other end. "And the carton has the eternity symbol etched inside. I don't know what they mean or if they're to leave a bread crumb trail."

"Well, over here we found someone else with an infinity sign in his briefcase and two messages in his pocket. I need that blasted key for those messages, or else it's gibberish. What if the key is just sitting in one of these churches? Hang it, Diana! I am so confused. I'm supposed to be calm and smart and collected, but . . ."

"Who's to say I am not a double agent?"

"You're too pretty."

"I don't want to be pretty. I want to be a threat." Diana joined Simon's immediate laugh, only to lower her voice. "Please tell me this is going to be worth it."

"Keep your eyes open. Except for right now. Go to sleep."

"I will."

But Simon didn't click off immediately. "You know, despite the fact that I am sending you on wild-goose chases, I consider you a friend. And I'm rubbish with friends."

"Yes. As I do you."

"You had right nasty bruises on your wrists when we last visited, Diana. I know you love your husband, but . . ."

The air heaved out of her lungs. "He . . . he has nightmares. About the war. He doesn't realize. I think h-he's reliving a moment again and again. And he assumes I am the enemy. He doesn't mean it. He feels worse about it than I ever could."

"I'm sorry for broaching a delicate situation. But I *do* care."

"Well, that's a first."

--- ∽ ---

Brent stirred a small whirlpool in his tea the next morning. What would their lives have been like if he had decided her secrets were too much of a wall? He would have every right. Not many men would settle for the precarious trust between them. He always regretted those thoughts the moment they crossed his mind, most often after a night that left him more tired than restless.

"Are you looking forward to seeing Silas?" Brent asked, noting her eyes on him.

"He always makes me think of my dad. Happy thoughts."

"Whatever you need to do to get that doctorate, Di, we'll do it. I'll tutor or . . ."

"Pawn a priceless relic?" Diana joked. "But what about the dusting and the hoovering and the baking and the six babies?"

"Six?"

"Poet's Corner has a lot of names."

He knew she was teasing, but his heart lit with the thought of it.

He wanted a family with her. He always had. But there had been a war and there was one secret after another. "They'll wait. Because you, my love, need to further develop that magnificent brain of yours."

⁓

Diana informed Brent that she would see Silas but only after sitting in on Brent's lecture. It had been so long since she first stumbled into his classroom to hear him frame concepts and ideas about Paul and the early church. That symbolic church had withstood just as much as the parish churches felled by the Great Fire and the Wren churches felled by the Blitz. And yet it was two thousand years strong. She hadn't fancied herself a religious person, but Brent's understanding and teaching of it were a magnet for her. She was always moved when he provided a historical and philosophical context to what he was teaching, then layered it with the sure personal conviction that made it his passion.

His father had been a vicar. And his grandfather before him. And his uncle, who raised him after his parents died, had prepped Brent for the church. But Brent's mind wanted to wrap around the Scriptures in a different way. "Besides," he told her, "I'm far too sarcastic to tend to a flock."

She leaned her head in her hand and watched as students were pulled into the context he provided to things that might have sounded dull as tombs from behind a dusty pulpit, but with Brent Somerville behind them they seemed new.

"Are you a professor here?" a student whispered beside her.

"I'm his wife," she said proudly as Brent extolled the importance of Paul assuming the languages of the countries he was visiting. Assimilating into the cultures and traditions so they could understand him and so his truth would hammer home.

"His taking the time to understand the worlds he wanted to reach," Brent said, "allowed him to have a voice that many would not have. He didn't have the whole frame of reference. He didn't have the whole picture. But he tried. That trust won him an audience and became the ember from which the church's fire spread."

Memories pulsed with the beat of her heels over the linoleum as she exited the lecture hall. Corridors she knew well, filled with the familiar wafting scent of cleaning supplies, books, and some indescribable concoction of tea and close quarters.

Diana approached Rick's office.

"Diana Foyle, what a pleasure."

"Diana Somerville," she corrected with a smile.

"Come have lunch with me. Like the old days." His smile was charming as he shifted the books and papers in his arms. He didn't need to work. He was rich as Midas, but he always said his brain needed a lark.

"I appreciate the offer." She looked over the books he was holding. A few on his usual fields of study. And a pamphlet in a language she didn't understand but with the same characters as on the piece of paper Simon had shown her, translated as *bird* and *steeple*. She thought back to the infinity symbol in the painting she had seen in his office. "But I have a previous engagement. Looks like you're preoccupied. I don't recall you reading Russian in our previous acquaintance."

"New lines of research."

"I'll leave you to it," she said cordially.

"I don't know what you see in him," Rick said once she was halfway down the corridor.

"Don't be so ghastly boring, Rick," she called over her shoulder.

Diana slowed near Silas's office. The door was slightly open and she needed only to nudge it open to be welcomed warmly. She knew Silas would be more than happy to discuss her continued studies. She stopped her hand on the doorknob. If she went in, she would be occupied for the rest of the afternoon. They'd talk about the past and Silas would reinstate her as a tutor. Everything would fall back into place.

Diana chewed her lip. She had promised Brent she would talk to Silas. And she would. She just didn't say *when*.

She had also promised she wouldn't visit another church without him. But how dangerous could it be if it was the middle of the day? Diana left the college and continued on a familiar route. Near High Holborn and Printer's Alley or Fleet Street, St. Bride's was the church of journalists and wordsmiths. Its full peal of bells rang over streets, narrow alleys, and courts familiar to readers of *Punch* magazine and Charles Dickens while meeting the neighboring bells of Andrew Holborn over the viaduct a short stroll away. It had always been a favorite of hers before she left and it took up several chapters of her ongoing dissertation.

Now, the gutted church was a mausoleum. Chairs shoved to the side from the services still held despite the missing roof and open access to the elements. Diana had read that alongside Roman coins and medieval stained glass, the bombs had erupted over 230 coffins from three different centuries. The bones of parishioners, the history of London enshrined in a moving tomb.

She stilled, looking up in the direction of the still-intact steeple. Its urns and gargoyles, its carved flames and flourishes. Twelve bells now gone had once solemnly tolled death and jubilantly chimed marriages. The bells had melted and fallen the night before their wedding. But the steeple still pierced the sky: singed and bruised yet distinctively Wren. She always thought it looked like a wedding cake.

She recalled her conversation with Gabriel Langer in Vienna and his warning that Simon used people without ever letting them completely in. That he gave a few pieces of a puzzle without ever fully pulling her in. But now she was curious of her own volition.

Why would someone use churches to pass messages? It was a question she had posited a thousand times in her head but now whispered aloud.

Steeples were an easy marker, she supposed, even the bombed ones. Activities continued: weddings and concerts even in open air before they were patched together. They were an immediate topic of conversation in rebuilding efforts—not only for their contribution to community morale but for historical preservation.

Then there was the matter of relics.

"Canterbury . . . City of pilgrims. And relics," Fisher had said, not wholly connecting the two before she explained their intersection. Rick knew relics. Rick knew pretty much everything, down to the churches she particularly fancied. Rick had a Russian pamphlet under his arm and an infinity symbol in his office painting. Rick knew London churches and *oleum medicina*. Rick smoked Piccadilly cigarettes and struck Brymay matches.

Having connected a few dots, Diana spun on her heel and started the familiar route back to Clerkenwell. She finally had something of use to tell Simon.

~ ❧ ~

When his shoes had sunk in the mud and Ross was snoring beside him, Brent used to mentally map his usual route to King's College as a way to keep from focusing on an itch in his sock or the penetrating cold. He would start with his favorite route from Clerkenwell on a bright fall day and paint the past so clearly he could hear himself reciting a lecture.

Now, back in the halls he'd imagined, the safe familiarity he longed for gnawed at him. He wondered if he had lost the magic that warmed his voice to enthusiasm for his subjects. He once loved the inevitable debates that would arise when they broached Romans.

But he still lost all inhibitions the moment he stepped behind the podium and any barrier between professor and student fell in their collective excitement. Many of his students had seen terror and war as he had. Many of his students were scarred. Many of his former students never returned, their papers languishing in a filing cabinet, unmarked and unread.

Many students had deserted their studies to care for babies made in haste before the bugle called and they signed their life's blood to King and Country. Many had made terrible vows and now slogged through the weight of their decisions. Those before him took the course as if it were a balm, a salve, and a salvation.

Brent could layer the Scripture with historical context and embroider it with his personal conviction, but at the end of the hour, while chairs scuffed over linoleum and men tucked their pens into their satchels, he had to believe that the right message would resonate with the right person at the right time. He always had before. And when it came to the inevitable undergraduate questions about Paul—Paul with that elusive thorn in his side that scholars and interested parties proposed as being anything from a stutter to celibacy—Brent was clearly out of his realm.

He left the lecture hall after his last late class and stuffed his notes in his satchel. Had he really been such a wonderful lecturer, or was he just finessing his power of memory and coloring the past as something he wished he could retreat to?

Brent left the college to see the starlight play with London—whole or in devastation—without recalling the nights he would squint and toss a few sardonic comments at Ross while imagining he was with Diana. Roaming with her, talking of everything and nothing at once.

"I fell in love with the idea of seeing everything through her eyes," he had said.

Ross, whose hoarse voice still broke through Brent's thoughts far too often, waking or sleeping. Ross, who seemed to watch his steps and inspired Brent to capitalize on every last experience. He took a rambling route home, hating himself for admitting he was biding his time before another burnt dinner and another night pretending to read essays or the paper while really wanting to talk to Diana, *really* talk to Diana. Did she treasure the time she had before he walked through the door?

November was fast on his heels as he took London in stride, the evening pitch dark far earlier than those endless late-summer nights before Diana had reappeared. At least then he could rail or pace or stare at the wall for hours without having her wonder if he was alright or hungry or wanted another cup of tea.

His reflexes heightened by war and more recently by Stephen Walbrook and Clement Danes pricked a warning over the back of his neck as he finally wove his way through Clerkenwell. He tipped his hat at the grocer, then smiled at the lady from two doors down who kept a badger as a pet. But then he made out a figure, tall and erect, lingering on the pavement, polished shoes crunching the dead autumn leaves underfoot and catching the sheen of the streetlight.

Something in the shadow's bearing put Brent on edge. He slowed his steps, darting his gaze up to his flat on the second floor. Still dark. Diana might not be home yet. He buried his worry under the possible explanation that she had visited Silas and they had fallen into old times. The man was a friend of her father's and almost a distant uncle to Diana. Time may have merely slipped away from her.

"Are you lost?" Brent stepped closer, eyes widening at the outline of the gun hanging from the stranger's hand. Brent took a step back when the stranger settled remarkably blue eyes on him.

"Inevitable," the stranger muttered after a moment.

"Pardon me?"

The man didn't move the gun away but wasn't fingering the trigger as tightly. "Inevitable."

"Can I help you?"

"Don't take this the wrong way, but you have in no uncertain terms ruined my career and perhaps my life."

Brent stalled a moment. The gun had dropped by the stranger's side but was still an easy motion away.

"Brent Somerville. Professor of theology. Carried stretchers in the war. Wounded and in hospital. Bloody bane of my existence."

"How so?"

"Married to the world's most inexhaustible authority on Christopher blasted Wren. And I thought if I do this *one* thing, I can do this *other* thing and ..."

"Sir, have you been drinking?" Brent flicked his gaze at the gun wavering in the man's hand.

"Not enough. I've been given a bit of a scolding. Then there's ... Well, no matter. Vienna. Beautiful city, have you been? Of course not. She always said you hadn't been. See, I didn't realize that Langer would be there too. Gabriel Langer. When I saw—Well, someone I went to see. Not him. Not that I don't like him. I do. I just never put the two of them together and ... I've ..." He looked straight at Brent and slurred, "Anyway, doesn't matter. Someone once said, '*When you're in love, you see it in other people.*' Maybe I'm seeing it too much."

The line sounded awfully familiar. Brent swallowed, then asked quietly, "Who said that?"

"Diana Foyle. Foyle like the bookshop in Charing Cross Road."

Brent felt a strange twist in his chest that sat at the intersection of anger and envy.

"She was talking about you. You and Wren churches. One or the other. For years."

Focusing on the weapon in the man's hand, Brent was glad he had arrived while the lights were still out, though he was equally puzzled and disturbed by the conversation and a man who knew his wife so well.

"I've just been in Vienna," the man continued. "There's no bell anymore. The one Diana liked. Sure you knew that."

Brent studied the man. His blue eyes on closer inspection weren't arresting or sharp, rather glazed. Brent was torn between wanting to ask how he knew Diana and wanting to send him and his gun as far away as possible.

"Do you want a cigarette?" He used the hand not holding the gun to reach for his breast pocket. "Oh. I've been terribly rude."

Fumbling out a cigarette, the man lit it and took a long drag. "My name is Simon Barre and I work for the British Secret Intelligence Service. At least I did. Or perhaps I still do." He lost his balance and almost fell.

"Are you alright? I . . ."

"I made the mistake of working unofficially with a civilian. Who you know, incidentally. Then there was the matter of the call from Vienna. Of course I went. Wouldn't you? I mean, if it were Diana? I would go for Diana and she's just a friend. Not to say that . . . I know she told me long ago . . . but never mind all of that. You don't know who *she* is. I told my direct supervisor I needed to go there immediately. *Immediately.* And did he listen? So now my agent is heaven knows where. I might just go anyway. Wouldn't that show them all?"

The moon spotlit his face and Brent watched his blue eyes widen at him. Simon sighed. "Where is she?"

CHAPTER 17

The last scene Diana expected to encounter when she returned home was Brent serving Simon Barre tea. She blinked it away as if a mirage and looked from Brent to Simon and back to Brent again. The world she had created with Brent and the world she had shared with Simon at Bletchley chafed.

"Simon!" she blurted.

Brent stepped next to her, kettle in hand. "Your friend was a little worse for wear when I found him outside, pointing a gun at me."

"I'm sorry?"

"The tea's strong," Brent said. "We'll sober him up in no time."

Simon had returned numerous times from his assignments in Vienna, and in all cases he was composed. He would work a lager for hours at the pub at Bletchley in order to keep complete composure, and he was always in control of what he offered those around him. She chewed her lip, taking in Simon's blurry eyes and the slight tremor in his hand as he lifted the mug to his lips.

"What did he say he was doing here?" she asked Brent while studying Simon.

"I didn't know you knew anyone in the Secret Intelligence Service."

Diana felt the air leave her lungs. She gave Simon a stern look, then stepped back with a broad smile. "Oh, this is wonderful."

"How is this wonderful?" Brent asked.

"I've never seen the man inebriated before," Diana whispered. "It works in our favor."

Brent raked his fingers through his red hair and it stuck up a little at the back. It needed a trim, but she didn't miss the army regulation length. "I don't understand."

"Because he can't keep me from telling you anymore." She squeezed Brent's hand, then joined Simon on the sofa. "Are you alright? This is *not* like you. What happened?"

Simon shook his head and took another long sip of the strong tea. It had the desired effect as his blue eyes cleared. "I don't want to talk about it."

"Let's get you home then. We can talk tomorrow." Diana thought a moment. "Ye Olde Cheshire Cheese? Elevenish?" She extended his hat. "Then we can discuss how Brent is now involved."

Simon pierced Brent with his blue gaze. "Is he?"

"He is now." Diana pulled Simon up from the sofa. "Up, up you come."

So there it was. She had wished and hoped for a dam to break, and the unflappable Simon Barre seemed the least likely suspect to open the next chapter of her life. But he had. Moments later, through the blinds, she watched his tall figure bend into a taxi on their street, his black hair catching the last sheen of the streetlight.

Brent occupied the seat Simon had vacated and motioned for Diana to sit beside him.

"What happened?" Diana asked.

"He said I ruined his life. Which I find highly unlikely considering I'd never met him before. But he also was upset about something he thought happened between a woman and Gabriel Langer, and then he started talking about you. How do you know him?"

"I worked in an administrative capacity in the war," Diana recited. "Translating for the Foreign Office. That's where I met Simon." She smoothed her skirt. "I know him probably as well as I've known anyone other than you and my friend Sophie Villiers. Something shook him tonight because his behavior was so uncharacteristic. Simon never lets down his guard. It takes a long time for him to trust people. He trusts me. But you . . . I think on some level he must have wanted you to know."

"Know what?" Brent pinched the bridge of his nose. "Di, my head is spinning. I have no idea what happened tonight. That intoxicated Secret Intelligence Service man knows my wife better than I do."

"No. He just knows one part of my life."

"He seems to know you quite well."

"We worked closely together."

"Closely?"

"Yes. A part of me would not have survived the war without him. You of all people know that I don't make friends easily. But Simon was a good friend to me."

"And he's the friend you did a favor for? The one who kept you from coming home?"

Diana nodded. "He is pursuing a Soviet agent called Eternity who he believes is linked to the churches here in the city and who has vital information."

"What kind of information?"

"The kind that could help promote the Communist agenda here in Britain. The kind of information that people would kill for. Simon thought as a civilian I could easily explore the churches without attracting any attention. If need be, I can speak to my historical research. But I also know the churches'—bombed or not— geographical locations and their proximity to other churches that might form a pattern. If I can see something familiar or recognize anything that seems out of the ordinary . . ." She stopped. "Simon believes Eternity is using the churches to meet with other influential men. And not just in London. In other cities."

"But why churches?"

"I don't know. Communal spaces? Public?" She shook her head. "I wondered as you do."

"This sounds ludicrous, Diana. Doesn't MI6 have their own highly trained men who can go on these dangerous missions?"

"They're not dangerous the way we're visiting them. Seeing the dome at Walbrook, looking into an ancient artifact . . ."

"But I don't understand why you're doing it. Patriotic fervor? You did your bit during the war, Di. Even if you can't tell me everything about it. But why is this the next phase of your life?"

She stared at him a long moment, aware of the weight of the questions and her own expectations. Aware that even though one door in her life was opening, it was still connected to the part of her blacked out from him. "Churches are part of our story. Yours and mine."

"And me?"

"You're smart. You're here. And Simon's actions tonight gave me the opportunity to let you in. So help me determine if any of it's related. Ancient vials. Matchboxes and cigarette packs. The words *bird* and *steeple*. A discarded telegram. Each item was left, I believe, for the next agent filtering into London. This is what I work with, and I keep hoping to find something that could determine the next church. Men have been killed for this."

"Then why would he involve you if he's your friend? And why would you promise him this?"

The silence settled between them as it had so often in the past weeks they'd occupied each other's space. She studied Brent's profile. When his eyes met hers, a spark jumped between them just like the spark that joined them that first afternoon in the churchyard, setting her heartbeat in motion and tingling her fingertips. The way his eyes drifted over her face told her he was exploring the same depth of connection.

"Why did you promise him you would do this?"

"He's my friend. You did all sorts of things for your friends during the war. I am sure of it. You haven't told me what, but I know you did. But we both know war throws people together."

"I did. Yes. We all made wartime promises." He didn't expand on them as she hoped he would. "This is beyond that loyalty."

"Maybe I don't want there to be another war. Simon says this is another war."

"Men have been caught up in controversial ideologies for years,"

Brent reasoned. "The loudest voice. The most progressive coming out of a time of violence." He took a beat. "I should have sent away for the spy kit in the *Boys' Own Adventure Stories* advert."

Diana employed the same careful study of the lines and columns of a church as she watched him. Lines creased his face and a hardness tightened the mouth that used to easily ply a smile. That easy smile was difficult to find in the man occupying her space now with scars and tired eyes.

It was possible to fall in love with the same person twice—she was sure of it. Because she was more determined than ever to fall in love with the man before her again and again, through his questions and reticence.

Sure, their promise to God and eternity was sacred, but Diana wanted to love him *beyond* the words she said before he shipped out. She wanted to love him as the Diana she had become.

Diana felt something click and settle in her chest. He hadn't driven Simon to the curb. Brent—*her* Brent—had invited him in for tea.

───────⁂───────

Brent realized that the war had made the woman standing here now, removing the tea accessories from the coffee table, into someone else. Simon Barre's revelation sent Brent reeling because he was certain that he didn't know Diana at all.

As she took the teacups to the kitchen, he noticed her coat was slung over the armchair and not hung on the rack. Doubtless she was surprised to see her friend, but it frustrated him nonetheless. A more reasonable Brent would recognize he was funneling his confusion into recognizing her limitations. An emotional Brent—who had kept himself in check while receiving her intoxicated friend— immediately leapt to her faults.

For one, she was a horrible housekeeper. Something he couldn't have fully anticipated when he proposed. Of course, there were the little things his mind tucked away in exchange for the attributes he missed. No matter how many times he explained the rubrics of the Hebrew alphabet, she *never* understood. And he hated the way she wrinkled her nose for other men when she giggled. Sure, she had told him it was a defense mechanism for when she wasn't comfortable with new people, but it clashed with her approaching him at St. Bart's, and in the middle of a spat he saw it as a slight rather than another sign that she held him above all.

Somehow their resonant problems—the secrets and her time away—crept under his collar again. He could focus on the attributes he chose to remember while she was far away. Diana was bright. Intelligent. Curious. So why was he focusing on a water ring on the table? Other than it hadn't been there before she moved back.

She had a lingering effect but only on those who knew what to look for. Most men would maneuver their transient glances over her curves and pretty face and turn—remembering the point of attraction while underestimating the woman. Instinctively he was proud of her. Humanly, it just allowed for more doubt to trickle in.

"Is it worth risking your life?" he said. "This thing you're doing for that man?"

"Yes."

He took a breath. "Is it worth risking mine?"

"No." No blink or beat. "Nothing is worth that."

"But that's what you're doing. By taking me with you. By doing this. Something you say men would kill for."

She was a breath from him with her chin slightly upturned. As infuriated as he was, that chin tilt stirred something in him.

Diana's gaze settled on Brent. Desperation and vulnerability warred in her eyes. He wasn't sure what she saw in his. Confusion? When she inched nearer, he reciprocated. He wanted to protect her. He wanted to connect with her beyond this man and this strange, unexpected twist in her story.

When she reached to touch his cheek, he slipped his arm around her waist. Her lips parted, and her eyes searched his. They met in the middle. He wanted to find the Diana of the churchyard they had explored together. Not this new Diana with her Simon Barre and her secrets.

She pressed into him so tightly he could feel her lines and curves. His palm followed the curve above her hip bone. The hour-glass figure of the Diana who appeared in his lecture all those years ago showed the lean years of war. Brent readjusted his recollection so the woman he explored was not a vision stored for a bloody dawn in a trench or an air raid but his wife, here and now.

Brent kissed her. His uninjured hand maneuvered from her shoulder to the slope of her waist. He kissed her again, starting at her temple, then skimming his lips over the curve of her cheek. Their lips met and their breath mingled as well. He savored the scent of her hair and the perfume she dabbed behind her ears. In this way they picked up exactly where they had left off: he could easily cross the t's and dot the i's.

He pursued her fervently until he felt her fingers beneath his shirt and over the buttons of his collar, slowly unfastening them. She moved to deftly pull back the fabric of his shirt.

Brent made a noise of protest against her mouth and nudged her hands away from him. "No." He disengaged and stepped back, her breath warm on his cheek and the feel of her fingers branded on the curve of his neck.

"I don't understand you." Her eyes radiated the full measure of her hurt. "I don't even know how badly you're injured. Or what happened to you." She tugged at the loose end of his collar. "For all that you tell me about the secrets I've kept from you, you are keeping several to yourself. If you need time, I'm patient, Brent, but I need you to *tell* me."

"This isn't about me."

"So this means we're back to where we started."

"How so?"

"Because you *said* you trusted me, and now you know I've had a very good reason for all of this. I had no choice." She leaned in again.

"Di, stop. Just stop."

"You know everything about me that matters. You trust me and you love me."

"You can love a person and still wonder who she is. This explains things, yes. But that man knows more about you than I do."

"You know everything that matters."

"So you say, but you are willing to go to great lengths for him. Danger. All of these secrets you trade. The lies you tell for him, and I couldn't even find you for a simple phone call." Brent took a step back and rebuttoned his collar.

He strode into the bathroom to get away from her for a moment, finding the tube of tooth cream snaked on the counter, leaving a mess in its wake, and a rolled-up towel beside it. He caught his reflection in the mirror. His eyes were stormy and his nostrils flared. He gritted his teeth for control.

The right part of his brain told him to shut the door, lean on the sink, and take several deep breaths. But he couldn't stop himself from hearing Simon say, *"Foyle. Like the bookshop on Charing Cross Road."* And he thought of the months when Diana's letters stopped while she was talking and laughing with Simon Barre.

Jealousy is for cowards. He wasn't jealous of her relationship but of the *time* Simon spent with her. Four years of an eternity pledged to his wife that Brent had lost. But the wrong part of his brain focused on her not being able to adhere in the slightest to who he was, what he had seen, what he expected.

He had promised he would trust her.

He held up the tooth cream. "I know you are a terrible housekeeper and that Mrs. Ratchet's pet badger two doors over is probably more competent in the kitchen, but for the love of God, Diana, you don't even *try*." He walked into the bedroom and snatched his pillow. "But I'm tired of our fight. It's been too long a day."

"*Our fight*?" Diana called after him. "*Our fight?* This is very much *your* fight. It isn't my fault if I am not the girl you sketched before you left. You could smooth out all of my lines and capture me exactly how *you* wanted. Is that my fault or yours? I changed, yes. We all did."

Brent returned to the living room and chucked the pillow at the sofa. He looked to Diana. Part of him wanted her to retaliate for his outburst. And by the fists bunched at her hips, the rapid breaths and the flush on her cheeks, he could tell she was thinking about it. He primed himself for her to rail at him.

Instead, her voice gentled. "Until the moment you tell me, until the moment you finally let me back in, you will wake up every night and grab my wrists when we share a bed. And relive it over and over. Because right now it is all just bottled up inside you. In the things you aren't telling me, right under your shirt collar. You can't do it alone, Brent. You can't carry that horror alone. Whatever it is."

Diana blew a strand of blonde hair from her face, then leaned in and kissed his cheek. "I'll get you a warmer quilt for the sofa."

Diana woke the next morning, alone, to sun streaming through the blinds and a nonburnt smell wafting through the slightly open door. She stretched and grabbed her robe.

When she stood in the kitchen doorway, Brent turned to smile at her. He looked far better rested than he did most mornings. She smiled at the rashers of bacon hissing in the pan and at sliced bread on the counter.

"Get the marmalade, would you?"

Diana collected napkins and cutlery and marmalade.

"Di?"

"Yes."

"I'll try harder." He set his plate on the table and looked directly at her, eyes softening while he painted her face. "I will. I'm sorry."

"I know this is not what you expected."

"But the best moments of my entire existence have been unexpected, haven't they? I never expected you in that churchyard, for one."

She set the items on the table. "I feel guilty when it seems that . . . parts of me are not what they were. That I would want to keep anything from you."

He lifted a forkful of eggs to his mouth, stopped, and nodded. "You're different, Diana."

"For better or worse?"

"For *different.* Just like you said. But I spent a long time staring at the ceiling wondering how I could expect you to accept how I've changed without accepting how you have. I was wrong."

Diana turned her fork over. "It seems like I am just feeling around in the dark. I don't even think Simon knows how this will turn out. But if we can stop these traitors . . . The stakes are higher than I am able to tell you."

They set out to meet Simon as planned, and while to Diana, the city exposed its potential, to Brent it was purgatory: buses waylaid around construction sites, roads and thoroughfares uprooted with bricks and barriers. In some cases Brent had to reroute his favorite shortcuts from Clerkenwell to King's and every last church they pursued in between.

Brent didn't say a lot to Diana en route to Ye Olde Cheshire Cheese, just off Fleet Street in Wine Office Court, for their appointed meeting with Simon, but the ease with which she brushed his arm and the fluid way he kept stride with her felt as natural as breathing. The silence between them settled as easily as it did when they roamed the city in its wholeness.

The tucked-away tavern was crammed with literary history.

Twain, Dickens, and Chesterton were once deemed regulars. The pub had three levels, but it was the bottom floor into which she and Brent descended, the smell of old wood and sawdust permeating the air and ancient tables stained with liquid rings filling the room. In the main-floor chophouse, Sydney Carton had once dined with Charles Darnay in *A Tale of Two Cities*.

Exposed beams, soot-swept floors, and grated fireplaces met the dank chill that only just kept the November wind from gnawing at them inside. Simon arrived in a smart navy wool suit, tugging at his tie, blue eyes unreadable behind their gold-rimmed glasses.

"A far cry from The Savoy," Simon said as Brent and Diana rose to shake his hand.

"It was rebuilt after the Great Fire," Diana replied as they sat. "Almost immediately." She stretched her arms out and looked around happily.

Everything made her happy this morning, Brent noticed. She had torn down a wall and in the process let him into her world. One that included Simon Barre.

"I'll see to the drinks, shall I? A pint, Mr. Barre?"

"Coffee."

Brent returned a moment later with a pint of dark lager, a coffee, and a precariously balanced lemonade for Diana.

"So it worked out then?" Diana smiled at Brent, accepting her glass. She lowered her voice. "And you made contact with your SOE agent?"

"Langer has been helpful." Simon took his coffee with an apologetic look. "I am very sorry for my abysmal behavior last evening, Professor Somerville. I have been intoxicated precisely two times in the whole of my sorry existence, the first at my college graduation party and subsequently last evening." He stared at his coffee ruefully. "What's more, it was highly unprofessional of me."

"You're human, Simon," Diana said softly. "We all make mistakes."

"We're living in times that don't allow us to be human, Diana. Humanity costs lives."

Brent took a long sip of beer, trying not to choke it down at the irony of Simon's statement. He was handsome and poised and Diana was completely at ease with him. He didn't recognize any attraction or flirtation between the two, rather watched two friends reunited in a new space and sharing a common interest.

"You know Brent teaches at King's, Simon. You can use him."

"Hold up." Brent set his pint down and flicked a look at the foamy rim left in its wake. "Use me for what?"

"What have you told him?" Simon narrowed his eyes at Diana.

"Everything I could without compromising either of us."

"I want to know how dangerous this is. What you're asking her— *us*—to do. I didn't fancy the man with a gun at All Hallows that first night, and I very much hated the one who grabbed her at Walbrook," Brent said. "And that first night, I thought I saw someone else too."

"You never said anything," Diana said.

"I thought it might be a figment of my imagination. Or a premonition."

"I have my own premonition," Simon said. "That what I am pursuing might be connected to King's. It's not the first time that academics have proven useful in Soviet causes." He looked between Brent and Diana. "You're safer together. As a pair. I can see that." Simon inclined his coffee mug. Really, the man was night and day from the figure Brent had encountered slurring his speech the evening before. "Are you aware of any Communist sympathizers at King's?"

Brent shook his head. "But I've only just returned. I've been rather preoccupied with classes, and it seems that politics and the like are second priority to just trying to keep our heads above water." He rimmed his pint glass with his finger. "The students have changed. Before . . . Well . . ."

He sensed Diana's gaze on him and concluded the thought with a shake of his head. "It doesn't matter. What matters is that you have Diana working for you in some capacity. And I won't risk her safety. So what do you need?"

"Rick Mariner is having a party." Diana broke the thread of their gaze and veered her attention back to Simon. "Brent can keep an eye and ear out at King's, sure, but what better way to see? I think that Rick might be involved. I wasn't going to say anything until I had something . . . anything, but now . . ."

Brent groaned. "I *loathe* Mariner's parties." He paused, pint in midair. "Or perhaps I merely loathe Mariner." He took a swig of his beer. "How did you know about Mariner's party?"

"He called the other afternoon. I plumb forgot to tell you. Because I hadn't thought about attending until now."

Simon sipped his coffee, his lips curved in a smile. "But you're the sort who can make do, Somerville? At a party?"

"Completely the sort." Diana raised her lemonade glass in Brent's direction, pride shining from her eyes.

"You can take a peek around." Simon looked to Brent. "Diana will tell you that I prefer to work on intuition."

"Hunches," Diana translated.

Simon nodded. "So, anything."

"Is everything alright, then?" Brent asked Simon pointedly. Simon mightn't have remembered his inebriated speech, but Brent did. To the letter.

"I don't even know what *alright* means anymore, Professor Somerville."

⚬⚬

Two evenings later, preparing for Rick's party, Brent had the distinct feeling he was stepping into the past yet as a stranger. Before the war Rick Mariner's faculty parties were a quarterly mainstay of his academic year. Everyone knew Mariner taught as a lark. Alongside his family money he had pawned a valuable artifact to afford his Mayfair town house. Money slipped through his fingers and paid for the charm that hung around his shoulders like a bespoke suit. More often than not after a few dances, he would retreat to the drawing room for cigars and unending debates with Silas Henderson, a history professor who eventually became Diana's supervisor.

As a rule students weren't invited, but not long after Brent had met Diana, she and a giggling friend of hers appeared. Brent asked her to dance and quickly learned that she was as talented on the floor as she was holding a tune. The posh band Mariner had hired was making "The Way You Look Tonight" hover on a wistful sigh: half melancholy, half longing. Brent had danced with several girls before Diana and wondered why previous songs were just a puddle of notes. He was so far gone on the soft silk of her dress and the smell of her and the way she tucked a long strand of blonde hair behind her ear. She got a little nervous with him. A blush flamed her cheeks, her nose wrinkled a little, and she fell back on Christopher Wren.

"It only took Wren ten days to present his plan for the rebuilding of London to King Charles the Second." She went on and on about his mathematical precision while Brent, dizzy with the feel and smell of her, was finding it hard to keep his instincts in check.

Tonight, the years pulled back with the damask curtain leading to Rick's salon. Fabric rations and a lack of sewing skill prevented Diana from wearing anything new, but the claret dress she wore might as well have been new, as long as it had been since he'd seen it on her.

Rick foisted a drink on Brent the moment he spotted him. "It's a '27." His voice directed them to look at the brandy label. "A very good year."

Brent smiled and raised his glass. "Thank you."

"And for you, Mrs. Somerville? Champagne?"

At Diana's nod Rick went to retrieve her drink.

"If you need me to sniff around, then you'd better dance with

Rick." Brent looked at her plainly. "You know you can get any-thing out of him. He's clearly already been into that decanter a few times."

Diana seemed unsure. She perused the faculty members, some new, some she certainly recognized from King's corridors and Brent's faculty luncheons. "But what will people say?"

"If you were going to run off with Mariner, wouldn't you have done it by now?" He winked at her. "I don't care what people say, Diana." He kissed her cheek and let his lips linger at her ear. "I'm all in." He pulled away to revel in her spreading smile. "Besides, you're a terrible dancer. It might rid you of him once and for all."

Diana beamed and walked toward Mariner. The more Brent saw her smile, the more the past settled.

Rick provided Diana with a champagne glass and she had his full, unguarded attention. Brent made pleasantries with several King's colleagues and clinked glasses with those he had surprisingly not encountered since his return. Where small talk had once been the weather or the price of flour, now it circled around where one served.

Mariner's abode was a regular Victoria & Albert collection: em-bellished with art and sculptures that offset the taffeta and cigarette smoke of the elite pressed into his impressive house.

Brent set down his unfinished glass and roamed past the cham-ber quartet to the hallway. The library wasn't hard to find and the door was left wide open, probably for curious visitors like himself. The immediate scent of a half-smoked cigarette and a lipstick-stained glass told him he wasn't the only guest with the idea.

He eased the door shut and clicked the inside lock on the door.

Diana had said to search for any indicator of an infinity sign. Mathematics wasn't Brent's field of study, but the symbol had religious resonance. *The Alpha and the Omega. The Beginning and the End.* From Revelation. Just like the words that—

Brent flexed his injured hand. Not tonight. He wouldn't think of Ross tonight. He would focus on the library and the cut of his wife's dress colored like tipped merlot.

Mariner had an impressive collection on pretty much every subject in fine gold-embossed volumes. Interspersed into the canvas of mahogany shelves and books was a collection of relics and art. Brent wandered to the desk, almost freezing at a soft thud and muffled laughter on the other side of the door.

When no one tried to enter, he looked down again at a neat tower of papers stacked on a blotter beside several expensive pens. His eyes caught on a sliver of paper peeking out. Diana's thesis. Brent rolled his eyes. Mariner was obsessed. Even Brent couldn't get through every long, loquacious page on Christopher Wren's use of light to present geometric symmetry.

Brent tucked Di's thesis away. Then he focused on the other papers. Mostly for the hammer, sickle, and star against a scarlet backdrop. He didn't know Mariner well enough to know if he was a Communist. Just an atheist who was always nagging Brent about his beliefs. He turned the top pamphlet over in his palm and saw an elongated 8. Whatever his wife and Simon Barre were pursuing, this might be part of it.

Whatever *it* was, it might be *something*. Brent folded the pamphlet and slid it in his jacket.

CHAPTER 18

S omerville sure had no issue leaving you in my arms." Rick's grip
was tight on her waist as they maneuvered around the dance
floor. "You're not tired of him, are you? Bored with countless stories
of his bravery and valor?"

He couldn't see her face, of course. Diana's chin was on his shoulder and her vantage was beyond him to the swanky flat and his
cherished antiques. "Brent doesn't much like talking about the war,"
Diana said. "You couldn't go, could you? On account of your eyesight? That must have been hard."

"They assume I was lucky."

When Diana couldn't think of any other response, she said, "I'm
happy you made it."

"We found different ways of engaging our minds. There is more
than one way to fight a war, Diana. Sometimes you need to fight a
status quo. An ideology."

Diana knew this all too well.

He almost lost his step but not quite, and he pulled her in sync
with him, directing her on the floor. "Never understood what you
saw in him."

"Rick . . ."

"If it was *just* an undergrad fascinated by older men."

"He's only five years older than I."

"So many of the fellows I know have a different way of approaching it." Rick provided ample examples of divorces and dalli-
ances. Many muffled against the rising crescendo of the band.

"We can't decide who we love, Rick."

"That sounds like a line from a film." He spun her toward the middle of the floor. Diana noticed a few eyes flitting their direction. Nonetheless, Rick should have chosen another partner by now. The song ended and they joined the smattering of applause.

"You were always more interested in how I looked," she joshed. The first familiar bars of a new song swelled, and Diana's heart lurched. Rick's arm clutched her around the waist, but she was slow at joining his rhythm.

"And Saint Somerville isn't interested in your looks?" Rick challenged.

"I wouldn't say that." Brent cut in and gently took Diana's arm and put his hand on her waist. She immediately felt at home, her shoulders relaxing.

"I say, if I had this goddess on the dance floor—or my bed, for that matter—I wouldn't spend my time in the library."

A dangerous glint sparked in Brent's green eyes and his grip on Diana tightened as he pasted on a sly smile. "I just ducked out for a bit of interesting reading. Di can handle herself against the shrewdest of cads. Fancied a page or two on geometric symmetry in Wren's city domes, as it happens. I forgot how robust your library is. And how specific to certain architectural treatises."

Diana glanced at Rick, who flushed and gave a quick bow before he turned away from them. "Why did I never notice he was such a brute?"

"You were young." Brent gave a one-shoulder shrug.

The song swelled. She fit into him like a puzzle piece. Diana had two left feet but never for this song. She never failed to find the rhythm for *their* song. "A Nightingale Sang in Berkeley Square."

"Don't hum, Di." Her husband's breath tickled her ear as he steered her in time. Instrumental bars replaced lyrics everyone knew by heart. Words about magic and birds and angels at the Ritz. Of two people in love, sure, but also of the love one felt for a city. Composed before that city crumbled and fell. "This poor song has suffered enough since you unanimously chose it for us."

Diana smiled. "I did choose it, didn't I?"

"You practically gave me a dissertation in its defense."

"Rick fancies he's in love with me." Diana placed her splayed hand on his chest.

"Rick Mariner doesn't know how to be in love with you."

A certain energy swirled through Brent tonight and loosened his steps. She cocked her head with a coy, flirtatious smile. "And you do?"

"I have always known how to be in love with you."

Diana's heart swelled and she pressed into him tightly. She couldn't remember the last time they danced to this song. She allowed him to direct her—firm hand on his back and broad shoulder a perfect fit for her head.

"Did Rick ever hurt you?" His deep voice reverberated through his chest. "Did he ever touch you? It never occurred to me that the lout was any more than talk."

"Would you defend my honor?" She tipped her chin up so their eyes locked.

"I'd die for it."

Diana nestled further into his shoulder.

"Reach into my breast pocket, Mrs. Somerville." Brent turned them toward the window.

"What did you find?" Diana asked playfully, reaching into his pocket and extracting the folded pamphlet. She peeked into it without attracting attention. "An infinity sign. Your bailiwick."

"Don't impress me with your Latin. It never worked with Rick." Brent spun her slowly and Diana arched an eyebrow. "Your Greek, on the other hand . . ."

He held her close, and when he shifted with the meter of the song, the stubble on his cheek brushed her forehead just as she turned to see a few women hovering by a table of wineglasses and a few men tucking into crystal tumblers. All watching them with a far deeper intensity and lingering gaze than they had when Diana was with Rick. It seemed the war made it unfashionable to be madly in love with one's spouse. After all, for all of the frantic kisses at train stations and hastily scribbled marriage certificates, *The Times* spoke to a rise in divorce filings. The preceding years made people too different and tore them apart. Diana pressed closer to Brent in defiance of any rift.

The end bars faded mournfully and Diana stepped back from Brent. She realized she hadn't talked to anyone but Rick and Brent since the party began. She disengaged her fingers from his and turned to the party. Smiling. Conjuring Simon Barre's charm and stepping into the fray.

"Silas!" Diana said brightly, seeing her old mentor in the foyer snatching a canapé from a passing tray. She held tightly to Brent's arm. She hadn't told him she had failed to see Silas the other day when they agreed she would go to his office. Fortunately, it didn't come up.

"Diana really needs to start her studies again." Brent shook Silas's hand. "As you know."

"Diana is an exceptional student." Silas smiled. "I'm so glad I gave you your father's book before . . . before all of this."

"Surely you have someone you could recommend her to."

"I will put you in touch with Walsh. Though he's a bit old-fashioned. He might not take to working with a student who is married to a faculty member."

"I don't know if I am going to be a student again," Diana said.

At the same time Brent said, "I'm not even in the same department, Silas. Surely you can do something. Your Cambridge connections perhaps? Diana's father was almost a legend. And she was one of your best students. I am not even saying that with bias. It's a fact."

"I will do what I can, of course." He smiled sadly between them. "In the meantime, how are you enjoying some restful domestic life?"

Brent turned to Diana with a knowing wink. "Diana can do something with eggs that seems an almost superhuman feat." Brent chuckled.

~⌾~

They weren't the first couple to retreat into the clear, cold evening, nor were they the last. When they neared Clerkenwell, the fallen steeples made the stars prick through more brightly, and the broken buildings stunted in their restoration just made the shadows more interesting.

Diana stopped him under a streetlamp and put a palm on his chest. "I told you that I am not ready to begin my studies again. What was that? You're speaking for me."

"We were at a party. Correct me if I am wrong, but you haven't seen your old supervisor, have you? We discussed it. And I thought you were going the other day."

"So because you assumed I hadn't, you thought you'd act on my behalf?"

"Did you go?"

"No. I didn't. Then I went home and saw Simon there and I knew very certainly it's not what I want. But you . . . you have an amazing opportunity here. Look at that pamphlet you found in Rick's office. You can help us get Simon what he needs."

"How can I help? It's not like Mariner and I are friends."

"Because if there's one sympathizer at King's, there will be others. Rick is popular. You know that."

"Is this what it will take to get you to continue your schooling?"

"I'm not trading with you, Brent. I'm asking you. I want to see this through for Simon, then we can think about next steps." Diana looped her arm in his. "Just pay closer attention. Eat lunch in the lounge."

"Sweetheart, if I were the sort of man who ate lunch in the faculty lounge, you and I never would have met."

"You'll start! Brent, the sooner Simon finds this man, the sooner we can get rid of Simon. Forever. Well, perhaps not forever, but at least reduced to a dinner now and then or a glass of sherry at Christmas. Please. He'll go back to just being my friend then. You'll see." He didn't respond. "Brent?"

"The war took your degree, Diana. You have to finish it."

"But you were always so supportive of what I wanted."

"And I still am." A car's headlights flashed and Brent took Diana's elbow and moved her from the curb.

"No. You're supporting what you want for me."

"You said yourself that tending house is not making you happy."

"So that's my only other option? Finish my degree or tend house?"

"What other option is there, darling? Work at Selfridges? Keep books? Your passion is waiting for you."

"My passion is right in front of me." She looked up at him. "And all around me. But why can't I have it in a way I choose?"

Brent rubbed the back of his neck. "Simon."

"I *know* that all I've been able to feed him is bread crumbs. But it's hard to do something for years that makes an impact and then . . ." Diana shook her head to finish the sentence and resumed walking.

"Listen to me," Brent said softly. "Stop for a moment."

Diana planted her feet and crossed her arms over her chest, bracing against the chill.

"You can preserve your churches by teaching people about their importance. Finish your degree, Diana. Silas will retire, but you have impeccable grades. You're so smart."

"I just don't know what I want. Seeing Rick. Being back at King's. I don't know if that's who I am anymore."

"I don't know if academia is who I am either, Di. But maybe I don't have a choice. Maybe it will just take more time to adjust. I think . . . I know we cannot expect to just step through as if everything was frozen in time. But we were on a clear path, and I don't want you to have any regrets."

"I know you want what's best for me."

"I truly do. Let's finish whatever this is for Simon. Can we agree on that? You help him find this Eternity and then we'll see about the necessary steps for you to go back. Alright? Di?"

But Diana had already strolled silently a few paces ahead of him.

———— ✑ ————

Diana spent the rest of the ramble home slowly finding herself after the last of the champagne had left her. Brent looked so handsome, and he was right. Maybe all she was doing with Simon was a tactic to help ease herself back into the life that she should want. It was all she had talked about. Having a home and family. It was all that the Diana who set off on the train to Buckinghamshire wanted. She tried to find that Diana in the mirror above the mantel as she unfastened her hatpin and wriggled out of her gloves.

Brent was finagling with his bow tie. He had always found it a challenge before the war, and now, with his injured left hand, it was even more difficult. It hadn't stayed straight all night and the memory made her smile. "Let me do that. Just like the old days when we came back from the cinema or a play."

His eyes stayed with her as she slid it from his neck. Her fingers lingered at his collarbone before she worked his top button. She pressed a kiss to his chin. She could hear his intake of breath, but then he smiled and stepped back.

"So, Rick Mariner."

"I thought we were pursuing another line of thought, Brent. The Brent of yesteryear would have very strong words if I interrupted this . . . erm . . . activity with a mention of Rick Mariner."

"Darling, Rick seemed genuinely surprised the day we presented him with *oleum medicina.*" He cast his gaze in the direction of the propaganda pamphlet he had set on the table near them. "Unless he's a very good actor. If that relic has something to do with this—"

"He's had several years to think and be swayed." Her fingers were featherlight in the hollow of his collarbone. "You and I, we . . . well, I'm assuming you had as much time to think about any ideology during the war as I did in the thick of it, which was none at all."

She undid another button, moved closer to him, pressed her lips to his chin. "So, Saint Somerville." Diana mimicked Rick's tone. "Are you interested in my looks?" Diana had chewed some of her lipstick off and curls spilled from their pins. She was certain her face powder bore the brunt of dancing. Her dress hung loose, where it had once filled out with curves unmarred by rations and stress.

Brent took her hands in his, studying the faint bruises on her wrists, then looked in her eyes. He raised their joined hands and kissed Diana's knuckles softly. "You look beautiful, Di." He slowly turned from her and resumed undressing in the bedroom.

Moments after, she joined him in the dark, having made quick work of her nighttime routine. "I don't understand you, Brent. I don't understand why you can't even look at me."

"Diana." He reached for her hand. "I was so happy to dance with you."

"Me too."

"Do you think it is easy for me to be so near you night after night? Especially on a night when you wore *that* dress?"

"I sometimes think when you look at me, you're reminding yourself that I'm the woman you married."

"But you aren't, Diana. You've changed. So have I. We're getting to know each other all over again. And it would be so easy to just give in to that." He smiled at the euphemism. "We were always so wonderful at connecting in that way. But I hurt you and I don't know who I am anymore. And I want something deeper with you."

"You never used to be this way."

"Diana, if we rebuild in one way, if I give myself completely to you, I'll be no better than the man who nearly fell off that bench at Great St. Bart's. Before, you would fall into me so easily. It was endearing, but I always knew there was something more to you. Maybe it will frustrate me to no end that you're calling the shots. That you're standing your ground."

He cupped her chin. "But I think I always saw the potential of this, Diana. I always wanted it. I'll love it, of course. And I'll fall in love with you as many times as I have to, to make it right. But I won't start there. That's like . . . rebuilding the dome at Walbrook before making sure the columns are straight."

CHAPTER 19

Brent lay on the sofa and stared at the ceiling. The bedroom door was open a smidgen, and sensing her behind it made him shift to the right and left, then roll onto his stomach and smother the sofa cushion. For all of his virtuous words to her and his refusal to hurt her again, it was nearly killing him. What if he kept deciding to hold on to one more secret or cross one more bridge before he felt ready? How much would he continue to exact of her and himself? He had married the most beautiful woman he had ever seen, and rewarded her with a chaste kiss on the forehead before bed.

When sleep finally came, it was without dreams or nightmare. When he woke, it was to Diana's voice on the telephone telling Simon about the pamphlet he found in Rick's office.

He went to lecture for the morning, having promised to meet her at a church over his lunch break. Though London looked different, he could have navigated the distance from King's to St. James Garlickhythe with his eyes closed.

It had always been one of Diana's favorites with its protruding chancel, something rare for a Wren church, and its abundance of light.

"The tower clock was destroyed," Diana said as she and Brent approached. "But the rest has stood up. Look! Even the Sunday hymns." A wood-encased sign listed the numbers of the upcoming order.

Thus, just as men in Savile Row suits rushed from Fleet Street offices under a sun-swathed and brilliant orange late-autumnal sky, they approached the church. The same temperate weather as when they first sat together in the yard at Great St. Bart's. He had promised to fall in love with her again and again—through any season, even as autumn yawned out the last of its sojourn.

Her reintroduction to the church after the loss of its beautiful inner architecture would hit her hard, the desecration a personal offense to her. A rector wandered nearby in a half alley where vintners and merchants used to barter their wares. Diana smiled. Brent tipped his hat. Soon sunlight streamed through the windows of Wren's Lantern and they had the sanctuary to themselves.

"Do you remember when I made you sneak in here before the Easter Sunday service?" Diana said.

"At five thirty in the morning. We picked the lock to the side door with your hairpin." Brent was amused. "You said you wanted to see if the sunrise lit up Wren's Lantern. You took little account of where you could *actually* see the sunrise in London."

Diana grinned. "You kissed me. Right over there. You said the light made my hair blaze."

"I said a lot of romantic things. I was young and in love and incredibly daft." Brent inspected a column.

"And you aren't now?"

"Incredibly daft?" he said dryly.

He strolled to the opposite side of the altar and peered up at the ceiling. With the exception of St. Paul's, it was the highest in the city. The floor of the south aisle still bore the damage of the bomb that had dropped inside but remained unexploded. Brent had read it had been detonated in the Hackney Marshes. He slunk to a relatively clean space on the floor, pulled his knees to his chest as a bit of a makeshift desk, and reached into his satchel for paper and charcoal. He began sketching with a technique perfected by so many nights in bomb shelters, his torch balanced precariously, his eyes accustomed to the dark from his years at the Front.

He focused on Diana, the curve of her cheek highlighted by her torchlight, the ruins of brick in disarray around her. His breath hitched. In the trenches or while tugging the end of a stretcher through the mud, he could sketch every feature in delicate lines in his mind's eye. He had memorized her face, the feel of her, how she looked when she peered up at him, her expression while recalling an interesting fact about the churches she loved. Even though part of her was shaded in darkness, his mind could color in what his eyes couldn't see.

Brent remained still when a figure entered the doorway. Didn't rise as he neared Diana, who clearly noticed his presence, speaking emphatically all of a sudden. "I think if we are to implement a system that ranks the buildings by their historical significance, we should consider those with potential as well as prior significance."

Brent slowly rose. "I agree." He stepped to join her. Unlike the man at Walbrook, the stranger didn't move toward them. Rather he kept silent and smoked. A rolled-up newspaper Brent could make out as *The Times* peeked out of his trench. He pushed the brim of his homburg back on his forehead and slowly unraveled the paper just as Brent and Diana's torchlight swathed its path.

Then he tucked the paper under his left arm and lit another cigarette, its orange ember at the tip like a small prying eye facing them a moment before he turned to the doorway and the double doors that led out to Garlick Hill.

Brent was so intent on his study of the stranger that when he moved his gaze, it landed on Diana, who had shuffled close to him.

"The matches. The mismatched cigarettes I found?" she whispered. "Did I tell you about those?" Her voice tickled his ear.

"No."

"He's got to be signaling someone. It's too rehearsed."

Brent nodded. "Shall we go?" he said in a louder voice for the benefit of the stranger.

"I think we've done all we're going to do for now. You have your sketches?"

Brent folded his sketch pad into his satchel beside the gun he had begun carrying on Diana's behalf as she tucked her notebook in her handbag. She cast a surreptitious glance at Brent and motioned with her eyes behind her. He took the hint, gave a curt nod, and double-checked. He took her arm as they walked out of the church.

Diana used the darkness and the construction barricades to her advantage and tugged Brent behind a pile of lumber. Together, they focused on the open doors of the church. Diana leaned into him as another figure appeared. A man of medium height who walked into the church as if he owned it.

A moment later the first man had joined him in the open door-way. "There were two people here. They left."

The second man chuckled. "Let me guess. A woman consulting on churches? Never mind. You're here now and all is in order. I want you to wait here for another half hour and someone will come to collect you."

"I thought you were to take me—"

"Ah!" the second man interrupted. "Some people are planners and others execute. I am the former."

There was a long silence between the men but an evident change in Diana. Her posture had straightened and the fingers on his arm tightened.

"Alright, Di?"

Her blue eyes pierced the shadows. "That voice. The man who joined him. It sounded *familiar* somehow." She shivered. "Too familiar."

~❦~

That night Diana told Brent he should take the bed. She'd sleep on the sofa. Her mind was turning and there was no point in his being uncomfortable when she was just going to stay awake and listen to the wireless anyway.

"It's not that comfortable."

"Then why are *you* sleeping on it?"

"Look at your wrists."

"Look at the shadows under your eyes." She blew a strand of hair that had fallen across her face. "Sometimes I think it has little to do with your hurting me and all to do with your wanting every last part of our relationship to be perfect. Even our making love. I don't look for perfection in things. And I don't care a hang about your scars."

"You know that—"

"I *don't* know." Diana wasn't angry. She was frustrated. He would keep dying on this hill and she would find herself being pulled further and further from him as he insisted that their sharing a bed would hurt her, would keep them from ever truly finding themselves. She wasn't sure how long she had to keep living for the little moments that mirrored their affinity before the war.

"I don't know, Brent. I lived without you for long enough. But what I *do* know is that bringing all of this up again tonight won't make anyone happy. I am going to call Simon. Please take the bed."

She rang Simon, and at the end of the conversation he said, "Listen. If it was Fisher, then I'm as distraught as you. He was my friend too."

"You're truly as surprised as I am?"

"I thought I had found my double agent. What I was hired for." Simon stopped a moment. "Maybe I was too close. Too involved? I don't know. It's not like I'm faring any better now."

"Simon, there are things here that are suspect. That *could* involve Fisher."

"Like what?"

"Mozart. I met Langer at a Mozart concert."

"Fisher could *not* have been in Vienna. You're just throwing out theories."

"How do you know that? Just because you didn't see him? That's what we do! We throw out theories! That's all you've done since this started. He knows everything about these churches, Simon, because he sat at a desk opposite mine for four blasted years. You keep speaking of this former SOE agent in Vienna. What have they found?"

"I can't discuss that with you."

"Listen, I might be tired or theorizing, but Fisher could work for him. He was bored."

"And he left Bletchley before all of us. On V-E Day. We were all out and drinking and toasting those large bonfires, burning everything on Churchill's orders so the Soviets would be left with zilch, and Fisher?"

"Wasn't there." Diana thought it best not to add that Simon seemed too preoccupied with Villiers that night. "And the very next day you told me you had the first whiff of this Eternity business in a while. You say this is a war of intelligence and ideology. This Cold War as George Orwell termed it in that newspaper article. Well, Fisher might just be a profile. Oh, Simon, the man's gait, his manner . . . you know him. He had that something that was so familiar."

"Did you see him clearly?"

"No, I couldn't flash my torch and give away our hiding spot. And the streetlights there are next to pitch."

Perhaps all of her friends were traitors. Fisher Carne. Rick Mariner.

Diana hung up the receiver and settled on the sofa, pulling a quilt to her chin. Perhaps the newspaper the stranger had in his pocket was the key to this Eternity puzzle.

Puzzles were all around her if she blurred her focus just a little. They were in Simon's cryptic messages and his requirements of her. They were in the Wren churches she visited under the guise of consultation, and her inability to find a succinct pattern in what she gleaned for Simon.

They were in the relic Brent gave back to Rick.

Fisher Carne would be a rather unsuspecting spy. None of the cloak-and-dagger stuff she saw in the cinema. He was so unassuming and a little awkward. About as primed for this sort of work as what she was doing for Simon. But he did have a mind like honey—everything stuck to it. He loved hearing about the little hunts her father sent her on. But if Fisher was a traitor, then it would make sense. Hadn't he mentioned that he knew Mariner? Way back all of those years ago.

The next morning Diana, asleep on the sofa, heard the shrill telephone while it was still dark outside.

"What now, Simon?"

"A man identified as Petrov was found at Magnus the Martyr last night strangled with wire."

Diana blinked, barely awake. "Pardon me?"

"Wire, Diana. Piano wire."

"Simon . . ."

"There was a message in his pocket. I can't crack it. But there was also a business card with the name Mariner. I'll bring it round when I have a chance. Petrov was supposed to be guest lecturing at King's. So maybe tell Somerville to keep his eyes open. Suck up to Rick Mariner? I don't know. And we need that key. I have two people on this and even tried to get Langer on it."

Brent appeared a moment later, tying his robe. "Who was that?" He blinked to adjust to the light she had just turned on.

"Simon. A man was murdered at Magnus the Martyr last night."

"That's horrible." He settled on the sofa.

Diana shivered and sat beside him, pulling the quilt she had used the night before around her. "Very. I think I might know who Eternity is."

"You know the man who killed someone with wire?"

She nodded. "He was so familiar to me, the man we saw last night."

Brent stared at her. "We were a few feet away from a murderer?"

"Yes." She yawned and shuddered under the blanket still wrapped around her shoulders. "He worked with Simon and me during the war."

"You have to let me return to sleeping on the sofa. I may have nightmares, but you're not sleeping at all." He rubbed her arm. "You're half freezing. You're out here . . ." He swallowed, spoke lowly. "Did I wake you last night?"

Diana blew a strand of hair from her forehead. "I am not sure, in those moments, if I should try to wake you up or if it's best not to startle you. I wish the army sent out pamphlets about this sort of thing. I'm sure many men are in your situation."

Brent ran his hand over his face. "I don't know what to do. I could seriously injure you."

"You can tell me what happened to you during the war."

"Would that really help or just make it worse?"

Diana lowered the quilt and played with the sleeve of her nightgown. She stretched out her arm and pushed back the fabric of her nightgown; her wrist still encircled by a faint band.

"I could break your hand and not even know I'm doing it."

"And yet you know that's not why we sleep in different beds."

"Di . . ."

But she wasn't going to press it. She stretched, wriggled out of the blanket, and met the rusty stubble at the curve of Brent's jaw with her lips.

A half hour later she cleared the breakfast plates and scraped toast crumbs into the rubbish bin. She helped Brent into his coat. She straightened the collar of his trench coat.

He leaned over and kissed her cheek. "Don't burn down the flat before dinner."

―∽―

Late April 1945
Bletchley Park

The frantic pace of the previous months and the constant jitter of nerves were replaced by rampant expectation. The headlines reported Hitler's suicide on the last day of the month and anticipation rippled throughout the Park.

Simon appeared at her workstation with a smile. "Almost time for a break?"

Diana glanced at the clock over the now-vehement radiator. Nodded. "I've fifteen minutes."

"Care for a cup of tea?"

She nodded. "Swear there's a ghost trapped in there," she remarked as they passed the radiator and took their mugs to an empty office in the corner. "You look tired." She studied him in the window light. "Simon, you're not half as bad as you think you are. You play all tough, but I know that deep down you are gelatin."

"You might change your mind. Diana, I need you to do something *very* important for me."

"How important?"

"It might mean not going home immediately after the war ends." Diana shifted. "What do you mean?"

"I need your help, and I believe you'll want to help me."

"This is a serious tone."

"You might not thank me right away, but you will. You'll see that—"

"Oh, hang it, Simon! If you're going to be cryptic with me . . . There's nothing you can do to convince me to stay in this wretched place after the war."

"When's the last time you heard from your husband?" Simon paused. "I have something that is of interest to you." The intensity in his gaze startled her so that she dared not blink.

Simon studied her, his eyes calculating.

"You're not Diana Foyle, are you?"

She straightened. "Pardon me?"

"You're Diana Somerville."

"I'm sorry?"

Simon reached under his tweed jacket and removed a file. His eyes locked with hers.

Her heart and constantly engaged brain imagined a thousand and one scenarios—none of which favored her husband being alive and well.

Simon casually set his tea on the table and adjusted his glasses. "I work for MI6. I was placed here to find a traitor."

"Why are you telling me this? Are you *allowed* to tell me this?" Simon had a propensity for being serious, but she had rarely seen such a grave expression on his face.

"I have access to any information I need. Including the welfare of some of our finest on the front lines."

Diana felt faint. "I don't know why I'm here."

"I promise you, Diana, that I would never lie to you about your husband's welfare. I swear it on my life. Do you trust me?"

"Do I have a choice?" She eyed the folder hungrily.

"Take a deep breath."

"H-he's dead, isn't he?" Her heart stopped. Her eyes welled with tears. "He's dead and you know. Some message. Some . . ." Where would she start? Her heart had already spelled out the beats of every finite syllable of his being dead before her brain could logically conclude a world without him.

He acknowledged the folder. "What would you do for this?"

"A-anything."

"I know that. And I want to help you."

Diana took a breath. She had spent so many nights awake, wondering as she studied the cracks in the ceiling what the worst would be. It was unimaginable. The worst would be learning that Brent was injured. Or scared or captured. Or just a shell of the man who pressed his lips to her palm amidst the crumbled brick of All Hallows. The worst would be finding that his voice was seized by terror, that he wouldn't offer her tea. That his eyes were vacant and his heart stale. That those seven words of love, not nearly enough in any language, had been extinguished.

Diana took a deep breath and peeled back the cover of the file.

There was a picture of Brent: a face in black and white whose color she could paint in, eyes bright and intelligent, shoulders broad in his uniform. A smile began in her toes and warmed through her.

She moved the photograph to the side and read the terse telegram of information that sank her heart to the bottom and drew her hand to her mouth.

Everything hurt. The overhead light, the tips of her fingers, the shrill sound of the radiator in the corner, the typewriter keys clacking in the next room, a telephone.

Her world shut down. "Two men from your husband's unit were wounded. One is dead and one is injured. And the paperwork is so shoddy that no one knows which is which. I have a contact in the war office who is close to sorting this out and I can help you. I can find out where they are. And who survived."

"In exchange for . . . ?"

"I have my reasons."

"How dare you use my husband as part of your *reasons*. I thought you were my friend. Why not use Fisher Carne or Villiers? Why me? Why did you tell me your secret?"

"I *trust* you."

"I was married just before I came here."

"You should never have told me about that bull's-eye church."

"Why?"

"Because it gave me an idea."

"What idea? Oh, right. Your reasons. How dare you sit there now tight-lipped?"

"I need you, Diana Somerville." His crisp voice used her surname emphatically. "And it looks like you need me too."

Diana looked at her cold tea. "You're right, Simon. I don't have a choice."

───── ❧ ─────

One evening a week later, Simon clicked his tongue at Diana's pale, thin face, the purple half-moons under her eyes. Villiers was watching her like a hawk and stabbed Simon with her gaze, mostly because she was annoyed, Diana was silent, and Simon was the easiest target.

Fisher was pale, too, Diana noticed, often with a slight rim of perspiration at his blond hairline. She tried to bring up her concern for their friend, but Sophie and Simon were too busy staring each other down while tapping their cigarette ashes in a silent, angry conversation across the pub table.

Fisher twisted a line of piano wire around his index finger.

"Why do you always carry that with you?" she asked.

"Never know when you might need it. It can slice through hard cheeses, it can measure, and seeing as no one has tuned the baby grand in the main house . . ."

She hadn't slept since Simon had shown her Brent's folder. At night she looked over the sketch of the churches he had given her on the train platform and then at a picture of the two of them. She tried to recall the feel of his hair in her fingers and the way his green eyes looked near gold in the sunlight. But the moment she drifted and closed her eyes, the uncertainty of two wounded men's conditions took over and she wondered if one of them was Brent. She tried to imagine how she would cope. Survive. Even live if it was without him.

She tried not to resent Simon with his secrets and his MI6 power, but it was hard to take directions from him day in and day out knowing he was the keeper of the most important thing in her life.

The next day he approached her at the kettle in the empty break room. His voice was soft. "This is the way I know how to do the right thing."

Diana could hardly speak. "Well, it's the *wrong* way to do the right thing, Simon."

"I'm worried about you." He squeezed her elbow. "You never eat. You never talk about Christopher Wren. When I first met you, you took everything in and you talked incessantly and tried so hard to reclaim the parts of your life before you came here."

"I had something to live for then. Simon . . . if you hear anything . . ." She blinked back tears.

Simon studied her a long moment, and try as she might, Diana couldn't read his clear blue eyes. "Brent Somerville is a lucky man."

So was Simon when it came to his relationship with Sophie Villiers. Then her eyes widened and her heart thudded, jolted to life again. Simon said "is."

He retracted something from his breast pocket. "So you'll go to Vienna for me?" He quirked an eyebrow.

"I'll go to the moon," she said, ready to lunge at him and rip the envelope from his hand.

The smile he gave her lacked his usual mirth. "I'm very happy for you, Diana. Truly."

With shaking hands she opened the envelope. Inside was a telegram whose curt words filled her with joy.

```
Barre. Ross killed. Stop. Somerville wounded
in action. Stop. In hospital. Stop. Will fully
recover.
```

Diana let the telegram fall from her fingers and threw her arms around Simon's neck, holding tightly as she dampened the shoulder of his shirt. When her knees began to give way under her, Simon took hold of her waist and led her to her chair.

She couldn't count the number of times she ran her finger over the telegram. Once she blinked away her joy that he was alive, she asked, "How wounded, Simon?"

"One thing at a time." Simon unfolded a piece of paper and placed it in her hand. "This is the name of the hospital where he's being treated."

"I-I can talk to him?" Her voice squeaked, but she didn't care.

"Why don't you take your lunch break now, Diana?" Simon's eyes were oddly bright. He truly wanted this for her. "And write a letter."

Diana poured her heart and tears onto paper that was almost translucent by the time she folded it into an envelope. How did you tell the other half of yourself, wounded and alone, that you couldn't be with him?

Diana had prided herself on keeping a stiff upper lip in front of Villiers throughout the interminable wait for news, but somehow the dam opened the moment she arrived home that evening.

"Whatever it is, Canary, it's not half as bad as the pudding in the canteen today. Come join me and I'll prove it." Her usual crisp glass voice was temporarily softened and she even pressed a kiss to Diana's head in a rare moment of affection. "It will all turn out. Things always do. Now let's eat terrible things and toast the fact that when you hit absolute bottom, you can only go up."

"Have you ever been in love, Villiers?"

When Sophie merely looked at her, Diana continued. "Because I was in love with Brent the moment I met him. And now, with all that is expected of me—and all that I have become—I sometimes wonder."

"If you're still in love with him?"

"No! Oh no. Not that. I sometimes wonder if I can be what he needs me to be. The man married a certain woman, and . . ."

"Canary." Villiers shook her head. "If he's anything but impressed at who you've become, then he's not worthy of you. You don't need him. You can come home with me. My parents have eons of space. You can live in the garden shed."

Diana smiled. She knew what she wanted: the same man she saw sketching in a churchyard. She just wasn't sure what she would have to do, say, or change about herself when this was all over to keep him.

CHAPTER 20

Diana met Brent at King's and together they strolled to St. Paul's for Evensong. Brent hadn't been inside the cathedral since before the war. He supposed stepping through its doors would tug him to the past. For unlike the other churches they had seen, this one remained relatively unscathed. And yet, as they found empty seats and sat, Diana didn't look at him like she had the first time they roamed the church together. She met his gaze straight on, shoulders slightly raised, and chin tilted upward.

"Did you find anything at the college?" She leaned into him once they had settled.

"Nothing out of the ordinary." He rolled the bulletin over his knee. "Almost *too* ordinary now."

The music began and the first bars of Mozart's Kyrie section of the Mass swelled. Diana was transfixed. But on closer inspection, he saw her eyes were glazed. Nostalgia for the church? For what they were the last time he crossed the threshold, when she was the girl in his sketches and he was light-headed as she hung on to him telling him every last thing about the church?

The music stirred something he couldn't translate through memory. At first Mozart took him back to the night he and Ross had heard "Ave Verum Corpus": that snatch of beauty in otherwise ugly surroundings. But when he turned to focus on Diana, she had drifted from him. Her shoulder no longer brushed his and she was slightly turned.

Perhaps it was unfair for him to expect her to let him in when he still tucked so much inside, but wasn't this place sacred to their love story? At least as sacred as their flat and All Hallows?

A new bar began and she slipped further. What was it about music and memory? He felt the need to comfort her. Let her know he was there.

"You're what my stupid heart will want always," Brent said softly.

"Even though I've changed?"

He looked around. "The church has changed, too, hasn't it?"

"But not too much. Just enough change to show what it lived through. To show it survived."

"Remember when you told me St. Paul's occupies a space where once there was a shrine to the goddess Diana?" he whispered. "Maybe that's why you love it so much."

"Maybe." She chewed her lip, shifted in her seat, and the music drew her again.

The piece was melancholy and reverent, certainly, but its effect on Diana left him at a loss. What did she hear in it? He was taking in the way the notes filled a sanctuary, familiar yet strange. From her body language and the light in her eyes, Brent imagined she was anticipating the next note. The next movement. All he knew was that she was experiencing a place she had once shared with him without him.

"Are you alright?"

"It just makes me think of someone. Of somewhere that . . ." She swallowed and folded her hands in her lap.

The chords filled the rafters and the next movement began. Brent looked around to see if he recognized anyone from their previous church visits. Something they should report to Simon. Perhaps the man she recognized. Her friend.

❦

An hour later, Evensong ended and the crowd spilled through the doors like an overturned vessel. The cathedral doors had seen coronations and funerals, had beckoned many. Now the throng moved single file past rows of chairs, curving slightly around the baptismal font and shuffling into the night.

Mozart lingered in the sanctuary, beyond the last legato note and minor chords of the soloists and musicians who were, like Brent and Diana, funneling outside.

Brent took a moment to look over his shoulder as they descended the steps of the church from Ludgate Hill and sloping down to Fleet Street, scarred but standing.

It certainly wasn't an opportune time to steal his arms around her and pull her in for a kiss. But he didn't fancy being at St. Paul's and not being completely in sync with her. So he embraced her tightly and pressed his lips to hers.

She kissed him back. Kissed him as an intercession between their idealization of each other and the broken people they were now. When she opened her eyes, however, their world was still uneven.

"What's wrong?" he asked.

"I kept thinking there must be some message in the music. From Fisher. The man we saw. The man I know. He taught me all about Mozart, Brent. This music was a friend to him." She stopped, reached into her handbag, and retrieved the program. "And when he introduced it to me, I began to look at it as a friend too. You see, Fisher loves numbers. He's a mathematician. There's a catalogue system that organizes Mozart's pieces. The Köchel Catalogue. This piece is #427. I only know that because he told me so often. Told me the composer wrote it for his wife, Constanze, so she would have a truly beautiful solo."

She shook her head. "See? Why I am so terrible at doing what Simon expects? I get emotional and fall into the past. My past with you, yes, but also with Fisher. A friend."

"It truly bothers you that he's connected in all of this, doesn't it?"

"Wouldn't it bother you? If your friend Holt or Ross or Tibbs . . . if you found out—?"

"It would. Funny, eh? The way we rely on people who share exactly the same experience?"

"Because no one else will completely know. I can tell you and you can tell me. But, I speak his language, Brent."

"You're not involved in what Simon is tracking. What he's involving you in. You're on opposite sides."

"And that pains me."

"Did you ever think that Simon needs you not for your impressive knowledge or your ability to connect patterns but because you are so emotionally involved? It must be nice for a man like that who has to work in hypotheses and patterns to know a woman who feels everything deeply."

They fell into pace silently.

"You're sure you were talking about Simon?" Diana said with a curve of a smile a moment later.

─── ✺ ───

Spring 1945
Italy

"Could you find me pen and paper?"

The nurse smiled in relief. He hadn't asked for either before. "You're finally going to write her," she said in broken English. "Of course."

"It's hard." He accepted the pen and paper when she returned.

"Everything's hard."

So he wrote a letter and sent it to the address that at this point was little more than a void. And alongside the pain and morphine drip, Brent became accustomed to the daily knife slicing because he hadn't spoken to Diana when week after week went by and his letter was never returned. One moment of self-preservation, of anger.

There was a letter, however, waiting for him when he finally arrived at the Clerkenwell flat just as he was healed. Meeting his crumbled city alone through a stream of servicemen. Brent snatched at the envelope shoved halfway under the door. He lifted it shakily and made out Diana's handwriting. He opened the door and found the flat much as they had left it—with a coat of dust, clean but stale air, still whole despite the bombs that fell throughout the Blitz and beyond.

The furniture was the same. The sketches he had left. The books Diana had hastily married with his own the day he pledged himself to her forever. The day he gave her every last piece of himself.

Brent set his rucksack on the floor and Diana's letter on the table. He wandered into the bedroom. The comforter was tucked in the way he liked and the light from outside still filtered through the blinds as it had when he closed his eyes in a dark, damp trench and tried to imagine its comfort.

The landlady had filled the larder when she learned he would return and there was tea in the cupboard. Brent opened the closet. Diana had taken much of her clothing, but her green dress hung next to his best suit. He slowly removed it and imagined how she filled it into life, how the fabric clung to her. He pressed it to him a moment and caught a whiff of her perfume and an undercurrent of a scent that was just *her*. She must still love him. She *must*.

He gingerly opened the letter.

Dear Brent,

I have tried to write this letter a hundred times. We used to be able to start anywhere in a conversation, and how ironic I don't know where to begin.

Other than to tell you at the very beginning that I miss you so much it feels like I've lost a part of myself, and every day I wake up to this horrible ache. That it makes it hard to breathe or sleep or eat. That I wish I were with you. That I had been with you when you were injured.

And other than to tell you that I love you. I love you. I love you. More than any word in any language. Seven or more.

And I cannot come home to you yet, even though it is ripping me at the seams.

Brent, I am begging you to trust me for all of the lost letters and all of the words I wanted to speak and haven't. There is a reason that has little to do with you and all to do with the war that took me away from you.

I need you to know that you are everything to me.

Brent wiped his eyes and read the letter again before he straightened his shoulders and put the kettle on the hob. Routine frightened him. But he met it as one did the most commonplace of nightmares. He'd patch up his life again. He stood unflinching at the chill of the solitary life before him. There was a distinct possibility that Diana would be tugged back into his world. There was hope that his heart would settle and thrum with the certainty of her.

But then there was all of the uncertainty too.

There was *Ross*.

Brent explored faith after Ross much as he did the mix-and-match tea bags in one of the patterned canisters Diana brought to his flat on their wedding day. Before Ross, he hadn't believed he could be drained of Paul's words recited to memory and sewn into revered theses. After Ross, he tried to reconcile the words that so confidently cut through his lecture halls with those that lay in the mud as his friend inhaled his last breath.

Brent spread his sketch pad on the kitchen table and pressed the tip of the charcoal so harshly he stabbed a hole in the paper.

You don't have time to think about Ross. You have no idea where Diana is.

But what sort of cruel equilibrium measured the wife he missed against the friend who exacted the promise that Brent would return to a home and a wife and be happy? Ross believed Brent had something to return home *to*. A real home. *Diana*.

A home beyond a few secrets or a possible betrayal. For what was Diana's absence other than a kind of betrayal? Even if she was still true to him, she wasn't *here*. He struggled to imagine how she would slip back into the current of his life, how she would suit the Brent Somerville scarred by war and unsettled by nightmares.

Usually Brent looked over a blank page as a road map his imagination navigated with charcoal, lines, and sure shading. Now, his fingers worked with a pace and confidence he hadn't felt since before the war. Though the subject matter was filled with things he had seen and couldn't blink away, the images seared on his mind. He shouldn't have to choose between them: Ross's memory and Diana's absence. But as the charcoal worked over the paper, it was not Diana's silhouette that came to the forefront. Just shadows and contours of what he and Ross had seen.

Even if he *did* know that he would rather risk a world in which he stepped into a churchyard on a sunny October afternoon. Even if it meant the loneliness upon his return, Diana's absence made his guilt dig deeper.

For the only thing that made Brent feel worthy of his friend's sacrifice was Diana.

He closed his eyes even as his fingers worked over the page. When he opened them, he had captured a fallen church bordered by a moat of stone. If he listened hard enough, he could even hear Mozart.

～♂～

November 1945
London

Having long since burnt Brent's breakfast and sent him out to his day, Diana spread the newspaper on her kitchen table and settled on a column speaking to women readjusting to the London they knew now the war was over. Women who assumed the roles of the men who fought far away and now were learning how to step back into their natural roles. A furtive look around the Clerkenwell flat and Diana was certain any talk of a woman's *natural role* was a moot point.

Diana knew Brent didn't expect that role of her. Yet she couldn't imagine lowering her nose to the crease of a textbook and many late nights with too many pots of tea formulating a new thesis. It was what Brent wanted for her. It was what she should have wanted too.

Especially because her life needed fulfillment beyond Simon's perplexing puzzles.

Alone in the apartment, Diana was riddled by the absence of sound: of telephones and telegrams, of typing fingers and a rickety radiator. There was the occasional lorry rumbling outside the window with a loose tailgate and often the sound of hammers restoring the shingles and rooftops on the nearby houses that hadn't been spared as hers had.

Mostly, she was aware of the absence of music. She turned the knob on the wireless until a BBC program filled the flat with Fisher's music. She closed her eyes and imagined Fisher sitting across from her.

Diana perused the bookshelves absently. So many of Brent's long treatises on theology, a Greek and Hebrew dictionary. One of her favorite letters from Brent's time at the Oxfordshire Barracks explained *ludus* to her, playful love, another Greek form of the word. In it, amidst sketches of churches and houses and a family of bunnies with a burrow near camp, he had listed some of the things he planned to do with her when he got home, worthy of the word. Taking her to a carnival and to Cambridge to row on the rambling river near his uncle's parsonage. Chaplin movies and tea and ridiculously fancy cakes at a tea emporium off of Leicester Square.

Diana ran her finger over the spines of the books on the shelf and stopped at the Ditchfield, then pulled it from the shelf. It was the book she had taken to Bletchley, tucking sketches and Brent's letters inside. It was the book she had taken into the Tube shelter on her wedding night.

She returned to the dining table and opened it. She smiled at the inscription in her father's handwriting. She brushed her palm over the worn edges and the endpaper of the cover. She flipped through the pages. Stopped on Poet's Corner and blushed as she remembered how she suggested naming her children from the gravestones in Westminster Abbey. A home. Children.

Diana set it aside in favor of an open notebook where she smoothed a fresh sheet. She listed all of the churches she and Brent had visited since her return. The churches that sewed up the course of her history. It was almost coincidental the way the churches she'd visited in hopes of helping Simon were notches and marks in the line of her life with Brent. Coincidental, maybe.

Most of the churches they visited were blessed by music or featured music. Maybe the promise was tied to music.

If Fisher saw churches only as buildings—as vessels for the music he loved . . . for Mozart—then perhaps that was a starting point.

Fisher. Diana always supposed he was superior to her. Inasmuch as she asked him for help. Inasmuch as she turned to him, assuming that everything he decoded or scribbled was truth. What if she gave him too much credit? They did the same job. They were, for all intents and purposes, equal in their work.

Maybe Fisher was just trying to do the best he could in a confusing situation. Silas said the war would be won by those who saw the world in a different way. Maybe Simon's war would be won by those who saw the world the same way.

CHAPTER 21

Many would say considering his experience that little could surprise Brent. Keeping his wife's hairpin in his breast pocket in hopes of breaking and entering a colleague's office at King's, however, was a new experience.

The days at King's blurred one into the next, often denoted only by the variance of his worry. He worried about Diana in a new way now that she had joined him at home, knowing what was expected of her given her association with Simon. Previously, it was the worry about where she was while he was back in his office and she honoring a promise. *A friend. A favor.*

Brent rubbed at the back of his neck, sore from another night on the sofa. Tired from another lecture where he couldn't shake the feeling he had slipped from conviction into recitation.

He was more social than usual too. Brent was never *anti*-social so much as he preferred escaping the small talk in hopes of finding a quiet nook with his sketch pad. But now he had far more than academic integrity in common with professors of various subjects. He had the war. It gave them all a conversational starting point. He spent his lunch hours in the cafeteria and his tea breaks in the lounge. He listened to theologies and philosophies and the perspective of men in fields completely different from his own in hopes of finding a similar rhetoric to that of Rick's pamphlets.

Most men were unified by service. But nothing he had heard or interpreted as a possible lead compared to Mariner's obvious association. If Rick wasn't about to open up, Brent would pick a lock and shove open the door.

Perhaps this would be the most important contribution since

Brent's return. For try as he might, he couldn't recognize the Brent Somerville once renowned as being young and bright and a rising star to watch. He began writing abstracts for possible books and lectures with even the possibility of guest appointments, but he'd lost his ability to judge whether his output was any good.

Now he was a man not an hour from breaking into a colleague's office. Mariner had been spending far more time at the college than usual. While Brent had always enjoyed late-night sessions if it meant a clean slate to begin fresh work the next day, Rick's tenure and his father's monetary contribution allowed him to keep more casual hours. Brent banked on the latter for stretching out the hairpin and turning the lock.

To make it worse, he had long given up feeling like a heel for preferring cafeteria food to Diana's cooking. And while it was standard fare and a little bland, it hadn't been scorched. They always doled out extra portions to him on account of his clean-cut looks.

He had just tossed an apple core in the bin next to his desk when student Sam Hunt appeared at his doorway. He waited while Brent looked over some initial notes.

"Well, your research is exceptional." Brent held the paper at arm's length. "And surprisingly familiar." He narrowed in on a reference. "Hunt, I'm not going to be on the committee approving your graduate thesis; you don't need to cite me."

"I read your doctoral thesis. From Cambridge. And most of your articles."

"That seems like a thousand years ago. As old as Paul."

"I'd never read anything about that verse on submission before. It was the only source that worked here." Sam pointed to a subsequent paragraph on the paper in which Brent interpreted Ephesians 5:22.

"It's quite dull of women just to submit to men all of the time, isn't it? Moreover, I don't think it's what St. Paul was trying to say." Brent smiled. "My wife's indubitably smarter than I am and Paul proceeds to say that husbands should love their wives as Christ loves His church, which is a submission of absolutely everything and all besides." Brent cocked his head to the side and studied Sam. "If you have a sweetheart who is scripturally inclined—"

"A fiancée."

"Just make sure you actually live it. I was a world-class idiot about it with my wife, but you seem sincere enough."

"Can I ask you something that has nothing to do with my thesis?"

"I'll try."

"When you saw your wife again, was it the same?"

Brent cleared his throat and shifted, playing with a button on his vest. He used to revel in the appearance of students at his office door. It spoke to their investment and their dedication. It often resulted in the most interesting conversations. Yet now? He was a stranger behind a lectern and now sat across the desk from an eager young man as changed as he.

Finally, Brent said, "Are any of us the same, Hunt? Are you the same?"

The young man had a walking stick—of course he was not. A weary knowledge was invisibly stamped on the countenances of all those who had served. Brent had immediately recognized it the moment he met Sam in class.

"No. But I thought with her being here I would return to something familiar."

"But your fiancée was *here* amidst all of the bombs and the poverty, hearing the worst on the wireless every day. Worrying about you every moment. You might not even hear the whole of her story." Brent heard himself and stopped. "All the nightmares you have. All you've seen. She can't experience that, but I'll bet she would have imagined."

When Sam spoke again, Brent was so lost it took the student's second mention of his name for Brent to look up. "So, if I have a preliminary draft for you by Monday, then? Just a prospective?"

"Hmm? Yes, oh, that's fine. Monday's perfect."

Brent tucked his papers into his satchel and retrieved Diana's hairpin from his pocket. Part of him that still reveled in the adventure comics he had read tucked into his uncle's attic as a boy relished the thought of breaking into an office. Part of him wondered why he still held on to a job and a world that were so clearly behind him.

The sound of his shoes on the corridor's waxed and polished floor echoed in exclamation of no other occupant in his familiar space.

Brent took the halls at a slow pace. He approached Mariner's closed door slowly. Then he stretched out the wire of Diana's hairpin into a straight line, slid it into the keyhole, and turned. Every click ricocheted through him until the lock gave way and the door budged with the press of his palm. Feeling a surge of pride, Brent stood back with a smile. He was better at this than he thought.

There amidst the showy display of artifacts, certificates, and even an honorary degree from a university Brent hadn't heard of before were pictures of Rick in full Phrygian cap and regalia posing with students, posing by himself. Brent chuckled. This man gnawed at him. There on the shelf was the portrait of St. Boniface, the saint carrying a staff that bore an infinity cross. Its religious meaning signaled the everlasting love of God. Its appearance in atheist Rick's office would have been ironic if Brent didn't know Simon looked at it as a calling card. A symbol linking sympathizers. The painting must have been what drew Diana's attention that first day.

Brent was careful with the history around him. Fascinated by it. Moving carefully among it.

There were only the night cleaners around, so he had no qualms about turning on the light. They wouldn't be able to tell which professor was which. He approached the shelf by the window where Rick had first held *oleum medicina* up to the light, feeling prickles over his neck and down his spine. The feeling of premonition cultivated during the war spread through him, and he froze at the sound of footsteps behind him. Too slow and intentional. Brent slowly looked over his shoulder.

Not the cleaning staff or even an irate Rick.

He didn't prepare for the figure to be so quick on the draw until he was pulled into a headlock, a tight metallic cord cutting deeply into his neck. He straightened and strained. He kicked and shuffled.

The wire cut into his neck and spots blurred in front of his eyes. Brent heaved a few panicked breaths. Suffocating, he coughed, swearing he could feel the dirt and debris of the battlefield all over again.

Brent had something to go home to. He had *her* to go home to.

He squeezed the assailant's wrists. The man yelped behind him and Brent tightened his grip until their roles were reversed. He got the upper hand and turned to face a medium-sized, nondescript man, features twisted in pain from Brent's force.

Brent gave the last surge of strength in him and shoved the man into Rick's desk, upsetting several papers and a few paperweights.

Providentially, Rick barged in. "Stop that! Desist!" The man sagged away from Brent and dropped the wire. "What is this all about? Somerville!"

The man swerved to Rick and wheezed, "Richard. Who *is* this?"

"Brent Somerville. He teaches theology. He is not part of any of this."

The man took him in as if for the first time. Staring at him long and hard. Brent felt the intensity of his eyes, as cutting as the wire. The man fell back, eyes still locked on Brent.

Brent gulped a few breaths and tugged at his collar. He didn't imagine the flicker of recognition and the puzzle on the man's face.

The man turned to Rick, rubbing at the wrists Brent had squeezed. "I don't fancy men half strangling faculty members. Kindly leave my office."

"Richard . . . we agreed."

"Kindly leave. Now."

Brent blinked in surprise. "W-we should call the police." He heaved a breath. "You know that man?"

Rick extended his hand to help Brent from where he was half bent over. Brent gripped it and straightened.

"What are you doing here? Did you break into my office? Pathetic, Somerville. I know you hate me—"

"I don't hate you."

Rick raised a shoulder. "If we call the police, it would be to report *you*. I was supposed to be meeting with that man tonight. *He* didn't break into my office. How did you . . . ?"

Brent showed him the hairpin.

"Oh. Someone didn't miss their *Boys' Own Adventure Stories*."

"I wanted m-more information about that relic." Brent sputtered the first lie that came to his mind. "For Diana's church consultations."

"Still on that?" Rick's furtive glance toward the desk drawer gave away the vial's location like the Sherlock Holmes story where a false cry of fire had a woman looking toward the thing most valuable to her. At the sense of danger or intrusion, even Rick Mariner couldn't keep a poker face.

"Thank you," Brent said sincerely after a moment, feeling at the garrote line on his neck. He slumped against the desk. "But I still am not going to leave my wife to you in my will." He flexed his fingers.

"You held your own. You're stronger than I would've thought."

"Years of rowing. Hoisting people over battlefields."

"Makes me want to avoid a row with you."

Brent cracked a smile he didn't feel. This was what Diana had felt when he almost broke her wrists with his grip. He squeezed his eyes shut for a moment until a wave of dizziness passed.

"About that man, Somerville. He's an old friend. He has some interesting philosophical ideas. We were supposed to be talking about—"

"*Oleum medicina*. Are you a Communist, Mariner?"

"I don't have time for politics."

"I found Soviet propaganda in your library and a man just tried to strangle me. Someone who is a notable member of Soviet sympathizers. No, don't ask me how I know that. I just do. Something is happening. You had that pamphlet in your home library. The St. Boniface painting when the last person in the world who cares about a saint is you. There is a man called Eternity . . ."

"What are you then, Brent? A spy?"

"I'm a ginger-haired professor of theology and you *never* let me forget it." Brent hoped his flippancy distracted Rick.

"Well, I was hoping the man could help me with a few transactions."

"What sort of transactions?"

"I like antiquities, as you know." Rick stared at Brent intently. "He was always trying to get me involved. In his life. In his ideologies. I'm the first to say that they've intensified since the time we were graduate students." Mariner stretched out his arms. "But you don't need any of that, do you? You're settled."

"Settled? What does *settled* have to do with anything?"

"I had a plan, Somerville. To make my father proud. Family. Heir. The whole lot."

"You can't possibly think that—You're talking about Diana, aren't you? What does she have to do with your association with a Communist sympathizer?"

"I'm used to getting what I want. Planning it in a straight line. And I didn't get the girl. I didn't go to war. I needed *something* to do."

Brent chuckled. It hurt. "I did get the girl, you're right. But she's not a girl, Rick. Diana is a woman. A strong and capable woman."

"Because I didn't fight when you did. And I should have."

"Now is not the time. As you said, I was half strangled."

"My entire life might have been different, you know? You meet a girl like that . . ."

"Oh, for heaven's sake, Rick. You did just save my life so I'll humor you. I didn't steal her from you because I didn't know she was yours. I simply sat down in a churchyard." Brent rolled his shoulders.

"Love and lust are two different things, and you don't love her." Brent nodded toward the painting of St. Boniface. "You love relics and history."

"And Diana."

"I can't help you there," Brent said quietly. "But as much as you annoy me, I don't want you to get caught up in all of this. That man is dangerous. He's killed men, Mariner. I know you don't like me, but trust me. Find somewhere else to get your fancy artifacts."

Rick nudged at his disrupted carpet with the toe of his shoe. "I should rat you out to the dean for breaking into my office."

"You should. But now you know I have a very good grip."

❧

An unfamiliar sleek black car was parked across the road from the Clerkenwell flat when Brent approached. Seeing Simon Barre step out of it, he startled and closed the remaining distance with a quick stride. "What are you doing here? Is Diana alright? She said she was staying in."

He studied Brent under a streetlight, then narrowed his eye on his open collar. "You look a little worse for wear."

"I was attacked tonight. By a stranger trying to garrote me."

"Blast!" Simon exclaimed. It was the first moment of genuine emotion Brent had seen in the man. "Are you alright?"

"I'll live. I'd rather not make a larger deal of it to Diana than necessary, if you don't mind."

Simon nodded and followed him into the flat. They ascended to the second floor, and Brent knocked softly before creaking the door open.

Something was clearly burning on the hob and Diana came from the kitchen looking delightfully flustered, cheeks flushed with the effort of her latest cooking disaster, hair in a kerchief.

"Brent! Simon!" Her bright smile smoothed when she gazed at

Brent. "What happened!" She dashed to him. "Are you hurt?" She peeled back his collar. "Oh my heavens!"

"I was attacked in Rick Mariner's office. Someone tried to kill me." Brent pinched his nose. He studied her suddenly pale face and rallied a little. "But, my love, it's nothing a cup of tea wouldn't fix."

Several moments later, Simon sat languidly in the armchair and lit a cigarette. Brent sipped tea, and Diana presented a plate of charcoal bricks trying to be biscuits.

Brent spread his hands over his knees. "I broke into Mariner's office." He looked at Diana while addressing Simon. "We had discussed it. I never should have given the vial to him in the first place. We've never really had a rapport . . . even professionally. But I do respect his dedication to the artifact."

"Rick didn't . . ." Diana put her hand over her mouth, muffling her voice. "He wouldn't . . ."

"Rick didn't attack me. It was another man. Someone clearly there to see Mariner. The same man we saw the other night at Garlickhythe."

"And you didn't stop him?"

"I was a little worse for wear and I guess I was more interested in having Mariner explain himself."

"But Fisher can't be Eternity," Simon said. "Because he is here and I don't recall his being in Vienna."

"But he's linked to him," Diana said. "So we just need to figure out how. He's in the city. He's clearly making himself known. It won't take long. I can draw him out. He'd want to see me, Simon. He's not doing a very good job of hiding himself." Diana huffed. "Why don't you get your men on it now?"

"There's still not enough. I'm still hypothesizing."

Brent held up a hand and gestured at his neck. "I have a wounded neck that proves otherwise."

Simon nodded. "I want to do this my way."

"Because it's gotten us *so* far." Brent rolled his eyes.

Diana opened her mouth to say something, then snapped it shut. Then she looked at Brent.

"You clearly have something to say, Di," Brent said.

"It might sound . . ."

Simon blew out a long rope of smoke. "Remember, Diana, whatever you see is valid. And valued."

"You sound like a propaganda poster." Diana picked at a piece of lint on her skirt. "What if Eternity isn't just one person? You saw that infinity sign as far back as Coventry, and it was easy to think this was one man. But what if it is several men? It could be a conclave of men. A circle."

"A ring."

Diana nodded. "And they all have equal share of the information. But each man is assigned to the place they would know best to help. I don't know! But perhaps Fisher is to accomplish certain things, not for a boss but for the group. And as more and more men join the circle—"

"They spread out," Brent concluded.

"But I have been to Vienna. Where are these men getting their orders? Who is calling the shots on where they pass this file? There has to be someone in the middle."

"I don't know. But Fisher always went on about the equality he wanted after the war. No one barking orders. About no longer needing to worry about who had more. Wouldn't that ideology of his warrant some sort of equal divide?"

"It would mean that men could easily spread out across the city, all of the same . . ." Brent puzzled a moment before he settled on a military term. "Rank."

Simon rammed the butt of his cigarette into the teacup he had long since relegated to being his ashtray. He sparked another. "But there is no pattern."

"We'll find it, Simon. Maybe even Rick Mariner is part of the pattern," Diana said, then looked to Brent.

"Rick said something to the effect of using the man for relics. You know that is his wheelhouse. I truly don't believe he cares a whiff about any ideology. He's only ever had one obsession." He looked up from his teacup and recalled what Rick had said about Diana. "Make that two," he added with a pointed look. "The assailant was familiar with our relic."

"Then perhaps Rick was the man we saw at All Hallows that first night. Or the man you thought you saw."

"I maintain Rick was genuinely surprised that we had it."

The conversation fell silent a moment.

"Well, if there's one thing Fisher loved, it was showing off to me," Diana said. "Look at him now using all of these churches. He's not exactly being subtle about it." She looked to Brent. "And now he's skulking around King's meeting Rick Mariner. He may not have known we were married, but he did know you taught there."

"Everyone knew you taught there." Simon nodded. "She never shut up about you."

Brent placed his empty cup on his saucer. "Flattered."

Simon eventually saw himself out, and Diana turned to Brent, who was arranging a blanket for the sofa.

"Oh, absolutely not. You're hurt." She stroked his hairline. "You get the bed."

CHAPTER 22

Diana woke early to painstakingly keep the eggs from burning. She gave Brent the entirety of their butter ration and ensured the rashers of bacon were just as crisp as he liked them. Not only was he hurt, but the attack the night before had stirred one of the worst nightmares since his return. He kept saying Ross's name amidst several mutters.

She had pulled her knees to her chest to listen, feeling guilty she was hearing snatches of a conversation that had little to do with her. Half a dozen times, she rose in the direction of the open door, only to stop by how much worse she would make it if he accidentally hurt her. She didn't fancy any more setbacks, but listening to him wrecked her just the same.

She didn't mention the dream, rather ensured his hat and coat were ready. "No more covert break-ins." She leaned up to kiss his cheek before she studied the line at his neck. "I don't fancy the outcome."

Once he was gone, she moved Ditchfield's book that had taken almost permanent residence on the dining room table to study the Köchel Catalogue Brent brought home from the library at King's a few days before. She closed her eyes to recall Fisher's workstation. The infinity symbol at his workstation was just a mathematical figure to her.

Was the Köchel Catalogue the key to crack what was hidden in Simon's file? She had now heard the Mass in C Minor twice performed since the war. Number 427. Could the four denote the fourth letter of the alphabet, the two the second, the seven the seventh?

She knew she was close. In her early time at Bletchley, she loved the anticipatory moments when she was confused and unseeing only to subsequently translate something. Then, with Fisher, when the static would crackle and she would clearly hear a line of command or directive.

She wasn't sure how long she had been sitting there when a knock sounded on the door, and she hopped up to open it.

"Mrs. Somerville."

She took the small wrapped package to the table. For a moment, the previous sleepless night and Brent's injury prickled at her, and she gingerly untied the string around it. She was only halfway through the wrapping when the telephone rang. Brent was meeting with Sam Hunt and would miss dinner.

Diana rang off and returned to the table, taking a deep breath and ripping the rest of the wrapping. A small box that might once have held a ring now sat in her palm. She opened it slowly to reveal a shiny, brand-new farthing. Under it was a small piece of paper that merely read *1800 hours*. The same time that the classical music program was often most clearly heard when she and Fisher had listened together. He could have just sent a telegram. But there was nothing dramatic about that.

Diana traced the profile of King George on one side of the coin and then the small bird sharing a name with her architect.

"You see, Diana, building a symphony is not unlike building a church. Ah! I got your attention. All of the movements are part of the structure. They build on one another, reusing the same themes and motifs. Not unlike some of your Wren churches. Take St. Paul's, for instance." She had never thought of music like that before Fisher mentioned it. She hadn't been able to hear a piece of music without recalling him since.

She looked at the Ditchfield book a moment. She could nearly recite the passages most familiar to her because of all of the time she and her father had spent perusing it. It implied St. Paul's was always an emblem of perseverance. Ditchfield's book called it "the great national Cathedral." It was at the crux of the city's annals, history, and culture just as it was at the center of Fisher and Diana's conversations.

Diana spent the rest of the day darning, baking, and attempting to take care of Brent's ironing. To her credit, while the collars were still creased, she hadn't burnt a hole in anything. She left a plate of cold cuts, cheese, and pickles for Brent and a quick note saying she was meeting an old friend.

The brilliant dome of St. Paul's was still the highest point in the skyline and the surrounding area: Paternoster Row where once a wall had six gates, two of which were once marked by St. Paul's Alley and Paul's Chain.

The links fastened to this chain were now severed by blasted buildings.

St. Paul's was gray-blue amidst the dark, very much as it had been since a white-haired Wren ascended to the top of its dome to give his final assessment, down to the pecking pigeons that cooed at her feet.

"Farthing for your thoughts, Diana?"

"Fisher."

"We're so intelligent our thoughts must be worth far more." He seemed happy to see her. At least, interested. His brown eyes sparkled in the dim light afforded them. "But I couldn't pass up the chance to give you a Wren."

"The most important messages we have are in music. In art. In literature. In history, architecture. Relics." She emphasized the last word.

"We always had the most interesting conversations, didn't we?"

It was surreal: reconciling this man from her recent past in a hidden corner of her life with the city she knew and loved. The clouds sank low over her wrecked city and yet the moon acted as a kind of spotlight, framing St. Paul's in eerie light.

Diana took a long moment to steady her breath. "Fisher Carne, a man who merely steals another's ideas—"

"Steals?" Fisher shook his head. "No. I am repurposing what we did. You and I, we listened to those radio interceptions day in and day out. Tediously straining for something that might *mean* something until the music happened." He let out a low chuckle. "And you and I, we found a way to make the war *beautiful*. I wasn't sinking in a trench somewhere and you weren't knitting something or ladling soup."

"You were my friend."

"I *am* your friend. I want no harm to come to you, Diana. Which is why I was so absolutely set off guard when I saw that Simon Barre of MI6 had lured you to Vienna."

"You knew he was an agent?"

"Of course I did. Do you want to live like Simon does? Always jumping at the slightest whistle? Always under orders he has trouble obeying because he sees the world outside of the lines? Never finding the courage to finally get the girl because he's so married to his job?"

Diana thought of the night Simon ruefully stared into his beer glass and told her about Sophie refusing his marriage proposal.

She shook her head. "No. I don't. But you are using everything I told you about the Wren churches."

"I'm an atheist, Diana. Why would I use churches?"

"Because they transcend faith! Because they are at the core just beautiful architecture and . . ." Diana stopped. Suddenly Fisher was a step—a breath—away. "You're laughing at me."

"That autumn afternoon at Great St. Bart's, you told me. A picture on your desk with a uniformed man. In a bombed All Hallows-by-the-Tower. You're a sentimental sort. I gave it a matter of time . . ."

Diana shifted slightly so they were facing each other, and unlike with Brent who had a head on her, she was even with Fisher's chin. "You realize, Fisher, that I understand you."

"Do you?"

"Because my mind works the same way, doesn't it? We were trained for that. My father said it was a blessing and a curse—my memory." She took a breath. "And I remember what I told you. Perhaps not precisely, but generally. And whoever is listening to you isn't adhering to the orders of an expert. No. You are merely a recitation."

"Maybe it's in what you *didn't* say."

She watched his expression. At first his eyes were unreadable. Then they sparked with something he probably hoped would be unreadable. But she was ahead. "Whatever I am involved in for Simon involves you. You're right that I was in Vienna and that I was working for him. But don't underestimate me." Diana stopped. "You were baiting me. Since you determined I was working for Simon."

She recalled chess rounds at the pub and Mozart over the wireless, Fisher explaining his favorite mode of decoding cipher that mirrored the scratch books of his childhood while Diana imaginatively scraped steeples in the sky. Fisher's profile was interesting angled under a slice of streetlight.

He had almost taken her *certainty* from her. What she believed in even beyond the structures that bound her to the memory of her father and her genuine passion. She raised her arm and slapped him hard against the face, her wedding ring drawing blood from the corner of his lip. Her eyes stung with tears.

Fisher recoiled a moment, held his hand to his throbbing cheek. "You're a fool, Diana."

She shuddered, breath moving in and out, her whole body on fire with anger and fear. "You almost strangled my husband. And you betrayed what I told you in confidence."

"I knew he looked familiar. From the picture on your desk. And maybe I just always knew from all of the times you talked about him. But I didn't know it was your husband when I hurt him." Fisher looked over her now-shaking form. "Go away, Diana."

"No."

"Wasn't the Americans' Liberty Bell fashioned at the same bell foundry as Great Tom and Great Paul up above us?" He tilted his head up to the grandeur of St. Paul's. "Go and find some American churches. Go anywhere. Don't throw your lot in with Simon Barre."

"No."

"I like you, Diana, but I will destroy Simon Barre, and I don't need you following him around like a lost puppy."

"I don't follow him around like a lost puppy."

"Much like you did Villiers," Fisher said.

This stalled Diana. Straight in her tracks. Maybe Fisher was right. She could leave. Villiers had left. She was going to North America. In Diana's mind Villiers was happily in New York doing whatever she did as the sun prismed the stories of the Empire State Building.

"When was the last time you heard from Villiers?" he asked.

"I haven't. Not since that last night. You weren't there."

Fisher gave a smug smile. "Of course I wasn't there. I was starting to put everything in motion. Just as I had started doing before the blasted war. I wasn't about to get called up and left for dead in some forsaken trench. Go away, Diana. Go far away."

"You think you're so clever. That because you used all of the things I told you, you're indestructible." Diana shook her head resolutely. "You forget, Fisher, that I spent as much time with you as you did with me."

"You're smarter than you're acting. I don't know if I would have the heart to kill you. No matter how important my cause." The honesty in his voice was cold. "But I do know where your husband works."

"You clearly didn't take all of this time meeting me just to recall old times. What do you want, Fisher?"

"To remind you that you have no obligation to Simon Barre. To warn you that you can still get out of this. I *do* like you, Diana. But I won't be as lenient the next time you and Somerville cross my path. Go back to your life. Your war is over." He tipped his hat and turned.

"Don't follow me. Don't be a hero. I give you my word that I am only going to my lodgings."

She stayed frozen in her spot until his shadow disappeared down the steps and into the street. She pressed her cheek against a classical column, soothed by the chilled cement that had withstood the zeppelins of the Great War and the bombs of the most recent war. She slid onto the steps, upsetting several pigeons that scurried to peck on another step. The most familiar part of her city stretched before her until Fisher's silhouette was reduced to a blip of shadow against the settling light.

She felt close to Wren here. *"See the columns and lines?"* Diana of yesteryear had told Brent when she dragged him from his lecture one autumn afternoon. *"Did you know that the funding of the cathedral was procured by a coal tax?"* A tear snaked down her cheek. And another.

She shrugged the last of Fisher Carne from her shoulders and straightened her spine to align with the rigid lines surrounding her. She couldn't be sure how much time had passed before she rose to hop down the steps. She took a last, longing look at Wren's masterpiece. She was overtired. She was scared. But she felt the enormity of the structure towering behind her. Brent would be worried about her.

"To build a church was to atone for a sin." It was what she had told Gabriel Langer at Peterskirche in Vienna. To build a cathedral was the ultimate embodiment of grace. She never wanted to be the woman who looked back and wondered if she could have appreciated something more, if she could have spent an extra few moments conditioning her heart and mind to recognize something so it might translate into fulfillment.

───── ⁓ ─────

Brent's appointment with Sam Hunt lasted far longer than he'd anticipated when he encountered the empty flat without any singed smell wafting from underneath the door. At first he assumed Diana had just popped out for shopping, but the note she left said otherwise. She was meeting a *friend*.

As the clock ticked onward, he began running his hand over his knee. She knew this man. This dangerous man. He wouldn't have held back from strangling her if she went to one of her churches alone. If she decided to play hero or *consult* on another church.

Brent furiously leafed through the Ditchfield book and rifled around the kitchen for any indication of where she might have gone. Three times he took his coat and hat from the hook and considered barging out into the night, dashing to every blasted church to find her, but what if she called?

His ears were so intensely peeled to the telephone, he almost imagined its ring. He poured a long finger of the scotch he kept on the side table and almost never touched. Then another. He uttered many frantic prayers and a few words internalized from his time with Holt and Tibbs.

He called Simon with the number Diana had affixed to the bureau in the front room.

"I'm sorry, Somerville. She's not with me."

"She could be anywhere. It's pitch dark out there. You have to find her. You have men there who can more easily get to the churches. Every last blasted church in this city. You have a *car*. I don't even own a car!" Brent had sold his car before the war. Petrol was hard to come by, and it wasn't as if he would be around to use it.

"Did she say when she would be home?"

Brent hated the man's distracted tone. "So help me God, Simon, if she is harmed in any way for all of this rubbish you drew her into, I will—" Brent stopped. Cursed.

"I get the general idea. I'm sorry. Truly."

"You don't think she would have gone to meet this Fisher Carne, do you?"

"I do. But I also know Fisher is fond of her. I trust that will keep her safe. Please do ring when she turns up."

It was well past ten when he heard the key in the door and his frantic anger was replaced with a relief that exhaled through the whole of him. He closed his eyes a moment and unclenched his injured hand.

He didn't allow her two steps into the hallway before smothering her in his arms. His lips found the tender curve of her temple and stayed there.

"I take it you were worried," she murmured into his shoulder.

He didn't let go for a long, long time. He wanted to press her against him for every moment he imagined the worst. For every infernal tick of the clock hand. For every scenario that found her ripped from him forever.

"Brent, I can't breathe." Her voice was muffled against him.

"I don't care. Neither could I for the past two hours."

She wriggled out of his arms and looked up at him, pushing her disheveled blonde hair from her face. "I have to call Simon. Then we can talk."

Brent beat her to the phone and placed a staying hand on the receiver. "You didn't call me, Diana. You didn't telephone to tell me you would be late. That I didn't need to imagine you lying in a church somewhere strangled by piano wire or that some man with a gun had shot you in the middle of Fleet Street."

He studied her face, unpinned hair, and stretched collar. "Are you hurt? Did he hurt you?"

"I'm fine." Her voice shook a little. "I just need to call Simon. It's important."

"So I am a part of this as long as you need me to be before you cut me out to tell Simon something?"

"Brent." She gripped his hand and moved it from the telephone. "Please. I will explain later. It's an emergency."

"If you pick up that phone . . . so help me!"

Diana rubbed her hand over her arm, then wrung her hands together, then circled her fingers over her sore right wrist.

Anger spread over the back of his neck and down through his arms. "You scared me to death! What was it you said at Walbrook? That you didn't want to be alone at those churches?" He waved a hand at her.

"If I had told you, you just would have come with me," she said softly. "I needed to see Fisher. Just me."

"I would have demanded to come with you, yes. So you saw him, then? The same man who strangled me last night?"

"He wouldn't hurt me. I had the gun."

Brent shook his head. "The gun you tote as if it's the latest fashion like a handbag or a scarf? The one you couldn't actually point at someone because you wouldn't be able to harm anyone? Not even in your own defense?"

"I'm not a coward."

"No. No, you're not. But you're daft! And if you think for one moment I will allow you to pick up that receiver before you sit down and tell me exactly where you were and who you met with and what happened—"

"Oh, be quiet, Brent. You scream at me enough in the middle of the night without my having to hear it when you're awake."

Brent stiffened as if slapped. When he recovered his power of speech a moment later, his voice was low. "Sit down and I'll make tea."

Diana shook her head. Her eyes had filled with tears. "I'm so sorry. I didn't mean it. I didn't mean it." She grabbed at his vest but he turned toward the cupboard.

"Sit down, Diana. Please."

When he handed her a warm mug, she pressed it to her wrist. The tears that had started earlier still trickled. "My hand hurts." She sniffed.

"You know I'd cut off my own hands rather than hurt you again. Please don't use that against me. I was angry, but—"

"No. No. It's because I slapped him."

"Pardon me?"

She gave a low blurt of air that almost sounded like a laugh. "I slapped Fisher. For strangling you. I slapped him *very* hard." She studied her hand as if surprised at the weapon it yielded. "And that's why it hurts."

Brent took her right hand in his, then lifted it to his lips. "You need to talk to Simon?"

Diana nodded. "I do. I need him to come round for tea."

"It's almost eleven o'clock."

"He'll want to hear this." She kept her hand in his and held it in her lap. "I'm sorry I scared you."

"It was like a physical illness. It was as if . . ."

"As if there's a stone crammed in your chest and all of your nerves are sparked at once and your mind isn't screwed on straight? It's like you feel guilty for breathing, if you remember to breathe at all? And anytime there is the slightest movement you imagine things? Like a mirage in the desert? And you hear the telephone ring even when no one is calling?"

Brent blinked. "Yes."

"I know the feeling."

CHAPTER 23

May 1945
Bletchley Park

Victory in Europe celebrations erupted with beer and tossed hats, confetti and loud horns that almost drowned out the sound of the shrieks and hurrahs from every hut and cottage surrounding the main house. Diana and Villiers headed to the overcrowded pub to toast their victory with sherry. Simon dropped by for a nip, but Fisher had already left.

"Odd Fisher didn't say good-bye," Villiers said in her distinctively smooth voice. But underneath, Diana suspected the loss. It was the end of an era. *Their* era. Their leaning on one another and forming a strong quartet to see them through raised glasses at lonely Christmases and nights bemoaning how everything seemed like an impossible failure. Like the myth Fisher Carne often mentioned. Sisyphus pushed the rock up and up the hill with enduring strength only to have it nearly topple him on its way down.

Would she ever have its equal in her life? Yawning through mornings after late nights and stealing to Hut 2 for watered beer and tea? Would she ever again sit in front of a machine that would bathe her in neon rays to compensate for the lack of sunlight or see bedsheets used in such inventive ways from togas to curtains in makeshift performances by an amateur theatrical league?

Bonfires had consumed countless papers, the glowing embers floating like orange bouquets into the waning dusk. Churchill ordered everything destroyed, and her work flickered like transient stars in large barrels across the estate.

The horns and the noise on the street beyond the manor lot

continued well into the night. The clock struck one and Diana, Simon, and Villiers were still at the overcrowded pub. She had drained the last of her sherry.

"Come. I want to show you something," Villiers said. They rambled from the village and back to the Park, across the slick dew of the manicured grass with the focal point the manor house. The pond was eerily still, glassy and dark as the moon hid behind a cloud. Diana shut out the ghosts of afternoon picnics and badminton games, the late nights when her brain still fizzed with analysis reports and snatches of music.

Villiers, with uncustomary loosened shoulders and spine, led them across the grounds. An exhaust pipe sputtered, a horn shrilled, and a few inebriated men let out wolf whistles in their direction, but Diana and Villiers ignored them. Simon glared at them.

The always-locked door to Hut 11 was open and swinging slightly. Villiers went ahead of them to push it open and Simon fell in step with Diana.

The first thought Diana registered as she stepped through the hut door was that they had cloistered a part of Villiers she never knew. Machines stood tall: disengaged with wires spiraling downward in a circle like dead snakes on the cement. Villiers called them Bombes and explained how they sparked and how the circular rotors clicked into life, and Diana for all of her listening and reports couldn't fathom how such odd-looking machines could be wielded by human machination. Villiers met these strange contraptions with her height and indomitable stature.

Colored cylinders with metal adornments patterned tall, broad boards that filled the warehouse-like structure.

"They needed tall women," Villiers said with flair, "to work these machines."

But all Diana saw were wires. Her brain was fuzzy from wine and lack of sleep and the adrenaline that coursed through all of them with the disbelief that it was all coming to an end.

"And now we all get to return to our normal lives shrouded in secrets," Diana offered as they made their way back outside.

"*Normal* lives? Nothing will be normal after this, Canary. Not one thing."

Simon lit a cigarette and held the pack to Villiers, who swiftly claimed one and pressed it to her lips. A moment later he flicked the match and two orange embers were eyes against the darkness. Diana waited and the night ticked on and Simon and Sophie smoked silently.

"Why does she call you that?" Simon asked Diana. "Villiers, why do you call her that?"

"Her hair," Sophie said.

Diana smiled. "Not *just* my hair. When Villiers first met me, I was stumbling here from the train station. I couldn't see where I was going and I was scared. And when I am scared I sing."

"Just like you," Simon said to Villiers.

"*What's* like me?"

"You like to label people and make them your own."

"I never labeled you."

Simon raised an eyebrow. "Didn't you? I clearly recall a time when—"

"Oh heavens, Simon, no use dragging all that out at this exact moment when we are . . ." Villiers's voice drifted.

"We are *what*, Villiers?"

"Amidst company."

"Stop circling each other!" Diana blurted so uncharacteristically. Simon's and Villiers's lit cigarettes stalled before reaching their lips. "Say something, *anything*!" She fell back a little. "Life is short. Too short. What if you never see each other again?"

"Not see Simon Barre again? Would I be so fortunate?" But she didn't disguise her wistful tone.

"You'll miss me," Simon said casually.

"Well, I'll miss both of you." Diana raised her chin. "Because you're my friends and I am happy that I got to know you. Both of you."

Simon flicked a few ashes from his cigarette before he dropped the butt on the ground and crushed it under his heel. "Never let anyone underestimate you. Even Fisher Carne knew that most of the time you were the smartest of the three of us." He turned to Sophie. "Villiers?"

Sophie stood still a moment, a faraway look shadowing her features. Did she wonder if the valuable purpose in their lives would be tucked away forever? Diana saw the slightest flicker of vulnerability in her friend's face.

"What are you going to do now, Villiers?" Diana asked. "We can stay in touch. In London. Or are you going home?"

Sophie looked between them and took a drag of her cigarette. "I thought I'd go abroad for a while." She was looking at Simon, and something cryptic Diana couldn't decipher passed between them.

Diana stared ruefully at her shoes. Did people often feel the same way watching Diana and Brent interact? She'd still have another long bout before finding out.

"Well, well, well. What's this?" Simon's triumphant voice drew Diana's attention upward. "Are those tears in your eyes, Villiers?"

"The night is damp. An ember from one of those bonfires is still stuck in my eye," she said resolutely.

Diana smiled. "It's okay, you know. You can have a moment, Villiers."

Villiers let her shoulders drop slightly. "I don't think anything will ever be quite like this again." She sniffed.

"I suppose not." But while his voice was solemn, Diana could see he was pleased his friend was showing such a rare display of emotion.

"Maybe that's for the best." Diana sighed.

"Maybe," Simon added.

Diana looked around the emptying grounds: some faces familiar and some not passed in shadow. She was a step closer to Brent and that should have inspired jubilation. Instead she thought about Fisher Carne. About why he left early.

Back home later, buzzed with champagne and the exhilaration of the night, she fell backward on her bed and closed her eyes to the spinning colors.

"Good-bye, Fisher Carne," she whispered in the dark that shrouded her packed cases. "I'll never forget you and I wish we had said a proper good-bye."

$\sim$

November 1945
London

"Hello, Somervilles." Simon appeared in the front hallway of their flat, dark-purple shadows under his eyes and a little pale, but still cutting a dashing figure in a bespoke Savile Row suit.

"Tea?" Diana offered.

He shook his head and addressed Brent. "It's the middle of the night. Please tell me you have something stronger than tea."

Brent procured a decanter from the side table and brought two tumblers.

"Where's yours? Oh come, Di. You need it." Brent reached for a third tumbler despite her head shake. "You're shivering."

When they were settled, Diana, with a finger of the liquid in her own glass, looked at Brent first and then at Simon. "I saw Fisher tonight."

"Alone, I take it. Judging by your husband's frantic phone call."

"Fisher is smart, Simon, but I guarantee he didn't care a hang about churches before he met me. That has to be a weakness. He's working on hearsay. Maybe there's no Soviet *agent* named Eternity."

"I've been tracking Eternity for a few years now."

"I know. But you haven't *just* been doing that. You've been organizing missions in London and Vienna you can't even tell me about. I sometimes forget that I only see one slice of your world. The one that involves me. It must have crossed your mind. You're always looking for patterns."

"I'm listening."

"Eternity has the file with all of that important information: the leads, the Soviet sympathizers, those in America who would donate. But how can he be in two places at once? Vienna and London, for example?"

"It is commendable that you're thinking outside the box, but don't you think I have tried to uncover the pattern?" Simon said.

"Don't patronize her," Brent said, interceding. "If you've come to these conclusions, then why didn't you tell her?"

"This is not the only city where I have traced him—"

"There's a lot about what you're making *her* do that shows that you might be making it up as you go along."

"Brent, it's alright."

"No. He's right," Simon said. "I apologize for my tone, Diana."

She nodded. "For one, the Innere Stadt in Vienna is full of churches within proximity to one another. Here in London we have several bordered by the London gates. For people returning from the war, from the field, from illegal access into the country, they would need a perimeter. Most of these men do not know London. Brent, remember the fellow we followed from Fleet Street?"

She looked between them. "Then they would need ways to signal one another so they could swap messages and learn where to meet a contact or where to find a safe space for the night. They could be on a scavenger hunt for a new meeting place or even to recognize a friend. If this is a ring, an establishment, then there would be different levels of power and not everyone would be granted the same level of clearance for some of the more top-secret messages. The exchanges of information beyond just establishing an infiltration."

"I'm listening," Simon said.

"We always look for patterns. What if music is a pattern? The list for the Sunday order of hymns. Fisher taught me about the numerology in music. If eternity is a ring of spies—or at least enthusiasts—they would need to have a common understanding. This goes in line with what Fisher is doing. Finding common places with easy access. People can move in and out."

Simon stubbed his cigarette into the coffee cup. "Well..."

"*Well*," Brent emphasized, "maybe this is the dead end. Maybe you have Diana roaming around churches and meeting this Fisher in the middle of the night and it means nothing."

Something flashed in Diana's eyes. The wheels in her head were turning. A theory not unlike her propensity for mixing churches and music, Mozart and numerology, lodged itself just as Simon flicked a match and lit another cigarette.

"You have no idea how much I need Diana," Simon finally said.

"You're right, I don't," Brent replied. "You're a smart man, Simon. A brilliant man by Diana's accounts. You work for the Secret Intelligence Service and no doubt did your bit for the war effort. But by all means, you lured an architectural historian from the Foreign Office."

"Brent!" Diana sent him a warning glare. "Simon, do you remember the old law of sanctuary? If someone was on consecrated ground and protected by the church they could not be harmed or incarcerated?"

"An old law."

"A very old law." Brent nodded.

"Maybe in practice. But in theory"—Diana warmed to her idea—"if Eternity is a ring of men moving through cities to find safety to protect themselves while passing on these official secrets, then of course the churches would make sense."

Simon nodded. Diana looked to Brent.

"What do you actually want of us, Simon?" Brent asked. "Diana keeps doing more and more for you, and I did what I could at King's."

He gestured to the scar above his open collar. "So far things have been alright. We saw that man with a gun. We followed a few people. There's definitely something ominous happening, but from what you've told me, Diana, you have fulfilled your promise to Simon. So why don't we take tonight as an end to all of . . . whatever this is?"

Diana swallowed. Simon's blue eyes settled on hers.

"I can't tell you everything. But you're important." Simon smiled at Brent. "And so are you, Somerville." He moved to rise.

"You can't be leaving," Brent said. "Then what was this meeting for?"

"I trust you, Diana." Simon sat back down. "I truly do. I have to go to Vienna. On orders. They like my setup there. They like Gabriel Langer." He shifted in his chair. "Langer might turn out to be more helpful than I could've imagined. I have an agent that, well, is not officially under my guidance but I've sort of unofficially taken that role anyway."

"Unofficial," Brent scoffed. "You seem to be quite good at that."

Simon ignored him. "I don't have the manpower to determine every man coming in and out of the city on your theory, Diana. No matter how likely it is you're correct."

"You only had an outline," Diana said.

"I only had a hunch," Simon corrected.

"I don't believe that." Brent shook his head. "What's truly in it for you? Why do you need Diana?"

"Her knowledge of the Wren churches—"

"No." Brent held his hand out to stall Diana, who wanted to intervene. "No. You could find *anyone*."

Simon stiffened and straightened his shoulders. "Luckily I didn't have to find anyone. I had *her*." He raised his glass to his lips and tipped more liquid down his throat. "Fisher likes you." Simon looked at Diana.

"He said he would destroy you, and I don't think he'll remember he likes me if I get in the way of that."

Brent slammed his glass onto the table. "Find someone else for your hunches, Simon."

"I wish I could. But Diana's not *anyone*, is she?"

And with a sad smile and a final drain of his glass, he left.

CHAPTER 24

December 1945

Diana knew end-of-term exams and the Christmas break had cleared out many of the students and faculty. The snow offered a fresh white blanket to the tumbled stones on the street, even as the first Christmas of the recent peace felt so different from others before it.

The merchants' shelves were still bare, clothing rations still in place, sugar and bread hard to come by. Tinsel and holly clashed against recently painted shop windows and women exchanged recipes with rather creative alternatives to the ingredients hard to come by.

Diana even found herself missing the small traditions she had shared at Bletchley: saving their sugar coupons, trying not to burn biscuits on the stove, having Fisher and Simon around for a small party and gift exchange.

And of course she thought back to the few times she had been able to meet Brent on his leave. They hadn't gone to London but had met in Brighton and even in Calais. Snow had fallen and carols sifted from candlelit churches in the few moments Brent and Diana wandered from their rooms. In those fleeting moments it was no longer his soft voice and their conversations that had been ripped from her but his physical presence. He taught her how to have several forms of wordless conversation, and while she cherished the obliterated lines between them, it made it harder and harder for him to be ripped from her when the train took them in opposite directions. Yet she had made the most of every second.

She supposed she was still making the most of every second.

Since the evening Brent had pressed her so close to him upon her return from meeting Fisher, she had noticed a difference. The line on his neck had faded and the bruises on her wrists were a ghost of a memory. While he still was adamant that he occupy the sofa, she occupied it with him for longer and longer even as the nights fell shorter.

Diana hadn't had another message from Fisher or a clear directive from Simon. Brent was intentionally pursuing her. She could sense him as strongly as she had that first night. She had pulled Brent to St. Bride's and Mary-le-Bow. They held a long afternoon at Magnus the Martyr, where carols echoed to the rafters and she wondered if each minor chord meant something. When it became clear that all that was on offer was music light in tone and hope burdened by the recent past, she allowed herself to enjoy it.

Snow sparkled in the sky as they walked into the early dark, adding a clean sheen to the city whose scars and bruises she saw all too clearly despite the busy traffic, people managing trees and holly boughs through the dark streets, and the festive lights on the corners.

Brent had been around more often lately, but she could tell a restlessness stirred within him. Was it because he missed his routine at school or because of his routine at school? When she had first met him, passion radiated from his voice and a light shone in his eyes when he talked about his lectures and his students. She certainly had his passion, but she wondered if his vocation still did.

The holiday season ushered in nostalgia, not for the recent lean and horrible years but for the last time the world seemed as calm and bright as the stanza wistfully caught by a violin bow from a street musician on the corner.

It wasn't until they slowed and she looked around that she noticed Brent watching her with intent. "What is it?"

"You."

Diana smiled. "What about me?"

"You don't see what I see, do you? When I step into those churches, when we're out here on the street." He interlaced their fingers. "You're seeing what it *could* be. What it's going to be. You're seeing the potential."

Diana merely nodded. She'd snatch all of the tender moments she could, knowing that eventually good things would be thrown in their path again.

They took their time on the way to the flat, allowing night to settle around them and the snowflakes to dissolve on the ground. The moment the key turned in their front door, the telephone rang. Simon Barre's former SOE contact had intercepted an encrypted message through his agent that he believed belonged to Eternity, which was addressed to London. They were just random letters in the Playfair cipher style and part of the message had been ripped away.

Brent took the opportunity to steal into the bedroom to make up for another sleepless night.

"So I've the date and time but no location," Simon said. "Tomorrow night. Eight o'clock. My understanding is that there will be a pass-off. I won't get back in time. I need you to find out where it'll be and go and get the file."

"How do you know it's going to be the file that will be exchanged?"

"I don't. Not exactly. It says *exchange*. Not of what."

"How did you decode it?"

"I didn't. My associate did. Train ticket stub."

"So this is not official."

"That man who died at Magnus the Martyr, Petrov? He was one of ours, officially looking into possible espionage activity in London. And my team believes they have enough to go on in terms of closing in on Soviet agents here. Agents who have nothing to do with Eternity."

He stopped talking, but Diana was too stunned to fill the silence.

"I'm not getting authorization because Petrov tried and failed and because MI6 is more willing to fund my work in Vienna. They like the small team I've assembled there. They won't risk me and they won't risk embarrassment. Langer and my SOE agent have a lead they're willing to pursue in Vienna. I can't be in both places at once. They feel that what they've found in Vienna deserves more manpower and takes precedence."

"What have they found in Vienna?"

"I can't tell you."

"Ha! That's rich."

"It could be a wild-goose chase."

"You don't say."

"Diana, if this file exists and if Eternity—agent—spy ring—exists, then we've won. Not just my hunch but my belief in you."

"And what if it's nothing?"

"Then it's nothing. This is my last shot at this. We've set up at the Sacher Hotel. I'm moving to Vienna for the foreseeable future."

"Oh."

"It's the last time I'll ask you for something other than a friendly tea."

"But you've been so sure of your pursuit of this."

Simon took a beat. "Apparently what's in the file affects four different countries. Gabriel Langer is trying his best. He and the agent I mentioned to you have established an operation here, but—" Simon groaned. "Anyway, we need the information that's in this file. You have to get it for me. But I can't decrypt the location of this bloody message."

Diana worked her bottom lip. Sunday night at eight. "Maybe I can figure it out. It's likely a church. Fisher clearly likes playing with us. Let me get a pen and paper."

He read the random sequence of letters to her and she drew out the usual grid that was the next step in making sense of the message while listening to him.

"Be careful, Diana. I'll get back as fast as I can."

"To pack."

"Yes." Simon was silent a moment. "I sometimes wonder if I made this all up because I wanted it to be true."

"You didn't make up Fisher garroting people with piano wire," Diana said. "Or nearly killing Brent."

"True. Maybe I just didn't want it to end. You. Theories. Problem solving."

"You're a Secret Intelligence Service agent. That's your whole life."

"It was nice to have someone else involved. Beyond briefs and meetings and orders."

"That's called friendship, Simon. I'd meet you for tea even if you don't send me to look in the shadows or consult on churches. Brent too."

"You mean that?"

"I'll find the location. Then you and I will pick up where we left off . . . as friends."

"Yes."

"You're allowed to be human, you know. Friendship is not a weakness. You don't need to barter or exchange for it. Did you ever think that if you had asked me this favor I might have done it anyway?"

When Simon didn't immediately answer, Diana thought of how she had said something quite similar to Villiers.

"Would you have?" he finally asked.

"We'll never know, will we? But I *am* your friend."

After she rang off, her mind was filled with long nights at the pub and the camaraderie she found when she least expected it with Villiers, Fisher, and Simon. A life she didn't share with Brent much as he couldn't share Tibbs, Holt, and Ross with her.

"What's all this, then?" Brent said over her shoulder a few moments later.

"Every scrambled message like this one needs a key. And we don't have it. Simon and Langer—his associate in Vienna—have determined something will happen tomorrow evening. The exchange of this file we have been in pursuit of, but they don't know where."

"Like a crossword puzzle?"

"It's not a crossword puzzle. It's a standard arrangement of letters attributed to Lord Playfair that is a common way of sharing an encrypted message. It's usually a word from a book or a message. But for now it will be guesswork."

"How did you learn all of this?"

"We had a lot of time on our hands. Fisher likes puzzles," Diana said.

Diana told Brent to go ahead and sleep in the bedroom while she played some more. She rapped her pencil on the table. Simon had entrusted her with a great deal. His job, it sounded like.

She spent a sleepless night at the dining room table, robe tied tightly over her pajamas in the middling dark, brewing several cups of watery tea. She was close. She rearranged the letters and scratched out a few possibilities, but the location evaded her. "Blast!" She crumpled up another piece of paper and tossed it across the table.

After peeling off a fresh sheet from the notepad, she pressed her pencil nub to the top and started a list of prospective places. This was Fisher. He would work within a certain radius and almost certainly within churches.

She hadn't realized she was drifting until she looked up from the pillow of her folded arms to find Brent at her shoulder. She blinked up at the clock, which was just chiming three.

"You have to go to bed, Diana. You have to sleep. You'll be ill if you don't." He gently gathered the hair at the nape of her neck and parted it like a curtain to press a gentle kiss on her neck. She slid around to turn into him and press her forehead into his shoulder. He rested his chin on her head. "I'm worried about you."

"You're one to talk," she murmured.

He smelled wonderful and he was so near their breath mingled.

She gazed up at him, and her wide, tired eyes must have had their desired effect. She yawned. "I can't move."

"Can't you?" The smile in his voice was warm. "That won't do. You need someone to carry you."

"Who could that be?" Her voice sounded thick and sleepy.

"Arms up, sweetheart."

Diana extended them and a moment and swoop later her legs were over the curve of his elbow and her head in the slope of his neck. "You're very strong."

"A blessing and a curse," he said dryly.

He laid her gently on the bed and adjusted the pillow beneath her head. Her eyelids were anvils. She couldn't tell if she was totally asleep or still hovering in a slight second of consciousness when she spoke to the shadow she sensed behind her closed eyes. "I fell in love with you the moment I heard your voice."

"Did you?"

Diana nodded against the pillow. "The very moment I heard it. I never wanted . . . I never wanted . . ." She drifted, the rest of her sentence tucked inside the smile she was sure still parted her face.

───── ❧ ─────

When she woke, she sat up too quickly, squinting in the light spilling through the blinds. Diana creaked the bedroom door open and tiptoed past Brent, who was sprawled on the sofa. She retrieved the milk bottle and the newspaper from outside the front door. She set both on the table with the intention of making tea and checking the social listings to see if anything of note was happening at one of the churches where a pass-off of the file might take place between Fisher and one of his group.

She turned to Brent and smoothed back his hair until the scar at his forehead was exposed. Sleep had shifted his pajama top, too, and Diana had full vantage of his parted collar, fallen open like a book at a favorite spot. Her eyes lingered a moment on the beginning of scars she had yet to see.

Had he woken in the night? She could often hear him through the open door and would jump up and check to make sure he settled. It would be worse if she approached him and risked him hurting her. Not that she was afraid of a few bruises on her wrists, but she knew the potential it had to rip the seams patching their relationship.

She pressed a gentle kiss to his forehead.

He stirred but not enough to wake. She left him where he was and put the kettle on. She gingerly turned the pages of the newspaper, passed headlines of reconstruction and the housing crisis, campaigns for political parties, and the rising price of bread and potatoes.

Then a performance of Mozart's Requiem that evening at Great St. Bart's. It would be dark and atmospheric and rather like the concert she had attended with Gabriel Langer those many weeks ago in Vienna. Music would distract from any meeting, and Fisher *loved* the Requiem. Köchel Catalogue #626. Requiem Mass in D Minor. Unfinished by the composer before his death.

"*Oleum medicina,*" she said aloud. The legend that Rahere might have brought a relic back from his pilgrimage to Rome. Yes, another thing Diana had told Fisher during their long afternoons working. She never anticipated conversations on relics would be made manifest upon her return to London. Couldn't have dreamt she would return to All Hallows and find holy medicine in the first moments of her reunited love story. The relic Rick had that Fisher wanted the night Brent was hurt.

"What's that, darling?" Brent said sleepily.

She closed his mouth with her own in answer. He threaded his fingers through her unbound hair as their lips met again and again.

"Fisher needed me to know," she said a few happy moments later, her head light, her heartbeat quickening.

"What's this about?"

"He needed someone to know how clever he was." She set two pieces of slightly burnt toast on his plate and placed the butter dish and marmalade beside it.

"So you know the location? You cracked your grid?"

"Yes." Diana's voice was tinged with pride. "St. Bart's, Brent. I told him about Prior Rahere. I told him about meeting you. That didn't necessarily mean the Roman churches I imagined: All Hallows or Walbrook or any of that lot. Not even Magnus the Martyr. Fisher chose the church I told him about. St. Bart's." She stared at her tea mug absently a moment. Then to a corner of the ceiling. "It's the perfect location. It makes me think that all along . . ." She stopped, apparently long enough for him to notice.

"Keep going."

"It's close to a hospital. St. Bart's isn't even a stone's throw away. It is tucked away from the main thoroughfare but still within the gates. Still central enough that you could direct someone unfamiliar to the city there by landmarks." It would be the perfect place for the exchange of information.

While Diana and Brent were prowling around Wren churches, Fisher had found a perfect hideaway.

Diana slid the paper to him across the table. "Mozart."

"Again?" Brent said.

"Still."

◦━◦

Brent remembered the hollow feeling of sitting in St. Bart's and deciding to trust her because he *loved* her and because he knew her war activity was a government-held secret. But Simon was in Vienna and they were in London. Brent had a scar on his neck to add to the war wounds on his forehead and left hand. He also had a very recent memory of waiting for her to return.

"This is different than the other times," Brent said. "Before we weren't guaranteed a meeting, but this is intentional—which means it is probably more dangerous."

"Of course it is. This is finally something *concrete*."

"Then we should leave it to the professionals."

"He asked me. And I gave him my word. I keep my word."

"I know."

"Thank you."

"I know because I went to Scotland Yard and learned you signed a piece of paper keeping your secret from me."

Diana froze. "I beg your pardon?"

"And if I ask what you did during the war and you tell me, then you are as good as a traitor. But what you are doing *after* the war is what is keeping us apart, Di." He grabbed her hand. "We are getting so close to being who we are *together*. This just seems like recklessness. With the exception of your meeting Fisher, I know you never once deliberately led us into danger. But this is the file men would *kill* for, remember? I know. I fought a war. Your friend tried to kill me."

"I have no secrets from you when it comes to anything at the core of who we are. I have not lied about my vows to you. I have never once acted against what I promised to you."

"Diana, can't you see? This is more than that. This is you deliberately deciding to put your life at risk." He used his left hand emphatically, and the melded fingers were more pronounced under the light. "You told Simon this man would stop at nothing to destroy him. Even *you* if you got in his way. Darling, doing this puts you in the way."

She swiped at her eyes. "Why didn't you tell me you went to Scotland Yard?"

"Oh, honey, if you want to play that game . . ."

"I warred with keeping a secret from you, sure. But with that secret I was able to do more for the war, more for you than I ever would have by staying here."

"For me?"

"I believed I was doing good."

"We all did what we had to do given the circumstances," Brent said. "But the difference, Di, is I never wanted to experience anything like this again, and you want to keep jumping in."

"My experience wasn't yours, it's true," Diana said softly. "I didn't have a horrible time looking at horrible churches and spending weeks in hospital. I didn't watch men die, Brent. I felt good at my job. And I made friends, just like you did. But I didn't . . ." She stalled. "I didn't lose anyone. The closest I came to losing someone was you. I didn't hear about your injury for such a long time. So I was worried sick about you, and you didn't need to worry about me, and I wonder if that is part of what's making this so difficult. We're coming *so* close."

"I deserve to worry about you. It's part of what we agreed to. Sickness. Health. War. It is my privilege, my dear, to worry about you. I will whether you are strolling out of our flat or nursing a common cold." He sighed. "You don't have to feel guilty because you were safe during the war. It's what I wanted. I don't want to tell you about my horrific experience because I don't want you to ever know. And I don't want you to live wondering if every last second will be your last."

"But I *did* live like that. For heaven's sake, we had bombs raining from the sky. At any moment we could have been invaded. I was *scared*. Not in the same way you were out there at the Front. But I was terrified: more for you than myself, I think. Because every time you left I had to try and imagine living without you again." Diana lowered her voice a decibel. "Decide what you want me to be, Brent. You think I should use my talent and then stop me when I am able to put that talent into action. I have been able to help Simon."

"By continuing everything I fought to stop. Don't you see? I had *one* job in the war, Diana. I carried wounded men with Holt, Tibbs, and . . . and R-Ross. We were *one* unit. We had to think together and act together. We had to share a common mind and purpose. And that focus was how we saved men. I made it through knowing I would come back to you. I arrived and you didn't. I know you cannot tell me all that happened during the war. And I know you were helping Simon, but I still don't know *why* he was more important."

She gripped his arm so tightly the knuckles on her hand were white. "I got sloppy, Diana. That's what happened. Because I was tired. And sick of it. It was raining and I lost my grip and that one wretched mistake . . . My fingers wouldn't grab and hold to my end of the stretcher and men *died* because of it."

He stretched the muscles in his wounded hand, then gestured at his left shoulder. "And I just have a few scars. And now I want to protect you because I couldn't protect Ross. And you want to do something stupid and dangerous."

"Our entire lives have been dangerous, Brent."

"But it doesn't have to be that way anymore. I can't hear a door slam without startling. It was one thing to pursue these men in public churches at concerts. It's another now that Simon is asking you to go into a meeting that could be potentially dangerous."

"But if we don't do it, then everything I did is for nothing. Everything I did for Simon."

"What about for me?"

"You don't understand."

"You gave to your country, Di. Just like me. You did work for the Foreign Office and signed the Official Secrets Act. You are brave and wonderful. But I fought for the right to protect you. And I lost a mate I couldn't protect. So it's in his honor I have to say we leave this for Simon."

"What if having *me* means having a woman who has learned how to be alone?" Diana took a breath. "I don't need to fall into you every second. I *want* to." She cupped his face. "There's a difference between my *needing* you and my *wanting* you. Can you handle that? I carried the burden of the act I signed . . . without you. But I am not the only one who is lying. Something happened to you on the Front.

And as long as you keep refusing to let me in, we will circle around each other. What I did was wrong, but you swore yourself to me and it means letting me into every last corner. It means letting me share all of you. But you won't. You'll keep fighting your war silently."

Brent let out a long breath. "I already fought my war, Diana. And I would go through every last horrifying moment and trench again if it means you are standing here. But us doing this tonight . . . I won't allow you to endanger your life."

"Allow me? Brent, listen to yourself."

"Di . . ."

"Because it's easier to cherish and hold your pain in a deep, dark place, isn't it? There's something almost reverent about keeping it to yourself. If it's your own, you don't have to be scared and you don't have to be vulnerable."

"No. I don't. And I never will." Diana took a long breath and straightened her shoulders before she consulted the clock in the kitchen. "I have to finish what I started."

"You would deliberately disobey me?"

"The Brent Somerville I married would never ask me to *obey* him. He'd want us to make all of our decisions together."

"There it is. The solution to the mystery we've been circling around since you returned from wherever you were. I am not the Brent Somerville you married."

The warmth of their morning drained. She dressed and affixed her green hat over her brushed and curled blonde hair.

Diana tilted her chin up. "I love you, Brent. I've loved you since the moment I met you and I will love you until the day I die." Her eyes locked with his as they stood silently.

"So you're going anyway?" His voice was strangled.

"He asked me. I am armed. It's a concert. There will be several people. It's far safer than the war we both fought, isn't it?"

When he didn't answer, she smiled sadly, swerved to open the door, and clicked it softly behind her.

CHAPTER 25

Brent stared at the closed front door for a long while. Looking back, he could see nothing that suggested she would deliberately go against his wishes. But looking back hadn't served him well, had it? Peering through Diana's lens, he should have seen the potential of her choosing to go anyway.

On some level he knew his stubbornness wouldn't last, that he would eventually give in, follow her to St. Bart's, and throw himself in front of her if it meant protecting her from her promise. But that level was buried under layers of hurt and anger. Did she not know what he had seen? What he continued to see when he closed his eyes or let his brain get idle? What form of love—Greek or otherwise—allowed for her throwing what he had been through back at him?

Because as much as he wanted to sink through the mud and listen to the moans and wails of the men whose lives were draining before his eyes for the good of King and Country, he needed a face instead of a platitude, and on the gray days when even faith was hard to hold to and the verses so impressed in his theses and so manifest in the churches she loved were too hard to recall, he just saw her.

He did a wonderful job of pretending to begin an abstract for a seminar on Paul's first trip to Spain. He turned on the wireless. As she was roaming the city at night, who might be following her? His chest closed in so tightly it was hard to recover breath.

If Diana hadn't stepped up to his bench in St. Bart's, would he have wandered from girl to girl, tasting their lips and feeling their curves with no certainty of commitment or eternity? Would he have found it as hard to return to London and reconcile the world he saw on the battlefield with the one he was trying to settle into like an overlarge sweater?

What she didn't realize and what he had been too stubborn to say was that the moment she clarified her stance on needing him and wanting him, he had fallen more deeply in love with her than he thought possible. Her declaration settled beyond the misunderstandings, the lies, and the cracks in their relationship. Diana was her own person. She was the woman some part of his heart had always imagined down to the stubborn tilt of her chin.

All of the words framed as odes when Brent made promise after promise on the field, after breathlessly setting down an empty stretcher and lifting his arms to the sky, failed. The bargains and pleas that he would never take her for granted or raise his voice at her again. And here he was deserting her? He thought long and hard, his hand hovering over the hat on the stand.

Not even a quarter hour after she departed, he followed her, unarmed, into the night ahead.

———— ✿ ————

Smithfield and Clerkenwell were historical neighbors with a hundred stories to tell, from Dickens to Rahere's pilgrimage to Rome, where he had been so moved by the ancient city that he'd built an abbey that withstood zeppelins and Henry VIII's desecration of the monasteries. In Great St. Bart's there was Bolton's window where the prior could peer out and watch the pious monks throughout their day. The music echoing over each stone at advent. And the neighboring St. Bartholomew the Less tucked into the narrative of this priceless square of London, serving the famous hospital where Sherlock Holmes had met Dr. Watson for the first time.

The yard stretched out to the ancient gatehouse and beyond, stripped of the light that spread over it the afternoon Diana had met Brent. Sleek cars and sputtering streetlights mingled with the promise of the church that held a wonderful moment of her past and the next step into her future.

She took a last few precarious steps through the yard she knew well, to a stone interface that looked like a patchwork quilt even before the war: a precursor of what all of the churches she loved might eventually look like when the rebuilding began.

As soon as she creaked open the heavy door and stepped inside, music caught the hollow hall in a net. She recalled the Requiem from one of Fisher's informal lectures. Diana straightened her shoulders and inhaled. She would do what Simon required. She felt in her waistband for her gun. Maybe Brent was right. Would she have the nerve to fire it? Or would she merely wander around with it as an accessory?

She missed the sure feel of Brent beside her, but the music was enough to fill her with courage at the moment. Even though she wanted him down to the toes of her shoes.

As she stepped through to the long aisles of the sanctuary, mournful chords blasted the tapestry of the ancient pillars and rafters. *"One thing about Mozart,"* Fisher would say, *"he's always surprising."* She sat at the very back in a cold, empty chair and surveyed the middling light in hopes of recognizing Fisher or one of the men who had shadowed the door of one of the churches she and Brent had attended since her return.

Sure enough, Fisher soon entered on the opposite side of the section in which she was seated. He casually removed his homburg and trench and slid into a seat five rows from the back.

As the chorus reached a discordant crescendo, Diana watched the man next to Fisher shifting in his seat while reaching inside of his jacket. The face was familiar. It was the Russian man who followed them before they subsequently followed him in the direction of Smithfield. Perhaps Great St. Bart's was his destination all along.

She felt the weight of the Russian man's cold gaze as he watched her intently. Fisher didn't follow the man's gaze. The Requiem always had an effect on him. The "Lacrimosa" movement, especially. She recalled it crackling through the wireless before smoothing back to the messages they were supposed to be hearing.

He blinked back to their world after the piece ended as if just returning from a faraway place.

Diana resettled her handbag on her lap. What was she going to do if she didn't find a way to intercept the inevitable pass-off? Point her gun and demand the folder be passed over to her?

This was a perfect place to do *any* business. It was tucked away and sometimes forgotten largely in part because it was unscathed by the war. Its patched exterior and cold stones within weren't the subject of propaganda or rallies to rebuild. It was almost hidden. But not *too* hidden from markers that would make it easy to find. For anyone unfamiliar with London, it could be a halfway house for safety. For sanctuary.

"Is this seat taken?"

Diana swerved at the soft voice at her ear, then smiled. "Brent."

She started to speak, but he placed a finger to his lips. She recognized it as the apology it was.

Together, they pretended to focus on the concert, but she could read the stiffness in his posture just as she was sure he could sense the accelerated thrum of her heartbeat. The fedora over his jostling knee nearly fell as he was having trouble keeping still.

She set her hand over his while he kept his eyes straight ahead. Diana dismissed the discordance between them. There was little time to feel petty about Brent. Each movement of music prickled the back of her neck. She could hardly sit still through the penultimate "Agnus Dei" and then froze when the final "Communio" movement saturated the tiles and inlaid tombstones, whose etchings were worn nearly to oblivion through time.

She stole several peripheral glances to the other side of the quire. The man with Fisher certainly had something tucked into his jacket. She might have been the least qualified person to sleuth about London, but it was clear that Simon was closing in on amateurs.

Another figure occupied the space opposite Fisher, but Diana didn't risk looking over completely. As such, she could only determine a third with nothing to distinguish him other than he had failed to remove his hat in church. The audience shuffled after the second encore. Diana, whose hand was now tightly on Brent's, knuckles white, waited. "Fisher is here." She inclined her head. "Someone is with him but I can't see his face. But he's wearing a hat in church! The man over there is the same one we followed and you confronted," Diana said. "I have watched that man since I got here, Brent. He's reached into his jacket several times. I think he has something."

"*The* something?"

She nodded. "And another man joined them." Brent started to glance over, but Diana put a stalling hand on his kneecap. "Oh look! The one man is leaving." She only saw his back as he slid into the chapel tucked into the north transept across from them, but it was the gait of the man who had followed them. "We'll split up." She felt under her blazer and blouse. "Take the gun."

"I will not take the gun, Diana."

"But, Brent . . ."

"But nothing." He pressed a finger to her lips. "The reason I am here at all is because you're asking me to. Keep the gun. I'll find Fisher and the other man." Brent's gaze searched the room around them. "Fisher never carries a gun, isn't that what you said? Just that bloody piano wire. I can handle him. You can't. I'll find that folder. Whatever the cost."

Diana reached up and kissed him on the cheek. "You're strong, Brent Somerville. Stronger than you know. *As* you know." She didn't want to fathom the sensation of her lips on Brent's jawline—as they were now—as a last kiss, but she accepted it. Leaned into it. "We can do this."

I can do this was so singular and cold to her. But *we*? There was a lot to wrap in two letters.

———— ✦ ————

Brent lingered by a column near the high altar as musicians finished returning their instruments to their cases and collecting their music and stands. While the view to the Lady Chapel and its ambulatory were blocked by the pulpit, he knew that was where they were headed and gave them a few paces ahead of him.

Brent strolled with a smile, pretending to look around as the last occupants filed out. He stared up at Bolton's oriel window—back to the grille and gate and hallowed space of the Lady Chapel beyond.

He tucked his fedora under his arm and strode confidently over the tile. His bearing and determination were something inherited from the army: *Even if you don't feel it, pretend. Make people feel as if you know every last thing you are doing.*

Nooks and crevices were nestled into the hallowed space of the medieval priory. A jigsaw puzzle as complicated inside as the patches covering its interface and the chapel itself a secret to the casual attendant. The enclosed stone of the chapel evidently a sound chamber so clearly did it preserve the echo of his footsteps the moment he crossed through.

Brent recognized Fisher immediately. Surprisingly, he had a gun exposed and waiting in his right hand. It wasn't until Brent strolled into moonlight provided by the broad arched windows that he fell back in surprise. A second man was there.

"Rick."

Mariner looked at Brent pleadingly. "I took your advice, Somerville. I came to tell him to find his artifacts elsewhere, that I didn't want anything to do with him."

"I don't know whether to be more surprised by that or seeing you in a holy place," Brent jested while trying to get his bearings.

"But I'm not too keen on his decision," Fisher said. "Your wife is the reason I chose this place. For meetings, to pass important documents. The other churches were an easy ruse to intercept men and lead them here. Once I had my eye on procuring *oleum medicina*, I got an idea. Diana once told me about a relic rumored to have been obtained by Prior Rahere during his pilgrimage to Rome." Fisher adjusted the gun aimed at Rick while quickly sweeping his gaze over the perimeter. "Nice place. She told me she had met the love of her life in its churchyard."

"I saw a Russian man one night," Brent said. "Doing a rather abysmal job of winding his way through London. But near Smithfield. I believe he's the man Diana is with now. She'll ensure she gets whatever file he collected from you."

Fisher didn't say anything. He didn't even look at Brent while explaining. "I was supposed to meet Mariner that night. At All Hallows. I confess I didn't make you out, but I knew Diana immediately. Four years and you learn a person's bearing.

"*Oleum medicina,*" Fisher continued. "It's worth a fortune. I *need* a fortune. There are influential men who want it. This can get me in with them in other places. At higher levels. You found it because he left it for me."

Fisher gestured to Mariner with his gun. "Exactly as we had planned. He would set it down just so and I would retrieve it. But he didn't do a very good job of hiding it or shutting up about it. Another acquaintance of mine showed up just as I left, clearly saw you two and left."

Fisher was the man Brent had sensed in shadow. And his acquaintance the one with the gun startled by a scene he wasn't expecting to find.

"He"—Fisher indicated Rick—"has some of the connections I want. But now he was *just* telling me he changed his mind." He cocked the gun. "Which is unfortunate, because he knows too many men and talks too much."

"I thought you didn't use guns," Brent said. "Just piano wire." He revealed the scar on his neck.

"You almost killed me. I figured it was about time I took precautions."

Brent startled. The man was two moments from firing at Rick. Brent considered yelling for help, but he didn't know what situation Diana was in. He was used to thinking quickly. He straightened his shoulders and fell on the man's weakness: They were all just amateurs in a game fashioned by war. They were all making it up as they went along. If Brent could speak to Fisher's incompetence . . .

"We met and followed the man you were with earlier," Brent told Fisher. "Mariner may have said a few too many stupid things, but it isn't like your other *associates* are competent. They stumble around in dark churches and tuck into trench coats like a Bogart film. It's not exactly a top-notch organization you're running here, is it?"

"London is a complex equation. It's a puzzle. A maze."

"London was *toppled*. It's easier to see your way around because there's more sky! You're sending them randomly around based on what you heard my wife say. Great St. Bart's?" Brent would ramble if it kept Fisher from pressing that gun any farther at Mariner or flexing his finger. "Not too far from the usual haunts of your run-of-the mill tourist. Not a far stroll from Fleet Street if you know where to go. Or if you look to St. Paul's as a compass. Good work on the St. Paul's Watch, eh? You heard about them? Diana never shut up about them. Dedicated their lives so the steeple and dome survived the bombs. It boosted morale. See, you must *hate* Churchill and the society we're attempting to return to, and yet you're appropriating that society for your gain. A tenuous one, I'll grant you."

Fisher scoffed. "You sound like your wife."

"How *dare* you pay me such a magnanimous compliment while you point a gun at my . . . friend? colleague? nemesis?" Brent chuckled weakly. "To Mariner. This is the longest the man has gone without talking. Ever."

Brent's eyes locked on Fisher. The man was prepped for a challenge and met him head-on. "*Try me,*" the flash in his brown gaze seemed to say. Brent didn't move, didn't flinch.

Rick cast Brent a pleading look. He was terrified. Brent knew the look from the war. Brent *wore* the look during the war.

Fisher surprised Brent beyond any instincts honed by war when he shot at the first word that left Mariner's mouth in a plea.

Mariner's limp frame sank to the stones.

Brent fell back. The Lady Chapel echoed with the sound of gunfire. He looked up at Fisher, who seemed as surprised as Brent. But he didn't drop the gun or let it droop to the side. Instead, he straightened his back and his arm and pointed it directly at Brent.

CHAPTER 26

Y*ou know what they say about the Requiem,*" Fisher once said.
"*That it is hard to prove its ownership.*" While Mozart had
started it, it was finished after his death.

There was a great deal you could hide. But in the end, no matter the illusion he created, his true self would always shine through. Right now it shone through in his being as ill-prepared for his current role as Diana was for hers.

Fisher wanted her to find him. Hadn't he implied as much the moment she ascended the steps at St. Paul's?

Diana wandered into the chapel to the side of the altar. Candles flickered and a lone woman knelt to pray under a large wooden statue of Christ on the cross.

To her surprise, the Russian man she had followed sauntered up to her. "There is so much speculation on who contributed to the piece. To the Mozart."

"It is just as important to acknowledge when sole ownership can direct too much attention." She paraphrased Fisher. "To leave people wondering about where everything comes in." He may have appropriated everything she had innocently told him to funnel a top-secret document through London, but Diana remembered everything he had told *her* as well.

She moved her arm behind her back in a casual stance and felt for the gun tucked in the waistband of her trousers.

"You're pretty, I'll give you that. He said you'd be here."

Diana didn't want to be *pretty*. She wanted to be a threat. She pointed the gun at the man. Her hand gave a little tremble. He was quite large and unnerving, but she kept the weapon pointed at him. "Give me the file."

"I don't have anything." He opened one side of his jacket demonstratively.

Diana flexed her shoulder and the barrel of the gun shifted over his chest, moving right to his heart. "Your folder!"

As if oblivious to the weapon, he strolled over. "You don't scare me." He stretched the sentence out. "You're a woman. Can't even hold a gun straight."

The gun wavered in Diana's hand.

He twisted her arm and she dropped the gun. Diana dashed to retrieve it, kicking at his legs, his ankles, anywhere she could thrash at him while he stayed her forearms. She strained against him but his hold was too strong, and all too soon he had her immobilized. While her brain railed at her defeat, her physical inability conceded to it.

But it didn't matter. The man had the gun now. Whether he was armed before was a moot point as the steel flashed in the waning candlelight.

Then she heard a gunshot and had no choice but to let the man get away while she ran in the direction of the sound.

❦

Brent straightened. Fisher stalled.

"I find it too much of a coincidence that we met *twice* in as many weeks," Fisher said unevenly.

How could the man take on a casual, conversational tone? Footsteps were approaching. Fisher had shot a man in cold blood. But Brent remembered all too clearly how quickly Paul's words had drained from him on the battlefield. You did what you had to in overwhelming moments.

"Stay back," Fisher ordered the congregation forming at the mouth of the chapel. "Stay back or I'll kill him."

Brent exhaled at the sudden stillness of the onlookers. A handful too frozen to move or holler.

"I almost miss the piano wire," Brent grumbled.

Fisher laughed too loudly. "See? You can make a joke even now. Diana said you were funny." Fisher cocked his head to the side. "You teach, don't you?"

Brent was surprised at how calmly his answers came considering a gun was aimed at his heart. "I'm rubbish at it now. It doesn't feel the same." He swallowed. "And I know what I'm teaching is important. There's eternity in it, for heaven's sake." He stopped at the irony of his sentence.

"It can't make you happy now. Your life. Your religion. What you teach."

Brent didn't dare move his head, but he did take in the small audience. What was the point of lying or putting on a show? "I feel that even with my graduate students, I keep sounding off as the man I was. Not the man I am now."

Fisher didn't lower his gun, but he did take his gaze off Brent for a moment to glance at the candlelit shadows across the Lady Chapel.

"I hadn't ever been to Bart's before, you know." Fisher focused on Brent again. "Before Diana. Just to the hospital. But not this little eyesore off of Cloth Fair. I only knew of it because of a story I heard. A love story."

"A love story." Brent's mouth twitched. "In a churchyard? Rather dull."

"That's what I told her. That she'd have a perfectly boring life. I'm a bit of a sentimentalist, you know."

"Not too sentimental. You're pointing a gun at the man whose love story you appropriated for your devious intentions."

Fisher cocked the hammer on his revolver. "And you were stupid enough to come here unarmed?"

Brent nodded. "I am. However, I have a relatively sharp charcoal pencil in my pocket."

Fisher stretched the arm holding his gun. "You can't be sleeping well." They might as well have been swilling whiskey at The Grapes. "Seeing all that you've seen. In the thick of it."

"No. I don't. I don't sleep well at all. Nightmares. Constantly."

"I might be doing you a favor. Ending your misery. They talk about the battle fatigue in the pubs. Things normal gents wouldn't say unless they've had a few pints and a sad song is playing. But you have someone depending on you."

"Yes. I do."

"So you have someone to live for."

Brent's pulse quickened. The conversation was an echo of one he'd had with Ross. "Yes."

"And I suppose you want the quaint little house and children and the whole lot of it?"

He wanted children with Diana named for the markers in Poet's Corner. He wanted what she showed him in the Ditchfield book, finger rimming the words describing cathedrals and churches. "Must sound frightfully dull but, again, you're talking to a man who gets kicks out of the Hebrew and Greek he teaches in New Testament theology."

"I've let my life get out of hand. And part of me thinks I can backtrack, but another part doesn't want what I had before."

"I can't help you there." Brent sensed movement at the bordering gate and swerved to see a man attempting to leave.

"I'll shoot him!" Fisher repeated, stopping the man in his tracks. "No running. No calling for help. It will be too late."

Had any of the stunned onlookers focused in on the slice of moonlight exposing Mariner's corpse?

"I should have listened to her," Fisher said. "I told her I would come here and sit on a bench and wait for a pretty girl."

Brent tried to swallow but there was a lump in his throat. "I don't know what to say. I didn't know you existed until recently."

Fisher shook his head. "Of course you didn't. Who would? I'm a mathematician who tunes pianos and fishes. No one ever noticed me until the war. Some men had everything and some nothing. Who wouldn't throw themselves into an ideology where all had the same?"

"I..."

"It was a rhetorical question!" Fisher snarled.

Brent had to give the man credit. He had just killed a man and his arm didn't waver once. Brent closed his eyes a moment. Thought of anything he *might* say to defuse the very near realization of his rather ironic and untimely death. "Except that you are Diana's friend. And as her friend you most likely wouldn't want to take me out of the equation..."

His senses heightened, Brent stopped at a strange feeling of something shifting, and his eyes widened. There was movement again in their small gallery of onlookers and Fisher wasn't taking it lightly.

Brent stared the man straight in the eye and even in the shadows saw a look of determination and hurt. A cold look. The look of a man who had given away everything.

His file had been exchanged. He could see the outline of its shape in Fisher's pocket. The man who had procured his artifact was dead.

"Don't do this," Brent said. "Don't. For *her*. I know you are fond of her. You remembered everything she told you. Your eyes soften a little when you speak about her."

"I envied how happy she was even in the midst of our tragic, horrible war."

That was when Brent knew he couldn't turn the tide except to steal a moment of acceptance. He couldn't run. He couldn't escape it. He couldn't plead with the onlookers too frozen and afraid of the man with a gun in a hallowed space.

He straightened his shoulders and thought of her. If he only had moments left, he wanted to think of Diana. Not of a woman nearby procuring a dangerous folder but a girl in a green hat turning in the sunlight outside. So he would . . . and *did* . . .

⁂

Diana sprinted through the hallowed sanctuary, sliding on the slick stones and inset grave markers. She listened for voices through the echoing din but heard only the clack of her heels as Prior Rahere slept in stone and Prior Bolton's window peered over her.

A small cluster of congregants lingered at the edge of the gate, but no one was speaking. Or moving.

"Let me through," she said frantically.

She spotted Fisher first through the slightly open wrought-iron gate opening to the Lady Chapel and slowed her steps. His gun was pointed at Brent with determined aim. She narrowed her gaze on the movement of his trigger finger. Her heart somersaulted. Fisher wouldn't blink before killing.

Brent was saying something in his even tenor voice, but Diana was too frantic to hear it. She didn't think twice before she hurtled through a few onlookers, through the partition separating the chapel from the sanctuary, and lunged at Brent, driving him to the ground with the whole of her weight.

The blast of the shot erupted the moment she shoved him out of the way.

CHAPTER 27

April 1945
Italy

Holt, Tibbs, Ross, and Brent usually worked a unit, and he and Ross were always in sync, holding the same end of the canvas-and-steel rectangle, hoisting wounded men over uneven terrain. He could anticipate Ross's next movements, knew from the slightest droop in his friend's posture if they needed to slow down.

"Padre..." It was hard to hear Ross over the chaos of bullets and artillery. The shrieks of men and the thundering staccato of guns. One moment he had complete control, and then Brent's end of the stretcher slipped, beginning a domino effect that had Tibbs and Holt swerving in panic to begin damage control.

Then there was nowhere to readjust. Brent hadn't dropped a sack in the grocer's; this was a barely breathing *man*. He fell back, his breath coming in galloping gasps. He hadn't been strong enough. The mud had been too deep and the gunfire too consistent. He thought he was steady. Then *why* had Brent let his guard down?

Ross attempted to restore order with Tibbs and Holt, lifting the sunken stretcher and finagling it, dragging it out of the worse of the murky puddles and to surer ground.

It might have worked, but a relentless barrage of bullets resumed.

Brent held Ross down, his hands tightening on Ross's wrists, fiercely determined to atone for his moment of weakness even as fire and mud fell around them. He felt the severity of the pressure through his arms and his back. Why hadn't he been able to hold as tightly moments before?

"Stay down." Brent gritted his teeth, covering him. He swiped mud from his eyes, coughing, and tried to fathom a world in which he wasn't sinking. The artillery was falling with shrill whistles around them and a grenade had settled near the slight mud pit they fell into.

"It's just more important for you to get home," Ross said.

Brent shushed him, prepared to take the brunt of the explosive himself while his friend was covered by the safety of the pit below.

"That's not how this works," Brent ground out. Ross had been injured from a previous bullet and Brent was stronger, if only by a smidgeon. So he would hold his mate down as anyone would have done in compliance with an unwritten code. Brothers on the battlefield.

It was stupid that through the hollow sounds of his last moments of life he would hear the refrain of Diana's stupid song. That nightingale worlds away in blasted Berkeley Square. But why shouldn't he think of the best thing in his life knowing that soon his light would be snuffed out and everything he feared for the past four years had finally found him?

He knew he was hurting Ross, tightening his iron clamp on Ross's wrists. But as long as he held him down, he could reverse his mistake. He could protect him. A soldier looked after his own. Brent would look after Ross at the cost of his own life.

And yet as he was thinking of Diana and aching for her, it hardly registered as Ross rolled over, hardly registered that he was no longer directly next to the shell, rather protected by another and the barrier of canvas and steel with enough sinking mud to keep him from bearing the full weight of the bomb blast. Hardly registered that Brent had underestimated Ross's wiry strength.

The wet-behind-the-ears kid who called him Padre and followed his every move had taken his last breath so Brent could exhale another.

Brent's head buzzed. He pried his eyes open and the moment came back. *You're the strong one,* Ross had said. The calluses on

Brent's hands from years of rowing kept his grip. His broad shoulders allowed him to keep a steady pace.

Brent didn't recall a lot after. Had he dreamt Holt and Tibbs yelling that they would be back presently after seeing to the barely breathing man in their care? The same man he had nearly dropped, beginning the spiral of events that left him in pain with Ross unmoving and battered beside him?

"Wh-what would St. Paul say, Padre?" Holt lifted Brent onto the canvas stretcher and waited for Tibbs to close Ross's eyes.

Brent gaped at him. Gaped at Ross unmoving and shattered beside him. Felt the stinging start to replace the phantom thud in his shoulder and the unbearable pain above his left eye. He stared down at his bloody fingers, then up at the raining sky.

He knew Paul's words like a lifeline. His heartbeat quickened and there was something. Just there. *Beareth. Believeth. Endureth. Hopeth.* All the words his mind and body and heart ascribed to Diana. But *where were they?*

"Padre?" Holt's concern was frantic.

Brent blinked and groaned, his eyes falling shut even though he wanted to stay awake and say *one thing* that might start to repair what he had done. No Paul. *No Paul* even. Brent could command a whole world from behind that lectern when it came to Paul. He could . . .

He had.

The words weren't just mouthed against the din of rapid fire and shouting men. They weren't lost in the barrage of rain and orders and calls and cannon fire.

Help me! A plea to the God he couldn't see beyond his lecture notes and Paul's insistence, the undercurrent of every Greek form of love and every last thesis and every letter to the Corinthians. Patient. Kind . . .

Help me.

Later, Brent awoke in a hospital in Italy amidst clean sheets, with four fingers instead of five, and morphine dripping in an IV to counter the pain of the burns on his side. All of Paul's words came back to him with a vengeance to mark the part of his heart irrevocably changed.

Brent's eyes adjusted to the light and he thought of her. For once he had stopped yelling Ross's name, in the blurry moments between waking and sleeping, he saw her. Only her.

But it doesn't matter. The only thing that matters is that when this is all over we will start. Truly start. London owes us that much. After all, we were generous enough to loan it our love story.

~ 🙞 ~

December 1945

Brent's shoulder throbbed, pressing into the stone floor of the Lady Chapel. Stunned, he registered footsteps echoing over the bricks before he could think or breathe or get his bearings. But Brent only cared about the weight on his back. His head buzzed.

Brent blinked. Fisher. The gunshot. *Diana.* Brent's eyes widened in panic and he gently shifted, heart shattering when he felt the sticky warm substance on his hand. The metallic smell. The feeling that life was slowly leaving through sinews and muscle. He knew the signs. It played every evening in his nightmares. But never her . . . Not *her.*

Brent grunted as he strained to disentangle himself without moving Diana.

"No. *No.*" Brent carefully repositioned her. She was pale, eyes closed, head falling limply back on his arm, blood trailing the left side of her face. "No!" Brent pleaded, then unraveled. He stopped, checked his breath, and inhaled deeply. "Diana."

With the hand not holding her upward, he placed two shaking fingers to her neck, dizzy with relief that her pulse was there. But she was losing too much blood. Brent laid her head down gently on the brick, wriggled out of his vest, and pressed it tightly to the gash at the edge of her temple, swabbing away enough blood so he could ascertain the damage while blinking tears away.

The world seemed to be closing in on him. He searched out the trail of the bullet on the side of her temple, through her red-soaked blonde hair. He made out a bit of bone beneath and his stomach rolled.

Her eyes fluttered open and she glanced around.

"You're alright, Di. You're going to be just fine. The bullet just grazed you." If she hadn't thrown herself in the bullet's path, he'd more than likely be dead on the floor. How could he live with her choice? *Ross's choice.* Though if their roles had been reversed, he would have done the same thing. He added more pressure to the makeshift bandage at her temple.

"Brent . . . ," she said weakly.

"Shhh." He cradled her head.

"I'm so sorry. I owed Simon because of you. Because of the hospital. He said he could arrange . . . He could find out where you were taken, and if . . . I did it for you. I promised him for you."

"I was a cad. I was angry. Don't talk. You're going to be fine."

Diana made a sound. Swallowed slowly. "B-but I'm so afraid you don't know . . ."

"Di, I can't hear you." Brent grazed her forehead with his lips, tasting the metallic tang of blood flowing too freely despite the pressure of his vest. He touched her cheek. "I can't hear you."

She didn't speak again. Her breath was light and she shivered now and then. He placed his coat over her. "I love you. If I've done this all wrong, I need you to know that," he whispered.

Love was complicated enough on its own without throwing war in its path.

Brent looked around frantically, blinking away what his mind saw as his eyes took in a church long drained of music but not of people.

He held her. Wasn't he trained for this? No. No amount of training could prepare him for cradling his wife's head as her breathing slowed from a bullet wound she took for him. Brent gently laid her head on the stone and disengaged.

Rising, his nerves sparked and his blood flowed just as they had any moment a wounded man was placed in their care. He blacked out the world, focused as if wearing blinders. His shoes didn't press through the weight of layers of mud, just grazed the stones he took in pursuit of help, soles clacking on sure ground at a pace he mightn't have thought possible while his memory took him through a tunnel.

When his voice fought through, it was quiet and uneven. "Can someone find help, please?"

The small crowd watching dispersed. Someone had had the foresight to ring for the medics and police before Brent's request.

He barely registered hearing Fisher had been arrested. He answered questions distractedly. A kind medic assured him several times that Diana would be just fine. Brent nodded, a weight sinking his shoulders.

He slowly walked from the Lady Chapel through the quire, casting a look at the chair he occupied when he promised to trust her through to the yard and into the night.

CHAPTER 28

Diana picked at the coarse, starched sheet of her hospital bed. Brent was glued to her side, but his eyes were bleary, hair matted to his forehead, shirt stained but hidden under his jacket. If she looked back at the fabric of the last seven years of her life, she would always be surprised by the way Brent's threads intersected hers: in a churchyard or lecture, at a train station, in pursuit of a Soviet agent named Eternity. Even if she could rewind her life to work through the insecurity and pain, she would hope it would cast her in his path. Again and again and again.

She had enough to occupy her time too. While Fisher had been apprehended at the church by the police and taken away, the file he was killing to protect had also been seized and somehow, even from another country, Simon Barre's influence stretched wide. The file was delivered to her in hospital and she would exercise her brain by spending the long days to recovery decoding it.

She looked up at Brent's bloodshot eyes and tentative smile and knew without a shred of doubt that she could *hope* and *bear* and *endure* all things because he was near. That where she ended he began. That the stop of a sentence, a premonition, or a word on the tip of her tongue would be fully realized by *him*.

"I'm sorry I left you without a gun." Diana studied Brent carefully.

"I'm sorry you got shot."

"Not actually shot." Diana smiled. "Grazed." She felt at her bandage. "I hope you didn't marry me for my looks."

"Not in the least." He ducked his chin to his chest a moment. Then he met her gaze. "*Agape.*"

"We did that one," she recalled. "All well. Everything seems like something new somehow, doesn't it?"

"It means the devotion of one for the help of humanity. Of others." Brent touched her cheek. "I don't know what you did during the war, Diana. Not truly and I won't ask. But I don't need to know to know that you have gumption in spades."

"You—"

"I feel like I've met you all over again."

Diana shifted, bunched the sheet in her hands. "You know, I was thinking . . ."

"Somervilles!" Simon appeared in the doorway, decked out in a fine suit with polished black shoes. He handed Diana a bouquet and set his fedora at the end of her regulation blanket. "Having a private moment?"

"As a matter of fact . . . ," Brent began.

Diana smelled the flowers. "You're in a good mood. Everything go well in Vienna?"

"I think I've won the respect of MI6. I have carte blanche to continue to build my little team for this task. Here and in Vienna." He turned to Brent. "When I met you. That night . . . well . . . something had . . . Anyway, with Langer and—"

"I'm glad it worked out," Brent interrupted. "But as you can see, Diana and I were having a conversation and . . . oh, so you're staying. Please, don't stand on ceremony."

Simon dragged a metal chair from the bed adjacent Diana's. Parking it next to Brent, he sank into it and crossed his legs casually.

Diana glanced at Brent, then handed the file to Simon. "Everything was encrypted. As you know."

Simon cursed under his breath and scrubbed his hand over his face. "Well . . ."

"She started to decode it," Brent said just as Simon flipped back the cover.

"How . . . how did . . . ?" Simon's fingers worked over the papers bearing Diana's cursive handwriting.

"Nothing a knowledge of Fisher's fondness for Playfair ciphers and Mozart wouldn't fix." Diana felt a little sad thinking of Fisher despite how he had killed Mariner and almost killed Brent. He so wanted something to believe in.

She had tinkered with a sequence of rough cubes she had produced, each bearing the distinctive grid pattern Fisher had taught her. "The Mass in C Minor. It was the one composition I found a pattern in. I heard it with Langer and then again here at St. Paul's. It's #427 in the catalogue and it's Fisher's favorite piece." She pointed. "There were three pages with vital information. I merely assigned each with four and two and seven. So the alphabet on page one began at the fourth letter—D—then the next at B, and the next—"

"G," Simon finished. He was watching her intently, glancing from the paper to her, then back again. "But what was the key? How did you find what words to use?"

Diana reached for the Bible on her bedside table. "Our atheist friend Fisher used a verse."

"Of course he did."

She leafed through and pointed. "Start there."

"Matthew 16:18," he read.

"'And I tell you that you are Peter and on this rock I will build my church,'" Diana recited. "I know that one. Married to a theology professor and all." She smiled at Brent. "Here's names, locations, and . . ." She felt a slight rush to her head and settled back against the pillow. "You'll figure it out."

"Thank you for this. Truly." Simon took the folder and smoothed out the pages before tucking it into his case. "Turns out Eternity is far bigger than we thought. More than just eight London agents. It's all across Europe. Soviet sympathy is rampant in Vienna. What's in this file is of interest to all four of the reigning Allied victors. Which is why I was thinking . . ." He looked to Brent before returning to Diana. "You could come to Vienna."

"I am a professor of theology at King's. I am not a spy. I have no reason to go to Vienna. Diana got you your precious file. More still, she translated it for you."

"My superiors believe I can stop this ring quickly from the inside without drawing a lot of attention. Someone else will keep an eye on London. I will focus on Vienna." He cast a pleading look at her. "Diana, I consider you part of that team now."

She rearranged her flowers, moving the daisies behind the carnations.

"Brent Somerville. I need you."

"I am not infiltrating a spy ring. Are you mad?"

"You can't have Brent, Simon. You can't take my husband to Vienna."

"You'll go with him. You can study there. You can wander around churches with Gabriel Langer."

"Absolutely not." Brent pounded his knee with his fist. "Whatever she promised you back at that Foreign Office, she has more than fulfilled. And while I will appreciate the neck scar from Fisher's piano wire, I won't miss the adventure. I've had four years at the Front and I really just want a nap."

Simon met Diana's eyes. "Did you tell him about our bargain, Diana?"

"Not in great detail." Diana swallowed at the memory. "Enough detail."

Brent ran his hands over his kneecaps. "Enough detail to know you bribed her with information about me." Brent's gaze swerved to Simon. "Why didn't you just tell her? She's your *friend*."

"Oh, believe me." Diana raised a brow at Simon. "We've discussed that."

"I think you owe me."

"Owe you?" Brent growled. The protectiveness she saw in Brent's eyes was worth every last thing she had done for Simon and more. "I owe her *everything*, including my life, and you . . . I owe you nothing. Were you attempting to ruin our marriage?"

"I can't ruin your marriage. It can't be ruined. She loves you too much. Wren churches and Brent Somerville. All I heard about for four years. Bring her with you to Vienna."

"I don't even speak German."

"Your wife does."

"I just got back. I can't take a sabbatical. They won't guarantee to hold my position."

Simon reached into his pocket. "A letter from the dean." He popped it into the front pocket of Brent's jacket. "And you have a position at the Universität Wien. You will be teaching Greek and Latin to undergrads. Attending faculty parties. Making friends. Going to meetings. Looking for men like Rick Mariner who are caught up in something over their heads."

"I am a Pauline scholar."

"He spoke those languages too," Simon said.

Brent frowned. "Diana, are you hearing this man?"

"You want this, Diana." Simon grabbed her hand. "Brent wants this too."

"No, Brent does *not* want this."

"Yes, he does," Simon continued, addressing Diana. "He *says* he doesn't, but I can see it in his face. He's trying to fathom how he can possibly spend another day supervising someone's dry thesis on Corinthians."

Diana pulled a loose thread on her blanket. "I wanted to start keeping house."

"You can! Hoover the flat. Cook. Eat rationed strudel and watery coffee."

"I don't know, Simon."

"I hear that Anton Pilgram is a favorite architect of yours."

Diana's eyes widened. "He did the altar at Stephansdom."

"See, Somerville? Your wife already knows the city. My former SOE contact is an agent there now and will take care of everything. Housing behind Stephansdom. Papers. The works. A few lecture opportunities in Prague and Brussels."

"You need to leave now, Simon. Your visiting hours are over."

Simon nodded, rose. "Do it for the war effort."

"The war's over, Simon."

"No, Somerville, it's not. Not mine. Not yours." He looked at Diana. "You know I care deeply about you and I am sorry you were hurt. You also know that you want to come to Vienna. I can tell."

Simon collected his hat and, just before he retreated, said, "Perhaps I'll see you there."

"It was so hard." Diana reached for Brent's hand once Simon was gone and held it fast. "Seeing everyone going home and knowing that I couldn't."

Brent smiled and lifted their joined hands so he could kiss her knuckles. "Do you want to go to Vienna, Di?"

"I want romance. I want everything I didn't get in our four years apart."

"The most romantic man I know how to be right now is the one who recognizes your abilities, Diana." He stroked her uninjured temple.

"You'd have to leave King's. Vienna is a dangerous place right now, Brent."

"We've found enough danger in London." He fingered the scar at his neckline. "Do you want to see those Pilgram churches?"

Her smile was automatic. "I love the churches there. But aren't you happy at King's?"

Brent studied her closely a moment. "It's hard to know what happy is right now."

"I want you to be happy. I want it to be like it was before the war."

"It can't be. Because I am not the same man I was then. You aren't the same either. It's a good thing, Di. You're finally given an opportunity to use gifts I bet you didn't even know you had." He quirked his lips in a smile. "You took a bullet for me. This is your call."

"That cannot be how we handle our decision making moving forward."

"But for this once . . . I've never taught Greek or Latin before. Or had ration-flour strudel. And there were moments, weren't there?" He shrugged. "It sparked something. Maybe you can do your graduate studies there. What? What is it?"

"I think Fisher made me realize how dangerous this ideology is. That it can grip men like Fisher who in turn lure men like Rick. What was it you told me once? That Simon needs my emotional perspective? Maybe that's all I need to bring with me. Well, not *all* I need to bring with me."

Diana leaned forward and raised her chin for a kiss, which he was happy to give, gently cupping her face in his hands.

"Did he almost ruin our marriage, Brent?" she asked several minutes later, not hiding the insecurity in her eyes. "Did *I* almost ruin our marriage?"

"How can you ruin something with such a strong foundation?"

"Simon means well."

"You want this, don't you?"

"The neighbor's pet badger startled me by the rubbish bins again the other night. Might be a nice change of scenery. And the churches. Karlskirche! Those ellipsoid roofs!"

"Then I suppose I'll be taking you on a rather tardy honeymoon. Presumably with terrible rations. Wrecked churches . . ."

"So, pretty much the same as here."

"Exactly."

CHAPTER 29

January 1946
London

When Brent told Diana about Ross, he did so slowly. One night at a time and without her providing a story in exchange. A few nights he was too exhausted to speak. Other nights, he would drift to sleep, then wake with a vengeance and grab her wrists much as he had held Ross's. But he was more easily roused now and she could more easily calm him.

It seemed that with the last barrier that fell between them, he was more willing to recognize she was truly there with him. She was stronger too. One night she surprised him by nearly holding his hands at bay.

Once, he had woken enough to apologize and gently kiss her hand and her lips and her temple and her chin, then he cracked a sly smile and kissed her right below the healed scar line near her temple.

Another night in the flat after he nearly chipped a tooth on her attempt at cooking a pork chop, he refused tea. "I don't fancy tea tonight."

She sought his eyes and held them. Then submitted to Brent's inclination to sweep her up wholly. Legs bent over the crook of his elbow, and very much like the moment she had laughed giddily over their threshold years before, she smoothed his hair back and kissed the scar on his forehead.

"There's one Greek word for love we still haven't spent enough time on."

Diana's cheeks flushed. "I am thoroughly willing to be an attentive student." She let her fingers hover over his lapel.

He looked down at her bruised wrist, raised it to his lips, and brushed it with a gentle kiss. "I am so sick of hurting you." He set her down.

"You were hurt too." She studied his two melded fingers, his touch featherlight on her wrist, then glanced at his left shoulder.

"Just promise me you didn't marry me for my looks."

"Oh, but I did." She undid his top shirt button and let her finger linger at his collarbone. "For your stunning green-gold eyes and your smile." She beamed. "And those freckles just at your forehead. Your aristocratic nose and your broad shoulders, of course." Another button. "And I also married you for your lovely speaking voice." She smoothed away a bit of fabric. "And because you are very smart and very kind." Another button. Then another. Another. "I've run out of buttons." Diana pouted as Brent held up his wrists.

"Cuff links," he said hoarsely.

"Right." She winced as she ran her hand over the scars on his shoulder and left arm and around his back.

"No more of this." He touched her cheek and wiped away her tears. "We've both apologized. We've no more secrets. It's just a memory now."

"A bad memory." She sniffed.

"So we make better ones. Besides, you love scarred things. Great St. Bart's for one." Brent lowered his forehead to touch hers. "I'm sure you'll make an exception for me too."

Over the next few days, Diana made several exceptions and several burnt dinners and several opportunities to help him with his shirt buttons.

Brent arranged to lecture at the Universität Wien and was already several chapters into a new treatise on Timothy. He still woke at night, often with a gasp of breath, pressing away whatever vivid scene impressed his mind. Often Ross, but more recently a scene in the Lady Chapel of Great St. Bart's with an outcome that didn't find Diana breathing evenly beside him.

He evened out his breathing and straightened his shoulders, blinking to focus in the dark. After pressing a kiss to her temple, he disappeared, often waking hours later on the sofa or returning to the bedroom and quietly pulling her into him for the last few hours before the sun—or more often the slate gray—announced morning through the blinds. She seemed deliriously happy.

~

Diana was packing when Brent appeared in the bedroom doorway.

"There's one more thing you should do before we leave." Brent led her to the dining table where he arranged a fresh piece of paper in the typewriter. Beside was an envelope posted to the Royal Society of Architects.

"What's this?" Diana asked.

"You've taken notes for two months now. I know part of them were just for show, but, Di, you can save your churches. That new grading system?"

She registered the blank page. How could she capture centuries in a few words?

One brick and another. Swiping through mortar, clearing debris. The churches, her sentinels, had tumbled into piles of rubble at her feet. The removal of felled planks and the designation of history. London would build and rebuild and rebuild again. Through zeppelins and blitzes and storms. St. Paul's would remain the highest point in the skyline. Great Tom and Great Paul would peal, warring to create the music of the sky that set Londoners about their day. The churches would draw attention to the skyline and inspire a gasp of awe.

London was beautiful because it had been broken. Not an eye-lash batted before it forged itself again.

To whom it may concern:

She accepted a cup of tea from Brent and flexed her fingers over the keys.

My name is Diana Somerville of King's College, and I would like to take this opportunity to provide my notes on the reconstruction of the churches that suffered the tragedy of the Blitz. In my humble opinion you should focus your efforts on rebuilding the churches (especially the Wrens—personal preference) before any other property in the cities proper of London and Westminster. You should funnel them into your grading system to recognize them as architectural treasures.

Doubtless you recognize their monumental impact. To build a church is to form a community and to stake a claim in history. What example of architecture more surely combines art, spirituality, and the beating heart of a people's hope than a place of worship?

Christopher Wren believed "all architecture aims at eternity." Our churches are our eternity. As London is restored, let it be around the sentinel of steeples and may its gray skies frame the toll of bells—cast in iron—pealing citizens to their day.

For as long as a populous finds its heart in the center of churches, so our nation will rise.

Our churches are our heartbeat.

A compass, just as her father had said.

If she ever lost her way, Diana could look to a steeple, could listen for a bell chime.

She almost wished Fisher Carne were there with her that

moment as she erected her shoulders and set her life and mind toward him. Because while others may completely ignore churches' history and the deft poetry that carved their columns and sloped their domes and spiraled and painted and buttressed their ceilings and showcased their light she would not. And she would reclaim them.

CHAPTER 30

January 1946
Vienna

I t was hard to hear Diana over the propeller of the plane even though she was talking incessantly about cream-filled pastries and the Baroque façades of the same color. For a pitch-perfect moment the lights below were pinpricks like the dome in Stephen Walbrook. It wasn't until they ascended over the spires and rubble that Brent could truly make out the voice beside him.

She pressed her nose to the glass to stare at London below: Tower Bridge and the Tower and St. Paul's standing sentinel, as it always had, above the maze of brick and upheaved stone. Churches sewed back together, the Thames a ribbon of gray through a city that would survive. Near what had been All Hallows-by-the-Tower and, of course, beyond his vantage, Great St. Bart's. They weren't as beautiful as they had been, but perhaps in some way their resiliency and survival made them more beautiful.

Brent took her hand and drew it to his lips. *"Pragma."* The engine roared through the dipping clouds.

She turned toward him and batted her eyelashes. "And what, *pragma* tell me, is that?" Her eyes lit with humor.

"Long lasting."

The plane proceeded through the afternoon sky, Brent unable to make out anything but a blur of clouds until the plane quickly dropped, along with his stomach. Suddenly the Danube sparkled below and in the distance waited the Baroque spires of the jewel of the Habsburg Empire for his discovery.

They landed and wandered through the terminal to the tarmac, where a driver saw to their luggage. Diana straightened the skirt of her smart two-piece suit and Brent inhaled. He had stepped outside of himself before. He could step outside of himself again. Diana held tightly to his arm, her nose and chin turned down, her blonde hair a perfect wave over her shoulder.

I need you like breath and sunlight and Paul's letters to the Greeks, he thought.

The driver said little as they wove their way from the airfield to the Innere Stadt to Domgasse: just behind the gothic spires where the zigzagged gingerbread roof of Stephansdom once towered over a street where Mozart spent the last of his florins and the last of his days.

The city was scarred as London was, rebuilding after blasts of bombs at the thirteenth hour, recovering from the false optimism that it would somehow make it through unscathed. Brent rolled his shoulders, took Diana's case, and surveyed the outside of a building still whole: tucked away, timeless, like the compositions of its famous resident.

"They call it Figaro House." Diana pointed to the building across the street from the flat Simon had arranged for them. "Because it's where he wrote the famous opera. Maybe we'll see his ghost."

"Maybe." Brent gave a sad smile. "But I think I've had enough of ghosts."

~ ❧ ~

"Let's go see a church." Diana's words were in sync with the heartbeat she could feel at her back, so close was Brent standing behind her. They abandoned their unpacking efforts and set off into the street.

The ruins of what had been the Nazi-occupied Hotel Metropole would wait. The cigar butts of the Soviet soldiers encamped at

Schloss Schönbrunn were swept under the carpet of her mind. She would see Vienna as it *would* be. It would rebuild like London and in a few years it would be as if nothing had marred it. The city still turned like a carousel around the famed Ringstrasse, and Diana blinked away the shadows of the blockades, the silhouettes of soldiers with rifles pointed toward the frosted rooftops.

Brent steadied her over the cobblestones, and she beamed at the churches that had survived—many far more blessed than her Wrens—as they turned in the direction of the Café Mozart. The statue of mounted Emperor Josef II stood grand against the stones and she had a perfect vantage of the Staatsoper: like a cake with arches and grand windows.

She stopped him in his tracks as they surveyed the scarred opera house. "I find it more beautiful now for the parts that have withstood everything. And for what I know it will become."

"How many architectural historians get to see everything rebuilt again from scratch?"

"Wren," she said with a smile just as they approached the Hotel Sacher, its opulence undiminished by occupation or war. Awnings with monogrammed initials stretched out like overlong eyelashes and offered the layered cream building a rich accent. Spit-shined windows like a hundred and one eyes peered down over the street below. While the Soviets in the quartered city had initially had reign of the hotel, it had recently been commandeered as headquarters by the British, and it was here that Diana would meet Simon's elusive contact.

"Is that you?" A clipped Mayfair voice was undercut by the purposeful rhythm of heels tapping out a pattern on the inlaid tiles. A woman, tall and regal, held herself like a baroness. Dark-chocolate hair framed a pale face; matching brown eyes were widely alert and countered by perfectly lined lipstick, the same intense red as the wallpaper. "Diana Somerville, née Foyle, like the bookshop on Charing Cross Road."

The wall sconces and chandeliers of Sacher's interior master-piece contributed to a canopy of made-up stars illuminating the blood-red wallpaper of the opulent hotel. Diana beamed at the woman's outstretched hand.

Diana flung her arms around Villiers and held so tight that her nostrils tingled with a wealthy rose scent. Strong arms squeezed her back. So Sophie was a former SOE agent? She had lived with the woman for four years and never knew. The war made great secret keepers of so many. When she disengaged, Diana swore she saw a flash of tenderness in her eyes. Because *no one else knew.* The war made quick work of solitary experiences.

Diana looked at Brent. The expression on his face let her know he had read between the lines. He knew exactly who was standing in front of them. The only woman who could throw Simon Barre so off his guard he would show up uncontrolled on their doorstep when he thought she was in danger.

But before she could make good on introductions, a soft foot-fall and shadow appeared and Simon arrived at Villiers's side with a soft touch on her elbow to announce his presence. One simple touch and Diana saw it all, a certain spark between them, with Villiers still trying to hide it.

"This is all very unofficial." Simon led them from the foyer to the adjoining café where a table was waiting.

Villiers turned to Brent and Diana and rolled her eyes. "As opposed to all of the *official* business you've been involved in. I shouldn't even be here. You shouldn't know any of this. But somehow Simon has made it alright. We'll swap *just* enough government secrets."

Strong coffee was delivered. Simon talked about all he had planned. Gabriel Langer would show Brent the ropes. Diana would continue to teach him German. Villiers was on a new line of work altogether. She couldn't speak about it in great detail. But she did give a hint.

"Artifacts. Of financial but also moral interest." She sipped her coffee. "That's what you get when you find yourself moving into a war of minds. But no longer Fisher Carne's mind. No, someone far more dangerous. Lout shot at you, didn't he? I knew I didn't like him."

"No, you didn't," Simon interjected, lighting a cigarette for himself and pressing its end to the one that Sophie lifted to her lips so hers ignited as well. The two set off bickering at each other for a few moments. It was like old times. Diana used their tangent to think of all the new beginnings she'd had since the war silenced her beloved church bells.

Now a city of cream and gold was her canvas. She leaned into Brent, who was watching Simon and Villiers with interest.

"Are they always like this?" he whispered, his crooked smile stretching wide.

Diana sighed. "Yes. Isn't it wonderful?"

She was pretty sure this was going to be her favorite beginning of all.

ACKNOWLEDGMENTS

While all of my books are special to me, *The London Restoration* is one of those rare and wonderful heart books that was an absolute privilege and joy to write . . . but it was also an immense and seemingly impossible amount of work. I was blessed with a team and support group that worked impossibly hard to ensure that *The London Restoration* was everything I had dreamed it would be and more.

I would like to thank my agent and friend, Bill Jensen, for the many luminous conversations that sometimes have to do with books but often have to do with opera and Mozart. Thank you for championing me and my career. I love having you on my side.

I would love to thank my team at Thomas Nelson who took a chance on me yet again and allowed me to pursue this book of Wren churches and Bletchley Park. They are as delightful in real life as in the millions of emails sent back and forth, and I cherish the support and friendship. Amanda Bostic, Paul Fisher, Savannah Summers, Margaret Kercher, Kerri Potts, and Laura Wheeler, you work tirelessly to ensure that your convictions are reflected in narratives with the propensity to change hearts and minds and I cherish working with you. Thank you so much for believing in me and putting up with my endless questions. I know you are as invested in my book as I am, and I am blessed to have you on my side. I truly feel at home with you.

Kim Carlton, my lovely editor, you are nothing short of brilliant. You believed in Brent and Diana through many (many) revisions and put up with me on numerous brainstorming calls and through my teary frustration and my less-than-positive self-talk. Your intelligence and perception made this book into something better than I ever could have dreamed. I treasure the long hours you spent (far above and beyond), and I have learned so much from you about how to shape a story but also how to approach work with a nonstop positive attitude.

Thanks mostly for being a dear friend. My life is better with you in it.

(To avoid copyright infringement, please insert the *Hamilton* lyric of your choice here).

Julee Schwarzburg, I will never *ever* forget what you did for me and my book. You went above, beyond, and tirelessly to assure that *The London Restoration* lived up to its potential. Given your reputation in the industry, I had always wanted to work with you and your experience—your knowledge and patience have made me a better writer. Thank you from the bottom of my heart for giving up your holidays for Brent and Diana Somerville. Thank you for seeing what I wanted this book to be.

Thank you to Lauren Schneider for her eagle eyes during proofreading.

Mike Ledermueller: my research assistant extraordinaire. You are a walking resource and library. My wonderful legitimate expert on Bletchley Park, any and all omissions or errors in the capture of this incredible world are, of course, my own. Thank you for being an all-around favorite human and for matching my enthusiasm for the daily activities of the extraordinary men and women whose intellect and tenacity forged a world we both love to explore. I raise my Hobgoblin to you.

Thank you also to Kat Chin for sharing my love of history and story for always texting when I need a smile and for being the best darn friend around. Love you, buddy.

Patti Henry, you are one of the very first people I discussed this heart book with, having kept it tucked closely to me for so long.

That breakfast and chat in Covent Garden is one I will remember for the rest of my life. Thanks for the constant and ongoing support.

Ken Polonenko: you helped me with Russian words, many of which were omitted from the final version of this book, but I will never ever forget the time you took in helping me.

My early guinea pig readers, Courtney Clark and Renee Chaw: thank you for taking the time to read an early version of *The London Restoration*. I enjoy your friendship and our many, many bookish talks. And Brent and Diana appreciate your time and enthusiasm.

A long, rambling conversation with Jonathan Spaetzel resulted in the creation of my made-up Roman relic *oleum medicina*, and I am so thankful to be surrounded by so many intelligent friends who help and listen until I find the perfect story element.

I don't believe I have had the opportunity to thank a book in one of my novels before, but I am happy that the first instance is in recognition of *High as the Heavens* by author friend Kate Breslin. I remember sharing a glass of wine and hearing the first inkling of the story at a writer's conference several years ago, but reading the finished product inspired me as a writer and a human. When I was first crafting the proposal for this novel, you were there to answer questions and give insight and I am so grateful for your generosity. Katie, it is for you that I lovingly named a hero Simon (who happily will move from supporting role to be the leading man in *The Mozart Code*) in honor of my love for that book and its inspiration.

Jocelyn Bailey, my friend, you teach me so much about the publishing industry and about life but also are a daily burst of sunshine. I appreciate your encouragement and support.

Allison Pittman, thank you for being constant and walking me through the dark times and feeling my highs as deeply as I do. I love you, Bucko. I cannot imagine life or writing without you a part of it.

Sonja Spaetzel, thank you, thank you, thank you. I literally do not know what I would do without you. You are my constant support system and listener and giggler. Spending time with you is a well of inspiration, and you make my heart happy.

Melanie Fishbane, thanks for long conversations and for talks that spark so much creativity. I love having you as a friend.

To Jared and Tobin, Leah and Annette, I so appreciate you. I have the best family ever.

Eva Ibbotson, I confess to snatching the surname Somerville from my beloved *The Morning Gift*. I hope I did the name justice.

Finally, to my parents, Gerry and Kathleen McMillan, who always told me I could do anything I set my mind to and immeasurably supported my dreams. You always believed that someday this book would come into existence: even when I couldn't see it. I remember one wonderful visit home when you gifted me with a large illustrated book of the cathedrals of England and Wales "for when you write your churches book." I nod to this cherished book in Diana's precious copy of the more historically factual Ditchfield book. But mostly in the fall of 2017 when I was at a crossroads as to what to write and do next I made one phone call home on a Saturday night (I know, I know I was interrupting the hockey game) and Mom said, "Your dad and I have been talking, and we think you should go back to London."

I went back to London, and *The London Restoration* would be nothing without that research trip. I try to never take for granted that I have that rare gem of a supportive family who truly believes that I should be writing and will do everything they can to support that dream.

DISCUSSION QUESTIONS

1. One of the reasons World War II fiction continues to resonate with the reading public is that many feel a personal connection to this relatively recent history, especially through familial ties. Do you know anyone who served in the war or lived through it? What are some of the stories from day to day life or the front that you are familiar with?

2. For Diana, the loss of the churches she loves feels like a death. To this day, bomb strikes result in the loss of priceless, ancient buildings. Do you believe that architecture should be treated as a casualty of war?

3. Committees established during the war in London discussed keeping the gutted churches in ruins as a monument to the war while others prevailed in ensuring that the historical churches were renovated to reflect the architect's initial vision. A trip to London offers views of both rebuilt churches and those overrun by gardens and time like the Priory of St. John in Clerkenwell and Christ Church Greyfriars in Newgate Street. What are some of the ways you would defend the decision to leave them as monuments and markers to the past? What would you say in defense of the decision to restore the churches honoring the styles of the original structures?

4. Diana and Brent feel an immediate affinity to one another when they meet at St. Bartholomew the Great. In many ways they are soul mates, best exemplified by the unique connection they have with the ancient church. Have you

ever met someone and immediately known that they would be sewn into the fabric of your life?

5. While Diana and Brent are both irrevocably changed during the war, they both find new ways to fall in love with one another. For Brent, this is best exemplified in his attraction to the chin tilt Diana has. Indeed, he thinks that in many ways the war has shaped Diana into the strong woman whose potential he always saw. What hints during the flashback sequences at the beginning of their relationship might Brent have drawn on in his imagining of a possibly more mature Diana?

6. Britons experienced higher than anticipated divorce rates during the postwar years as men returned from war estranged from the wives who did what they could on the home front. While Diana and Brent certainly have moments of uncertainty, they are determined to make their marriage work: especially because, like the churches, it has such a strong foundation. Why do you think Brent and Diana's marriage survives?

7. Diana makes some interesting friends at Bletchley Park who end up influencing her life—for good or ill—long after the war. Fisher Carne, of course, and Simon and Sophie Villiers. Were there instances throughout the book that revealed the true identity of Sophie? Of Fisher?

8. Rather than ask Diana out of friendship if she will help him find Eternity after the war, he bribes her with information about Brent, leaving her with little choice but to accept his bargain. Do you think that Diana would have helped Simon even if he did not provide her with the promise of critical information about Brent?

9. In *The London Restoration*, the city Brent and Diana love is as much a starring character as the human characters in the book. London is a city known to many even if they

haven't had the opportunity to spend time in it. The fairy
tales and nursery rhymes (such as "Oranges and Lemons")
as well as the popular structures such as Big Ben and
Parliament and the Tower of London are familiar to most.
Wren's masterpiece, St. Paul's Cathedral, for one, is part of
our cultural consciousness. What are some of the stories
you associate with London either in modern or historical
times? Do you associate famous examples of architecture
with them?

10. The title, *The London Restoration*, not only refers to the
rebuilding of a city but to the reconstruction of Brent and
Diana's marriage. In what ways does the rebuilding of their
city mirror the time they are spending getting to know one
another again?

11. Many of the men and women at Bletchley Park were chosen
and successful because they saw the world through a
different lens and approached problems in a different way.
Indeed, Brent tells his friends he fell in love with Diana for
the prospect of seeing the world through her eyes. Can you
think of an instance when you approached a problem or
question through a lens special to your experience or view
of the world?

12. Brent and Diana often use the seven Greek forms of *love*
as a means of reflection and the many ways they love each
other. Doing an easy Google search, can you think of a few
of the forms of love not covered in the book that reflect
their relationship?

ABOUT THE AUTHOR

Rachel McMillan is a history enthusiast, lifelong bibliophile, and author of the Herringford and Watts series, the Van Buren and DeLuca mysteries, and the Three Quarter Time series as well as the nonfiction books *Dream, Plan, and Go* and *A Picture-Perfect Christmas*. Rachel lives in Toronto and is always planning her next adventure.

Facebook: RachKMc1
Twitter: @RachKMc
Instagram: RachKMc